PRAISE FOR
SUSAN CRANDALL'S NOVELS

SEEING RED

"4 Stars! Crandall weaves a tight and suspenseful story that will have readers guessing until the last chapter. Poignant in places and nail-bitingly tense in others, this is one of those books readers will want to finish in one sitting."

—*Romantic Times BOOKreviews Magazine*

"Exciting romantic suspense...Readers will enjoy this tense thriller."

—*Midwest Book Review*

"A fast-paced thriller that will keep you guessing...*Seeing Red* will lead you down a fear path of horrific crimes that could happen anywhere."

—**TheRomanceReadersConnection.com**

"Another fascinating story by the talented Susan Crandall...*Seeing Red* is a riveting tale that you won't want to put down...Highly recommended!"

—**RomRevToday.com**

"Compelling...well-written...The suspense was fast-paced and the romance was irresistible...The book was hard to put down...Most definitely an author to keep your eye out for."

—**BookPleasures.com**

more ...

PITCH BLACK

A KISS IN WINTER

"Everything a contemporary romance reader wants in a book."

—*Midwest Book Review*

"A very character-driven story, *A Kiss in Winter* is a tale of family expectations and disappointments."

—*Romantic Times BOOKreviews Magazine*

"Complex characters, intricate relationships, realistic conflicts, and a fine sense of place."

—*Booklist*

"Great characters, a touching relationship, and exciting suspense."

—*Affaire de Coeur*

"Brilliant characterization, edgy suspense...a tension-rich mystery."

—**ContemporaryRomanceWriters.com**

ON BLUE FALLS POND

"A powerful psychological drama...*On Blue Falls Pond* is a strong glimpse at how individuals react to crisis differently, with some hiding or running away while others find solace to help them cope."

—*Midwest Book Review*

more ...

"Readers who enjoy...fiction with a pronounced sense of place and families with strong ties will respond well to Crandall's...sensitive handling of the important issues of domestic violence, macular degeneration, and autism."
—Booklist

"Full of complex characters...it's a well-written story of the struggles to accept what life hands out and to continue living."
—Romantic Times BOOKreviews Magazine

PROMISES TO KEEP

"An appealing heroine...[an] unexpected plot twist...engaging and entertaining."
—TheRomanceReader.com

"FOUR STARS!"
—Romantic Times BOOKreviews Magazine

"This is one book you will want to read repeatedly."
—MyShelf.com

MAGNOLIA SKY

"Emotionally charged...An engrossing story."
—BookPage

"A wonderful story that kept surprising me as I read. Real conflicts and deep emotions make the powerful story come to life."
—Rendezvous

"Engaging...starring two scarred souls and a wonderful supporting cast...Fans will enjoy."
—*Midwest Book Review*

THE ROAD HOME

"A terrific story...a book you will want to keep to read again and again."
—**RomRevToday.com**

"The characters...stay with you long after the last page is read."
—**Bookloons.com**

BACK ROADS

"Accomplished and very satisfying...Add Crandall to your list of authors to watch."
—**Bookloons.com**

"An amazingly assured debut novel...expertly drawn."
—**TheRomanceReadersConnection.com**

"A definite all-nighter. Very highly recommended."
—**RomRevToday.com**

SLEEP
NO MORE

SUSAN
CRANDALL

FOREVER

NEW YORK   BOSTON

This book is a work of fiction. Names, characters, places, and incidents are the product of the author's imagination or are used fictitiously. Any resemblance to actual events, locales, or persons, living or dead, is coincidental.

Cover art and design by Rob Wood
Book design by Giorgetta Bell McRee

Forever
Hachette Book Group
237 Park Avenue
New York, NY 10017
Visit our website at www.HachetteBookGroup.com.

Forever is an imprint of Grand Central Publishing. The Forever name and logo is a trademark of Hachette Book Group, Inc.

Printed in the United States of America

First Printing: January 2010

10 9 8 7 6 5 4 3 2 1

For Allison, my daughter, my friend.

Acknowledgments

Once again I am indebted to others for the successful completion of this book. Thanks to Melissa Crandall for the hours of poolside brainstorming; it was a great summer. And to Karen White for both in-person and long-distance chats; you helped keep me on track. To my son Reid, a great writer himself, for pushing me in the right direction when I called when faced with various forks in the writing road. And of course, to WITTS (Alicia, Brenda, Garthia, Pam, Sherry, and Vicky), best critique group *ever*. I can't imagine writing a book without you all.

I thank Dr. Walter Beaver for his help and insight to Alzheimer's and dementia, and sleepwalking—as well as all of those other topics that popped up as we chatted.

No suspense would be complete without questions answered by the ever able crime scene writers group.

Mega-appreciation to my fabulous editor, Karen Kosztolnyik, for her keen insight and direction; and to those in the Grand Central family who lend their talents to making my dreams come true. Thanks to my agent,

Annelise Robey, whose eyes lit up when I described this book idea to her over breakfast.

And most of all, thanks to my family: Bill, Reid, Allison, and Melissa, for their endless support and for listening to my shameless whining about something I truly do love to do.

SLEEP
NO MORE

PROLOGUE

The house where Abby Whitman's family lived wasn't like the plantation houses in the movies. There were no sweeping staircase and grand foyer. The house *did* have two sets of stairs. The second was at the back of the house—it had been for servants "back in the day," as Abby's daddy said. The foyer stairs was fancier, sure, but it was no Tara.

It was at the bottom of the foyer stairs that Abby's mother stopped her and held her by the shoulders.

Confused and disoriented, Abby tried to pull away. She didn't know why panic was squeezing the breath from her lungs. She shouldn't be afraid of Momma.

"Abby. Abby, stop," her mother's voice was quiet, but Abby heard something underneath; a dark whisper of fear.

Abby's eyes began to focus. Her mother was smiling, but her eyes looked scared. Momma was never scared.

Abby's stomach took a roller coaster plunge.

"You're sleepwalking again, sweetie," Momma said. "Let's get you back to bed."

That was when Abby saw the heavy front door

standing open and understood why Momma was so upset. Abby had been outside in the dark. Outside where there were gators and snakes and a river to drown in. Outside where there was quicksand and woods to get lost in.

Every night when she went to bed, Abby promised herself she wouldn't sleepwalk. And then she prayed that God would fix her. Promises and prayers weren't doing any good. This was the second time in a week Abby had wandered in the night. The last time she'd woken up in the hayloft in the barn.

When they reached the top of the stairs, Great-Gran Girault was there waiting.

Abby had been hoping now that she was eleven she'd grown out of being scared of Gran Girault. But sure as the moon, she hadn't. Gran had to be a hundred; tall and thin with weathered skin sagging on her bones. Her white hair was always in a bun—even when she was in her nightgown.

She lived in Louisiana, where they believed in things like evil spells and devil's curses. One time when she was visiting, Abby had found a little pouch under her pillow one morning. When she'd opened it, it had tiny bones and some dried weeds and a rock in it. It smelled funny. Momma had been really mad when she found out.

Almost always when Gran looked at Abby, it was with a frown.

Now Gran looked at Abby with a frown so intense it made the hair on the back of her neck prickle.

"I tell you, Betsy," Gran said, her voice like sandpaper on rocks, "you need to do somethin'. It ain't natural, her creepin' 'round here in the night like she does. Starin' eyes like she's possessed."

"Shush, Gran!" Momma kept them walking right past Gran.

Abby's room was next to her sister Courtney's. She was six and everybody always said she was "cute as a button." Court never went sleepwalking. And Gran Girault *never* looked at her with a frown.

Momma tucked Abby into bed and kissed her on the forehead.

Abby pulled the sheet up to her chin, clutching it like it was a rope that might keep her tied in bed. "Gran hates me."

Her mother ran a hand over Abby's hair. "Gran is old and confused. You mustn't pay attention to her. Besides, she's going home tomorrow."

The smile on Momma's face said she was happy about it. That made Abby feel just a little better.

"Good night." Her mother left the room, closing the door behind her.

Abby rolled onto her side, determined to stay awake all night. That way she couldn't sleepwalk. At first she didn't even blink. But soon her eyelids grew heavy. She tried counting the flowers on her wallpaper. But they started to run together.

She closed her eyes—just for a minute....

When Abby opened her eyes, it was daylight.

A car door slammed outside. Daddy was taking Gran Girault to the train station. Abby got up and watched the car pull down the lane, feeling like a dark and dangerous storm had finally blown away.

Always at Sunday evening dinner, right before grace, Abby's family lit the oil lamp that was as old as their house. It was tradition; her daddy told her it was in honor of those Whitmans who'd gone off to war and never come home. It had been a custom he was passing along, just like he would pass this house to Abby someday.

Today was Abby's first time to light the oil lamp. Naturally, Courtney had a hissy over it. She never liked it when Abby got to do something she didn't—which wasn't often.

At bedtime, Court was still pouting. And Abby climbed into bed with a smile on her face. She could hear Momma in the next room, telling Courtney that when she turned eleven, she'd get to light the lamp every other Sunday.

Courtney whined that it wasn't fair. Abby hoped Momma and Daddy wouldn't give in like they usually did. Abby had had to wait until after her eleventh birthday. Court should have to, too.

Abby drifted off to sleep feeling really good; not only did she get the special privilege of lighting the lamp, but Gran Girault wasn't here to give her the stink-eye if she happened to go sleepwalking again. It was a good day.

Abby opened her eyes. Stinging smoke caused her to close them again. An orange glow flickered in the fog of smoke. There was heat at her back—and the sound of crackling dragon breath.

She opened her eyes in tiny blinking slits to see where she was. Darkness and smoke blotted out everything.

For a second she stood there, panic squeezing her chest. Then she remembered. She dropped to her knees. The smoke wasn't as bad here. She even recognized the living room rug.

She'd been sleepwalking.

The fire was in the dining room.

She had to get everyone out!

She opened her mouth to yell for her parents, but breathing in felt like a cat was clawing her lungs. She coughed until she nearly threw up.

Suddenly she heard Courtney screaming. In the back of the house. On the other side of the dining room.

Abby tried to crawl through the dining room, feeling her way along, but it was too hot. She turned around and started crawling back the way she'd come, but she bumped into a piece of furniture. It was hot. So hot. So painful.

In a panic she got to her feet and tried to feel her way to the door. The smoke tore at her lungs. She smelled her hair being singed.

She had to get out.

Courtney was still screaming.

Abby thrashed forward, flailing her arms. She heard china break.

And then she found the door.

Help Court. Wake Daddy.

Dizziness made her stumble. She felt like she was trying to breathe underwater.

She tripped over something and fell face-first onto the living room rug.

The crackling was getting louder.

She heard Daddy calling her name, over and over, until she couldn't hear anything at all.

CHAPTER 1

Life can so often be divided into before and after. Not by the little wrinkles and frays of daily wear, but by monumental events that rip cruelly through the fabric of a finely woven existence. It happened to everyone. Abby Whitman understood that. But she also felt she'd had more than her fair share of befores and afters; befores and afters that had thrust her onto unforeseen roads, leading to generally uninvited futures.

Some called it fate. Some called it luck. Great-Gran Girault had gone so far as to call her cursed. The first time Gran said it, Abby's mother had called Gran Girault a superstitious old kook from the backwater Louisiana swamp. And man, had that set off fireworks between Abby's parents. At least the argument had taken Great-Gran's condemning eye off Abby long enough for her to slip out of the house to the refuge of the old, overgrown rice fields where she could live in a world of her imagination; one where little girls did not do things in the night that they couldn't recall the next morning.

Now Abby was a grown woman—and she realized

that curse still clung to her with a tenacious grip. As she stood in the muted gray dawn that cast her small kitchen in gloom and shadow, she once again felt as if the jaundiced eye of Gran Girault was on her, and her stomach did a slow, nauseating roll.

Muddy prints left by bare feet trailed across the white kitchen tile like dirty accusations. They began at the dead-bolted back door and moved toward the living area.

Abby knew what she would find even before she kicked off the slippers she'd absently slipped on as she'd gotten out of bed. Even so, the dark smears between her toes and the grime following the crevices of her skin set her heart into a thoroughbred-out-of-the-gate gallop.

In a panic that was far too late to be of any value, she sniffed the air for smoke. Then she took off on a frantic circuit of her tiny house. All doors and windows were locked. She found no ignited stove burners, lit candles, overheating curling irons, or overflowing plumbing fixtures. Nothing unusual except those muddy footprints that became fainter as they went up the stairs to the half-story that housed her bedroom.

She followed them. Reaching her bed, Abby stared at it for a moment. Then she flipped back the covers. Her breath left her lungs in a rush as she looked at the mud-smeared sheets.

Straightening her spine and ignoring the trembling in her hands, she slowly lowered the blanket, pulling it up to the head of the bed, as if she could tuck this nightmare in and drive it back into sleep.

With slow and heavy footsteps, she retraced her previously panicked path through her tiny house, the converted brick summer kitchen had been spared when her family home had burned.

At some point over the past few years her reason for living out here had slipped from front and center, shifting so slowly into her peripheral vision that she'd barely noticed. She'd allowed herself to be diverted by the pleasure of restoring the old gardens of the plantation. Here in this secluded place of atonement, she'd somehow found peace.

But this morning the branches of gnarled oaks against the gray skies outside her windows looked menacing and the isolation had an air of desperation.

The dark realization settled upon her. Fate had just doled out another before and after:

Before I started sleepwalking—again.

She'd been free of the disorder for her entire adult life. It was a demon thought exorcised at puberty; gone and yet never fully forgotten.

As Abby stood in the early morning silence, she realized that this particular demon's reappearance did not feel wholly unexpected. The fear of the disorder's return had been a dark shadow that lurked in the fog every night when she closed her eyes; the *real* bogeyman under the bed. And it was the reason she would always live alone.

An isolated incident, she assured herself.

Why now?

Stress and hormones; Dr. Samuels had listed both as likely triggers for sleepwalking. There was only so much a person could do to insulate a life from such things, and Abby had employed them all. Still, stress had come crashing into her carefully constructed life with the unexpected death of her mother a few weeks ago.

Her gaze was drawn back to the footprints.

Vulnerability raced up her spine on spider's legs. She'd been outside. In the dark. Alone. Unaware.

Doing what?

It was a question she wasn't sure she wanted to answer.

She opened the back door and stepped onto the small stoop. The early April wind plucked loose hairs from her ponytail and snaked beneath her robe, drawing goosebumps on her bare legs. The marsh grasses leaned in unison and the distant surface of the Edisto River ruffled like tide-sculpted sand. Clouds boiled overhead, blotting out the rising sun, promising a storm before the day concluded.

The garden hose normally hung on a decorative hook near the back steps. It was unwound, the end disappearing into the squared boxwood hedge that bordered the main garden.

She crossed the coarse grass, the dew of early morning turning the dirt between her toes once again to mud.

Water cascaded over the lip of the birdbath like a fountain. The slap and splatter of it hitting the soggy ground reminded her of the way rain used to roll off the gutterless roof of the old plantation house that had been her family's for generations—the house she'd burned to the ground. It was a sound that conjured both comfort and regret.

She returned to the stoop and shut off the spigot with a firm hand, just as if this was a normal morning and she'd just finished watering. Then she marched back inside, refusing to look back at the hose winding like a snake into the hedge.

An isolated incident. That's what she had to believe.

As she closed the door behind her, she looked at the footprints on the tile, then at her dirty feet, both grating reminders of a raw vulnerability she'd hoped never again to experience.

Gran had been right. There was something unnatural about Abby—and she hadn't grown out of it at all. She couldn't let her father know. He thought she'd been cured years ago. In fact, she couldn't let anyone know. Everyone in Preston already looked at her as the girl who'd burned down an irreplaceable historic treasure; the girl who'd nearly killed her own sister. The looks would return. Old ladies would once again shy away from her. Mothers would keep their children out of her path.

She went into the bathroom and started the shower. If only she could wash away the stain of fear as easily as she did the mud on her feet.

Sometimes Jason Coble thought it a cruel twist of fate that he, a psychiatrist who spent his days untangling other people's emotions and assessing their mental health, had missed the signs of his now ex-wife's alcoholism for so long. Sadly, it hadn't been his professional skill that had guided her into recovery. It had been his harsh threat to seek sole custody of their children. Nothing else had broken through the stone wall of Lucy's bitterness and denial.

In reality, there was little chance of his getting guardianship of his stepson Bryce, whom Lucy hadn't allowed Jason to adopt. But their daughter Brenna was another case altogether.

Not that he wanted to live that way, with hostile court battles and ugly scenes. What he *wanted* was Lucy sober and an amiable coexistence that would nurture their children. Generally that's what he'd achieved—so far. But it was a tightrope-balancing act. In order to safeguard that balance, he had to keep up constant covert observation of Lucy's state of mind and her behavior. It was an unpleasant and unalterable fact of life.

Today he lingered on the fringes of Lucy's family as they gathered in the tiny narthex of St. Andrew's before Vera Marbury's funeral. The loss of her Grandmother Vera had hit Lucy hard. It showed in her brittle posture and the jittery movement of her hands.

Jason's feet shifted on the well-worn slate floor of the old church as he looked for signs that she'd found her consolation in a bottle of vodka. She was very good at disguising it.

He walked across the narthex.

Stepping behind her, he touched her elbow and leaned close, getting her to turn. "Hello, Lucy."

"Jason." Her eyes narrowed. Clearly, she'd figured out what he was doing; maneuvering her so he could smell her breath for alcohol. It was a dance they'd done more times than he could count.

He looked at his ex-mother-in-law, Constance. "I'm so sorry about your mother. Vera will be sorely missed."

Constance nodded as regally as a queen. "Thank you, Jason."

Lucy said in a chilly tone, "You don't need to be here."

Jason glanced at his seven-year-old daughter. She was looking at them with measuring eyes. He gave her a smile and a wink and received a bashful head duck in return. It broke his heart to see how far she had retreated into herself in the past year, since the finality of the divorce had officially broken their family in two.

"But I do," he said to Lucy. "Vera was Bryce and Brenna's great-grandmother. We're family." Sometimes

Lucy got so tied up in her own emotions, she forgot that her children had feelings, too.

Bryce stepped forward and gave Jason a quick hug. "Thanks for coming, Dad."

His seventeen-year-old stepson only called him Dad when he was feeling particularly vulnerable. His biological father had died of testicular cancer when Bryce had been only two. Lucy had been adamant about keeping her first husband's memory sacred. Jason had honored her decision, but even without adoption papers he felt as much Bryce's father as Brenna's.

Lucy turned her back on Jason. "You won't be sitting with the family."

Constance spoke up in a tone that left no room for argument. "If Brenna wants her father to sit with her, that's where he'll sit."

Surprised by her support, Jason nodded his appreciation. He knew Constance held him one hundred percent responsible for the divorce, that she considered it abandonment of the vilest kind. For better or worse, he'd taken the vow—and broken it.

He held out his hand to Brenna. She cast a skittish glance at her mother before she reached out and took it. But Lucy was walking away, diverting her attention to the flower arrangements being set at the front of the nave. She might not like being overridden by her mother, but she didn't have the backbone to defy her openly. It used to make Jason angry for her; he'd seen his ex-wife run roughshod by her mother enough to understand that Constance was part of Lucy's problem. But today he was selfishly grateful.

Bryce gave Jason an apologetic shrug and followed his mother.

Jason clasped his daughter's hand. "Come on, Peanut. Let's go sit down for a bit."

She smiled up at him, showing the adorable gap where she was missing a couple of teeth.

A lump gathered in Jason's throat. How was it possible to love someone this much?

He squeezed her hand more tightly as they walked into the sanctuary. He hadn't been inside St. Andrew's since Brenna's baptism. The church smelled of aged wood, lemon polish, and incense.

In her bleakest moments, Lucy liked to blame his refusal to convert to Catholicism (and his ambivalent approach to religion in general) as a major stumbling block in their marriage. Lucy liked to blame lots of things that took the spotlight off her own behavior.

Father Kevin Ferraro approached, meeting Jason and Brenna in the main aisle. "Good to see you, Jason."

They shook hands. "It's been a while."

Jason and Father Kevin were in the same golf league. Here in South Carolina there were few completely golf-unfriendly months, but this spring had produced one. In the past weeks the priest looked to have lost weight; his cheeks were hollowed and his eyes appeared sunken. Jason wondered if the man was ill.

"And Miss Brenna"—the priest placed a gentle hand to the top of her head—"have you been keeping up with your studies for your Parish School of Religion class?"

Jason knew the man used the full name of the class because he assumed Jason was ignorant of the abbreviation. But Jason was well aware of Brenna's love of her PSR studies. He was proud of her dedication to her spiritual responsibility, even though he sometimes worried that she used it as an escape.

"Yes, Father." Brenna smiled proudly, but her voice was barely audible even in the silent sanctuary.

"Wonderful. Wonderful," Father Kevin said. "Pretty soon you'll be old enough to be an altar server. We need more little girls like you here at St. Andrew's."

The priest moved on. Jason and Brenna took a seat in a pew near the rear of the church, and began quietly discussing what Brenna was learning in PSR. Listening to his shy, lonely little girl, Jason wished other less introverted parts of her young life could also inspire that kind of light.

Abby's morning had been so hectic that the muddy footprints were relegated to the periphery of her mind. Even so, the implications of their presence stuck there like a festering splinter as she rushed the last flower arrangement for Vera Marbury's funeral from the back of her van to the side door of St. Andrew's.

As always, Maggie was there on the doorstep to greet Abby with a wide smile. Father Kevin was guardian for his niece, a blue-eyed teen with a bright spirit, sharp wit, and Down syndrome. Maggie was Abby's right-hand gal for all events that required flowers at St. Andrew's.

Maggie crossed her arms over her chest. "You're late."

"I know, I know. Can you unwrap these and take them into the sanctuary?" Abby handed the bouquet to Maggie. "I have to go pick up Dad for the service."

"Sure, but you'd better not come in late. Uncle Father doesn't like it when people come in late."

Abby waved as she hurried back down the steps, smiling at Maggie's name for her uncle. Her parents had been killed in a helicopter crash two years ago while on a relief trip for Children of Conflict, the organization they'd founded to assist orphans of war-torn areas in Africa and the Middle East. They'd left both Maggie and COC in Father Kevin's capable hands.

Because everyone called him Father, Maggie had decided calling him Uncle Kevin wasn't respectful enough for her; Uncle Father was born.

There were ten stoplights in Preston. Abby had to drive through seven of them to reach her father's house. While sitting at the fifth, her cell phone rang. She glanced at the caller ID. Her sister always called at the worst moments.

"Hi, Court."

"I was just thinking you need to hire someone to wash Dad's windows. I noticed when I was home for the funeral how dirty they are. Mom would have a fit."

At sixty-three Betsy Whitman had been taken by a massive stroke, her death a shock without warning. The funeral had brought about Courtney's only trip back to Preston since she'd left the day after she'd graduated from high school.

Courtney didn't give Abby a chance to respond before she added, "You know I'd do it myself, but…" She paused. "Well, you know how it is with people in Preston…." Her voice slid into that tone that chafed Abby's ass like wool underwear.

"I'll take care of it." She immediately regretted her sharp tone. After all, it was her fault Courtney felt uneasy in Preston.

She bore horrible scars from the fire and had always felt everyone here strained to see them, no matter what she did to cover them up. The plastic surgeon had done what he could, but he'd reminded them at every operation that childhood burn scars were the worst. There was only so much medically possible.

Courtney now lived like a hermit in a cinderblock house (as fireproof as she could get) in New Mexico. Both decisions she wouldn't have made if Abby hadn't been sleepwalking and set the house on fire.

The light turned green and Abby crossed the intersection.

"Have you seen him today?" Courtney asked.

"Not yet. I'm headed to his house right now."

"Abby! You are *not* taking him to that funeral!"

"He wants to go." Vera Marbury's daughter, Constance, and Betsy had been close friends.

"It's too soon," Court said direly. "He's not up to it."

Court always had such grim predictions. She lived over fifteen hundred miles away and rarely talked to their father because it made her "sad." How in the hell could she assess his emotional state?

"If I don't show up to get him," Abby said, "he'll just go by himself. I don't want him going alone. Listen, I'm here; I have to go. I'll call you later. Bye." Abby disconnected the call, shame and aggravation scrapping like selfish children for the upper hand.

She stopped at the curb and honked the horn; he was supposed to be watching for her.

As she sat there, she looked at the windows. Crap, they *were* dirty.

She hoped she wouldn't have to concede Court was right about the funeral, too.

Her dad's front door remained closed. Abby shut off the car and hurried inside the house. She found him in his favorite chair, the newspaper in front of him.

When he heard her come in, he lowered it and smiled. "There's my girl."

"Ready to go?"

For a brief second, he looked blank. Then he put down the paper and rose from the chair. "Of course. Ready."

When they got outside the front door, her father reached into his suit pocket. "Uh-oh. No keys." He opened the door again.

"I have a key," she said. "I'll lock up."

Her dad continued into the house. "I have to find my keys."

Abby glanced at her watch. "Dad, we're going to be late."

"I'm sure I left them on the kitchen counter," he called back to her.

A full minute passed and her father didn't return. Abby went inside.

She found him in the kitchen, ripping open drawers and rummaging through them.

"I can't find my keys!"

"It's okay, Dad." Abby smiled to herself. Her mom had called him the absentminded inventor. Even though he'd been a science teacher his entire career, he constantly dabbled in the basement working on one project or another. The man was brilliant, but seriously could not find his socks when they were on his feet. "I have a set. Let's go and I'll help you find them when we get back."

"But I need to know where they are." His voice held an unusual edge.

"They're probably in a jacket pocket. We'll find them, but we need to go or we're going to miss the service."

"No! I have to find my keys!" With increasing agitation, he opened the flour canister, looked in, and shook it.

"Stop and think about what you were doing the last time you had them." She started looking, too.

Three minutes later, she found them—in the medicine cabinet in the bathroom when she'd decided she needed something for a rapidly escalating headache.

She dashed back into the bedroom, jangling the keys. Her father had every pair of pants he owned out on the bed, searching through pockets.

"Where were they?" he asked, his face beaded with perspiration.

"Medicine cabinet. You must have had them in your hand when you came home from the drugstore and put things away."

He blinked. Then he shrugged. "Must have."

"No matter. Let's go." She hurried him to the car and headed back across town.

As she drove she thought about her Dad looking in the flour canister. He was absentminded, but that seemed out there even for him. Surely it was just the panic that had made him do something so incongruous.

The funeral was small. At ninety-one, Vera Marbury had outlived most of her contemporaries. During the organ solo before the service, Abby stole a look at her dad out of the corner of her eye. He sat with his hands relaxed in his lap and a serene look on his face. Being here was not catapulting him back into raw grief. At least that was one *I told you so* Abby wouldn't have to hear from her sister.

The last breathy notes left the brass pipes of the organ and Father Kevin stood. He began with a prayer. It was a long one.

Unused to such forced stillness, Abby shifted in her seat. Her foot began to jiggle.

Her father's hand closed over hers. He whispered, "Easy, Jitterbug."

He hadn't called her Jitterbug in years. It was the nickname Abby's mother had given her even before she'd been born, saying that Abby had been incapable of a still moment even in the womb.

Abby looked over at her dad. A melancholy smile graced his face and an unshed tear pooled in his eye.

She tensed. Was this the beginning of an emotional landslide?

Then he winked and Abby released the breath she'd been holding.

She returned his smile and squeezed his hand. She also stilled her foot—at least for the moment.

There was much to admire in a Catholic funeral. Having it in the church that had seen many of the significant events of a person's life felt right, the completion of a circle. And the ritual was comforting. Not to mention it allowed a person to move around; stand, respond, sit, kneel, sit, stand. Catholic aerobics.

When time came for communion, non-Catholics Abby and her father remained in their pew. She noticed that Jason Coble, Lucy's ex-husband, also remained behind, the only one left in the family's seating area.

Abby had always thought he and Lucy were an odd match, but could never say exactly why. Not that she knew either of them all that well. Even though Betsy and

Constance had been close, Lucy and Abby had not. Lucy had been a few years ahead of Abby in school, but even if they'd been the same age, Abby doubted they would ever have been more than passing acquaintances. Lucy was breathtaking; an exotic hothouse flower, a beautiful contrast of pure, delicate white and vivid fuchsia. Abby was a common carnation; a filler flower.

Abby studied Jason Coble for a moment. She couldn't associate him with any plant or flower. He seemed much more like the earth that nurtured all living things. A silent source of strength; not all flash and glitter like Lucy's first husband.

Jason Coble wasn't from Preston. Lucy had met him while she'd been visiting a friend in Savannah. He was a nice-looking man; calm, confident, maybe a little stiff. He reminded Abby of a youngish college professor—in an Indiana Jones kind of way.

After receiving communion, Brenna returned to her seat beside her father. Her face looked as peaceful as any angel. Lucy was right behind her, crying and trembling so hard that Bryce had to support her.

After the service, Abby and Maggie remained in the sanctuary, sorting which flower arrangements would go with the family, which to the graveside, which to the local nursing home, and which would remain in the church.

As Jason and Brenna exited the sanctuary, Brenna hesitated, her gaze on her mother. Lucy was sobbing inconsolably, a tissue pressed to her mouth. Brenna looked up at Jason, her eyes filled with her conflicted allegiance.

Jason squeezed her hand and nodded. "Go on, Peanut."

"Love you, Daddy," Brenna said as she let go of his hand and slipped away.

"You, too, baby," Jason said softly.

Bryce was supporting Lucy by the arm. Brenna took her other hand, offering all of the comfort her little heart could hold.

Jason watched, thinking that even for Lucy this display of grief was overblown. He suspected an emotional fissure that most likely did not have its origins in her grandmother's passing. And emotional fissures for Lucy quickly became chasms. He'd have to keep a close eye.

Constance went to Lucy. As she did she shot Jason a look that said she'd extended her olive branch as far as she'd intended. He was no longer a part of this family picture.

He took a step back into the sanctuary and leaned against the doorjamb.

That was when he saw Betsy's daughter Abby. Her nearly waist-length dark hair was pulled away from her face in a wide clip, keeping it out of the way as she moved quickly and efficiently, sorting through the flower arrangements. Even with it held back like that, it flowed with her movements, falling over her shoulders like mahogany silk.

He wondered if it was as soft as it looked. An itch in the center of his palm urged him to find out.

That reaction took him by surprise. He hadn't felt the desire to touch a woman for a very long time—his complicated life just didn't allow those feelings to surface.

And yet, here he was, unable to look away from Abby Whitman.

She had the build of a woman who used her muscles, but somehow he doubted it was at a gym. She seemed the type to get her exercise outdoors. He liked that. It was natural, not the artificial toning and tanning Lucy had always subscribed to.

But it wasn't only Abby's appearance and energetic nature that drew his eye. It was the way she interacted with Maggie. She was neither coddling nor discounting—the two ways most people dealt with Maggie. She and Abby were working as a team, Abby directing matter-of-factly, yet kindly. Their mutual respect was as clear as the bells ringing in the church tower.

In that instant, Jason decided there was much to admire in Abby Whitman, beyond her reputation for artistic brilliance in her work.

He started down the center aisle, feeling as if fate was directing his feet, his unexpected attraction outweighing his reservations.

Abby had just pointed Maggie toward a sturdy white amaryllis that would go to the nursing home when she heard a footfall behind her. She glanced over her shoulder. Jason Coble stood in front of the first row of pews with his hands in his pants pockets.

Something flashed on his face when they made eye contact, as if he'd been startled by her turning.

He was even better-looking up close. But there was something more about him, a calm self-assurance that was far from arrogance. She'd been right in her assessment that he was like the earth, sustaining, giving.

He offered a friendly smile and gestured toward the flowers. "May I give you ladies a hand with those?"

Before Abby could respond, Maggie straightened with the amaryllis in hand. "Thank you. No. It's our job."

Jason gestured with a tip of his head toward the

narthex. "I wanted to give them some time. My presence tends to make Lucy more upset...."

Abby gave a nod of understanding, surprisingly pleased to have an excuse to keep him around for a while. She told herself it was simple curiosity.

She looked to Maggie. "If Dr. Coble helps us, we'll be on our way to Tidewater Manor that much sooner." Maggie loved visiting the nursing home when they delivered the flowers.

"Maybe I could help with the heavy ones," Jason said. "Of course, Maggie will need to tell me where they go."

Abby waited while Maggie made up her mind, fighting the urge to make the decision for her and accept his help.

After a moment, Maggie held the amaryllis out to him. "This goes by the side door." She pointed to the open door to the church office.

Jason nodded and took the plant.

As he started toward the office, Maggie called out. "Don't drop it."

"Yes, ma'am." His tone said he had a smile on his face.

Once all of the flowers that needed to be transported were out of the sanctuary, Maggie looked at Jason and said, "You did a good job."

He smiled in a way that brightened his entire being. Abby had always thought him reserved; certainly the picture Lucy's mother had painted of him to Abby's mother was that of a critical and unforgiving man. But what Abby had seen firsthand said he was anything but.

He put a hand on his chest and bowed slightly. "Knowing how serious you are about your work, I take that as a high compliment, Miss Maggie."

Maggie started toward the office. "Don't get a big head."

Abby winced. "Maggie can be a harsh taskmaster."

He smiled again. "Just glad I lived up to expectations."

Maggie called from the office door, "Ready to go, Abby?"

"I'll be right there." She turned to Jason. "Thanks for the help."

He gave a smile that exposed dimples Abby hadn't noticed until now. His hands pushed back his jacket and disappeared into his pants pockets again. He glanced toward the narthex. "My motive wasn't entirely selfless."

She returned his smile, reluctant to walk away. "Well, we appreciate it anyway."

With a nod, he took a step backward, then hesitated. "I was sorry to hear about your mother."

"Thank you."

His probing gaze locked with hers. "Unexpected deaths are always most difficult."

Looking into his eyes, she felt the jittery agitation that had been thrumming just beneath the surface of her skin all morning suddenly calm. The choppy ripples in her soul smoothed to a peaceful stillness. "It's taking time, but we're all adjusting."

"Your dad doing all right?"

Abby thought of this morning's overblown panic over his missing keys. "It's hardest on him. He and Mom always did everything together—"

"*Aaaaabeeeeee.*" Maggie called anxiously through the door.

"I'd better go. Thanks again." She stepped around him

to retrieve her purse from the first pew. As she did she brushed his arm and felt a little ripple of expectation.

When she looked up, her dad was coming toward them. She slipped her purse on her shoulder and waited.

With a smile, he shook hands with Jason. "Tom Whitman."

"Jason Coble . . . we've met, but it's been a while."

Her dad nodded. "Are you here with Abby?"

What an odd question.

"No." Jason cast a glance at Abby. "No, I'm Lucy's ex-husband."

Her dad's smile faltered, then quickly recovered. "Ah, yes." He turned to Abby. "You go on, sweetie. Constance and John want me to go with them to the place where they bury people."

The place where they bury people? What in the hell was wrong with him today?

Jason quietly prompted, "You mean the cemetery?"

Her father blinked and shifted his gaze away.

"Dad?"

After a moment, her father said, "They'll take me home after." He kissed her on the cheek. "I'll talk to you later, sweetie."

Unsure how to respond, she watched him walk away.

When she glanced at Jason Coble, the look in his eyes said that she might have reason to worry.

CHAPTER 2

After two extra games of checkers with Mr. Deveraux, Maggie insisted on polishing Mrs. Farnham's nails because she'd promised the last time she and Abby had been at Tidewater Manor. While Maggie took care of Mrs. Farnham, Abby polished Mrs. Farnham's roommate's nails. Abby could swear word spread faster at Tidewater than it did at Beanie's Cafe in downtown Preston. One by one, ladies trickled in to Mrs. Farnham's room, creating a traffic jam of walkers and wheelchairs. They came with questioning brows and hopeful gazes.

By the time Abby and Maggie left the facility, they'd done all of the resident ladies' nails, with the exception of Miss Turnbull, who, although Maggie was worried about her feeling left out, was in a coma and needed to have the color of her nail beds monitored.

As Abby drove through the rain back to St. Andrew's, Maggie grew uncommonly quiet. After a while, the sound of the windshield wipers thumping back and forth seemed to amplify the uncharacteristic silence. With a glance across the car, Abby said, "You certainly made those folks happy today."

Maggie kept her gaze on the windshield and sighed. After a moment, she said, "Do you think when Uncle Father dies I'll have to live at Tidewater Manor?" The pronunciation of her Rs was always thick, but when she was upset the impediment became more pronounced.

"Why would you ask that?"

With a shrug, Maggie shifted her gaze to her lap. She was picking at her cuticles. "I heard him talking on the phone to someone about it."

"Oh, Maggie, I think you must have misunderstood —"

"No!" Her head snapped up. "I. Heard. Him." She punched her blunt index finger into the palm of her other hand to emphasize each word.

Abby started to argue that Maggie's uncle wasn't going to die anytime soon, he was only in his mid-fifties after all, but stopped short. He had lost weight. He looked as if he wasn't sleeping well. Maybe he *was* sick.

She asked, "Do you know who he was talking to?"

"No. When he saw me he got mad and told me to go in the other room and close the door."

Mad? Father Kevin *mad* at Maggie?

"Sometimes adults make arrangements for their children...plan way ahead, just in case something unforeseen happens. Maybe he just didn't want you to worry over nothing."

Maggie slid Abby a sideways glance, pressing her mouth into a line of disbelief.

"There's no reason for you to worry about going to Tidewater. When the day comes that your uncle can't take care of you, there are lots of people in Preston who love you and can—"

"*I* take care of Uncle Father. He told me God knew he needed someone to take care of him, that's why He sent me." Defiance glittered in her eyes. "I take care of Uncle Father. I can take care of myself." She crossed her arms over her chest.

"Yes, you can." Abby agreed, deciding it really wasn't her place to be having this conversation with Maggie. "You do a good job of taking care of all of us."

"Darn right." Maggie's gaze returned to the road ahead, her mood seeming to lighten now that she had that off her chest.

When they arrived back at St. Andrew's, the rectory next door was dark and the light was on in Father Kevin's office.

"You don't have to walk me in," Maggie said. "It's raining."

"No problem. I need to measure for garland for the Ostrom wedding." A good excuse for going in to have a quick word with Maggie's uncle about Maggie's concern.

"But it's late."

With a wink, Abby said, "Which it wouldn't be if *someone* would have let Mr. Deveraux win at checkers sooner."

"He cheats." Maggie opened the van door. "You can't let a cheater win." She slammed the door and hurried with thudding steps up to the side door of the church.

Abby caught up just as Maggie swung open the door. The gloom pressed close in the oak-paneled hallway. A flickering shimmer of candlelight came from the sanctuary at the far end. Off to the right, Father Kevin's office door was ajar, allowing a sliver of light to fall onto the slate floor. She could see him pace past the opening, talking on his cell phone. He appeared agitated as he disappeared from view.

Abby had just opened her mouth to suggest to Maggie they wait before barging in on him when she heard his groan followed by a sharp bang and clatter.

"Uncle Father!"

Fearing his collapse, Abby rushed past Maggie, beating her through the door. Her toe hit the cell phone lying on the floor, sending it skittering across the slate.

Father Kevin spun around, his face wet with tears, his mouth a twist of agony. "Maggie?"

"I'm right here, Uncle Father."

With a trembling mouth, he raced across the room and crushed his niece to his chest. "Praise God! You're all right."

"What's wrong?" Abby's heart began to settle back into its proper place as she slowly bent to pick up the phone.

Father Kevin turned his face toward Abby, seemingly reluctant to release Maggie from his arms. "It's late. You didn't answer your cell."

"Oh!" Abby, her own hands shaking from the adrenaline rush, reached inside her purse. "Sorry. I forgot to turn it back on after the funeral." She turned the phone on, its cheerful welcoming tones ringing hollowly in the room.

Father Kevin pressed a kiss on the top of Maggie's head and mumbled, "You're all right."

"We didn't mean to worry you," Abby said.

Father Kevin straightened and released his niece. He

drew a deep, shuddering breath. "Sorry. I overreacted—with the rain-slick roads and all."

As Abby handed him the cell phone, his eyes still held the glitter of agitation and his face was shiny with perspiration.

"Are you all right?" she asked. "Let me get you some water."

"I'm fine. Fine." He put a hand on Abby's arm and took a step toward the office door, escorting her out. His hand was trembling.

Maggie said, "I'm going on to the house."

Father Kevin's head snapped her way. "No!" He paused. "I'll only be another minute here. We can share the umbrella."

Maggie shrugged and flopped into the worn leather chair across from his desk.

He walked Abby to the office door. "Thanks for taking Maggie along. She always enjoys it." His voice had the tone of manufactured casualness.

"They all love to see her come." Abby didn't have the heart to bring up the question Maggie posed on the ride home. "And she's great company for me."

"She's a special girl." He looked toward his niece with heartbreaking tenderness. Not really surprising. Maggie could stir protective instincts even in the most callous heart.

"Yes, she is." Abby agreed. The sheen of perspiration seemed to be disappearing from his face. "You're sure you're all right?"

He nodded and put one hand on the doorknob, giving Abby a gentle nudge with his other. Clearly he was embarrassed by his behavior and was anxious to get her on her way. "Good-bye, Abby. And thanks again."

"Good night, Father." Abby moved through the open door and it closed quietly behind her.

She glanced toward the sanctuary on her way out. A dark figure huddled at the kneeling rail. Candlelight reflected the pale oval of his face. He was not bowed in prayer or gazing at the crucifix, but staring directly into the hallway where Abby stood. The instant their eyes met, he turned away and bowed his head.

Feeling like an intruder on the man's solitude, an eavesdropper on his prayers, Abby hurriedly headed for the side door.

Yet another feeling ran just beneath her embarrassment, the nagging of something being off, out of place.

She nearly turned around and went back to knock on Father Kevin's door to make sure he knew someone was in the church. Recalling the look in his eyes as he'd hurried her out his office reinforced the fact that she was a visitor here; she needed to leave both the parishioner and the priest to their privacy.

As Abby got in her van and started the engine, it dawned on her what had bothered her about the man in the sanctuary; he still wore his hat.

Let Maggie get one look at that and she'd make certain the poor guy wouldn't make that mistake again.

Jason leaned back in his desk chair and rubbed his eyes. It had grown dark nearly an hour ago. The desk lamp in his office was the only illumination in the house. He got up, stretched his arms over his head, and shut the lamp off. If he was going to eat, he'd have to go out. The kitchen was bare, as it usually was on the weeks when he didn't have Brenna. He wondered why dining out by himself felt less lonely than grocery shopping for one. He supposed it had something to do with living in a small town; invariably, he ran into someone with whom he could have at least a passing conversation.

The rain that had begun during Vera's burial had settled in like an uninvited relative. Jason ducked his head into his collar as he hurried to the detached garage, thinking that Lucy was having enough trouble with her grief without dreary weather compounding it. She'd seemed to fold in on herself as Bryce had helped her to the family car at the cemetery.

Jason put up the garage door, but before he started his car he dialed Bryce's cell phone.

"Hey, Jason." The "Dad" vulnerability of earlier in the day had apparently departed. The tinny sound of iPod earbuds filled the background. Jason could picture Bryce sitting there with one of them plucked from his ear and dangling on his chest.

"You really need to turn that thing down; you're going to ruin your hearing."

Bryce sighed loudly, but the music disappeared.

"I was just calling to see how everyone is," Jason said.

"Fine."

"Are you still at Grandmother's?" As with her name, Constance refused anything short of proper. She was the only person in the world to call Lucy *Lucinda*.

"No."

"Been home long?"

"A while."

Jason could hear the shrug in his son's voice. He longed for the day when Bryce would emerge from his teen years and participate in more than monosyllabic conversation again.

Jason asked, "Mom holding up okay?"

There was the slightest beat of a pause. "Yeah."

"Can you expand on that?" Jason prompted.

"She laid down for a nap after we got home."

"She's still sleeping?"

"Um, I'm not sure."

"What's your sister doing?"

"Watching a Disney DVD."

"I was just headed out to get some dinner. You and Brenna want to come?" *And while I'm picking you up, I can check on your mother's sobriety.*

"No." The answer was unusually curt, even for Bryce.

Before Jason could say anything else, Bryce added in a tone that bordered on apologetic, "I really think we should stay with Mom. Besides, we already ate. Grandmother sent home a bunch of food people carried in to her house."

"All right, then. Tell Brenna I'll call her at bedtime." He paused. "And Bryce...call if you need me."

"Right. Bye."

Jason ended the call feeling more disconnected and isolated than he had in a long while.

The sand and gravel parking lot at Jeter's Restaurant was jammed with haphazardly parked cars. It looked like a junkyard jigsaw puzzle with ill-fitting pieces. Not for the first time, Abby thought that a little organization might help. She knew that Sam Jeter didn't want to risk losing the mature trees that grew at random both in and around the lot by paving it, but it seemed he could somehow define the parking spaces. At the very least, he could reserve a spot for carry-out orders.

She wove through the maze of bumpers and taillights and finally found a place to squeeze in her van. One of these days she'd be able to afford a second vehicle, something small and fast, easy to park; she wouldn't have to drive this logo-branded beast everywhere. Of course, her sister—who designed said logo—was quick to point out that the van was inexpensive advertising, a mobile billboard, which was necessary since Abby's business was run out of the old carriage house on the family property and not where anyone could see it. Truth was if folks wanted flowers in Preston, it was Abby or the Internet. Courtney just liked the idea of her artwork on constant display.

The rain had stopped. As Abby gathered her purse, drips from the trees hit the top of the van, echoing like a drum. It was a lonely sound that served to remind her she'd be eating by herself again tonight.

Jeter's was a jack-of-all-trades eatery, family dining mixed with a small arcade, a pool room, and a bar. There was a wide porch on the side with wooden picnic tables; empty tonight because of the weather. The place was Lowcountry through and through, complete with rough-sawn wood, corrugated galvanized steel, and buckets built into the tables for the crab and shrimp shells. Out back was the big smoker for the pulled pork and ribs.

When Abby entered, she was pinned against the door by the crowd of people waiting for tables. The din of dozens of conversations was punctuated by the occasional child's squeal and clack of balls in the pool room. Everything was overshadowed by too-loud music.

She was in no mood for chaos. Today had been filled with too many unsettling events. Dad. Father Kevin. Worst of all, those damn muddy footprints. With the distraction of her work day over, these things had become a toxin invading her thoughts. The festering splinter of her sleepwalking was throbbing with each heartbeat. It whispered a cadence of condemnation that matched the rhythm of her pulse.

And beneath that, reaching across time, was the echo of her sister's screams—

"Are you all right?"

Abby blinked; the cries of pain and terror faded back into the past, sliding beneath the lively sounds of Jeter's. The hostess stood in front of her with a concerned look on her face.

While Abby had been lost in thought, the path to the bar had cleared.

"Fine." Abby forced a smile and moved toward the bar. "Just picking up a carry-out order."

The barstools were nearly all taken. A knot of people were having an animated conversation in front of where she normally picked up her order.

As she stepped up behind an open barstool, she made an effort to avoid making eye contact with anyone. The problem with small towns was when you wanted to grab and dash with your dinner someone invariably sucked you into an unwanted conversation.

Sam noticed her from behind the bar and nodded. He finished mixing a drink and then grabbed a brown paper bag from near the register. Before he reached her with it, a voice on her left said, "Did you and Maggie get all of the flowers delivered?"

Even with a simple question, Jason Coble's voice soothed her ruffled nerve endings and all thoughts of avoiding conversation evaporated.

"We did," she said, turning to him. "Thanks to your help, Maggie had time for an extra game of checkers with Mr. Deveraux."

Sam set the bag with her dinner on the bar and Abby paid her bill.

Jason eyed the bag. "Dinner for one?"

He was wearing an oxford shirt with rolled-up sleeves and jeans; looking less like Indiana Jones and more like the kind of professor college girls fell wildly in love with. Quiet. Confident. Hot.

"As a matter of fact, yes," she admitted.

He gestured to the empty barstool next to him. "Join me? I'll buy you a beer to go with whatever's in that bag."

His semi-sad smile tugged at her heart. She imagined the loneliness in his eyes was reflected in her own.

The appeal of eating in her empty house was diminishing by the second; the whole idea suddenly felt more like exile than sanctuary.

It bothered her a little that his presence could change her once-set mind so quickly. Even so, she sat down next to him. "Thanks, I believe I will."

Sam came back and handed Abby real silverware and a napkin. She ordered a beer; Jason made certain it went on his tab.

As Sam walked away, he shot Abby a wink. She responded with a perturbed stare. Damn busybody. This was why she ate at home.

Jason, seemingly oblivious to her eye war with Sam, reached over and pulled the top of her bag open. He peeked inside. "Maybe you have something better than boiled shrimp in there."

Abby drew the bag to her. "I do." She looked at him sternly. "And I don't share."

He leaned close when she opened the Styrofoam container, breathing deeply as the steam rose from her pecan-honey-glazed fried chicken. "Didn't expect a skinny girl like you—"

She thumped the top of his head with the back of her spoon.

He jerked upright, surprise in his eyes.

"You get over there and peel your low-fat shrimp." She shooed him away with a flip of her fingers.

He laughed and the shadow of sadness seemed to lift from him. It felt nice to have boosted his spirits, and she realized he'd improved hers as well.

They talked of inconsequential things for a while. Jason's dry humor engaged her completely, keeping her thoughts away from dark places. He finished his beer and ordered another. Abby declined a second, but ordered coffee, just to have a reason to stay.

There was a lull in their conversation as she stirred cream into her coffee. She toyed with the idea of quizzing him about her father's lapses—who better to let her know if she had reason to worry than a psychiatrist. But tonight he wasn't a psychiatrist. He was just a guy in a bar; a charming guy who made her laugh and forget her own worries. Why drag things down? Besides, it would be like asking for free professional advice. Wrong. Wrong. Wrong.

"What are you thinking about?" he asked.

She lifted her coffee cup. "About how many sit-ups I'm going to have to do to keep that fried chicken from being the straw that popped the button on my jeans."

"Liar."

The sip of coffee she'd just taken made a U-turn. After she dabbed her mouth with a napkin, trying to recover ladylike composure after nearly spewing coffee out of her nose, she turned to him with a raised brow. "I beg your pardon?"

His teasing hazel eyes held hers. "Liar." He said it slowly and distinctly.

"Well, I heard what you said. I was giving you a chance to save yourself."

"Am I on dangerous ground?"

"Let's just say that the last boy who called me a liar got a black eye, and I got a trip to the principal's office."

He pulled a frightened face and held up his palms. "Let me restate. Something's on your mind and it's not fried chicken."

"Ooooh, *Doctor* Coble, I didn't know you were psychic, too."

He laughed and shook his head. "Sorry. Didn't mean to pry. I guess it's a hazard of the profession." He paused and his gaze grew softer, concerned. "It's just that you looked so sad." His hand came close to her face, as if he was going to touch her cheek. He hesitated, then withdrew and wrapped his hand around his beer.

She sighed and buried the tingle of anticipation she'd felt when she thought he was going to touch her.

"It's been a long day is all."

"Yeah, it has." He sounded as tired as she felt. And

she hated the fact that she'd dragged down both of their moods.

Jason paid his bill. Then he picked her jacket up off the back of her bar stool and held it for her. "I'll walk you to your car."

She almost told him there was no need, but she wasn't ready to part with his company just yet. So she slipped into her coat with a nod of thanks.

He held the door for her and they stepped out into the dim light of the parking area. The moon was overhead, its light muted in the gauze of breaking clouds.

She said, "Looks like the rain's finished with us tonight."

He looked up. "Looks like it. Which way is your car?"

"Over there." It was nearly blocked from sight on the far side of a large bush where the parking lot merged with the woods.

Jason took her elbow and started that way. "I want to thank you," he said as they walked.

"Thank me?"

"For staying to have dinner with me. Next time I'll buy more than just your beer."

"Next time?" She stopped, tilted her head, and looked at him.

"Yeah, I'd like there to be a next time."

"Me, too." They stood there like a couple of teenagers for a long moment.

A car horn honked, making them both jump. Someone was trying to back out of a space; Abby and Jason were in the way.

When Jason's gaze broke from hers, she was relieved

from the unexpected, and unsettling, intensity of the moment.

With a hand raised in apology to the driver, Jason moved them along toward her van. It was getting darker with each step away from the building.

"Don't you know a lady shouldn't park in a dark and hidden spot like this? What if I wasn't here to walk you out?"

"I take care of my own self."

"Seems I heard Maggie say the same thing to her uncle today."

"Ah, but I can back it up—remember the kid with a black eye."

A hand went to his chest in feigned shock. "What kind of Southern belle are you?"

"The cast iron kind that's used to ringing solo."

His laugh echoed off the trees as he opened the door to her van. The sound crawled deep inside her and nested near her heart, humming inside all the way home. She felt its presence as she went through her nightly routine. And when she crawled into bed a short while later, she placed her hand on her chest and swore that residual laughter was radiating a heat of its own.

CHAPTER 3

Awareness crept close, wielding a club which it used to pound the inside of Abby's skull.

A frog croaked incessantly, its voice like sandpaper on her brain. And it was close. So close. Under her bed?

She shifted and heard gravel raining from her ceiling.

Then she realized she was sitting—and listing to the right. Her feet were wet.

She opened her eyes—or eye; the left one refused. Raising her left brow to elevate the upper lid, she managed a useless slit. Her right eye began to focus. There was a greenish glow in front of her. A dashboard. *Her* dashboard.

The white deflated balloon of the airbag hung from the steering wheel.

A cool, damp breeze moved past, sending a clammy shiver down the back of her neck.

She lifted her hand to her head. With her movement, gravel ticked as it hit the interior of the van. Not gravel, she realized. Broken glass.

The windshield was intact. Dead ahead, the illumination

from one headlight, the right one, glowed just beneath the surface of the brown water. Tendrils of mist curled from the water's surface, twining through clumps of tall marsh grass. The world beyond was wrapped in impenetrable darkness.

The window in the driver's door was missing, which accounted for the glass bits.

Her head throbbed with each sluggish heartbeat.

She touched her temple, then held her fingers close to the meager light from the dash. They were dark. Blood.

That frog continued to croak, louder.

"Shut up!" She was rewarded with a slice of fresh pain in her head, much worse than what the frog had caused. Nevertheless, she felt better for having yelled at it.

The clock on the dash said three-fifteen. The last thing she could remember was Jason Coble walking her to the van in Jeter's parking lot. Hours ago.

She tried to lean forward but the seat belt held tight.

With trembling fingers, she fumbled to release the seat belt buckle. It came undone, but did not retract. She slid it off her left shoulder and the metal plate on the belt clanked against the door panel, startling the frog into temporary silence.

With effort, she pushed open the driver's door. It moved cumbrously, not because of the pressure of water on the outside—it wasn't deep—but because she was fighting gravity. The van's right side was at least two feet lower than the left.

For a moment, she sat there, putting off getting into the water. She hated swimming in anything where she couldn't see what was swimming with her. She never got more than ankle deep at the beach. The marsh looked like something from a horror film, dark, misty, and endless.

But it couldn't be endless. She'd driven her van into it. The road couldn't be very far.

She slid off the seat, her pencil skirt riding up her thighs. She eased lower, until her feet met with solid ground—solid being an overstatement. What was underfoot had the consistency of tapioca pudding. The cold water was deeper than she'd expected, up to her thighs.

Common sense said the road had to be on the left. Unless she'd been spun around. There were no visible lights in any direction.

She listened. Nothing but crickets and frogs. No traffic noise to orient herself.

The shock of the cold water began to clear her head. Her cell phone!

She turned around and boosted herself back into the tilted van by grabbing the door frame.

Her purse wasn't on the passenger seat. Reaching toward the passenger floorboard, she hit water almost immediately.

"Crap."

She started to shiver.

Groping blindly in the water, she located her purse.

Not much chance the cell would work. She dug through the soggy contents of her bag anyway and located the phone. She pressed several buttons before she gave up on there being a glimmer of life in it. She threw it back in her purse, opened the glove box, and retrieved a flashlight.

"Please let these batteries be good."

When her trembling fingers flipped the switch, the light came on. "Thank you, God."

With flashlight in hand and her purse on her shoulder, she once again lowered herself into the water. She swept the flashlight three hundred and sixty degrees. Nothing but tall grasses on the far side of the van. There was a fairly dense woods to the left, hulking trees draped with Spanish moss beneath which grew a tangle of under-growth. That had to be the direction of the road.

Steadying herself with one hand on the open van door, she pulled her left foot out of the muck and her shoe was sucked off her foot.

Don't think of the snakes.

Slowly, she put her bare foot on the marsh bottom again.

She took another step that cost her right shoe. One more step and she wouldn't be able to steady herself with the van's door any longer.

No choice but to go forward.

Fighting the drag of the water and the pull of the mud, it was slow going. The more she tried to not think of all the things that lived in marshes and ponds, the more snakes and gators dominated her mind.

There! Did she hear something? She halted and held her breath.

Definitely. A rustling in the vegetation. The lap of a water ripple against something solid.

She held perfectly still until the chattering of her teeth told her she had to move—take her chances of attracting a gator or die of hypothermia.

There is no gator. Get moving.

Almost to the first scrubby tree. Just a few more steps—and she didn't hear a gator thrashing behind her.

Gators don't thrash until they have you—

Something bumped against her leg.

With a scream, she tried to run. The mud held onto her

feet and she pitched headlong into the water, losing both the flashlight and her purse.

Her feet broke free and she flailed toward the trees, anticipating the painful chomp of a gator or the sharp sting of poisonous snake fangs.

Neither came.

She pulled herself out of the water and up a short slope by grasping handfuls of tall weeds and low branches.

Once at the grade of the narrow road, she took several loping steps, then collapsed onto the ground, gasping and spitting out brackish water.

After she caught her breath and was certain no gator was on her heels, she stood up and looked around.

Giant old-growth trees lined both sides of the road; ghosts of Spanish moss shifted in the breeze. Beneath the arching boughs, scrub and squat palmettos were so dense it was difficult to even see the water she'd just fled. Looking around, she couldn't believe she hadn't hit one of the thick trunks or gnarled low-reaching branches as she'd veered off the pavement.

Long fingers of fog rose from the marsh, reaching across the narrow road in several places. The road itself was unlined crumbling asphalt, barely wide enough for two small cars to pass one another. Definitely not the road between Jeter's and home, but it could be any one of a dozen roads in the general vicinity of Preston.

Had her van been in the marsh for hours and hours? It was impossible to see from the road; no one passing by would notice it without really looking for it.

Turning in a circle, she couldn't decide which way she should start walking.

Then, far down the road, she saw light. Headlights.

The twin dots increased in size so quickly that she knew the vehicle was coming fast.

Help. Someone was here to help. It was a miracle out here at this hour on a weeknight.

Before the vehicle was close enough for its headlight beams to illuminate her, it stopped so suddenly she could hear the tires skid on the pavement.

"No!" She tried to trot that way, limping, waving her hands over her head. "Help!"

The headlights swung around in a reckless three-point turn.

Abby slowed, staring at red taillights that were receding as quickly as the headlights had been approaching.

"Come back...please..." She stood shivering in the center of the road; dizzy, barefooted, her wet blouse clinging to her.

Suddenly a strobe light reflected off the foliage around her. She spun around. An emergency vehicle, lights flashing but without a siren, was coming from the opposite direction.

"Thank God." She raised her hands and waved.

The police car stopped a few feet in front of her and its driver door opened.

Abby walked toward the officer who was no more than a silhouette against glaring lights.

"Miss?" he called. "Are you all right?"

"Pretty much," she said. "My van ran off the road."

"I'll radio for an ambulance."

"I'm really okay."

But her protest went unheard; he was already talking into the radio attached at his shoulder.

Then he said to her, "You can hang up now."

"What?"

"911 dispatch is still on the line with your cell. You can hang up; free up the line."

Obediently, Abby reached for the purse that wasn't on her shoulder. "It's in the water—dead."

His hand once again went to the microphone attached to his shoulder. "You sure that line is still open?"

Dispatch's crackling answer came over the radio. "Yes. I can still hear the frogs."

"But not us?"

"No. Are you at the scene?"

He looked at Abby. "Did you call 911?"

She shook her head, dread building in her chest.

"Then somebody else is out here."

CHAPTER 4

Abby stood there, looking at the officer as if she couldn't understand what he'd just said. But she had understood. It was just too awful to face. Someone else was out here. Someone who had called 911—someone too injured to get out of the car and come to the road as she had.

Another fact sunk in. If the 911 call had recently been made, as the arrival of the deputy probably indicated, she hadn't driven into the marsh hours ago on her way home from dinner.

But what reason would she have had to be out here in the middle of nowhere in the dead of night?

Those muddy footprints came to mind.

Oh shit.

"Which direction were you coming from?" the officer asked.

She hesitated. What if she *had* been sleep-driving? It seemed preposterous, but so did a lot of other things she'd done while asleep. "Um, I don't remember." She felt the lump on her forehead. "I don't remember what happened at all. I don't even know where we are." She pointed, "My van is over there, pointed that way."

He nodded and then spoke into his radio again, "Is the person on the line responsive?"

"No," the 911 operator said. "There's been no verbal communication at all. Just an open line."

He signed off his radio and looked at Abby. "I want you to sit in my car and wait for the ambulance." He took her elbow and urged her in that direction.

Once she was in the back seat, he retrieved a blanket from the trunk and wrapped it around her shoulders. "You stay here. The ambulance will be here soon."

She nodded mutely. Her tongue felt too thick to speak.

She watched him through the windshield as he walked away. He became more obscure as he moved out of the headlight beams, shining his flashlight on the pavement and searching the woods on either side of the road. Soon all she could see of him was the sweep of the flashlight beam.

Suddenly, the light veered to the right and disappeared into the woods.

Someone is out there. Someone is hurt. It's all my fault.

Abby jumped out of the car, dropping the blanket to the ground as she tried to hurry toward the place the officer had disappeared. Dizziness kept her from moving in a straight line. Her bare feet slapped the pavement, every footfall shot a drumbeat of pain through her head.

In the distance behind her, she heard the thin wail of an approaching siren.

Abby struggled to move faster.

Off to the right, the opposite side of the road from the marsh, she caught the flicker of the officer's flashlight through the woods. She stumbled in that direction, sliding down into the ditch next to the road, and then scrabbling back out the other side. Every sliding step was punctuated by a sharp stab or a rough scrape.

The officer was kneeling beside a motorcycle, the flashlight shining on its bent front wheel and twisted handlebars. Then she saw it wasn't just the motorcycle; a person lay beyond it. He wasn't moving.

The officer looked up. When he saw her, he moved the light away from the wreckage and shone it on her, blinding her from the sight of what she'd done.

He hurried in her direction. "I told you to wait in the car."

"Is...is he...?" She couldn't finish the question.

"What's your name?" he asked as he took her shoulders and turned her back toward the road.

"Abby Whitman."

"From Preston?" He started them walking, keeping his body between her and the man on the ground.

"Yes." Although she'd known the truth the instant she laid eyes on the still form and the unnatural angles of his limbs, she forced herself to say, "Tell me! Is he—"

"I'm Deputy Trowbridge. You have any ID?"

"I lost it in the water. I fell...dropped my purse..." Her words accelerated as she spoke, as if in defense. "...it had my driver's license—"

"It's all right."

She offered, "The registration is in the van."

He held onto her upper arm as they crossed the roadside ditch. It didn't feel nearly as deep or as steep with his assistance.

When they reached the road, the EMS unit was pulling

up behind the squad car. Deputy Trowbridge walked Abby straight toward it.

"Carl will take care of you," he said as he handed her off to one of the paramedics. The other walked away with Trowbridge.

Abby stood rooted in place, watching the deputy and the paramedic walk down the road following the bobbling beam of the flashlight. They weren't moving at a frantic pace.

As she watched their slow progression, a scream built in her chest. She gritted her teeth to keep it inside.

Carl the paramedic had picked up the blanket she'd dropped on the road and wrapped it around her again. "Let's go check you out." He gave a gentle nudge toward the EMS truck.

Abby wanted to run after the deputy, to demand the answer to the question she could barely comprehend, but her leaden feet moved toward the ambulance.

"Are you in much pain?" Carl the paramedic asked as they walked slowly toward the truck, his steadying hand on her elbow.

She shook her head; her jaw clenched against the scream, against the fear of irrevocable actions.

As they got closer, the rough rumble of the engine drowned out all other noise, and the sharp smell of diesel burned her nose and turned her stomach.

Carl helped Abby into the back of the truck; the diesel smell was less strong here, the lights blindingly bright.

He checked Abby's pupils and asked her a dozen questions which seemed aimed at assessing her cognitive skills. She answered absently, her mind whirring with the reality of what she'd done, while at the same time clinging to the thin hope that the motorcyclist was in better shape than he had appeared; he'd called 911 after all.

A few moments later, Deputy Trowbridge appeared at the open back doors of the truck. "I need you to take a sobriety test, Ms. Whitman."

"I haven't been drinking." Even though she couldn't remember anything of the past few hours, she was pretty sure her driving impairment wasn't caused by alcohol.

"Are you refusing to take the test?" he said coolly.

"I ... no, I just haven't ... of course I'll take it."

By the time Abby had taken the breathalyzer, two additional sheriff's department cars had arrived. The new deputies blocked off the road with a portable barricade topped with blinking yellow lights.

The other paramedic returned with his kit and no victim. They closed the back doors and headed toward the hospital with Abby sitting in the back. As they drove past the road block, she saw the coroner's van arriving.

Dear God. The worst was true. Her sleepwalking had finally killed someone.

Bryce awakened to realize he was still fully clothed on top of his comforter. It was three-thirty a.m. Light shone through the space between the bottom of his bedroom door and the carpet. His mom never left the lights on after she went to bed.

He nearly turned over and went back to sleep, but that light nagged him. Was Mom still up? Was she okay?

He should have spent the evening with her instead of shut up here in his room. But man, how much could a person take? All he'd wanted was some time without drama. And Mom was drama in spades.

He got up and opened his door. The house was silent. Bren's bedroom door was opened just a crack, as always. He tiptoed close and peeked in. Bren was sleeping on her side, facing the door, that little stuffed dog she'd had since she was a baby tucked beneath her chin.

His mother's bedroom door was open. When he looked in, the bed was made, the comforter rumpled from where she'd napped earlier. The door to the master bath was open. It was dark.

She'd been such a freakin' mess today. He'd been embarrassed for her at the funeral; he didn't like Jason seeing her like that.

Had it bothered *her* that he had?

Oh God, had she done something...?

Bryce dashed to the master bath and flipped on the light.

It took him a moment to realize the image he'd re-created in his mind didn't exist—not this time. The bathroom was empty.

Still quivering inside from his adrenaline rush, he went downstairs. The lights were all on, but the living room was empty. So was the kitchen. He checked all of his mother's old hiding places and was relieved not to find a single vodka bottle.

Where the hell was she? It was too damn cold to be outside.

He checked the garage. Her car was gone.

Shit. This was not good.

It was nearly eight a.m. when Abby finally had her release papers from the Emergency room in hand. It had been a grueling night, made worse by the doubt in

Deputy Trowbridge's eyes every time she answered his questions with, "I can't remember."

It was the truth. And she wasn't about to start speculating aloud to the police until she'd had some time to see if her memory would return. Was sleep driving even possible?

As the ambulance had driven away from the accident scene, it had taken two sharp ninety-degree turns back to back and Abby had finally figured out where she'd had her accident. Suicide Road. That was what people called it anyway; Abby had never known it by any other name. It was little used except for those who sought the thrill of high-speed turns, since its main purpose was to link a couple of boat launches on the river.

And it wasn't far from Abby's house; in fact, she and her sister used to ride their bikes on it when they'd been kids.

That proximity to home made her even more suspicious that she'd somehow been driving while asleep. How would she ever know for certain?

She couldn't remember anything after leaving Jason in Jeter's parking lot. Where had she been in the hours between nine p.m. and shortly before three a.m.? She *was* wearing the same clothes—but she'd gotten dressed while sleepwalking more than once in the past.

The hospital had drawn blood for a full drug screen. Abby didn't take drugs. If something showed up, that might answer her questions; but not in a way that was any less disturbing than sleepwalking. The only thing she'd consumed had been at Jeter's, sitting beside Jason Coble—a man with a prescription pad.

No. There was no way. She would have seen him put something in her drink. And she'd felt fine as she'd walked to the van.

Sleepwalking was the most likely answer. Perhaps when she got home she'd find proof she'd been there after Jeter's. Until then, she was keeping her speculation to herself.

The ER doctor had assured her that it wasn't uncommon for an accident victim not to recall the time prior to an accident. And, he'd said, she might never remember more than she did at the moment.

She'd killed someone and couldn't recall a scrap of it. God! Even if the accident investigation didn't lay blame at her feet, how could she live with that?

So far the police wouldn't even tell her who the man was.

The glimpse she'd gotten of that lifeless body had branded itself on her brain. It was there with every blink of her eyes, with every breath she took.

Fatigue buzzed wasp-like in her head. Her thoughts were like puzzle pieces shaken in a box.

"Do you have someone to pick you up?" The nurse's voice startled Abby out of her thoughts. She realized she'd been standing in the middle of the ER hallway with her papers in hand, no doubt looking lost and confused.

"I can call my Dad."

The nurse smiled and pointed toward a wall phone. "You can use that phone there. Just dial nine first."

"Thank you."

In order to get her dad there without alarming him, she told him she was delivering flowers at the hospital and had a flat tire, asking him to come and pick her up. Then she left the ER and walked through the hospital to the main entrance and waited.

* * *

Bryce awakened to someone poking him on the shoulder. He rolled over and almost fell off the living room couch.

He blinked.

It was daylight.

Bren was standing there holding her stuffed dog. "Are we going to school today? I can't get Mommy to wake up."

"Where is she?" He kept his voice even, kicking back the panic clawing at his back.

"In bed." She looked more puzzled than scared.

A dozen alarmed questions popped into his mind, none of which he'd ask his baby sister. "You go on and get some cereal. I'll check on her."

For a long moment, Bren stood there with a look in her eyes that scared the shit out of him—a look that said she trusted *him* to make it all right.

He touched her shoulder. "It's okay. Go on."

As soon as she walked into the kitchen, Bryce raced up the stairs two at a time. Shit. He'd waited up for his mom to come home and fallen asleep on the couch. If he'd stayed awake...

He skidded to a stop at his mother's open bedroom door.

She lay diagonally on the bed on her stomach, wearing only her underwear. Her face was turned away, her clothes in a heap on the floor.

Bryce swallowed dryly and walked into the room, steeling himself for the worst.

Slowly, he reached toward her arm, fearing the same cold, unyielding feel of Grandmother Vera's skin in the

casket. Now he wished he hadn't touched his dead grand
mother. But he'd been so curious....

His fingers made contact with his mother's skin.
Warm. Alive.

His breath left him in a rush and dizziness washed
over him.

"Mom." He shook her hard "Mom!"

She mumbled and swatted him away.

It was a routine that was sickeningly familiar. There
would be no waking her until she slept this one off.

Bryce left the bedroom and closed the door.

He had to get Brenna ready for school.

"Abby?"

Abby turned away from the glass doors that led to
the entrance portico of the hospital. The movement told
her that she'd been still too long; her sore muscles were
beginning to tighten and cramp.

Jason Coble stood there, wearing a hospital ID tag, a
dress shirt and tie, and black slacks. He looked just as hot
as last evening—but in a much more professional way.

His greeting smile faded. "Oh my God, are you
all right?" he asked, eyeing her bruised and butterfly-
bandaged forehead. "What happened?"

"I had an accident." She bit her lower lip to keep from
saying more. The knot arose in her throat again as she
thought of that poor man lying in the woods. But she'd
held herself together this long; she was determined not to
break down until she got behind the privacy of her own
door.

She tucked her hands behind her back as the trembling
began once again. Her dismissal papers rattled slightly as

they shook against the back of her skirt. She hoped Jason didn't notice.

He walked closer. "In a car?" He raised his brow and pointed to the stains and mud crusted on her clothes.

"My van went into the marsh." She looked down at herself. "This happened when I walked out." Walk being a relative term, she thought.

"But you're all right? You've been checked out in the ER?" His hazel eyes reflected the concern in his voice. She felt foolish for even flirting with the possibility that he'd drugged her while they sat in Jeter's last night.

"Yes. I'm just waiting for my dad to pick me up."

"How did it happen? The accident, I mean. Was it on your way home from Jeter's?"

"I don't think so. I lost consciousness." She touched the throbbing bump on her head. "I really can't remember anything."

"And they're letting you walk out of here! You should be held for observation—"

"I'm fine." She cut him off firmly, even though the very uttering of it shot pain through her head and tensed sore muscles in her neck.

He stood there with his hands on his hips, glaring. And the man had one forceful glare.

"Really, I'm all right," she said. "They checked me over completely—X-rays and everything. I have the papers here to prove it." She held up her dismissal forms. "Besides, some of us small business folk don't have the luxury of health insurance."

"Lack of insurance is no reason for negligent care." He looked as if he was going to pick her up and carry her back to the ER and demand they admit her.

"Dr. Morris gave me all of the lecturing I need."

His eyes narrowed. "So he *wanted* to admit you."

"No, he didn't. Not exactly. He mentioned the possibility. When I said I'd rather not, he didn't argue. He just had me sign an extra paper."

"Abby!"

"I'm *fine*! I just want to go home and go to bed." She realized she sounded like a whiny child, but seriously, if she didn't get home soon she was going to have a breakdown here in public. She added, "And I'll go see my family doctor tomorrow morning if I'm feeling anything more than sore."

He gave an exasperated sigh, but at least he no longer looked as if he was going to go caveman on her. "Is there anything I can do?"

"You're sweet to offer, but no." *Now go away. I want to be alone—just in case the growing cracks cause me to fly into a million pieces.*

"I'll stay with you until your dad comes."

The last thing she needed was explaining all of this to her dad in front of Jason. She pointed to the hospital ID. "I'm sure you have doctor things to do."

"Nothing that can't wait."

It appeared he was determined. And she was too tired to fight anymore. So she fell quiet, watching out the front doors again.

Jason surprised her by following her lead and letting silence rule the moment. And, as he stood quietly by her side, he had the same calming effect on her as he had yesterday in the sanctuary. After a few minutes, her tension ebbed and fatigue took the upper hand.

She must have swayed on her feet, because he took her elbow and said, "I think you should wait sitting down."

"I don't understand why Dad isn't here yet. He was at home when I called; ten minutes away."

"How long ago?"

She looked at the clock over the reception desk—her watch had fogged over and stopped working—and was surprised to realize how much time had passed.

A sickness bloomed in her belly. "Nearly an hour ago."

CHAPTER 5

Abby explained to Jason how she'd lost her cell phone in the marsh. She told it dispassionately, but he saw the anxiety in her eyes and tension in every muscle of her body. She must have been terrified out there in the dark, disoriented, hurt, and alone.

It was clear by her scant details that she didn't want to talk about the accident. Jason respected her privacy even though he desperately wanted to know what had happened to her—and, he realized, not because of simple curiosity. For some reason he *needed* to know everything about her.

He swallowed his questions, handed her his Black-Berry, and suggested she call her father again. "Maybe he got...distracted."

The sharp look she shot him before she dialed confirmed his suspicion that Abby wasn't completely unaware that something could be going on with her father's mental health.

Jason watched the worry in her eyes intensify as that call went unanswered.

Dear God, he wanted to hold her, assure her that her

nightmare of a night would not turn into a hellish day. When he'd laid eyes on her moments ago she already presented such a tragic picture that he'd had to make a conscious effort not to reach out and comfort her. That contusion on her head had to be killing her. Her white blouse, the same one she'd had on at the funeral yesterday, the one that was fitted and oh-so-flattering, was untucked from her skirt, dirty, and torn slightly at the shoulder seam. She wore tan non-skid hospital socks instead of shoes. And that long, beautiful dark hair was matted and tangled at the ends.

And now she was scared to death for her father. Unfortunately, Jason thought that fear was likely warranted.

He inched closer.

"No answer." She punched the "end" button and handed the phone back to him with a frown. Her eyes roved the lobby, as if she was deciding her next move.

"Does he have a cell?" he asked.

"No. Refuses to get one. He had Mom's account cancelled after she died and donated her phone to a battered women's shelter."

"And you said you didn't tell him about the accident?"

She shook her head. "I didn't want to upset him before he got in the car."

Good thinking. "Wait just a minute."

He left her and stepped over to the reception desk. He gave Janet Baker, the woman on duty, the name and description of Abby's dad and instructions to call Jason's cell if he showed up. He also asked her to have Emergency call him if Abby's father arrived there, either as a patient or looking for Abby.

Then he sent a quick e-mail from his BlackBerry cancelling lunch with a colleague.

When he returned to Abby, all of the lethargy that had enveloped her when he'd first walked up had disappeared. She was bouncing on the balls of her feet and twisting her dismissal papers into a tight rope in her hands.

"All right," he said. "Let's go."

She looked at him with startled eyes. "What?"

"I'll drive you to your dad's house. Maybe he just stopped someplace and we'll pass him along the way."

It was clear that she could see through his pretext; but she played along, clinging to her denial just a little longer.

"What if we miss him and he shows up here?" she asked.

"I've told Janet to call me if he does." He inclined his head toward the reception desk.

The woman sitting there gave Abby a smile and a reassuring nod. It did nothing to soothe her agitation.

He could see the argument rise in Abby's eyes, then quickly fade as her worry overcame her independence. "Okay."

On the way out the door, she said, "You think there's something wrong with him, don't you?"

"What makes you say that?"

"The look in your eyes." She paused.

He was normally much better at masking his thoughts. Or maybe Abby just read him more easily than most people. "Let's find him, then we'll deal with whatever comes next."

He was glad she didn't ask any more questions.

When they got to his car, he opened the passenger door for her. She slid in, giving him a naked glance that tore at his heart. After he closed the door, he looked at her through the window for a moment. He wanted to fix this—not as a psychiatrist, but as a man. He wanted to restore that cheerful spark in her eyes that he'd seen last night. Last night, when he'd felt a connection unlike anything he'd experienced with a woman in a long, long while.

His own house wasn't in order. His invitation to future dinners had fallen out of his mouth before he'd fully engaged his brain. He had no business even thinking about getting involved.

And yet, here I am.

He could guise his actions in just being a good Samaritan all he wanted; his true motives were pounding in his veins like a primal drumbeat.

He'd find her father, then he'd back off. It was the only fair thing to do. She had enough to deal with without heaping his issues on top of her own.

With a self-disgusted grunt he walked around and got into the driver's seat.

Abby scanned the lot as he pulled out of his reserved parking space. "Dad drives a Black Explorer with tan trim around the wheel wells."

At this time of day the lot wasn't crowded. There was no black Explorer.

Jason pulled onto the street. "Should be easy to spot, then."

He watched oncoming traffic. Abby looked down the side streets and checked parking lots as she directed him toward her father's house.

Jason asked, "Have you noticed changes in your dad lately?"

"You mean like that 'where they bury people' thing yesterday?"

He nodded, keeping his eyes on the road, looking for the Explorer.

"He looked for his lost keys in the flour canister. He was in an absolute panic." Her voice held a sad resignation. "Mom had been doing most of the driving. Still, it was so unlike him to get that worked up over something like misplaced keys." She sighed. "I suppose I should have been watching him more closely since she died."

"They did a lot together, your mom and dad?" he asked.

"Everything. Since he retired, they even sold the second car."

Jason nodded, thinking the best specialist for Alzheimer's and dementia was seventy-five miles away from Preston.

"This is it, on the right." She pointed toward a white two-story with a wide front porch. "Pull in the driveway. His car should be in the garage."

Jason did as instructed. Abby was out of the car and trotting toward the detached garage before he got his key out of the ignition.

She opened the side door, leaned in, and popped right back out. "His car's gone," she called as she hurried back toward where Jason stood with his car door still open.

"Let's check the house anyway to be sure he isn't here," he said.

"His car is *gone*."

"What if he loaned it to someone? What if it's in the shop?"

"Why wouldn't he have told me when I called for a ride?"

Because he might not have remembered. "It'll only take a second. Check the house."

"I don't have a key."

"Let's make sure the door's locked."

Looking annoyed, Abby walked over to the back door. Jason followed a few steps behind.

She gave him a this-is-a-waste-of-time look as she put her hand on the doorknob. That expression changed to surprise when she turned the knob and the door swung open. "He always locks the door."

"Dad?" she called as she stepped inside.

A quick search of the house confirmed neither her dad nor his car keys were there.

They returned to Jason's car and backed down the drive.

He noticed someone sitting in a gray Chevy Impala across the street and half a block down. "Is that a neighbor?"

Abby followed his gaze. "I can't see well enough to tell with those tinted windows. I don't recognize the car."

"Maybe he saw your dad leave." Jason got out. He hadn't taken two strides in that direction when the car pulled away from the curb.

Jason held up a hand to stop him.

The car accelerated on past.

Jason got back in the car with Abby.

"Maybe he didn't see you," she offered. "Lots of the neighbors are elderly."

"Maybe." *Only if he was too blind to drive.*

"Take me back to the hospital."

He looked at her. "Janet is watching for him there. Is there anywhere else he goes on a regular basis?"

"The post office. The grocery, I guess."

"We'll check there." He backed the rest of the way out of the drive and headed toward town.

They didn't find her father's Explorer at either place.

Jason asked, "Friends?"

Abby bit her lip. Her toes were tapping against the floorboard and her hands had once again picked up those hospital papers and wrung them into a sweaty pulp. "John and Constance Zeiss are really the only people he's spent any time with since Mom died." She looked at him with wariness. Clearly his ex-mother-in-law had let her opinion of him be known.

"Hey, it's a public street. We'll drive by and see if his car is there."

The appreciation in her eyes made it seem as if he was making a Herculean sacrifice. He assured her, "It's okay. Constance hasn't come after me with a rifle...yet." He winked and was rewarded with a smile.

Tom Whitman's car wasn't at the Zeisses'. At Abby's suggestion, they checked Abby's mom's grave at the cemetery. No luck.

"I think I should drive you home. You can get cleaned up and...," he stopped, unwilling to finish.

"What? What are you thinking?"

"You don't have your cell. Your home number is the only way he, or someone on his behalf, can get in touch with you."

"On his behalf," she echoed weakly. "You mean the police. You think something's happened to him."

"It sounds like he's had some confusion already. Sometimes people get disoriented while driving. Sooner or later, they usually ask for help."

She closed her eyes, accepting his words with the

strength he'd already grown to expect from her. "All right. Take me home."

Bryce was in the kitchen making himself a sandwich when his mom walked in.

"Why aren't you at school? And where's your sister? Why didn't someone wake me?" she asked, her rapid-fire questions holding a tone of accusation. She always went on the offense like this when she feared she'd been caught.

He set his knife in the sink. "Bren's at school—I drove her. And we *did* try to wake you." He wasn't going to explain why he wasn't at school. She had no right to give him any shit about it.

She pushed a hand through her hair and sighed, her demeanor changing in a heartbeat. She was pale, her blond hair dull; she looked almost translucent, as if she was fading away. "I'm just so exhausted. All of those days at the hospital…the funeral…." She went to the refrigerator and got out the half-and-half. Then she kissed his cheek as she passed on her way to the coffee maker. "You sweet boy, you made coffee."

"Where'd you go last night?" he asked, fingers tensing on the edge of the countertop.

He saw her jaw tighten before she turned to look at him. She had that *don't sass me* look on her face. "I went to see a friend."

He snorted.

"Things have been very difficult for me, and you know it." That angry tone was back. "I just needed a little time for myself."

"Is that what I should tell Grandmother?"

Her pale blue eyes snapped to his face. "You called Mother?"

"She called here." He leaned against the counter, glad to see the panic in her eyes.

"What did she want?" Her hands trembled as she brought the coffee cup to her lips.

"To see how you were."

"Oh."

"Don't worry, I didn't tell her." He knew his grandmother would only make the situation worse; she always did. Still he wanted to kick his mom's ass right now.

"Tell her what?" she straightened, looking defensive.

"That you snuck out in the night and went drinking."

"I was *not* drinking! I told you, I went to see a friend."

"And I suppose the side mirror on your car fell off by itself." It had been hanging by the wiring when he'd gone into the garage to get his own car to drive Bren to school.

"I stopped at the ATM. I got too close and clipped the post next to it."

Because you were drunk.

If Jason found out, it would ruin any chances at all of their family getting back together. The drinking had torn it apart. If his mom stayed sober long enough, Jason would come home.

Bryce wanted to yell. He wanted to shake her. He wanted to break something.

Instead, he picked up his sandwich and headed up to his room, slamming the door behind him.

"Oh, my gosh, there he is!" Abby said when Jason turned at the painted sign for Abby's Flowers at the end of the lane to her house.

Tom Whitman was leaning against the driver's door of his Explorer, parked in front of the flower shop, which was closer to the main road than the little brick cottage where Abby apparently lived. Off to the right, in front of the cottage, were the ruins of brick steps that led to nothing. Beyond that was what looked to be a formal garden in the making.

A very unusual place to live, he thought. But then, Abby wasn't a usual woman.

Jason pulled in next to the Ford.

Her dad took one look at her as she got out of Jason's car and grabbed her into his arms. "What happened to you, Jitterbug? I've been sittin' here waiting forever. I thought you had a flat tire."

Abby was visibly relieved. "I needed you to come to the *hospital*, not here."

"I thought you said you needed to make a delivery to the hospital." He put a gentle thumb to her forehead. "What happened?"

"It's a long story," she said. "I'll tell you after I get a shower." She turned and looked at Jason across the hood of his car. "Thanks so much for your help."

Abby's dad walked toward Jason. "Tom Whitman." He extended his hand in introduction. "I appreciate you helping my little girl."

Jason saw the stricken look on Abby's face. "I'm Jason Coble. We saw each other yesterday at the funeral."

Tom slid a quick sideways look at his daughter, then chuckled a little uneasily. "'Course. I remember now."

The look on Abby's face said she saw through the lie. "Dad, you have a key to my house, could you go unlock it? I'll be right there."

He nodded to Jason and walked toward the cottage.

Abby's stark gaze met Jason's. "What do I do?"

This time he didn't stop himself. Jason reached out and took her hand in his. "He'll need to be evaluated. If you like, I'll make some calls."

"Can't you do it?" she asked, squeezing his hand.

"I can, at least the initial evaluation, I thought you might be more comfortable with a specialist. There's a doctor in—"

"No." She said it quietly and firmly, with all of the control he'd seen her use to disguise her fears. "I'm more comfortable with *you.*"

Tell her no.

"All right. Tomorrow afternoon. I don't have any patients booked. Two o'clock work for you?"

She nodded, holding his gaze. "Thank you." Then she turned and walked away.

Jason didn't date; he already had his emotional hands full. Abby Whitman had already crawled more deeply under his skin than he should allow—and astoundingly quickly. His invitation to have dinner again had come out of his mouth at a weak moment; borne of the most enjoyable evening he'd spent in a very long time. And he was afraid Abby would induce many of those moments. Treating her father would only lead to further temptation.

He watched as she walked to the cottage, knowing in his heart he was making a mistake.

CHAPTER 6

Maggie listened as Abby's recorded voice answered. Something was wrong. Abby was supposed to be here by now. She'd said she would come before Mrs. White, the housekeeper, got here. Mrs. White had already been here for fifteen minutes.

Maggie had gotten up extra early to be ready. She and Abby were supposed to make a special garland today. It had to be made all by hand. This would be the first time Maggie got to help *make* the flowers, not just put them up.

But Abby hadn't come.

And she wasn't answering her phone. Maggie had left messages at both numbers. Abby always called right back, even when she was real busy.

"Who are you calling?" Uncle Father was grouchy today. He looked sick.

"Abby." She hung up the phone.

"You shouldn't be bothering her all of the time." Now he sounded plain mad.

Maggie opened her mouth, but nothing came out. She was Abby's helper. Abby *needed* her.

Uncle Father came and put his arm around her. Maggie leaned away and looked in the opposite direction.

"I'm sorry." It was his regular Uncle Father voice. "I didn't mean to snap. I'm not feeling very well today."

"Are you dying?" Maggie wasn't going to ask. But it just came out. Now there was no way to swallow the words back up.

Uncle Father looked like *she'd* yelled at *him*. "Why would you ask such a question?"

Maggie wasn't going to admit she'd been listening when he talked on the phone. That was the worst of bad manners.

She looked at the floor and shrugged. Nobody ever made her answer when she did that.

"Maggie, dear. I'm just feeling a little off today. It's nothing to worry about."

Maggie blew out a breath that puffed her cheeks. She'd been so worried. He must be okay. Uncle Father never lied.

"What about Abby?" she asked. "Something. Is. Wrong." She pointed her finger into her other palm with each word so Uncle Father understood this was *serious*. "She always calls me right back."

Maggie felt the grouchy come on him again. His arm tightened around her shoulder. He gave her a little shake as he said, "Enough about Abby." He took a deep breath that sounded like it might suck all of the air out of the room. "I'm sure she's busy. Now you need to go do your studies."

"But—"

"No buts. To your room."

Maggie left the kitchen and stomped up the stairs. But she stopped when she heard Uncle Father's cell phone ring.

She knelt down after the turn in the stairs where Uncle

Father couldn't see her. It was bad to listen. But it could be Abby.

Uncle Father answered with his grouchy voice. "What do you want?"

Maggie listened harder. Uncle Father was never rude.

He said, "I told you I'm taking care of her." He was quiet for a minute. "That would be entirely the wrong way to handle it." He was quiet again. "She doesn't know...Yes, I'm painfully aware of what's at stake." He hung up.

Maggie wondered, *What don't I know? And why won't he tell me?*

Then it struck her like a hammer. Her ears started ringing and she couldn't breathe. He *is* dying.

She swallowed down the cry that tried to come out.

She tiptoed up to her room and closed the door. Then she lay down on her bed and cried into her pillow.

Drawing on a reserve she hadn't been aware she possessed, Abby kept herself from falling to pieces in front of her father while she told him about her accident. Even as she began to recount the aftermath, she was weighing whether or not to admit her fear of sleep-driving. She didn't want him to worry—not to mention she didn't *ever* again want him to look at her the way he had after she'd burned down the house. And yet, she didn't want to outright lie to him either. Luckily he made it easy by not asking why she'd been out on Suicide Road in the middle of the night in the first place.

That non-reaction was the only hint that he wasn't entirely himself. He'd acted perfectly normal otherwise. So normal and connected that she thought perhaps she'd been overreacting with her assumption something was wrong with him. She'd been exhausted, distraught, and in pain when she'd called him from the emergency room. Perhaps she hadn't been clear that she wanted him to come *to* the hospital.

"You're sure you're all right?" he asked once again.

Truth was, her equilibrium was shaky at best and she was so drained she could barely hold a coherent thought.

Since he wasn't letting it go, she worked up more than the single word "fine" she'd used the past two times he'd asked. "Just a killer headache and some sore muscles." She cringed at her choice of adjective—killer. Was she?

He seemed to read her thoughts. "It was an *accident,* Abby. The police didn't say anything that made you think they suspect you were criminally negligent, did they?"

She shook her head.

"Then let's not view this as anything more than what it was, an unfortunate accident. Motorcycles are so danger-ous. If that fella had been in a car with a seatbelt on, he probably would have walked away like you did."

But he didn't. And I can't remember.

"Accidents happen, baby." He held her close and rubbed her back. "There wasn't anything you could have done to avoid it."

"You don't know that—"

He took her shoulders and held her away from him. He looked into her eyes. "I know *you.* If you could have avoided an accident, you would have. Remember when you drove Mom's car into the ditch to avoid hitting a squirrel?"

She nodded. Her mom's car had sustained twelve hundred dollars' worth of damage; the squirrel only an adrenaline rush. Her dad had said that squirrel was the forest equivalent of the six-million-dollar man.

But this hadn't been a squirrel. This had been a man. And she *hadn't* avoided killing him. She shivered.

He wrapped her in a warm gentle hug. "You go ahead and take your shower. Then you should get some sleep."

"Um, I really have some things I *have* to do today. Can I borrow the Explorer?"

He looked at her from beneath beetled brows. "Sleep. You need to sleep."

I may never go to sleep again.

"I'll take a nap as soon as I have things at the shop under control." She paused. "I *promise*."

"Why don't you let me take care of the shop for you today? I can make your deliveries."

She needed him home where he'd be safe. And she needed to talk to the sheriff's department. If she told him where she was headed, he'd insist on going with her. She wanted to keep his stress to a minimum until she had an opinion from Jason about her dad's mental health.

She decided she'd talk to her dad about that appointment later. She'd thrown enough at him for the moment.

With a hand on her hips for emphasis, she said, "I can only imagine the arrangements you'd put together. You can't even get dressed without Mom—" she cut herself off.

He looked away, blinking.

Putting her hand on his back, she whispered, "Sorry."

He sniffed and looked at her with unshed tears in his eyes. "It's all right, Jitterbug." He kissed her on the forehead. "Go get your shower."

Moments later, Abby had the water in her shower

cranked nearly as hot as it would go. She stood under the scalding spray. As she watched the skin on her chest bloom crimson, a choking sob broke free. She slapped a hand over her mouth, stifling the sound from traveling though her tiny house to her father's concerned ears.

That sob was quickly followed by another that erupted from the very center of her body. Dizzy, she staggered backward until her back hit the cold tile. Her knees buckled and she slid down the wall until she was folded in the corner of the shower stall.

The hot water pelted the top of her head and her shoulders as she curled deep into herself, wrapping her arms around her knees. Breathy sobs shook her body with their intensity.

She huddled there until the water ran cold and her tears were spent. And still the anguish in her heart remained branding-iron hot.

On Jason's way back into town, his cell phone rang.

"Dr. Coble," he answered.

"Jason, this is Ken Robard, I need you to come to the house as soon as possible. Kyle has been," the man paused, "killed. Jessica's had a complete breakdown."

Jason had been treating Jessica Robard for severe depression for over a year. Somehow they'd managed to keep her treatment private even though Ken Robard led a very public life.

Their only child, Kyle, was a sophomore at Duke University. Jason wondered if the boy had fallen into drug use while on campus. Jesus, Jessica was in no shape to withstand a blow like this.

"I'll be there in ten minutes, Senator."

* * *

Abby ignored her father's insistence that she stay at his house, telling her she was in no shape to drive. Which was probably true. But she convinced him to loan her his car anyway. She needed answers and there was only one place to get them.

It was nearly eleven-thirty. Her plan had been to go directly to the sheriff's office and see what she could find out about the accident investigation. At the very least, she wanted the identity of the man on the motorcycle. Not that it would make things any easier, but it would fill in one of the many unknowns about last night.

However, as she drove past St. Andrew's guilt moved her foot to the brake and turned the Explorer to the curb. Maggie had left three worried messages on her home voice mail—and Abby hadn't taken the time to call her back.

Father Kevin's car wasn't in the driveway of the residence. Abby went to the door anyway; sometimes he left Maggie at home when he was going to be gone for a short time.

Maggie's face brightened when she opened the front door, then quickly clouded over. "What happened to your head?"

"I had an accident in my van last night and bumped my head. That's why I wasn't here this morning."

Maggie's brows drew together. "I've been worried. I've been calling your cell phone *all morning*. *Even* after Uncle Father told me to stop."

"I'm sorry you worried. I lost my cell phone in the accident—that's why I stopped by. I wanted you to know I'm okay."

"What about the garland?" Maggie was just short of pouting.

"We'll have to do it all tomorrow. How about I pick you up at eight in the morning? We can work at the shop all day and have the flowers ready for the wedding Saturday morning."

Disappointment creased Maggie's innocent face, but there was no way Abby could focus on work today.

"Please help me tomorrow," Abby said, "There's no way I can get it done in time all by myself."

Maggie brightened. "All right. I don't want you to get into trouble with Mrs. Ostrom; she's grouchier than Uncle Father is today."

Abby chuckled. "Mothers of the bride are always grouchy right before a wedding." She gave Maggie a quick hug before she turned and went down the steps to the street. "Thank you. I don't know what I'd do without you."

Maggie called, "Neither do I."

By the time Abby reached the nineteen-sixties yellow brick one-story building that housed the sheriff's office, all traces of the smile Maggie had sparked had faded.

The sun beat through the Explorer's windshield, making the car stuffy and uncomfortable. Still she sat there for a long while before she found the courage to get out and face the culmination of her darkest fears.

CHAPTER 7

As Abby entered the lobby of the sheriff's office, which was in the county seat seventeen miles from Preston, she realized this was the first time she'd ever been inside a police station of any sort. Going through the door, moving from bright sunlight to wholly artificial fluorescent, from the heat of the sun to the cool interior, intensified the sense of vertigo that had been growing over the past hour. She had to pause with her hand on the door handle and wait for the spinning to stop.

Once she could move forward in a straight line, she did so, taking in the lobby area. It wasn't at all what she'd expected, given their mostly rural county.

Instead of stepping into Andy's office in TV's Mayberry, she walked into a room with a dozen battered vinyl chairs, some mended with color-matched vinyl tape. Instead of a wide counter or a reception desk manned by a kind-faced grandmother dressed in a seasonal-themed sweater, there was a four-by-four Plexiglas window on her right. It had an intercom mounted on the wall next to it and a slide tray like you'd see at a bank's drive-up window. Behind that was a man in a deputy sheriff's uniform.

A sign indicated the jail was through a door on the left side of the lobby.

The deputy behind the glass looked up when Abby approached. "Can I help you?"

His voice sounded tinny through the intercom.

She started to speak, but only produced a froggy croak. What was a person supposed to say in a situation like this? Should she just blurt out that she wanted to know who she'd killed?

She cleared her throat. "I'm Abby Whitman...I was in an accident last night...."

He nodded. "What can I do for you, Ms. Whitman?"

"I just wanted to know if...if you can tell me anything about the investigation—who else was involved?"

"Just a moment." He got up and walked away. A few seconds later the door in the same wall as the window opened and he said, "Please come in."

Behind the solid door was what appeared to be an ordinary office with cubicles and a couple of private suites.

"Have a seat." He pointed to one of two chairs outside one of the private offices. "I'll inform Sheriff Hughes that you're here."

"Thank you."

The deputy returned to his desk and picked up the telephone.

A short time later the door to the private office opened. Abby only knew Sheriff Hughes from his campaign posters and photographs in the local paper. He was a bear of a man with grizzled gray hair. He looked much larger in person.

"Ms. Whitman. Come in."

Once she had declined a beverage and was seated across the desk from him, he said, "I'm glad to see you're all right." His serious gray eyes traveled to the lump on her forehead.

"Thank you." Guilt weighed down her gaze. She had trouble meeting his eyes. "The man on the motorcycle...he didn't make it, did he?"

The sheriff shook his blockish head. "No, I'm sorry, he didn't. He was pronounced at the scene."

Abby sucked in a shuddering breath and gripped the edge of her chair. "So there's no way to know what happened?"

"Deputy Trowbridge said you have no recollection of the accident or events preceding. Have you had any improvement in your memory?"

Was there accusation in his voice? Or was she just projecting her own conscience on his words?

She shook her head and her sore neck muscles screamed in protest. She stopped and answered verbally. "Unfortunately, no. The last thing I can remember was around nine o'clock when I left Jeter's."

He nodded, looking almost sympathetic. "We may have some luck figuring out what happened, at the accident scene at least. There is a state crash investigation team working on it. They're usually pretty good about determining how an accident happened."

She straightened her spine and looked him in the eye. "Good. I need to know."

"It's early yet, but I can contact you when I receive their report."

"I'd appreciate that."

"Unfortunately, once we pull your van from the marsh, we'll have to keep it in the impound lot until the investigation is complete."

"I understand." She swallowed and forced herself to ask the hardest question. "The man on the motorcycle—who . . . ?"

Sheriff Hughes leaned forward, placing his elbows on the desk and lacing his thick fingers together. "Nineteen-year-old Kyle Robard."

Abby's breath rushed out of her lungs. She felt as if she would deflate right here in this chair, shrivel and curl onto the floor, ready to be tossed in the trash.

"*Nineteen*," she echoed in a whisper. *Kyle Robard.* The name sounded familiar. Then it clicked into place. "Senator Robard's son."

"Yes." That single word hung in the air like a prison sentence.

Could this get any worse?

From the moment Jason heard how Kyle Robard had died, he felt as if someone had wired him to an electric current. God, why hadn't Abby told him there'd been a fatality? Did she even know it yet?

Once he had Kyle's mother sedated, Jason said to the senator, "She should sleep for several hours. I doubt she'll be in much better emotional shape when she awakens." He looked Ken Robard in the eye. "It's going to be important that someone stay with her at all times. At least for the first few days. I still feel she'd be better off in a facility—"

"No!" The senator glanced toward his sleeping wife and lowered his voice. "I *said* no hospitals."

Jason looked into Ken Robard's eyes. "I'm serious about this. She isn't to be left alone. She's already tried—"

"I understand!" The senator blew out a breath. "I'll make certain she's watched."

"Call me right away if you have any concerns."

"Of course. Thank you for coming so quickly...and for your discretion."

Discretion. The word made Jason want to sock the guy in the mouth. Ken Robard had put his political career before his wife's well-being too many times to count. Discretion. As if Jason would run out and sell this information to the highest bidder. The senator needed a serious adjustment in priorities.

As Jason left the Robard master bedroom, he had to concentrate on decorum in order to keep from sprinting toward his car.

Once behind the wheel, he couldn't shake the image of Abby in the hospital lobby; bereft, alone, hurt. It probably wasn't any of his business. He would likely be overstepping his bounds. But the thought of her dealing with this alone stabbed at his heart with a thousand tiny needles. Even in their short acquaintance, he'd seen her strong independence and the protectiveness she had of her father. She *would* be dealing alone.

He had to at least check on her.

He turned the key and put the car in gear. Then he headed straight back to Abby's house.

Although the electric buzzing in his veins continued, Jason felt a sense of relief when he saw Tom Whitman's Explorer parked next to Abby's little cottage. At least she wasn't alone physically; mentally was another thing altogether. He doubted she would allow herself to lean on her father, not completely, not with his own mental health already an issue. Jason could offer that kind of friendship; a supporting shoulder, someone to help talk things through.

Did she already know of Kyle Robard's death? Or would he be the one to deliver the news?

He got out of his car, knocked on the door, and waited for either Abby or her father to answer. It'd be easier to tell her father first— that was if he was in a good cognitive frame of mind. Then her father could break the news to Abby; bad news was always less sharp when delivered by someone who cared and sympathized with you.

That thought made Jason realize, if *he* didn't care and sympathize, he wouldn't have driven like a madman to get here. Nor would he have cleared his schedule for the rest of the day, just in case Abby needed him.

The door swung open. It was Abby, not her father. She looked surprised. She also looked like she'd been crying. Good. All of that restraint this morning had him worried.

She didn't say anything, just looked at him with those wide bourbon-colored eyes. They had the dull, trauma-tized look of someone on emotional overload.

"I hope I didn't wake you," he said. "I thought perhaps your dad would answer."

"I took him home. And no, you didn't wake me."

She didn't invite him in. Suddenly, Jason's conviction that she needed him, that he had a reason to be here, evaporated.

Still, he pressed on. "May I come in?"

She hesitated for a moment, her expression unreadable. Then she opened the door wider and turned away, walking leadenly to a sofa set before a huge brick fireplace. There were a dozen wadded tissues on the wood-plank floor and a rumpled fleece blanket spread out on the cushions.

Jason closed the door softly and followed her. That sofa was the only place to sit, other than the stools at the island that separated the living area from the kitchen. He wondered if the limited furnishings were to keep the small space uncluttered or to make a statement of solitude.

Abby seemed to accept his presence without question as she curled into the corner of the sofa with her legs folded on the cushion beside her. She drew the blanket over her lap and on up to her chin.

Her gaze moved to the empty fireplace and fixed there. She didn't say anything.

There was something disturbing about her complete stillness. He didn't know her well, but he'd seen enough of her to know she was always in motion. She radiated waves of surplus energy in the way that athletes did body heat.

He studied her, lifeless eyes rimmed with sleep-deprived dark circles, pale fingers clutching the edge of the blanket as if it were the only thing keeping her from flying off into the stratosphere.

She visibly shivered.

Fresh firewood sat stacked on the wide brick hearth.

"Are you cold?" he asked. "I could start a fire."

She nodded, a single motion, no more than a dipping of the chin. Her stationary gaze never wavered.

Jason shrugged out of his jacket and laid it across the

arm of the sofa at the opposite end from Abby. After he unbuttoned the top button of his shirt, loosened his tie, and rolled up his shirtsleeves, he went silently about building a fire.

Once it was going well, he stood and brushed his hands against one another.

"That's nice. Thank you," Her voice sounded small and broken. Not like Abby.

"Can I get you anything? Something to drink?"

A weak smile curled her mouth. "Shouldn't I be asking that? I'm the host."

"I didn't come to be entertained," he said quietly; a normal voice might somehow startle her, loosening her grip on the blanket that bound her to the here and now.

After a beat or two, she shifted her gaze from the flames and looked him in the face. "Why did you come?"

The helplessness he heard in her voice shot an arrow of pity right through his heart.

He felt intrusive enough, barging in on her solitude. So instead of sitting on the sofa, he sat on the coffee table in front of her. "I didn't want you to be alone." It was as much of the truth as he'd admit at the moment.

She looked down at him and her detachment drained away as if washed by a hard rain. Tears slipped from her eyes, silent and unnoticed. They rolled down her cheeks.

She sounded as if she'd choke on her grief when she said, "I killed a boy."

Without thought, he moved to the sofa beside her. He gently pulled her against his shoulder. She resisted for only a half-second; he felt her surrender to grief and to the comfort he offered in every muscle of her back and shoulders.

For several minutes there was only the crackle of the fire and her breathy sobs. He'd never felt so utterly impotent—even though he knew this kind of grief, this kind of guilt, had to run its course as surely as a fever must.

She cried past the moment when her hot tears soaked through the fabric of his shirt, past the moment when she became limp against him, until, he guessed, there were no more tears left in her body.

Slowly, she pulled away from him and reached for the box of tissues on the table. She did it without so much as a glance at him, and he knew she was embarrassed.

"Abby, look at me."

She did, with obvious reluctance; dabbing her nose as her eyes met his from beneath the sweep of her dark lashes.

"I came because everybody needs a shoulder to cry on," he said, speaking more frankly than he'd planned. "And I...I wanted to be yours."

When she would have looked away, he put a finger under her chin and held her gaze. "You've been through a horrible experience. You need someone."

"I'm fine, now." She straightened. "Thank you."

He heard the dismissal in her tone. But he wasn't going to be pushed away so easily. She'd been through a trauma and it was bound to get worse in the days ahead.

"Do you know who the boy was...the one on the motorcycle?"

Stiffening, she looked at him warily. "How did you know he was on a motorcycle?"

"It's a small town. I work at the hospital."

"Then *you* know who it was."

He nodded. "Do you?"

She closed her eyes and swallowed. "Yes. I stopped by the sheriff's office this morning."

"It may not have been your fault, Abby. He was nineteen and on a motorcycle. On that road he was most likely going far too fast." He left it there, hoping she'd tell him what *she'd* been doing on that road and why she hadn't told him in the first place that there had been another party involved in her accident.

She didn't. In fact, she didn't say anything more at all. The vulnerability he'd seen in her before she'd given way to tears retreated behind a curtain of stark independence.

He finally asked, "Have the police made any determination about what they think happened yet?"

"An investigation team from the state police is working on it." Her tone did not invite further questions.

She looked terrified—as well she should be. Jason knew to what lengths Ken Robard was willing to go to prevent sullying his family's golden name.

But there was something else in her eyes that bothered Jason. She was pulling away with an air of self-preservation. She was deliberately keeping something from him.

She suddenly got to her feet. "Thank you for coming by."

Thirty seconds later, Jason found himself back in his car. She'd been polite and appreciative as she'd shown him out. Even so, he had the feeling that a door had been closed between them. One that wouldn't be opened again.

CHAPTER 8

The ringing of the telephone startled Abby awake. The book she'd been reading slid off her lap and landed on the floor with a soft thud.

She hadn't meant to fall asleep, had been fighting against it. Orange embers of the dying fire glowed in the hearth; she'd been asleep a while, then.

The phone rang again. She reached for it with fumbling fingers and she looked at the clock. Two-forty.

"Hello." Her voice was raspy and the word barely understandable.

There was no response.

Abby cleared her throat and repeated, "Hello?"

The only response was a slobbering indrawn breath. She heard noise in the background, music.

"Is someone there?" she asked, her heart kicking against her breastbone.

No answer, only a thin and unintelligible whine, a pitiful cry that spoke of intense suffering.

The image of her father lying on the floor taken down by a stroke shot into her mind.

"Dad? Do you need help?" She got to her feet and looked for her shoes. "Dad! Is that you? I'm coming."

A choked sob responded.

Abby frantically looked for her cell phone to call 911; the EMS could get there faster than she could.

Shit! She didn't have a cell!

"Dad, hang up. Hang up and I'll call for help."

The garbled moaning finally began to form slurred words in a whispery voice. "W-why...wh-whyyyy... please...oh pleeease...." There was a sharp intake of breath. "...please don't tell...p-pleeeease...."

There was a clatter and the line suddenly went dead.

"Dad!" She immediately dialed his number.

It rang once.

Twice.

I should have called 911 first.

Just as she was about to disconnect, he answered. "Hello?" His voice was gravelly from sleep, but clearly understood. Not the voice of moments ago.

"Dad? Are you all right?"

"'Course I am, Jitterbug. What's wrong? You sound upset."

A shuddering breath left her. "I just got a call...I thought it was you."

"What kind of call?" Protectiveness sharpened his tone.

She thought about the voice. "It must have been someone drunk dialing—or maybe kids messing around." Her knees felt weak with relief and she sank down on the couch again.

"Maybe I should head out there—"

"No need," she cut him off. "I was only upset because

I thought something might be wrong with you. But you're okay, so I'm okay." Or she would be when her heart slowed back into a normal rhythm.

"I'm coming anyway."

"Dad, I don't need a babysitter. It was just a random call. Besides, I have your car."

He huffed. "Never shoulda let your mother talk me into selling the other one."

Now that sounded like the dad she knew. She chuckled. "I'm sorry I woke you. I'll call you in the morning."

"You'd better."

"Night, Dad."

"Night, Jitterbug."

For a moment, Abby sat on the couch with the phone in her hand. That voice slithered around in her mind, wrapping her nerve endings in acid. The more she tried to force it out, the more tenaciously it clung. Although it hadn't been more than a rough whisper, it had been so intense, so filled with pain. It reached something primal in her, something instinctive that immediately wanted to recoil.

I'm exhausted and making too much of this.

She got up off the couch, shaking her arms to rid herself of the creeps.

At least that call had awakened her. She wasn't taking any chances of sleeping again until she figured out some way to safeguard against leaving the house in the middle of the night.

Yesterday when she'd come home from the hospital, at least one of her questions had found an answer. Although she had no recollection of the time between when she left Jeter's and when she awakened in the swamp, the evidence was there to prove she'd been home. Her bed had been unmade; she never left her bed unmade. An empty milk glass sat on her nightstand. At that point, there had been no surprise left in her, just a heavy, dull acceptance. There had been no reasonable explanation that put her on Suicide Road. So she didn't fight the unreasonable any longer. Sleep-driving. God, how much more dangerous could she get?

For now, she had to stay active to avoid falling asleep again. Tomorrow she'd tell the police her theory and go from there.

Surely sleep-driving constituted some form of negligence. Would they charge her with a homicide?

The thought sent a shaft of new fear through her heart. But she had to do what was right and accept the consequences—something she'd known all along, but hadn't truly faced until now. At least if they locked her up, she wouldn't be able to unwittingly hurt anyone again.

She put on her garden shoes and let herself out her front door. She'd get a head start on that garland for the Ostrom wedding. It might be the last ceremony she ever did flowers for.

As she walked toward the carriage house in the velvety darkness, a deep sadness settled in her chest. And if that sadness had a voice, she realized, it would sound just like that scratchy, desperate voice she'd heard on the phone tonight.

At seven-thirty a.m. Abby was making much-needed coffee in her kitchen. The only sleep she'd had since the accident was that unintentional nap last night. She was so tired her bones ached—or perhaps that was from the accident. She hoped the coffee would at least clear her foggy head.

Hearing a car pull up in front of her house, she went to the front window and looked out. The lane ended about forty feet from her front steps, as it used to stop in front of the big house. Deputy Trowbridge was getting out of his cruiser and putting on his hat. The slanting sun glinted off the brass nameplate on his chest, stabbing her eyes with a shaft of light. He reached back in the car and pulled out a small plastic box, then headed for her door.

She hadn't noticed before how young he was. He looked more like a fresh army recruit than an officer of the law. He moved with an air of arrogance that reminded her of his skeptical questioning at the hospital, spurring a streak of defensiveness in her.

Last night's resignation ducked behind her dislike of his attitude and the irrational hope that he was here to tell her the accident investigation team had concluded that Kyle Robard had been responsible for the accident, that he'd been drinking, or high; that she had been the victim.

Her mouth went dry as she took a deep calming breath and opened the door before he knocked.

"Ms. Whitman." He tipped the brim of his hat. "I apologize for the early call, but we have a few questions about the accident." He didn't sound at all sorry; he sounded as if he was going to relish every moment of what he was about to do.

She stepped back and opened the door wider. "Come in."

As he stepped across the threshold, he removed his hat. Abby wondered why he put it on for the short walk to the door in the first place. Probably for intimidation.

She realized he was just standing there, waiting.

"Please, sit down," she said.

He sat on the edge of the seat at one end of her sofa. Because it was the only place to sit in her living room, she sat at the other end.

His gaze moved from her face to her hands and back again. She realized she was twisting them in her lap. She tucked them beneath her thighs.

"First of all, we need your fingerprints, in order to help sort out the scene," he said.

When she didn't respond right away, he said, "Unless you have an objection...?"

"No. Of course not."

He opened the plastic box and took her fingerprints without further comment. When he was finished, he handed her a packet holding a towelette.

He settled back on his end of the couch, silently watching her while she cleaned the ink off her fingers.

Finally he spoke, "Have you remembered anything more since we last spoke?" There was a cutting edge to the way he said "remembered" that stuck like a thorn in tender skin.

She sat up straighter, biting her tongue to keep from snapping at him. She managed a calm, "No." It was true. She hadn't *remembered*.

He didn't respond for a long moment, just pinned her in place with his glacial stare.

Finally, he said, "I see."

He seemed to be waiting for her to elaborate. She didn't.

As he pulled a little flip notebook from his pocket, he

said, "We've drawn a few conclusions. We were hoping you'd be able to corroborate them."

"As I said, I don't recall anything. But if something you say sparks a memory, I'll certainly tell you." Why couldn't he have stayed away? She'd feel so much more comfortable talking to Sheriff Hughes in his office, coming in on her own, not cornered like this.

"The accident happened shortly before three a.m. just prior to the 911 call—not near the time when you say you left Jeter's." He looked at her with expectation that set her teeth on edge.

"And you established this how?" She was hungry for solid facts.

"Kyle Robard was with a friend in town until two-thirty. Left there alone. The medical examiner established a time of death that backs this accident time."

Time of death. She thought of that poor boy using the last of his fading strength to call for help and she flushed hot with nausea.

Trowbridge noticed. "Are you ill?"

"Who wouldn't be sick thinking of that poor kid's death?" She held his gaze, refusing to let him fluster her further.

He didn't respond, but made a show of jotting down a note.

"You say he'd been with a friend. Is it possible that he'd been drinking?" she asked, cringing a little at the naked hope in her voice.

"We haven't gotten all of the test results yet." He looked at her like she was trying to blame the dead. "Do you have any recollection at all of someone else, a third party, at the scene?"

The question took her by surprise. "No. I didn't even know about Kyle until you—found him."

Deputy Trowbridge went on before she uttered another word. "There must have been someone. Kyle Robard *could not* have made that 911 call."

"But you found his phone with the 911 line still open."

"The medical examiner determined that Kyle was killed instantly. So there was either someone else on scene, or you made that call yourself."

For a moment Abby sat in stunned silence.

She looked into the cold hearth and thought back through the events of that night. She remembered waking in the van—dry except for her feet, leaving the vehicle, thrashing out of the swamp. Then the deputy arrived almost immediately. There hadn't been any time for her to find Kyle Robard and use his cell to call for help, even if she'd known he was there.

She looked back at Trowbridge. The smug look on his face clenched it. She wasn't going to give him anything. She'd go to straight to the sheriff with her confession. "I didn't."

"You said you couldn't remember most of that night. Perhaps you found him, called for help, and don't recall."

"No. I awakened in the van, went to the road, then you arrived. I'm not missing any bits of memory in that area." *At least I don't think I am.* Her memory seemed to be getting foggier, not clearer.

"You think on it for a while." His tone was one a person would use on a naughty six-year-old. "You were in shock. There could very well be things missing from your memory *after* you awakened in the vehicle."

She could only imagine his reaction if she admitted she suspected she'd been sleep-driving.

She said, "Maybe someone stopped, found Kyle, called for help, and left. That makes more sense to me."

"It's possible, but not likely. We're checking his phone for fingerprints. Perhaps that will solve the mystery." He raised a brow, as if waiting for her to confess.

"Perhaps," she said stiffly.

"You say you got out of the van and went to the road. Did you return to the van after you exited the vehicle?"

"No . . . well, yes. I got out, realized I left my purse and cell phone, climbed back in."

"Through the door?"

"Of course."

"It was still open from your initial exiting?"

"Yes."

"Do you know how the driver's side window got broken?"

"No. When I awakened there was glass all over me, so I assume it broke as I drove off the road."

He made a note, and then closed his notebook. "You said you lost your purse and cell in the marsh."

"I did—after I got them out of the van."

He stood. "All right. That's all for now."

"Do you have any idea yet what happened?" She stood and followed him to the door, reaching around him to open it.

"We're still working on it." He put on his hat, then he looked her in the eye. "You'll be sure and let us know if you have any clearing of your memory, won't you?"

"Of course." She closed the door behind him, turned the deadbolt, and sagged with her back against it. Her tired

mind was scrambling her thoughts until she was beginning to doubt herself. Was she forgetting something?

Who made that 911 call?

Even if sleepwalking explained her lack of memory, it
didn't answer that question. Could someone have stopped
and then just left Kyle's dead body in the woods? Who
could have been so callous?

Abby looked out the front window, resting her throbbing forehead against the cool glass.

As Trowbridge's brake lights brightened at the end
of her lane, she suddenly remembered those headlights,
fast approaching and making an abrupt U-turn just as the
deputy had arrived. With everything that happened afterward, she'd forgotten completely about them.

Could they somehow be connected?

She wasn't about to call Deputy Trowbridge and tell
him. She'd save it for the sheriff.

CHAPTER 9

This morning, Uncle Father wasn't in the kitchen making pancakes as usual. And Abby was going to be here soon. Maggie had to be ready.

She went back upstairs to look for him.

She heard him whispering prayers. His bedroom door was open. Uncle Father said it was always all right for her to come in if the door was open. But she stopped. He was praying. Praying was private.

Uncle Father had two crucifixes in his bedroom. One over his bed where everybody had one. And one on the wall beside the closet door.

Below Jesus-by-the-closet was a little table with two candles. One for Maggie's mother and one for her daddy.

That's where Uncle Father was praying. On his knees. His face was bristly. His eyes were closed. He was rocking back and forth with the music of his words. Maggie couldn't understand any of them.

She stood at the doorway waiting for him to notice her. Maybe she should just go away.

Then she heard him make a little sob sound.

She went in and got on her knees beside him. She put her arm across his shoulders and bowed her head.

"Don't be sad, Uncle Father," she whispered. "I'll help you pray."

He made a low sound that wasn't prayer and wasn't words. He leaned forward and put his forehead on the floor.

It scared her but she didn't leave. She even kept her hand on his back.

She said, "God will help you."

He sat up and wiped his cheeks with his hand. He looked at her with a smile and said, "*You* give me strength, Maggie love."

"You better now?" she asked.

"Yes. Thanks to you."

"Good. I'm hungry."

He laughed a little. "I didn't realize it was so late. Let's go make pancakes, then."

They made the pancakes together, but Uncle Father didn't eat any.

The doorbell rang.

"That's Abby!" Maggie jumped up and put her plate in the sink.

"Abby?" Uncle Father said. He sounded funny, not quite surprised, but different. Maybe he was still sad. "Why is she here?"

Maggie sighed. "I *told* you. We have to make a wedding garland today."

"Oh. Yes. I guess I forgot."

She kissed his cheek. "Will you be all right without me?"

"Of course. Now you run along. Don't keep Abby waiting."

"You don't want to go to the door and see her?"

"Not this morning. I haven't even shaved yet."

She was so excited her feet wanted to dance. Today she was going to do everything on her own.

"Okay. Bye." She hurried out of the kitchen.

She was so happy that Abby hadn't had an accident again today.

This was going to be the best wedding garland ever made.

Abby sat across the workbench in the carriage house from Maggie, thinking there was no way she would have all of the arrangements ready for the wedding tomorrow. Her exhaustion made it so she had to think and rethink every move; work that normally came naturally now was an act of conscious will.

Maggie's chatter had ceased. Her tongue was caught between her lips as her blunt fingers worked wires slowly and meticulously around the flowers and magnolia leaves. Abby was happy for the silence. Her fatigue was making her irritable. She didn't want to take it out on poor Maggie.

Abby's cell phone rang. She'd stopped at the Verizon store to get a new one on her way to pick up Maggie this morning. It felt like having the ability to walk restored after a stint in a wheelchair.

She looked at the number on the screen. It was Dr. Samuels, the physician who'd taken care of her as long as she'd been alive. She'd left him a message earlier today. He was only practicing part time now, after having retired and unretired twice already. Naturally, he didn't have office hours on Friday.

She got up, leaving Maggie to continue working.

Once she was out of Maggie's earshot, she answered.

"What can I do for you, Abby, dear?" Dr. Samuels's voice sounded thinner, less robust than she remembered. It had been well over a year since she'd spoken him.

"I think I need to see you," she said. "I've . . I've been sleepwalking again." She figured explaining her theory on sleep-driving would be better if delivered in person.

"You don't say." He sounded surprised. "After all this time?"

"Yes."

"Hmm. Losing your mother so suddenly most likely triggered this recurrence." He paused. "When did it start?"

"As far as I can tell, Tuesday night."

"Most likely you were experiencing it to some extent before that. Have you been continuing your strict bedtime routine? Have you been taking your supplements?"

Back when he'd treated her for sleepwalking as a child, Dr. Samuels had developed a regimen in an attempt to curb her sleepwalking. It consisted of an unalterable routine for retiring at night: always at the same hour; no TV, no exercise, no reading thirty minutes prior to bed; a hot bath followed by ten minutes of silent meditation (of course at age nine Abby had no idea how to meditate, so just sat with her eyes closed for ten minutes and pretended); a magnesium supplement and a glass of milk immediately prior to lying down.

Abby couldn't say with any certainty that it helped. She continued to sleepwalk until she'd passed puberty, although perhaps with less frequency. She'd probably just grown out of her sleep disorder as Dr. Samuels had initially predicted. Still, she had never varied from this routine. It was just one of the reasons she'd never spent an entire night with a man.

"Yes to both." She felt hope deflating in her chest. "Aren't there new drugs or something?"

"A few. But honestly, I don't like the side effects."

Could they be worse than driving around killing innocent people?

He went on. "And I haven't read much that leads me to believe they work in most instances. There is a sleep lab now at the hospital down in Savannah. Maybe we should set you up there for some tests."

"I was hoping for something more immediate," she said.

"Abby, there just isn't anything immediate that can be done."

"I've read about hypnosis—"

"Oh-ho, I'm sure there's aplenty out there who'll take your money. But I don't put much stock in hypnosis to alter sleepwalking."

Tears of frustration pushed for release. "I'd like to see you anyway."

"I think that sounds like a good idea. How about Tuesday? You can call and talk to Charlotte on Monday for a specific time. Then we can work on getting you into that sleep lab."

"Is there any way I can see you today?"

"I'm sorry, but that's just not possible. I'm already at the airport. I won't be back until late Monday."

She closed her eyes and exhaled. "All right. See you Tuesday."

God, she couldn't go without sleep that long. She'd have to figure out some way to make it safe.

Jason called the Robard house to tell the senator he was on his way to check on Jessica.

"Jessica is fine," Ken Robard said. "She doesn't need you."

"Wonderful. I'd like to speak to her."

"She's sleeping."

"I'll stop by then."

"No," Robard said. "You can't come here. TV reporters are camped out in front of the house. Kyle was supposed to be at school...he came back home to see a girl. We didn't know anything about it. Reporters are trying to make more out of it than it is. We don't need more speculation—"

"My concern is your wife's welfare. If I can't come and see her, I'll send an EMS unit to your house. See what the media makes of that."

"You can't do that."

"Watch me."

"You're dismissed from her case. I'll find a new doctor."

"Fine. I'm still sending the EMS."

Jason heard a huff on the other end.

"Don't stop and talk to anyone. You're coming as a family friend. Is that understood?"

Jason disconnected the call. If Jessica Robard was "fine" this morning, it'd be a miracle. Sometimes Jason got the impression Ken Robard would have been happier if his wife's suicide attempt had been successful. A grieving widower played better to the public than a man with a wife suffering from an ongoing mental illness.

Sheriff Hughes looked across his desk at his young deputy. "What makes you think she's lying?"

"The evidence for one." Trowbridge sounded surprised that the sheriff even asked. "Plus, it's obvious by her demeanor. She's hiding something. I don't buy it for a second that she doesn't remember *anything* after nine p.m."

The sheriff generally trusted his first impressions; and his said Abby Whitman wasn't telling them everything, either. Still, Trowbridge in his inexperience wasn't looking beyond that gut response.

"What would be the point?" Hughes asked. "Her blood alcohol and drug screen came back clean."

"Maybe she knows who the third party is and is protecting him."

Hughes thought of the theory the state team had come up with thus far. There was a third vehicle, or at least a third person, either involved in the accident or there immediately after. They'd found footprints near the body that were too large to be Abby Whitman's. Unfortunately those prints were such a mess it was going to take the lab a while to tell if they had a shoe tread worth anything.

Those prints, along with the post-mortem 911 call, were clear indicators of a third party. They also backed Whitman's accounting of post-accident events; that she had just come out of her vehicle at the time Trowbridge arrived. The question was did she *see* anyone?

"It's possible that she's protecting someone, I suppose," Hughes said. "We both know the Robard kid had a need for speed. Maybe he was racing someone at the

time—someone who called for help and fled the scene.
So maybe it played out just as Ms. Whitman claims."

Trowbridge's eyes clouded with skepticism. Hughes
suspected he wanted to be *right* more than he wanted
the truth. He had the intelligence and drive to be a good
officer; he just needed to develop a little patience—and
a lot of humility.

Hughes said, "The investigation team says there's
something about the positioning of the two vehicles that
doesn't add up with their initial thoughts. They're working up some computer re-creations and examining the
damage on the motorcycle and the van. Maybe we'll have
more specifics by tomorrow."

"What about Senator Robard?" Trowbridge asked.

Unfortunately, Trowbridge had been in the room when
the senator had made his most recent call demanding
charges be brought against Abby Whitman.

Hughes looked at his deputy sharply. "The senator is
not your problem. And I don't want a word of his phone
call to pass the walls of this office."

Trowbridge had the sense to appear contrite. Truth was,
he had trouble keeping work subjects out of his personal
conversations. Hughes had called him on it more than
once—minor stuff, but it was a bad habit to get into.

Hughes redirected the conversation. "Did you speak
to the priest?"

Trowbridge nodded. "The prayer card found near
the motorcycle was from a funeral at St. Andrew's on
Wednesday. Lucky for us it was a very small funeral. I
have a list of about sixteen that the priest remembered;
the rest I need to get from the guest registry. The family
already has that. I'm headed out this afternoon to start

checking them out." He looked quite satisfied when he added, "Abby Whitman was one of them."

"We'll see if the fingerprint on the card matches hers," Hughes said.

"How about those on the cell phone? Do we have any idea how many unidentified prints are on it?"

"A couple that are good enough to match. But until we have something to match them to, they're useless."

"We have hers, at least. We'll be able to tell if *she* was the one who made the call. Then maybe we can prod her memory."

Hughes didn't like the enthusiasm in Trowbridge's voice. He also didn't see what reason Abby Whitman could have for denying making the call for help.

He said, "One step at a time. For now, I want you to check out the local body shops, see what's come in new since yesterday. The state says there's white paint on the handlebars of the bike. They're comparing it to the van, but in case it doesn't match we'll have someplace to start."

Trowbridge left the office and the sheriff picked up his phone and used the intercom to the officer on the desk. "Don't put any more calls from Senator Robard through. Assure him we're on top of the investigation and will be certain to call him the minute we have anything."

Jason sat at his desk, finishing his notes in Jessica Robard's file. When he'd arrived at the Robard house there had been two news vans parked on the street. Two cameramen and two reporters had immediately scurried his way when he'd slowed to pull into the long driveway. They'd probably run his license plates and have his identity figured out by the five o'clock news.

Maybe that would be for the best. Then Ken Robard wouldn't make his decisions about his wife's health based on keeping her condition a secret.

It had been a damn good thing that Jason had insisted on seeing her. She was supposed to have been sleeping in the master suite; she was supposed to have someone with her at all times. But when Jason and the senator had entered, the bed had been empty.

A frantic search followed. They'd finally found her in the attic—only because she knocked something over and the thud gave away her location. She'd unpacked what looked to be Kyle's entire childhood. Around her on the floor were empty boxes, piles of stuffed animals, baby clothes, Boy Scout uniforms, baseball jerseys and an array of mitts, trophies, blue ribbons, and a scattering of Star Wars toys. She was smudged and sweaty and had fought them every step of the way as they'd taken her back down to the bedroom.

Jason had adjusted her medication and lambasted the senator for leaving her in a room by herself. The incident did seem to have rattled the man. Enough so that Jason trusted his promise to have someone with Jessica at all times.

Jason closed her file and looked at the clock. It was nearly two. Would Abby actually show up with her father for their appointment? After the way she'd withdrawn yesterday, he doubted it.

It was probably just as well; there were others who specialized in Alzheimer's treatment. And he didn't want to complicate things further with Abby by treating her father.

As that thought entered his mind, he asked himself just what he was hoping for in that relationship. Good sense said one thing while his desires were in stark contradiction. He'd been blinded by his own emotions before. Unfortunately he hadn't been the only one to suffer.

Just last night when he'd spoken to Brenna on the phone before her bedtime, she'd asked again when he was coming home. He'd thought at least that issue was behind them. When he'd probed more deeply, he discovered that Bryce had told her if they were all very good, things would work out. Brenna had then told Jason that she'd been good and she prayed every night for Daddy to come home.

When she'd said it, Jason had thought his heart would shatter with its next beat. But his heart kept pumping—and his innocent baby girl kept hoping.

He scrubbed his hands over his face. Nope, he had no business inviting anyone else to his emotional circus.

He heard the outer door open and close. Jason didn't employ a receptionist; the size of this town kept his practice too small to need one. Which was the same reason that his office was located in the back of his residence.

He heard Abby's assuring voice as she spoke to her father.

She'd come.

He couldn't tell if the feeling in his gut was excitement or trepidation as he walked into the tiny waiting area to greet them. The second he looked at Abby, he realized it was excitement—no doubt about it. He was extraordinarily happy to see her, no matter what circumstance had brought her here.

Shame followed right on the heels of that thought. She looked exhausted; he had no right finding pleasure of any sort as a result of her difficult situation.

Jason looked at her father. He appeared calm. Jason wondered how Abby had convinced him to come. How much had she shared with him about her concerns? God knew, this had the potential to be an ugly scene. But somehow Abby had handled it in a way that her father didn't seem threatened.

Tom Whitman shook his hand. "I'm only here to satisfy Abby. She's been such a worrywart since her mother passed. I'll tell you right now, I've never been sick a day in my life. Can't even remember the last time I needed a doctor."

"It's good of you to humor her, sir." Jason smiled. You're lucky to have such a wonderful daughter. Please, come into my office."

Once Abby and her father were seated in the chairs across from his desk, he handed them a clipboard with health history forms.

"The first thing I'd like is for you and Abby to fill out a general health questionnaire, list all dietary supplements and medications you're taking—"

"I don't take any medication. I'm healthy as a horse."

Jason nodded. "That's good. It'll help narrow things down. I just need it in writing for my records."

Abby took the clipboard and began writing. She asked her father very few questions; clearly she had a good handle on his daily life.

When she was finished, she had her dad review and sign it. Mr. Whitman handed it back to Jason. As he took it, he glanced over at Abby. Her face held utter trust mixed with such stark hope that he nearly flinched. God knew, he didn't want to be the one to have to shatter that hope.

"I'd like to have an hour alone with you, Mr. Whitman."

Jason shifted his gaze back to Abby. "Feel free to leave, if you have things you need to do."

Abby did have something to do. She was so damned exhausted she could barely keep her thoughts from tripping over one another. Before she could sleep, she had to insure that she wouldn't be able to leave the house while sleepwalking. On the way here she'd gotten an idea.

"All right. I'll be back in an hour." She took her dad's hand and squeezed it. "Thank you."

"Anything for you, Jitterbug."

At the use of her nickname, Jason gave her a smile— one that said he had a nickname for his little girl, too. Abby thought of how gentle and attentive he'd been with his daughter at the funeral. Jason Coble was a good man.

Too bad she could never let herself care for him; that fact had just been reinforced with the reoccurrence of her sleepwalking. Gran Girault had called it years ago: there was something fundamentally wrong with her and it would never go away.

Pushing away self-pitying thoughts, Abby left the office and headed to the hardware store.

She parked in an angled spot on the street a half-block from Cottrell's Hardware. As she walked toward the store, a gray Impala with darkly tinted windows drove by. She'd seen it parked in front of St. Andrew's when she'd dropped Maggie off. It seemed to slow as it passed her.

Or maybe she imagined it. There was something creepy about those ultra-dark windows.

Oh for heaven's sake. I'm getting paranoid.

She had to get some sleep, get her mind back in order. She entered the hardware store and found what she was looking for; there were only two door alarms on the shelf. They were dusty, as if they'd been there for quite some time. She took them both. She also picked up two double-keyed deadbolts.

As she checked out, she looked out the front window and saw that Impala cruise past again. The hair on the back of her neck rose.

Good God, Abby. He's just looking for a parking spot.

"Find everythin' you need, Miss?"

Abby turned to the clerk. His kind eyes looked out of a face that reminded her of a shriveled apple. "Yes, thank you."

"You gotta make sure you line them two pieces up real good now when you put 'em on your doors."

She nodded.

"They work on magnets, you know."

She didn't really care, as long as they worked. Her head throbbed and her eyes felt like she'd been in a sandstorm. She wanted to get back to Jason's office before her dad was finished with his tests. Then home. She wanted to sleep a bit before she finished the flowers for the wedding tomorrow.

"Need bat-trees? These run on bat-trees, you know."

"Oh, I didn't even think." She looked at the label and reached for three double packs of nine-volt batteries hanging on pegs just below the countertop. "Thanks, I'd have been mad if I got home and discovered I needed these."

He nodded. "We don't sell too many of these add-on door alarms, but you're the second person buyin' 'em this week."

"Really?" People here rarely locked their doors, let alone armed them with alarms.

He nodded. "Must be all of the stuff they're putting on

the evenin' news and magazine shows. Folks *round here* don't need alarms. Yep, gotta be those magazine shows if it's even got Father Kevin worried."

"Father Kevin bought door alarms this week?"

"Sure did. Damn—pardon, Miss—doggone TV. Got people all worked up. Scared of their own neighbors."

If only it was her neighbors she was afraid of, instead of something dark deep inside herself.

Abby sat next to her father, across the desk from Jason Coble. Her heart was beating too rapidly. She reached across and took her father's hand.

She couldn't tell from Jason's expression which way his findings had gone. The child in her fought against adult logic. If there wasn't *something* wrong, they wouldn't be sitting here right now.

Jason rested his forearms on his desk and clasped his hands on top of the file with her father's name on it. "I want to start by saying this is not conclusive, what we've done today.

"The general neurological screening assesses reflexes, coordination and balance, eye movement and muscle strength. I didn't note any significant deterioration beyond what is age appropriate.

"In a situation such as yours, Mr. Whitman, with the recent loss of your wife, depression could be playing a role—"

"Good God! A man can't grieve for his wife now without it getting a label put on it?"

"Dad. . . ." Abby squeezed his hand.

"Mr. Whitman, I understand your frustration. There is a difference between clinical depression and grief. Your grief is entirely natural and justified. Sometimes it can camouflage other, more serious health issues. We're just trying to sort everything out."

Her dad rubbed a hand over his face. "Go on."

"Our exam today on your mental function does show some memory issues as well as some minor decreases in cognitive function. But these findings could be the result of any one of several disorders. There need to be lab tests conducted to rule out ailments that could result in memory loss and confused thinking."

Abby's father let go of her hand. He leaned forward in his chair and said, "I'm *fine*. I can't see how those tests prove otherwise; they were just a bunch of silly questions. Everybody my age forgets things now and again."

"We're just making sure, Dad. I know you don't like going to the doctor, but Mom would want to make sure you stay healthy."

At the mention of her mother, her father's mouth snapped closed.

She nodded for Jason to continue.

"Like I said, we need to rule out potential causes."

Her father stood up abruptly. "I'm *fine*. Not as young as I used to be, but fine nonetheless. I don't need more tests." He walked toward the office door. "Thank you for your time."

He went out and closed the door loudly behind him.

Abby sat there, looking from the closed door back to Jason. "Should I go after him?"

"Does he have car keys?"

"No."

"Then wait a minute. Just so you know, this isn't an unusual reaction."

"How long do you think he's been...slipping?"

"There's no way to tell. I will say that it isn't unusual for a family member to take up the slack, so to speak, thus hiding deterioration from others."

"Mom? You think she was hiding this?"

"Possibly. It's likely that it came on gradually and she just adapted without a conscious decision to do so."

Abby thought of her mother's insistence on selling their second car—and the fact she'd taken up the driving.

Jason got up and walked around the desk, sitting on its edge right in front of her. He looked into her eyes. "Listen, Abby, if it is Alzheimer's, I think he's in early stages. Now's the time to get him on a treatment to slow down the progression. He needs someone other than me to confirm the diagnosis and render treatment."

"It sounds to me like you know what you're talking about. Can't you order the tests, then we can go from there?" The thought of putting her father, vulnerable as he was right now, in the hands of a complete stranger bothered her. And after her conversation with Dr. Samuels earlier, clearly he wasn't an option.

"I'm *not* the right doctor."

"But you've said yourself there isn't a specific specialty dealing with Alzheimer's."

"No, but there are neurologists with much more experience with it; that's who you want treating him. I'll do a little checking around. I promise you," he took her hand, "I'll find him the best."

The warmth of Jason's hand made her realize that her own were like ice.

"Look at me, Abby."

She did.

"You look like you're hanging by a thread. You need

to take care of yourself, too. He needs you to be healthy and strong."

Hanging by a thread. If you only knew.

As she sat there, feeling the warmth of his hand, looking into the depths of his eyes, she asked, "Do you have experience with hypnosis?"

The confusion on his face made her realize how out in left field her question was.

He said, "I have, yes. But I don't think it'll help your dad—"

She pulled her hand out of his and stood. "Of course not." Cold feet ran off with her sleepwalking confession. Did she want Jason to know? Would he ever look at her the same if he did? "I was just grasping at straws, I guess."

He moved as if he was going to put a hand on her shoulder, then stopped, letting his hand fall to his side. "I know how difficult this is. I'll call you as soon as I find a doctor for him."

"Thank you." She hurried toward the door and opened it. Just before she walked out, she stopped and almost turned around.

There was something about him that made her want to trust, made her yearn to hand over the mess of her life and have him untangle it.

And yet, showing her vulnerability frightened her almost as much as her sleepwalking did. Hypnosis would be the ultimate exposure of her weaknesses, her faults; it would be total surrender of her privacy.

She took a breath and walked out of the door.

As she left the house, she thought: *He's not the right doctor for Dad…but what about me? What if Jason Coble holds the key to exorcising the darkness living inside me?*

CHAPTER 10

Bryce headed downtown after school. This was one of the few days he'd be able to do whatever he wanted. He usually had to go straight home to babysit Bren—just one more benefit of having divorced parents.

Even when Jason had been living with them and Bryce's mother had stayed home, he'd always gone straight home after school. He'd never known what shape his mother would be in by the middle of the afternoon. More times than not, he'd had to look after his sister *and* clean everything up before Jason came home and discovered how his mother had spent her day.

But today he was free. His mother had taken time off work because of Great-grandmother Vera's funeral—and Jason sure wasn't coming home.

It was great not to have Bren tagging along when Bryce went to the comic shop. He'd recently gotten into collecting. He couldn't afford many of the old ones, but he liked a couple of the new series. If he kept them long enough, they'd be as valuable as those old ones were now. They were an investment. His mom just didn't get that.

She said he should be doing something more "productive" with his time. Like she had room to talk.

When he walked into Hi Flying Comics he ran into Toby, the cool dude he'd met here a couple of weeks ago. Toby had dropped out of college when he figured out how much money he could make trading and collecting comics and action figures and stuff. He traveled all over buying and selling, hitting shows and auctions. His grandmother lived in Preston; that was why he was here now.

"Hey, Bryce." Toby always remembered him. That was one reason Bryce liked him. He also never acted all weird when Bryce had to bring Bren along. And he never treated Bryce like a stupid kid. Lots of older dudes who hung out here had a rod up their asses.

Bryce knocked knuckles with him. "What's up, dude?"

"The usual. Buyin' and sellin'."

"How's things with you?"

"Been better," fell out of his mouth before he censored it. Why hadn't he just said, *Great. Fanfuckintastic?*

"No shit? What's the deal?"

Bryce shrugged. "Family crap."

Toby nodded; he clearly understood family crap. That made Bryce feel a little less like a douchebag.

Toby said, "You look like you'd like to break somethin'."

He nodded. He hadn't thought about it that way, but that was *exactly* how he felt.

"Do it, man. It'll make you feel better. Just go out there and beat the shit out of somethin'." Toby slammed his fist into the palm of his other hand. "Hey, I'll even take you. I know just the place."

They left before Bryce looked at a single comic.

*   *   *

When Bryce arrived home at four-forty-five, his heart nearly jumped out of his chest. A sheriff's car sat in front of the house.

He thought about driving on past and coming back after it was gone.

But he quickly realized this couldn't have anything to do with what he'd done; it was impossible for the police to know and be at his door, at least not yet.

So if this wasn't about him, it had to be his mom. Had she been picked up for a DUI in the middle of the day? God, had Bren come home after school to this?

When he bolted through the front door, his mother was in the living room with a deputy sheriff. They were both standing there, looking at him. His mom's eyes were bloodshot and wet with tears.

He felt his neck get hot. *Cool it. They can't know.*

His mom's voice sounded all jittery when she said, "This is my son, Bryce."

The deputy nodded. "Do you drive, Bryce?"

"Yes, sir." He glanced at his mom. She was looking at the floor and biting her thumbnail.

"And you attended your grandmother's funeral on Wednesday?" the deputy asked.

"Yes, sir."

"Where were you on Wednesday night between two and three a.m.?"

His mother said, "I told you he was here in bed. It was a school night, for heaven's sake."

The deputy continued to look at Bryce.

"I was here," Bryce said. "I didn't leave the house after

we got home from the funeral." *I couldn't have been out then if I'd wanted to; it'd have left Bren alone.*

"Did you attend school on Thursday?"

"No." *Why did this guy give a shit if I'd gone to school or not?*

"Why?" the deputy asked, looking sharply at him.

"I overslept." Bryce shrugged. "So I decided to stay home. It had been a crappy week with the funeral and all."

"All right," the deputy said. "Thank you both for your time."

Bryce's mom walked him to the door.

When she returned Bryce asked, "What was that all about?"

His mom went into the kitchen for a tissue. He followed.

"Kyle Robard." She dabbed her eyes and blew her nose. "This is just so awful. He was so young...." She sniffled. "His poor father...."

"*Why* was that deputy here?" he pushed.

She straightened. "They're looking for someone who was at the accident scene. Apparently Betsy Whitman's daughter, you know Abby, the florist, was involved. But they think there was another car."

"What does that have to do with us?" he asked, searching her eyes for a lie.

There it was. Deceit. A flash behind a shadow. Bryce had seen it enough to recognize it.

She said, "Nothing, baby. Nothing at all."

His stomach was slowly tying itself into a pretzel. "What did you tell them when they asked where *you* were that night?"

"I told them I was at home, of course." She spun and walked out of the room. "Dinner will be ready in an hour."

Bryce stood there openmouthed. He thought he just might puke.

All of the talk at school today had been about how twisted Kyle Robard's motorcycle had been; there'd been a photo on the front page of Thursday's newspaper. Kids had been speculating on how fucked-up Kyle's body must have been if his bike was such a mess. There was even a pool going on whether or not the casket would be open or closed at the funeral.

It had made him sick. But not as sick as realizing that his mom had just lied to the police.

The telephone rang, startling Abby out of a deep sleep. She looked at the clock. Six-thirty p.m. She'd been asleep for two hours. Her alarm clock was set for eight p.m. so she would have time to work on the Ostrom wedding flowers. It seemed somehow safer to sleep in the daylight.

She answered on the third ring. "Hello?"

"Dad just called. He said you took him to a psychiatrist. Said you're trying to prove he's crazy. What the hell, Abby!"

She closed her eyes and rubbed them with her thumb and forefinger. When did this all get twisted in her dad's mind? When she'd left him he'd been accepting of the idea that he needed more tests.

"I'm not trying to prove he's crazy, Court."

"But you made him go to a *psychiatrist*?"

"It's not like I tied him up and dragged him there. I asked and he agreed to go."

"Why did you ask? What's going on?"

"He's been forgetting things...getting confused. I just took him for an evaluation. It was no huge deal."

"Bullshit! You think he's losing it and it's no big deal!"

"Court—"

"Why didn't you call me! Didn't you think I should *know* he's got Alzheimer's? I should have been part of this. I *certainly* could have figured out a way not to upset him so much."

"We don't know he has Alzheimer's at all. And he was fine when I left him." He'd been convinced it was all unnecessary, but he hadn't been upset. "Was he still upset when you got off the phone with him?"

"No. I got him calmed down. I promised him I wouldn't let you stick him in some nursing home."

"Jesus, Court, I never said *anything* about a nursing home. Is that what he thinks? Did he *say* it?"

"Not directly. But I know that's what he was worried about. So I nipped it right there."

No, you planted the idea. "There are several things that could be causing his symptoms, so he's getting more tests."

"Were you *ever* going to call me?"

"Yes, after I had some idea what was going on. I didn't want to worry you unnecessarily."

"He's my father, too, Abby. You can't just go around making these decisions by yourself."

She took a deep breath and let it out. "I'm sorry. I didn't mean to make you feel like I was making decisions without you. It just seemed—"

"Like you could do it all your way. Just like Mom's

funeral. Listen, if you don't want to take care of Dad, I'll bring him here to live with me."

Oh yeah, the emotionally crippled taking care of the mentally impaired.

Abby immediately wanted to slap herself for that thought. After all, it was her fault Courtney was emotionally crippled.

"You're jumping way ahead," Abby said, forcing a calm in her voice she didn't feel. "See, this is why I didn't call you. You always get all dramatic—"

"So which is it, Abby?" Courtney's voice was razor sharp. "You wanted to protect me? Or you didn't want me to get *all dramatic*?"

Both. "I knew you wouldn't want to come to Preston. And it just seemed better to do some of the preliminary things before I called you. I'm sorry. I didn't mean for you to feel shut out."

Courtney was silent for a long moment. "When is he getting these other tests?"

"I'm not sure. Dr. Coble wants to refer him to a doctor with a good track record with this kind of thing. He's doing some checking for us."

"I think you need to take him to Savannah. Maybe even Columbia."

"Relax, I'm sure it'll be someplace other than Preston."

"What's that supposed to mean?"

Abby bit her lip. "Nothing. I'll let you know as soon as I have a list of doctor's names."

"Well, you're not going to leave dad by himself until then, are you? You should stay with him."

Under the current circumstances, it was probably more hazardous for her father to be sleeping under the same roof with her than staying alone. "I have his car at the moment, so he's not driving."

"Well, we both know how dangerous home can be, don't we, Abby?"

Abby squeezed her eyes shut and gritted her teeth. She pretended she didn't get Court's innuendo. "I don't think he's in danger. He's just…slipping. I don't want to make him feel worse by hovering."

"Honestly, Abby, I don't understand you at all."

"I'll call you tomorrow. I have a wedding, so I'll be in town early to check on Dad."

"I'll be waiting." It sounded very much like a threat.

After she hung up the phone, she buried her face in her hands and growled in frustration. Then she threw her head back and yelled, "God, she pisses me off!"

Since the day Courtney was born, Abby's relationship with her had been a disappointment. At three, Abby had been so excited about a baby sister that she and her mother had crossed off the days on the calendar in the month before Courtney's arrival.

Had she known the upheaval that was ahead, Abby might have relished those final days as an only child.

Courtney had been a difficult, colicky baby who had grown into a stubborn—and occasionally spiteful—child. When she was seven, she'd taken all of Abby's stuffed animals, including the Pound Puppies, and thrown them down the old well because Abby wouldn't give her the giant blue teddy bear she'd won at the carnival. That bear had been a cheap-ass thing that really hadn't meant anything to Abby (certainly not as much as her Pound Puppies). She should have just handed it over. She'd lost all of her beloved collection and been left with the garish blue monster whose color rubbed off on the wallpaper as a constant reminder.

It wasn't that their parents hadn't tried to curb Courtney's behavior. But no amount of punishment seemed to have any effect.

Then came the fire. And punishing Courtney for anything became unthinkable.

Abby went into the bathroom and washed her face with cold water.

She had work to do. Happy work. She couldn't let her anger with Courtney bleed over and ruin Alexa Ostrom's wedding arrangements.

Abby grabbed a snack from the kitchen to take out to the shop. Then she retrieved the key for the double-key deadbolt she'd put in today from the little china box on her coffee table. Before she opened the door, she turned off the electronic alarm she'd also just installed. It wasn't a perfect solution, but it had given her enough peace of mind that she'd been able to rest.

Too damn bad Courtney had had to wake her up and ruin it.

At four a.m. Abby had the flowers finished and tucked safely in the cooler. If she went to bed now, she could get a couple of hours' sleep before she had to load up and head to town. Working with her dad's Explorer instead of her van it was going to take two trips.

Her body screamed for a long and deep sleep. But two hours was all she'd chance. Fewer REM cycles, less chance of sleepwalking.

As she walked across the dark space between the carriage house and her cottage, she sensed movement off to her right. She turned quickly, but didn't see anything under the big trees lining the lane to the main road. Most of this property had grown quite wild in the past fifteen years, since the loss of the main house. The woods pressed close and the undergrowth was dense, although this early in the spring it wasn't as solid as it soon would be.

She waited a moment, straining her eyes in the darkness.

Too tall to have been a gator or a raccoon. Must have been a deer.

Even as she had the thought, the skin on her neck tingled. She walked just a little more quickly toward her cottage. As she moved, she cast glances over her shoulder, in the direction of that shadowy motion. She listened carefully for movement and heard only normal night noises and her own exaggerated breathing.

Once inside the door, she locked it behind her and turned on the alarm. Without turning on the lights, she looked out the front window. She spent a couple of minutes searching for a sign of that deer—just to assure herself that it *was* a deer.

Finally, she turned away unsatisfied. She left the lights off. Her eyes were well acquainted with the darkness; navigating the short way to the sofa was easy.

She did little more than kick off her shoes before she lay down. Going through her bedtime ritual and climbing into a real bed felt like a surrender to sleep. She would not completely surrender.

Stretching out her aching muscles and resting her head on the toss pillow felt so good she let out a little moan.

She was asleep before she drew two more breaths.

She was driving through the fog and she was

unnaturally afraid. She slowed her van; the road was nothing but twists and turns. Her hands ached from gripping the steering wheel so tightly

A deer leapt from the woods beside the road.

She hit the brakes.

The tires squealed.

She stopped just short of the deer, her heart beating rapid as hummingbird wings.

The deer stood there for a long moment, just staring at her through the windshield. The fog rolled around his shoulders like a cloak, then wreathed his head like a halo.

His lips were moving. She watched them intently, trying to figure out what he was trying to say.

Something startled him and he leapt away, disappearing into the night.

But the halo remained. It glowed white, then red.

Abby drove toward it, but never seemed to get any closer.

Then the red and white halos separated.

And suddenly they weren't halos any longer. They were taillights. Right in front of her.

She swerved—

An electronic screaming startled Abby awake. She sat up, blinking. She was in her living room. On the sofa.

The front door was open.

The piercing wail of the alarm stabbed her ears.

She jumped up and hurried to the door, reached up, and flipped the switch that turned off the alarm.

Had she...?

No. She'd been on the sofa when it started; there was no delay on this alarm.

She looked out into the darkness.

Was that movement near the carriage house?

She slammed the door closed. As she reached to lock the deadbolt, she realized the key wasn't in it. Hurrying to the little china box on her coffee table, it was there, right where she'd left it.

I could not *have opened that door.*

She checked the frame and the lock. Everything appeared intact.

With trembling fingers, she slid the key in the deadbolt and locked the door.

She snatched up the cordless phone and dialed 911. As she did, she hurried from window to window, her heart racing.

Nothing. No movement. No lights from a vehicle in the lane.

She stood frozen near the front door, eyes never leaving the lane outside as she waited for the police.

CHAPTER 11

The sun wasn't yet up as two officers from the sheriff's department—fortunately, neither of which were Deputy Trowbridge—searched outside Abby's house with flashlights. Then they combed the nearby woods. They didn't discover a prowler. She hadn't really held much hope that they would; not after that screaming alarm. Even if he hadn't made a clean getaway, it was way too easy to hide in the acres and acres of dark woods.

The officers went to check the carriage house while Abby waited inside her locked cottage. She watched them move across the yard in the blue and red strobes of their cruiser lights. She clutched the edge of the draperies when they separated and she saw their flashlights disappear around opposite corners of the carriage house.

Just days ago she'd thought she would never feel more vulnerable than she did when she'd discovered she'd been sleepwalking again. She'd been so wrong. This was a million times worse. Vulnerable, violated, and victimized.

What if I hadn't installed that alarm?

Images of rape and murder raced through her mind, hitching her breath in her chest.

She didn't breathe easily until the officers reappeared together at the nearest corner of the building. They moved back toward her cottage, flashlights sweeping in wide arcs around the perimeter of the yard.

She let them back in.

"The carriage house is locked," Jones, the deputy who'd arrived in the first car, said. "All of the windows are intact. I'd like you to come out and walk through with me to make certain nothing was taken from inside. Officer Bigelow is going to take a look around the rest of the property. Are there any other lanes that lead in from the road?"

"No. This is the only one."

Jones nodded and Bigelow left.

She asked Officer Jones, "If the carriage house door is locked and the windows aren't broken, why do we need to go through it?"

"You said the deadbolt on the house here was locked, is that right?"

"Yes. As I said before, I was a little spooked when I came in. I'm certain I locked it."

"There's no sign of forced entry on this door. Either the guy used a duplicate key, a bump key, or picked the lock. Could have done the same on the carriage house."

"No one has keys. I just changed the lock." Her stomach turned thinking of someone huddled out there in the dark picking her lock.

She got her keys and walked beside Officer Jones to the shop. That same skin-prickle feeling of being watched that had bothered her more than once recently settled on her. Her imagination, she knew. They'd searched the area already. There were no vehicles parked nearby. Still, she moved just a little closer to the officer.

A thorough search of the carriage house yielded nothing amiss. They returned to her cottage. Officer Jones took fingerprints from the door.

"I'll need to take yours for comparison," he said to her when he'd finished.

"Unfortunately, you already have them...from the accident Wednesday night."

"Ah, yes, the senator's son." He packed up his fingerprint kit as Abby fought to block out the image of Kyle Robard's broken body. "Ms. Whitman, do you have a boyfriend?"

"No."

"An ex-boyfriend?"

"Not unless you go back a very, very long time. What does that have to do with anything?"

"It's looking like this was personal. If they'd been after money or credit card numbers, they'd have broken into the shop. With the car outside, unbothered, they knew you were here—"

"It's not my car, it's my father's." She realized even as she said it, it was a ridiculous statement.

"Have you had any problems with an individual lately?"

"No."

"Nothing with the business? Creditors? Unhappy customers?"

"No." She was starting to feel like a character on *Law & Order*.

Unfortunately, this wasn't fiction. Whoever had broken into her house was as real as it got.

There was a soft knock at the door before it swung open and Officer Bigelow reappeared.

Both Abby and Officer Jones looked at him expectantly.

"Ms. Whitman, there are several broken headstones and a monument that has been tipped over in that old cemetery out near the road. A lot of the grass is mashed and there are relatively fresh tire marks in the pull-off from the road. Do you know if that damage is new?"

She thought of the six-foot-tall stone monument to her great-great-grandfather. It had stood undisturbed for a hundred and fifty years. "It has to have happened since last Sunday. I was in there cleaning up, getting ready for mowing season."

"Did that cemetery have any ironwork; urns and such?"

"Yes. I think there are four or five urns. And the fence and gates."

He nodded. "Fence is there. No gates. The high price of scrap metal has been spawning lots of this kind of theft. We'll check the cemetery more thoroughly when it gets light. Take some photos of the damage. If you'd make a list of what you think is missing and send it to the department, that'd be helpful."

"All right."

After the officers left, Abby locked the door and armed the alarm before she took a shower.

As she stood under the hot spray, one question kept resounding in her head: *Who would want to do this to me?*

She didn't have anything worth stealing.

Personal. The police thought it was personal.

No matter how she looked at her life, she just couldn't see who would want to harm her.

She froze in mid-shampoo as a thought slammed into her mind: *You* did *kill a senator's son.*

Right. And he hired a hit man to get even. Seriously, she had to get some real sleep; she was losing her grasp on reality.

She shut off the water. If she didn't stop thinking like this, she was going to lose her mind completely.

On Jason's way to pick up Brenna for their customary Saturday breakfast, he called Father Kevin. It rang long enough that he'd just about given up when the priest answered.

"Hello, Father, I'm going to take Bryce and Brenna out to the driving range this afternoon. Do you want me to touch base with the catering staff at the club, make certain everything is in order for the fundraiser while I'm there?"

A couple of months ago, Father Kevin had seemed overwhelmed with the task of organizing the golf fundraiser for Children of Conflict that had been held every May for the past ten years. It was easy to understand; his burden had more than doubled since the death of his sister and her husband two years ago. So Jason had stepped in this year, making phone calls and doing errands.

The exhausted sigh that came over the phone took Jason by surprise. Father Kevin loved this event and the ability it gave him to contribute to his sister's organization. He'd managed to recruit golfers from all over the United States to participate, even a few celebrities.

"Yes, I suppose that would be a good idea," Father Kevin said without his usual enthusiasm.

"Is something wrong?"

"No. Nothing. Thank you for helping." The line went dead.

Worried over this uncharacteristic behavior, Jason nearly called him back, but decided to wait until this afternoon, after he'd spoken to the caterers. Then he'd have a reason that wasn't pushing beyond the boundaries of the priest's privacy.

Jason was more than a little surprised to see Brenna and Bryce standing on the front porch when he pulled up. Bryce had already declined the breakfast invitation, but that wasn't unusual. What was unusual was that he was up this early.

Before Jason even got the engine shut off, Bryce was walking Brenna down to the curb. Jason studied his step-son carefully, wondering what had prompted this change of mind.

But Bryce didn't climb in the front seat. He opened the rear passenger door for his sister.

"Hello, Peanut," Jason said.

"Hi, Daddy. Bryce said he's not going to hit golf balls with us this afternoon. Can't you make him?"

Jason ducked to look at Bryce across the car. "You dumping us?"

He threw Brenna an annoyed look and gave an offhand shrug.

Brenna said, "Yes he is. He's not doing his part for the good of this family."

Jason cringed at her choice of words; it was a phrase Lucy used to get her way.

It seemed to hit a nerve in Bryce, too. He said, "All right! I'll go."

"Good," Jason said. "Sure you don't want to grab breakfast with us?"

"I'm sure." He straightened and Jason lost sight of Bryce's face.

Jason called, "We'll be back at one to pick you up."

Bryce closed Brenna's door.

Jason watched him as he walked back to the house. There was something different about him, something heavy and just a little dark. It was evident in the way he moved.

Jason was anxious to spend the afternoon with him, to see if he could get his son to open up.

At eight a.m. Abby parked the Explorer at the side door of St. Andrew's. Maggie came out, her face lit with excitement. Her chunky little legs moved more quickly than Abby had ever seen them. She met Abby at the rear hatch of the SUV and threw her arms around her.

"This is the best day ever!" she said, as she nearly squeezed the breath from Abby.

Abby hugged her back. The feel of Maggie's sturdy body lent a calm warmth that was very much needed.

"All right, Maggie, let's get ready for this wedding."

Maggie took a box with the pew arrangements and headed for the door. "We did a good job. Mrs. Ostrom *can't* be grouchy today."

"If she's grouchy, it certainly won't be our fault," Abby said, knowing the odds of Mrs. Ostrom, mother of the bride, acting like a woman with bees in her bloomers was pretty darn high.

When they entered the sanctuary, Father Kevin was placing fresh candles in the candelabras onto which Abby would add bows and flowers. His back was to her.

"Good morning, Father," she said.

When he turned to face her, he looked at her with haunted eyes sunk deep into their sockets. Abby sucked in a breath. It had only been three days since she'd seen him, but he looked so much worse.

She set down the flower arrangement she was carrying and stepped over to him.

"Abby," he said, There was a peculiar edge to his voice, as if he was expecting something, some reaction from her.

"Are you all right?" she asked.

He blinked, slowly, the way a person does when he's been pushed past the point of exhaustion. For a long moment, he just stood there.

Finally he cleared his throat and said, "That's what I should be asking you—after your accident." His sluggish gaze moved to the butterfly bandage on her forehead.

"I'm fine." Although she realized she hadn't looked much better than Father Kevin when she'd put on her makeup this morning. "But you're not looking well at all." She laid a gentle hand on his coat sleeve.

He studied her face, as if looking for something deep in her eyes. "Life gives us all trials." He paused. "We must accept them."

"Is there anything I can do for you?" she asked.

For a moment his gaze sharpened, as if she'd surprised him. Then he reached out and took her hand. "You're already giving me a priceless gift. I thank you."

He turned away and walked into the hall that led to his office.

A priceless gift? Her involvement with Maggie?

Abby watched him disappear into his office, more worried than she'd ever been for him.

* * *

Once the frantic preparations to the sanctuary and the hall where the reception would be held were complete, reality began to knock on the door of Abby's consciousness. Not only was she troubled by the break-in, but that dream she'd been having when it occurred kept buzzing around in her mind. The details of it had grown hazier as the daylight hours progressed, yet it chafed like a prickly clothing tag, nagging and prodding for attention.

Could it have been more than a dream? Could it have been scraps of memory from the accident? Had she swerved to miss a deer?

There was only one person she knew who might help her figure it out. But first she had to go and check on her dad. Courtney would no doubt have a fit because she hadn't made it there before the wedding. With the break-in and the police, there just hadn't been time. Abby *had* called him on her way to the church and he'd sounded his old chipper self.

She found him in the back yard, fertilizing the azaleas.

When he saw her he smiled and gave her a kiss on the cheek. "Abby, my girl, glad you're here. I'm starving."

She'd been bracing herself for the litany of accusations that Courtney had passed along yesterday. But it was as if nothing had changed since Abby left him yesterday afternoon.

Relieved and just a little confused, she went inside and made them a late lunch. Had Courtney made it all up? Was it her sister's anger and not her dad's that was the whole issue? Or had her father made those accusations and forgotten them?

While they were eating, she broached the subject of further testing.

"Jitterbug, I told you I'd do it."

Should she ask him about calling Court?

No. It would upset him either way. It'd either dredge up emotions he'd forgotten, or it'd make him angry with her sister.

He went on, "Whatever it takes to smooth away those worry wrinkles of yours." He ran a forefinger between her brows and then tapped the tip of her nose. "You'll never catch a husband if you look like a prune." He winked.

"I'm not looking for a husband and you know it. I live alone for a very good reason."

He sighed. "Abby, you can't let what happened ruin the rest of your life."

"It ruined Courtney's." Her sister lived like a hermit in a cement block house filled with smoke detectors. Abby would not take the chance of sleeping under the same roof as another person. One burn victim on her conscience was enough for a lifetime. God, when she thought of the horrors her sister had been through, those months in the hospital...

"Your sister is making her own choices."

"Choices she wouldn't have had to make if *I* hadn't set that fire." Those were words she never uttered. Never. Hearing them come from her lips was like the sting of whip strikes on her soul.

"You aren't responsible. It was the same as a lightning strike, no one could have predicted or prevented it. It just happened." Her dad reached out and put a hand on her shoulder, squeezing reassuringly. His capacity for forgiveness constantly amazed her. She'd nearly killed her sister, had put their entire family at risk, and had destroyed the family home.

He added in a soft voice, "That's in the past, Jitterbug. Let it go. You haven't been sleepwalking for years—"

She stood abruptly; her chair scooted noisily across the tile. "I have to get going. Do you mind if I keep the Explorer a few more days?"

"Of course not."

"Do you need anything from the store?"

"Can't think of anything."

She put her plate in the dishwasher, and then leaned down to kiss his cheek. "Just give me a call if you do."

He grabbed her hand before she walked away. "You be careful out there, Betsy."

She stopped cold. "I'm Abby, Dad."

He blinked. "Of course you are. Why are you telling me?"

She gave him a fierce hug and left.

As she got in the car, she assured herself that her father had been perfectly normal all through her visit—until he'd called her Betsy. It probably wasn't a big deal. Mom used to call Courtney and Abby by the other's name all of the time. Occasionally she had even called Abby Scooter, the dog's name.

It was a natural slip of the tongue. That was what she kept repeating all the way to her car.

On the way to Jason Coble's house, the radio gave a news update that struck her like a fist in the gut.

"...*police are now looking for the driver of a third vehicle in the investigation of the early Thursday morning accident that took the life of nineteen-year-old Kyle Robard, son of Senator Ken Robard. Police stress that at this point they are only looking to question that driver.*

Services for Kyle Robard are scheduled for Wednesday at Randall and Roberts Funeral Home in Preston, the senator's hometown."

Abby switched off the radio as she pulled to the curb in front of Jason's house. For a long moment she sat there, staring at the tree-lined street but seeing the wreckage of a motorcycle illuminated by a flashlight beam.

She dry swallowed two extra-strength Tylenol in the useless fight against a fatigue headache. Her eyeballs felt as if they were swollen to twice their normal size and covered in flannel. Twice today her heart had started beating so fast that it felt like a hummingbird in her chest.

Would she be able to sleep when she got home? Or would images of twisted motorcycles and visions of burn scars appear every time she closed her eyes? Would memories of dreams join with her newfound fear of intruders to keep her awake?

Abby buried her face in her hands and rubbed her eyes.

When she lifted her face and reached for the door handle, she saw in the side mirror the tail end of a gray Impala cross the intersection behind her.

She spun to look, the quick movement making her a little queasy.

The car had passed from view.

God, you are *getting paranoid. There have to be dozens of gray Impalas in Preston.*

Someone broke into your house. Nothing imaginary about that.

Enough! She smacked the steering wheel with both hands. This was getting her nowhere.

She got out of the car and immediately the world began to swim before her eyes. She took two staggering steps and bent at the waist, laying her head on the Explorer's warm hood.

The last thing that registered before the world went black were hands grabbing her shoulders.

CHAPTER 12

A bby could hear before she could see. A man was saying her name.

"Breathe deeply, Abby." She obeyed. "There you go," he said. "And again. Now open your eyes." He was patting her hand—not gently. She was sitting, leaning back against something warm and uneven.

The Explorer tire, she thought. She was sitting on the street.

The face before her was a blur. But the voice had already registered. Jason.

Her eyes began to focus. He was hovering close. His hazel eyes were concerned, but his lips curved in a slight smile. "Hey there." He stopped slapping her hand, but continued to hold it.

Abby heard a car roll slowly by and a man's voice call, "Y'all need help?"

Jason called back, "Thanks, we're okay."

The man called more loudly, "Miss? You all right?"

"Oh, boy," she mumbled. Could this get any more humiliating? "Fine, thank you, sir."

It was a moment before the car moved on.

Just over Jason's right shoulder a smaller face appeared, haloed in blond curls.

Oh yeah, it could get more humiliating.

Beneath a pink visor, Brenna's hazel eyes were replicas of her father's. "Is she okay, Daddy? She looks really white."

"I'm okay," Abby said and started to gather herself to stand.

"Whoa, there. Just sit for a minute," Jason said.

"I'm in the street."

"Not a busy one. Bryce is right there making sure all the cars know you're down here."

Abby rolled her eyes. "Fabulous." *Wouldn't want anyone to miss me lying on the street in front of the shrink's house.*

Jason laughed and the sound of it began to bring warmth back to her body.

"Okay, now, Bryce, you get on Abby's other side." Jason moved to one side and got a good hold on her upper arm, as if she was going to need serious hoisting to get off the pavement.

She cast him a discouraging look. "I can get up on my own."

"Well, you certainly got down there on your own," Jason said. "Why not let us just make sure you don't have a repeat performance?"

Another car rolled slowly past with a woman looking wide-eyed and curious out the passenger window.

She sighed. "Just get me off this street."

Bryce moved to her side. His grip was much more tentative than Jason's, and he stepped quickly away once she was vertical. From the corner of her eye, Abby saw him wipe his palms on the legs of his jeans.

Jason held tight, and hooked one arm around her waist so she had no choice but to lean against him.

"Head rush?" he asked quietly, his breath close enough to tickle her ear. That hint of intimacy sent a shiver over her body that he must have felt—and misinterpreted—because he tightened his grip.

"No food. No sleep. Bump on the head. I'm okay now."

"Uh-huh." Jason turned and said, "Bryce, can you pull my car in the drive?"

She now saw that Jason's Altima was pulled crookedly to the curb behind the Explorer, as if he'd swung to the side of the street in haste.

She thought of those hands on her shoulders as her world had started to fade. If he hadn't grabbed her, she'd probably have split her head open on the pavement.

"You've certainly got good timing," she said, looking up at him. His face was as close as a lover's; the late afternoon sun showed the slight stubble of his beard coming in much lighter than his brown hair.

"Nobody's ever accused me of that before." He leaned to her ear and whispered, his hand squeezing her waist slightly, "I'm damn glad I had it this time." He started moving them toward the sidewalk. "Bren, would you carry Abby's purse?"

Abby straightened. "I don't want to intrude." She hadn't even thought about the possibility of him having his children. She hadn't been thinking about anything except discovering if her dream would reveal the truth about the accident. "I should have called first. We can talk later."

Bryce said, "Um, I really need to get home. I have plans."

Jason shot Bryce that same glare she'd seen in the hospital lobby.

The boy turned wordlessly and walked to the driver's door of Jason's car.

"Really, Jason," Abby said, trying to put a little space between them. "I'm fine now. I just got a little dizzy."

"We're going inside." Jason's voice took on a take-no-prisoners alpha-male tone, a tone Abby normally wouldn't tolerate. But the way Jason used it, it made her feel safe, looked after.

Bryce slammed the door on Jason's car—hard. Abby felt the slightest tightening of Jason's muscles in response.

Once they were inside the house and Abby and her purse were seated on the loveseat in the living room, Jason went to get them something to drink. He disappeared through an old-fashioned swinging door between the dining room—which was across the entry hall from the living room—and the kitchen.

Brenna sat on the sofa with her arms crossed over her chest, looking at Abby with curious eyes. "Are you a friend of my Daddy's?"

Abby thought of the evening at Jeter's, and the possibilities that had hung in the air between them—before her life went completely out of orbit. "Yes, I guess I am."

"You guess?" She wrinkled her brow.

"Yes. We're friends, your dad and I."

"Oh," she sounded disappointed. "I thought maybe you were here because you're sick. Daddy's a doctor, you know."

The sound of the back door slamming was followed by harsh whispers coming from the kitchen. Glasses clinked, masking the words.

"Yes," Abby said. "A very good doctor."

Jason came into the room with a tray. On it were two glasses of iced tea, a juice box, a can of Coke, and a sugar bowl. He held it in front of Abby. "Take your pick."

Brenna's gaze was on the juice box. She looked a little nervous, but she didn't say a word.

Abby lifted a glass of iced tea from the tray. "Thank you."

"As un-Southern as it may be, it's unsweet," Jason said, nodding at the sugar bowl.

"I'll keep your secret. You might be run out of town." She knew he'd been living in Savannah before moving to Preston, but before that? "You're not a Yankee, are you?"

"Half, but only by blood," he said. "My father was from Michigan."

"Grandpa died before I was born," Brenna said.

Abby looked at the little girl, who immediately looked away. "I'm sorry to hear that," Abby said. "One of my grandpas died before I was born, too."

Brenna kept her eyes averted and started fidgeting with one of the toss pillows on the sofa.

When Jason offered the beverages to Brenna, she looked adoringly at him and took the juice box. Abby remembered being that age and thinking that her father could fix anything, like he was super-dad.

"Peanut, would you mind taking this Coke back into the kitchen? Have Bryce get you some graham crackers to go with your juice."

Brenna shot a mistrustful glance toward Abby. "It's

almost time for us to be home. Mother doesn't like us to be late."

"Please. I need to talk to Abby for a minute."

Brenna slipped off the sofa and picked up the Coke can from the tray. She turned down the hallway instead of going through the dining room as Jason had.

Jason took the other glass of tea and sat on the sofa.

Abby set her iced tea on a coaster on the table next to her. She wasn't going to drag this out any longer. "I came to see you because I need help, and I can't wait until next week for office hours."

A slight shadow flickered across his face. Disappointment? "Help with whatever caused you to collapse out there on the street?"

"Yes, sort of. Remember when I asked if you had experience with hypnosis?"

He nodded, leaning forward and holding the glass in his hands between his knees.

"It wasn't for Dad. It was for me. I've been," she paused, hating even uttering the word, "sleepwalking. I read that sometimes it can be helped with hypnosis." She left it there, waiting for his reaction before she revealed the entire hideous truth.

"Abby—"

"Please don't say no. I'm desperate, or I wouldn't be here right now."

He took a deep breath. "What I was going to say is that I don't feel comfortable treating you. Not when we're...friends. I can refer you—"

"I don't have time to wait for referrals! I need help. Now. I'm doing things...." She couldn't quite bring herself to list them out loud.

"I know sleepwalking is frightening," he said. "But treatments aren't—"

"*My* sleepwalking," she thumped her palm against her chest, "is more than frightening—" She sucked in a breath that came back out as a sob.

That sob was followed by another.

Jason moved to sit on the arm of the loveseat and put an arm around her.

She allowed him to pull her close, turning her face into his chest. Within seconds she was mortified by, yet unable to halt, the break in the dam of her tears.

Bryce left Bren in the kitchen watching some stupid show on the Family Channel. He walked down the hallway toward the living room. He was tired of sitting around here waiting. He was supposed to meet Toby in forty minutes.

This wasn't Bren's weekend with Jason, so she'd be going home, too. Bryce wanted to make sure he had time to assess his mom's "mood" before he left Bren with her. He'd been pretty sure there was something more than orange juice in her glass this morning.

He stopped cold just outside the living room. *Holyfuckingshit*. They were on the love seat. Jason's arms were around her. His head was bent over hers.

Bryce flashed hot.

Stupid bitch. She was going to fuck *everything* up.

"Jason!" He was gratified by the way Jason jerked upright, looking guilty as hell. "I need to get home."

Jason got up and walked over to him. Abby turned away and started rummaging in her purse. Bryce heard her sniffle. Just like a girl to manipulate with tears.

"Listen," Jason said quietly, "I need to stick with Abby

for a while. You go ahead and take your sister home. Use my car. I'll have Abby drop me by to pick it up later."

So not what I had in mind.

"What do you want me to tell Mom?"

Jason looked at him as if he was speaking a foreign language. "That I'm helping someone with an emergency."

Bryce glared into Jason's eyes. "Like a doctor emergency?" It sure hadn't looked like it.

Jason huffed. "Whatever it is, it's private. Which means you don't say anything to anyone about it—except to your mom that I'm dealing with an emergency."

Bryce wanted to say that his mom had cried buckets of tears and Jason had never treated it as an emergency.

He spun around and stalked into the kitchen. "Come on, Bren. Dad's done with us."

Bren looked up at him, confused.

"I am not *done* with you." Jason was right on his heels. He gave Bryce the stink-eye. "Either of you."

Bryce grabbed the keys off the kitchen counter and stood by the door.

Jason knelt in front of Bren and said, "Your brother is going to drive you home, so you're not late. I need to stay here and help Abby for a while. Okay?"

As if she said no you'd change your mind—big freakin' hypocrite.

Bren got up and hugged him. "I guess so."

Bryce wanted to yell at her. But she didn't know that Jason was in there hooking up and had decided it was more important to stay with that woman than to take his own kid home. What if Bryce hadn't been here; would Jason have stuck Bren in a taxi and sent her off by herself?

"Come on, Bren."

"I appreciate you doing this, Bryce," Jason said, as if Bryce was taking out the trash.

Bryce put a hand on Bren's shoulder and opened the back door.

"I'll call you before bed, Peanut."

"'K, Daddy."

They got into Jason's car. "Put your seatbelt on," Bryce said over his shoulder, as he started the engine.

"I *am*. Holy moly, give me a second. Why are you being such a jerk?"

He didn't say anything. Bren didn't need to know the truth.

By the time Jason came back into the living room, Abby looked like she had herself back under control. He was ashamed that a little piece of him wished she still needed his arms around her.

He wanted to help her, but he did not want to be her doctor. He knew through Constance that, even though her family had kept it quiet, Abby had set the fire that burned her family's home while she'd been sleepwalking. This was an issue that wouldn't be easily resolved. The roots went deep. It would take a very long time to unearth all of them.

He sat down on the sofa, a safe distance from the temptation to touch her.

"I sent the kids home," he said. He wanted her to feel at ease and not have to censor her words because of young ears.

"I feel terrible for interrupting—"

"You didn't cut anything short," he said. "It was time for them to be home. You'll drop me by to pick up my car later?"

"Of course." She dabbed her nose with a tissue and cleared her throat. "I'm really sorry—" she flipped her hand with the tissue in the air "—about all that. I'm not really like that."

"Like what?" he asked.

"Hysterical. Dramatic." She kept her gaze on her hands, now in her lap twisting that tissue the way he'd seen her twist her dismissal papers. "A basket case."

"I didn't see any of those things. I saw a woman who's been pushed to the breaking point. We all have one, you know."

"Well, I prefer to reach mine less publicly. Not..." She shook her head dismissively.

"Where you can't hide it."

She stiffened and sat up straighter. "Where I can't keep it private. There's a difference."

He gave a half-chuckle when he remembered what she'd said in the parking lot at Jeter's. He repeated it to her, "You're a cast iron belle who rings solo."

Her chin came up. "You make it sound like a short-coming."

"Maybe if you'd let yourself lean on someone, that breaking point would come later rather than sooner."

"Hey, we don't all have that option. I have good reasons for living the way I do." She crossed her arms over her chest and fixed her gaze somewhere outside his front window.

He sighed. "I didn't mean to sound like I'm criticizing. I'm offering to help. Let me be the person you lean on."

Her guarded gaze snapped back to him. Oh, how he wanted to move across this room and hold her. If only he could take away some of the pain in her eyes. But he kept himself planted where he was. He wouldn't get anywhere by pushing her.

"I'm hoping you came here because you trust me," he said. "Let me help you, Abby. At least until you get past all of this upheaval." He couldn't offer more; he was in no position to make promises, and he didn't think Abby was in the mood to accept them.

She bit her bottom lip for a moment, looking at him with indecision in her eyes. He tore his gaze away from the sensual pose of her mouth, and concentrated on her eyes.

Finally, she said, "I do trust you."

A shimmer of gladness glowed in his chest. He was certain Abby didn't trust many people, and having her admit it aloud was a coup. It amazed him how edgy he'd been sitting here, waiting for her response.

He held her gaze when he said, "I want you to trust me completely. Without reservation."

She nodded. "You're the only one I know who can help. You're a psychiatrist...."

The hopeful luminosity in his chest flickered out like a candle flame starved for oxygen. "Abby, I can't treat you."

She shot to her feet. "I thought you wanted to help me!"

"I do. I want to support you while you deal with all of this crap that's landed in your lap. But as a friend, Abby, not as a doctor."

Being her doctor would prevent any chance that they could ever be more. Now wasn't the time for them, he knew that. But he wasn't willing to cast out the possibility forever.

"In case you haven't noticed, I'm coming apart at the seams." She paced back and forth in front of the fireplace. "You don't even know the extent of my problem. Maybe I need you as a doctor more than I need you as a friend."

He shook his head. He had to make her understand. "I don't do good work when I'm emotionally involved." Lucy had proven that.

She scoffed. "You can only treat people you don't give a rat's ass about, is that it?"

"You're twisting my words. What I'm saying is, once we establish a doctor-patient relationship, there won't be any starting over once things settle down for you. We can't go back to that night at Jeter's."

For an instant her face softened and she looked at him the way she had when she'd admitted she'd like to have dinner with him again.

Then her fear returned. It was so obvious it might as well be a vaporous cloud that shrouded her body and obscured the light in her eyes.

"I said I'd take you as a doctor—and forfeit the friend." Her voice was trembling and he hated that veil of fear with everything he had in him.

He got up and went to her. Taking her hands, he pulled her squarely in front of him. "Abby, for me there's no choice. I've already crossed that line with you. I'm already emotionally invested."

This time her face didn't soften. She looked at him with cold reserve. "You won't think that after I tell you what I've done."

CHAPTER 13

Abby pulled her hands from Jason's and moved back to the safety of the corner of the love seat. He'd said he was emotionally invested. She couldn't dismiss the cascade of sparks that admission set off inside her.

But it would come to nothing. It didn't matter that his presence quieted the spinning, tense fear in her core. It didn't matter that while he'd held her in his arms it had taken an act of conscious will to prevent herself from clinging desperately to him, from engaging in something inappropriate and ill-timed; simply because he had the ability to take the pain away.

Jason had shown himself to be a caring man—with his children, with her father...certainly with her. But there was something more between them than caring and comfort. Even throughout these past days' ordeals, in the odd quiet moments, the memories of that moment in Jeter's parking lot stirred secret desires. Jason had danced on the edge of her fatigued mind, flirting with fantasies she didn't have the energy to suppress.

He was a man whose every breath was an unconscious

announcement of his masculinity. There was something carnal in the way he moved, the curve of his mouth, and certainly in the way he looked at her. But he buried it beneath a stringently controlled exterior. She recognized it simply because she'd constructed the same sort of defense against sexuality in herself.

Of course, her defense was for an entirely different reason. And it served a very important purpose. Even if they somehow found themselves in a relationship, it wouldn't be the kind that Jason deserved. It would be a relationship of halves; for she could never leave herself unguarded, never indulge in a twenty-four-hour-a-day commitment.

He stood there looking down at her for a long minute. Even his gaze could arouse things in her body that had been dormant for a very long time.

She looked away, knowing that if he sat next to her, her will would dissolve; she would bury those dark truths about herself. She would be weak. Selfish. She would take what she could for the moment and reality be damned.

Finally, he returned to the sofa across the room. His face showed confidence. Confidence that said whatever she was about to tell him, he would not be shocked, he would not turn away from her.

That look would not last. And once she revealed the whole truth, he would never look at her the way he was now, or the way he had at Jeter's.

Jason deserved someone worthy of that look of confidence.

So he had to know it all.

She began, starting her tale at the moment she came to

in the swamp. Then she led him through everything that happened afterward, step by horrid step. Her breath came short as she told of the deputy saying there had to be someone else out there in the darkness. She lost her battle with tears when she described seeing the motorcycle—and Kyle Robard.

That was the only time Jason moved throughout her telling. He leaned forward in his seat. Abby noticed his hands were locked together and his knuckles blanched white, but he didn't move closer or interrupt.

A little part of her wanted him to stop respecting her wishes and haul her off to bed, erase her reality entirely before she revealed the truth. She waited.

He stayed where he was.

She pressed on, knowing it would change the way he looked at her forever. "I think the reason I don't remember anything before I came to in the swamp is because I was sleepwalking...sleep-driving, that is."

"Abby, it's not uncommon to not recall an accident after it happens. Especially if you've lost consciousness."

"But it's not only that I can't recall the accident," she said. "I don't remember anything after I left you at Jeter's. When I got home from the hospital, it was obvious I'd gone to bed...to sleep."

"Again, not uncommon. It happens." His tone was not in the least argumentative or mocking. "Have you had problems with sleepwalking recently?"

"I think it started after Mom died. The only time I know for certain was the night before the accident. I only know that because I left the hose running and a trail of muddy footprints when I came back inside."

She closed her eyes. She'd thought the image of those

muddy footprints had been haunting. Now there was something so much worse emblazoned on her memory. "You have no idea what it's like to do things you're unaware of, things that are entirely out of your control, things that can hurt someone else."

"I can only imagine how terrible it must be." He was quiet for a bit. "But Abby, sleep-driving? That's a complex activity. And you made it pretty far from home before you...encountered trouble."

"Don't you think it's possible?"

"Of course it's possible. Just not very likely. Since you think you don't remember the accident because you were sleep-driving, it would follow that you *should* be able to recall going to bed if your amnesia is because of the sleep-driving. Your memory loss is most likely associated with the accident itself."

Made sense—if she was a normal person.

"Jason, I had absolutely no reason to be out on that road in the middle of the night. I hadn't been on it since I moved back out there."

"Why *did* you move back there?" His gaze was sharp enough she swore she could feel razor cuts on her skin. He almost seemed angry.

"It's the perfect place for my business...and Dad let me have it rent free until the flower shop got going—"

"Abby." He sighed and rubbed his hands on the thighs of his jeans. "Constance told me about how the fire was set. Why would you choose to go back there and face that ruin every day?"

"I told you why," she said, unable to keep the defensive tone from her voice. "My business—"

"I don't believe that's the reason at all. I think it was

because your sister moved away and you no longer had a daily reminder of what happened. You think you deserve to feel guilty. You're punishing yourself."

"Stop shrinking me! Where I choose to live is not the issue here."

"You can't have it both ways, Abby," he said, his tone a calm contrast to hers. "You asked me to 'shrink' you."

"And you said no!"

"I said I can't treat you. And I certainly can't hypnotize you. But I can speak to you as someone who cares about you. The fact is, I'm a psychiatrist; I can't change the way I think."

She scrubbed her hands over her face. "Okay." After a deep breath, she raised her gaze to meet his once again. "Okay. But leave where I live out of this. I need to figure out a way to stop this sleepwalking. If hypnosis can't fix me, maybe it can help me remember the accident." Her voice slid down to an exhausted whisper. "I have to know what happened."

"Abby, if you were sleep-driving, you won't ever remember. Hypnosis won't bring memories of that night forward because you never made those memories. Your conscious mind wasn't engaged. If you want to know what happened, I think you're going to have to rely on the police investigation. They're looking for a witness; maybe he'll come forward."

"You know? You know that a third person made the 911 call?"

"I don't know anything about the 911 call. Deputy Trowbridge was here, asking where I was that night. He said some evidence at the scene indicated someone who'd attended Vera's funeral had been there, so they were questioning everyone. I wondered why that was a clue they were following, since you'd attended the service. But clearly there's more to it." He rubbed his chin. "If a third person made the 911 call, why don't they just trace that phone?"

"Because it was made from Kyle's phone," she said, "which was found near him...his body. But they determined he'd been killed instantly."

"Then that caller took precautions not to be identified," Jason said thoughtfully.

"Maybe he didn't have a cell," she offered.

"Possibly. But that doesn't answer why he didn't stay until the police arrived."

"Maybe it was a kid afraid to be caught—out when he was supposed to be home, underage drinking, something like that."

"Could be. That person is your lead. That's where you'll find your answers, Abby. When they find the caller—"

"What makes you think they will?"

"Because nobody can keep something like this bottled up. And this is a small town. It's going to come out."

"Deputy Trowbridge thinks I made the call and don't remember. If they're looking for a third person, does this mean they didn't find my fingerprints on the phone?"

"Maybe. It may also mean the lab hasn't confirmed the results yet. I'm sure the police are under pressure. They have to do something visible and proactive. Kyle was a senator's son. Unfortunately, big wheels produce deafening squeaks. I see it time and again when I work with GBI—"

"With what?"

"Georgia Bureau of Investigation. I started doing consulting work for them when I lived in Savannah. I still do occasionally."

"You helped solve cases—like those guys on *Criminal Minds*?"

"Nothing nearly that thrilling. Just offered professional input to investigations and did some court testimony. It was interesting work."

His professional life in Savannah must have been more fulfilling than what he found here in Preston.

"Do you ever consider going back?" she asked.

He shook his head. "Bryce and Brenna are here." He sat in silence for a moment, then stood. "Did you tell the police you think you may have been sleep-driving at the time of the accident?"

"Not yet," she said. "I still want to try hypnosis. If I wasn't sleep-driving, couldn't that uncover what I was doing prior to the accident?"

"Possibly. I have someone I can call who uses hypnosis frequently. We'll have to drive down to Savannah."

"We?"

"Yeah, we. I'm not letting you do this alone."

He left the room and returned a few minutes later. "She'll see us tomorrow afternoon, but she won't be available until five."

"Tomorrow's Sunday."

"She's doing it as a personal favor."

A little voice asked how close this "she" was to Jason that she was willing to do personal favors. Not that Abby had any right to have such a thought.

She said, "Thank you."

"You look exhausted. How much sleep have you had since the accident?"

"A couple hours here and there. I've been afraid to."

"Denying yourself sleep isn't helping your cause. The more tired you are the more likely you are to sleepwalk."

"I know. I know. Yesterday I installed some of those magnetic alarms on my doors to wake me if I try to go outside."

"So why didn't you sleep last night?"

"I had a wedding today, so I worked until about four this morning. And then at five, the front door alarm went off." She'd effectively pushed the incident to the back of her mind, but now a chill crept across her skin as she thought of waking to that screaming alarm and her door wide open.

"Sleepwalking?" he asked.

"No. There's no delay on the alarm; I was asleep on the sofa." *And totally defenseless.* Her stomach went sour and her mouth dry. "The door was open and the key wasn't in the deadbolt."

"Jesus, Abby! Someone broke in?" He jumped to his feet, as if to protect her after the fact.

"Thank God, the alarm scared him off."

"You called the police?"

"Yes. They didn't find anyone. Apparently whoever it was either picked the lock or used something called a bump key. The lock is good as new."

"And freaking useless!" He was pacing in front of her. She hadn't thought of that.

"Abby, I don't like this at all. Not on the heels of the accident and the publicity."

"It had nothing to do with the accident. How could it?"

"We were just discussing that the third person didn't want to be found."

"But I don't remember anything. I didn't see anyone."

"They don't know that."

She shook her head. "This isn't one of your convoluted GBI cases. This is Preston. I had an accident. I know the sleepwalking idea is off the wall, but there's no big web of deceit or hidden conspiracies at work."

"Until we know differently, we're going to act like there is."

CHAPTER 14

"You're staying here tonight," Jason said for the third time, standing nose to nose with Abby.

And for the third time Abby said, "No. I. Am. Not."

At least her anger had put some color back in her face. She was probably the most stubborn woman he'd ever met; but there was nothing selfish about her obstinacy.

She'd already tried to make him believe she'd stay at her dad's. But that was a lie easy to see through. She was terrified of harming someone while she was sleepwalking. No way would she put her father in that position. The same for hotels; not that there were any in the vicinity of Preston.

He went on, "You might as well give up this argument, because I'm not backing down. You can't stay at your house, not until the police have a better handle on this break-in. And I'll make certain you're safe from your sleepwalking. You'll be able to let go and sleep. You need it."

Jason understood her fear. Although taken to the extreme, it was justified. Even before her suspicion of sleep-driving and having an accident resulting in a fatality, there had been Courtney. Childhood burn scars were the very worst—and apparently Courtney's involved her arms, neck, and the side of her face. Not places easily concealed.

Survivor guilt was a powerful and destructive thing. Seeing those scars every day would have been like Abby peeling a scab off a deep self-inflicted wound. Courtney's burns might heal, but the damage to Abby never would.

And once Courtney had left Preston, Abby had felt the need to punish herself with another constant reminder.

"You can't protect me from me," she said. "I'm not backing down." She poked him in the chest with her index finger hard enough that he took a step backward. "I *never* sleep with anyone else under the same roof."

He didn't call her on just negating the lie about staying with her father. That wasn't the battle he had to win at the moment.

He said, "I'm a light sleeper. We'll set things up so I have plenty of warning if you're up and moving. You can stay in Bren's room. It's right next to mine so I'll be able to hear."

She pressed her lips together and shook her head. She was so fatigued that she swayed on her feet.

For a long moment they simply stood there and glared at one another.

He settled his hands on his hips. "You'll stay here if I have to tie you up."

Suddenly her mask of stubborn anger cracked and a near hysterical cackle burst forth. "Isn't that against the law?"

"You can have me arrested after you've had a good night's sleep."

Her out-of-control laughter bubbled on, giddiness born of exhaustion. He knew it was only a matter of time before her mood swung the other way.

"I'll take your lack of response as capitulation." He picked up her purse and shoved it into her midsection. "Let's go get your things."

He walked out of the house with confident strides, hoping she was following. He didn't dare look back to see; that might open the door for more argument.

Once out the back door, he held it open. She walked past him without looking at him, her purse still clutched against her body where he'd thrust it.

She was silent when he opened the passenger door of the Explorer. And still when he climbed in behind the steering wheel.

As he started the car and pulled out onto the street, he cast sideways glances at her. She had something cooking; her capitulation was much too sudden and her silence as eerie as the green calm before a tornado.

Well, she could scheme all she wanted. He wasn't losing this battle.

When he made the turn that led out to her house instead of going toward Lucy's, she showed her hand.

"I thought we were getting your car," she said.

He looked over at her. Her posture had stiffened as she looked longingly at the right turn he hadn't made. "We're going to be together until after we get back from Savannah, so there's no need. We'll get it tomorrow."

"You told your kids you'd pick it up."

"Yes, I did. I'll let them know I'll be getting it tomorrow when I call Brenna at bedtime."

"But..."

"You're too exhausted to drive."

"But…"

"Why, Abby, I'm beginning to think you were planning on giving me the slip once you had me out of this car."

She huffed and crossed her arms over her chest. "As if you couldn't figure out where I'd be."

"Ah, but you were thinking about it. Admit it."

She jerked her head so she faced the passenger window.

"You know I'm right. Staying with me is the only logical solution for now. Home's not safe. You don't want to upset your dad. I'm it."

She kept herself turned away from him. "I think you're enjoying this macho bossy bullshit."

He grinned. "How am I doing at it?"

She huffed. A moment later she mumbled, "You really can't hold me against my will."

"Hey, it's only for twenty-four hours, most of which you'll be asleep. You'll hardly notice." He paused. "If it makes you feel any better, I'll turn myself in to the police as soon as we get back from Savannah."

"Ha-ha."

After a bit, he said, "Seriously, Abby. This is the only solution I can think of for now. If you'd like, you can stay at your house and I'll keep watch outside."

She finally looked at him. "You'd do that, wouldn't you?"

He nodded. "Whatever it takes to keep you safe and let you get some sleep."

She groaned and leaned her head back against the seat. "All right. I'll stay at your house. Just for tonight."

The sun had set but light still clung to the day when Jason turned into Abby's lane.

The change in speed and direction roused her from a doze. She exhaled loudly. "Oh. We're here."

"We are." When he'd seen her head bob a few minutes ago, he'd almost decided to just keep driving as long as she slept. But she needed real sleep, not cat naps—or car naps.

"Can you stop at the shop first?" she asked. "I need to check my messages."

He stopped the Explorer in front of the carriage house. "Hold on a minute. It's getting kind of late. I want to call Brenna." He pulled out his cell phone and made the call.

Abby stepped outside the car and leaned against the fender.

Lucy answered.

"It's me," Jason said. "I need to talk to Bryce before I tell Bren good night."

"He's out." She put down the phone with a clatter. He heard her calling Brenna to the phone.

"Daddy! Bryce made me spaghetti and Cheez Whiz and Oreos for dinner."

Jason shuddered. "Did Mommy have some too?"

"She wasn't home yet."

"I see. But she got home before Bryce left, right?"

"Yeah. He was mad because she was late. He called her a bunch of times."

"Can you tell Bryce something for me?"

"Sure."

"I won't be picking up my car until tomorrow morning."

"'K."

"Sleep tight, Peanut."

"Don't bite the bedbugs." She giggled.

She'd gotten the phrase turned around as a toddler. Now it was their little joke. "Can I talk to Mommy again?"

"Mommmeeeee. Bye, Daddy."

"What?" Lucy said.

"You weren't home when it was time for Brenna to be dropped off."

"And *you* didn't drop her off," she said sharply.

"Did something come up? You should have called me and I would have kept her."

"She was with Bryce. And it's none of your business why I wasn't here."

He came straight out and asked, "You're sober?"

"Jesus, Jason! I have a life. Just because I'm not home doesn't mean I'm out drinking!"

He really didn't have a leg to stand on. He'd sent his daughter on home without confirming she was there. Still, it pissed him off. Spaghetti and Cheez Whiz for dinner.

"Just let me know if you can't be there next time and I'll keep her with me."

He hung up before she said anything else.

When he got out of the Explorer, Abby looked his way. "Everything all right?"

"Fine."

She cast a dubious look his way. When he didn't offer more, she pushed herself away from the car and headed to the shop.

He waited while she unlocked the wood-framed glass door, which was the only mark of the twentieth century he could see on the building. The window next to the door was a nine-over-nine with weathered wood and flaking glazing. The original carriage doors were intact at the end of the structure. They looked like any ten-year-old with the slightest bit of determination could break into them; the deadbolt on the glass door was almost laughable.

Clearly whoever had been on this property in the wee hours of this morning wasn't looking for cash or credit card numbers.

"Are you coming?" Abby's voice broke into his thoughts. She was standing there holding the door open for him.

He stepped inside and looked around the dark interior.

"Wait here so you don't break your neck," she said as she stepped around him.

"Hold on," he said, but she kept going.

She walked across the space with no regard for the deep gloom—or anyone hiding in the shadows—her feet no doubt guided by years of habit.

"Abby. Wait." He took two steps before his shin hit something hard enough to leave a bruise. "Ouch! Son of a..." If this was her idea of caution, he was glad she'd agreed to stay with him.

The lights came on and Jason's tense muscles relaxed.

Abby looked back at him. "You okay?"

Jason looked down. His attacker had been a two-foot-high plaster garden gnome. "Fine."

She went about her business and Jason looked around. Abby's floral arrangements were unlike any he'd ever seen—not that he was an expert, but he'd been to enough

funerals to know what the standard was. He was curious
about the space that fueled her creativity.

The place smelled of old timber and eucalyptus. The
entire area was open. A counter and cash register sat near
the far wall.

There was a large walk-in refrigerator beyond a wide
worktable. Bits of greenery littered the top of the table
and the floor beneath. There was a rod sticking up at
one side of the table filled with spools of colored ribbon
aligned like the colors of the rainbow. Nearer the door,
where he was standing, various pottery, glass vases, and
garden ornaments were neatly displayed.

The building had a wood plank floor, old enough that
wide cracks had grown between them and deep sloping
grooves had been worn in the traffic paths. The exposed
beams supporting the roof had clearly been hand hewn.

Realizing this building's age, he understood the incredible loss Abby felt over the destruction of the main house.
Constance had said the Whitmans never planned to
rebuild on the site; what was gone was irreplaceable. But
Jason wondered if Abby's father had chosen to move to
town in order to lighten the load of his daughter's sense
of guilt. As for her move back here...God knows the
woman could wear a man down with her arguments.

He looked at her behind the counter, getting a pen and
paper to write down her messages. Her dark hair swept
past her shoulder and hid her face. She seemed so slight,
and showed incredible emotional and moral strength. But
she had to find a way to forgive herself, or she would
never find true peace. He wanted to help her achieve that.
Then maybe she would allow herself to live a full life that
included living with someone she loved.

She pushed the button on the answering machine. Just as the voice began speaking, Jason realized he should never have let her come in here. Why hadn't he been thinking?

"This is Kathy Richardson. I'd like to order flowers for Kyle Robard's funeral. Randall and Roberts Funeral Ho—"

Jason hurried around the counter and hit the "stop" button.

Abby was sucking in huge gulps of air. The pen had fallen from her shaking hand.

She pushed him away and swiped a vase off the counter. The explosion of broken glass was like a gunshot in the room. She pressed the heels of her hands against her forehead and paced across the glass, grinding and popping it into smaller pieces.

"Abby! Stop!"

She was shaking her head in agitation, still moving across the bed of broken glass.

"Abby!" He reached out and grabbed her arm, stepping into the glass himself. "Stop. The glass."

He pulled her away from the area of the floor covered by the shattered vase.

She allowed him to lead her only so far, then removed her arm from his grasp and put some space between them. All of her angry energy turned inward. Her face took on a stony calm, her eyes focused somewhere other than in the reality of this moment.

She faced the window, her arms wrapped around her middle. Her shoulders rose and fell with her breathing. This silent withdrawal was more unsettling than any tears he'd seen her shed; he wanted her to let him in, not retreat further.

He chanced resting a hand on her shoulder blade.

When she didn't pull away, he ventured further and gently turned her toward him. Her gaze moved from the window to the floor.

"Abby, look at me."

She swallowed roughly and raised her eyes to meet his.

There were no words that could take away the pain that reached from her eyes deep into her soul. So he pulled her against his chest with one arm and pressed her head into the crook of his shoulder. "I'm sorry. I'm so sorry," he murmured.

Her body trembled slightly and her arms wrapped around his waist. She remained eerily silent.

He held her more tightly and stroked her hair. "So sorry, baby."

After a minute or so, and much too soon for Jason, she took a deep breath and leaned away from him.

"I'm okay now." She patted his chest. "I'm all right."

He framed her face with his hands and looked into those wounded eyes. He felt himself moving before he had time to censor his actions. She held perfectly still...until his lips touched hers. Then her hands clutched his shirtfront, pulling him closer.

He tasted the salt of her tears and his heart broke just a little.

She kissed him back, her mouth soft and yielding beneath his.

He could feel the flutter of her pulse where the heel of his hand rested on the side of her neck. He couldn't help but hope he was the reason for its accelerated rhythm.

One kiss blended tenderly into another. His body

awakened and he realized how long it had been since he'd held a woman. He wished this moment would last, neither going forward nor back, so he could linger in the possibilities.

When she pulled away, she lowered her gaze and bit her lower lip.

He smoothed her hair away from her face, hooking it behind her ear. Then he slipped a finger beneath her chin and tilted her face up. Even in her current state of exhaustion, she was lovely beyond words.

She looked at him steadily, her seeming shyness disappearing. "I know I've sounded like an ungrateful snot. I'm sorry," she said. "Thank you for being here; for helping me."

He smiled and felt as if he'd crossed a bridge she didn't allow many people to find, let alone cross. It was safest to let her get used to this new intimacy one quiet step at a time. He simply said, "You're welcome."

She reached up and caressed his cheek. Then she let her hand fall away and looked at the glass on the floor. "I'd better get the broom."

"Abby," he said and she stopped. "Do you want me to listen to the messages for you? I can call all of them back and tell them they need to order from somewhere else."

She rolled her lips inward and bit them. He wondered if she could still taste him as he tasted her salt and sadness.

After a second, she said, "No. The viewing won't be until Tuesday and the service Wednesday. Let me think about it until tomorrow morning."

"Good idea." He watched her walk away, marveling at her strength. He glanced at the machine. There were twenty-four messages. She was going to need every bit of that strength.

Once they had the glass cleaned up, she locked the shop and they drove the Explorer a hundred yards to her cottage.

The front door was draped in the deep shadow of evening and the giant magnolia that stood nearby. That was why he didn't notice the door was ajar until the weak high-pitched tone reached his ears.

Abby halted, hearing it, too.

He quickly pulled her back and stepped in front of her. "Was this locked?"

"Yes."

"The alarm is battery powered?"

"Yes."

The tone was weak and faltering. Clearly running out of juice.

"Go back and get in the car," he said. "Lock the doors."

"Only if you go with me. We can call the police."

"There isn't another way for a car to come and go, is there?"

"No."

"I don't think they're still here. We haven't seen a car, even out on the road when we turned in. Besides, they would have heard our car doors by now and gone out the back."

"Then let's go in," Abby said. She pulled out her cell phone, as if it was a weapon. "I'll have 911 ready."

He went up the brick steps and pounded on the door frame. "Hey!"

"I thought you said they were gone," Abby whispered.

Jason wondered why she kept her voice low when he'd just shouted.

"Just making sure," he said, and thumped the door again with his fist.

He waited, listening. Nothing but the pitiful thin whine of the magnetic alarm.

He said, "Stay right behind me."

He pushed the door open with his foot, and reached to the left, where he knew the light switch was.

The bright illumination stung his eyes when the ceiling fan light came on. The place wasn't more than one big room with a loft overhead, so he could sweep the area easily. Everything appeared in order.

He reached up and turned off the alarm switch. Then he grabbed Abby's hand to keep her close. With his other hand he picked up a heavy candlestick off the bar between the kitchen and living area.

They systematically checked all of the closets and the loft. When they turned the light on in her small bathroom they found the only trace of the intruder. Written across the mirror in wide red marker were the words:

you tell
you die

CHAPTER 15

Tell ... tell ... tell....

The word had been echoing sluggishly in the back of Abby's brain for the past twenty minutes. She wanted to scream, "Tell what?" and maybe it would stop. Right now her only hope of discovering what someone feared she would tell lay with Jason's friend in Savannah.

She needed to get up and move, to shake off this feeling of victimization. But every time she did Jason cautioned her not to touch anything. So she'd limited herself to one tiny section of sofa cushion and settled for bouncing her knees. As for Jason, he looked like he wanted to break something, and it intensified every time he looked at her. It seemed prudent to stop drawing attention to herself.

When the police arrived they were different officers yet again; Fisher and Haggerty this time. They'd come with a serious demeanor and a full crime scene investigation kit, thanks to Jason. Abby had gathered through his conversation with the sheriff's department that he had a

working relationship with the locals as well as his old
GBI contacts in Savannah.

The officers were being exceptionally thorough—
probably because Jason kept a critical eye on their every
move. Even Abby, in her diminished mental state, could
tell it was beginning to piss them off.

Officer Fisher sat down to question her. She could
barely hold her focus, often missing a question entirely
until he repeated it. He was beginning to look at her like
she was impaired in some way.

Not that it mattered. These were the same gamut of
questions she'd answered this morning. She had no new
answers.

Officer Haggerty continued to gather physical evidence. Abby watched him move about her house with a
camera and a fingerprint duster out of the corner of her
eye.

Would they ever finish and get out of here? Her adrenaline rush had passed. She hadn't thought it possible, but
she was more drained than before.

Jason paced, alternating between cautioning Fisher to
take it easy on Abby and prodding Haggerty to be vigilant
in his work. Abby had the feeling that if Jason hadn't had
some connection with the sheriff already, they'd have
asked him to wait outside by now.

Fisher asked, "Any idea at all what the threat is referring to?"

Jason stopped dead in his tracks and looked at Abby.
They'd discussed it while they'd waited for the police.
Although she'd been slow to come around, Jason's idea
really was the only thing that made any sense.

She said, "Maybe it has to do with the accident I had

the other night. We think whoever made the 911 call to
report it from Kyle Robard's phone thinks I saw him, and
he doesn't want to be discovered."

Tell...tell...tell.... There was something hovering in
Abby's mind, shrouded and just out of reach. When she
concentrated on it, trying to figure out why it kept plagu-
ing her, it relocated deeper into the fog.

"Interesting theory." Fisher's brows drew together.
"You said he? It was a man then?"

"I used the masculine for the sake of simplicity," she
said, her head beginning to pound more severely and her
vision blurred. "I didn't see *anyone*."

Jason said, "Now that you know there's been a threat
to Abby, how about pushing the lab work through?"

Fisher visibly bristled, but his tone was civil when he
said, "Dr. Coble, we have to rely on the state lab. I'm sure
they're processing things as quickly as they can."

"I've been involved in enough cases to know how this
works. You *can* speed up the process."

"That's not my call, sir." The last word sounded like
a restrained warning. "We don't have the resources that
your GBI has."

Abby wondered how Jason would have dealt with
Trowbridge's attitude. Or maybe Trowbridge wouldn't
have had an attitude if Jason had been here yesterday.

Haggerty said, "I have everything I need." He put his
camera back in its case. "Except I'd like to take that mirror to the lab."

He pulled out a screwdriver from his kit and looked at
Abby with expectation.

"Help yourself." She knew even after she got the
marker off of it, she would never be able to look into that

mirror again and not see those words; they would remain ghosts in the glass.

Fisher's cell phone rang. He pulled it out of his pocket and looked at the ID screen. "Excuse me." He got up and walked over to the kitchen. "Fisher."

Jason returned to his pacing, but Abby could tell he had his ear tuned to Fisher's conversation.

She wasn't able to decipher anything other than that it was a short exchange.

When he hung up, he returned and asked Abby, "Officer Bigelow wanted me to ask you if you own a silver iPod?"

"No. Mine is white. Why?"

"When he came back to search the cemetery earlier today, he found one in the grass near the big monument."

"Cemetery?" Jason asked, looking at Abby.

"There's an old family cemetery near the road. Someone vandalized it sometime in the past week."

"And you didn't think this was worth mentioning?" Jason asked.

"It's been a long day, Jason."

"I know. I'm sorry. It's just that it could be a clue to who is doing all of this."

"There have to be hundreds of silver iPods around," she said, thinking this was as good as no clue at all.

Jason brightened. "But they won't all have the same fingerprints on them, or the same songs and video clips."

"You got it." Fisher gave him grudging acknowledgment. "Barring registered fingerprints, the video clips might be our best bet."

"Have they examined it yet?" Jason asked. "Do they know if the prints match the ones they took from Abby's door this morning?"

"Too soon." There was just a hint of challenge in those two clipped words. He stared at Jason for a moment, waiting.

Jason had his hands on his hips and a frown on his face, but he kept his mouth shut.

Haggerty came out of the bathroom, Abby's mirror in a large clear plastic bag. She turned away so she didn't have to see the words again.

As Fisher opened the door for Haggerty, he asked, "Are you planning on staying here, ma'am?"

"No. I'll be staying in town."

"Good idea." He picked up the rest of the gear and walked out.

Abby moved to the front window and watched them load their cars. The darkness seemed heavy and thick between her house and the road a quarter of a mile down the lane. Jason came and stood just behind her, resting a hand gently on her shoulder.

One after the other, the two cars did three-point turns to head back out of her lane. Watching gave her a sense of déjà vu. Those headlights the night of the accident had seemed so insignificant. But now...

"After the accident, before the police got there, I saw headlights coming—from the other direction. They stopped and turned around very abruptly. Maybe it was the person who made the call coming back, and he turned around when he saw the lights of the police car coming."

His grip tightened on her shoulder. "Did you tell Trowbridge?"

"I didn't remember until after he'd left. I was going to talk to the sheriff again and tell him. But things have been so crazy."

"Did it get close enough for you to tell anything about the vehicle?"

She shook her head. "It's probably useless information."

"We'll still tell the sheriff."

Abby leaned back against him. She welcomed the word "we." Even if it was only temporary, she wasn't in this alone.

"Test it," Abby said.

Jason sighed, stood on tiptoe, and pressed the button on the upstairs hall smoke detector. It sent out a piercing wail.

"Satisfied?" he asked. God, would the woman ever give up and go to sleep? It was nearly ten p.m. She could have been in bed an hour ago.

He'd taken the front door alarm from her cottage, replaced the battery, and installed it on Bren's bedroom door. Now he'd just tested all of the smoke detectors in the house.

Abby still didn't look comfortable.

"Believe me, this is all overkill anyway," he said. "I used to wake up when Bren turned over at night."

"Make sure there aren't any matches in the room."

"It's *Brenna's* bedroom. She doesn't smoke and I don't allow her to burn candles in there."

She just stared at him with her arms folded over her chest.

"All right." He went in and opened drawers he'd never opened; invaded his daughter's privacy in a way he never had. Then he returned to Abby in the hallway. "No matches. No lighters. No illegal fireworks. No concealed firearms. Now, please, go to sleep."

She caught her lower lip between her teeth. She was eyeing the doorknob. "Can you turn that around so it locks from the outside?"

He put his hands on her shoulders. "Abby, I want you to be able to relax, but I will not lock you in that room."

A small smile came to those beautiful lips. "I thought you were willing to tie me up."

He kissed her forehead. "So tempting...." He stepped away, his hands itching to touch her. "There are fresh towels and a new bar of soap in the hall bath. I think Bren has some shampoo in there, but it smells like bubblegum and makes my stomach turn."

"Then maybe you'll smell me coming before you hear me."

"Abby—"

She laughed. "I was just kidding. Besides, I have my own shampoo."

He thought of the light gardenia scent as he'd held her. Heady and intriguing.

He made himself walk away. "Good night. Let me know if you need anything."

She smiled. "Good night." He was halfway down the stairs when she called, "Jason."

He turned.

"Thank you."

She disappeared into the bathroom before he could respond.

Bryce walked into Jeter's. It was late enough that most of the families had cleared out. The arcade was filled with lame high school freshmen. But the pool tables in the back were occupied by beer-drinking adults.

It felt good to bypass the arcade and head to the pool table where Toby was chalking his cue. Bryce hoped some of the little dorks in the arcade noticed the company he was keeping and spread it around school. Could increase his cool factor exponentially.

Toby lifted his chin in greeting. "Thought you might not make it."

"Had some stuff to do." Part of that stuff had been feeding his little sister dinner and tracking down his mother.

She'd finally answered her cell on his third call. She had some story about meeting an old friend for coffee and losing track of time. He'd wondered if that old friend's name was Smirnoff. But she'd seemed stone sober when she arrived home. Weird, but sober.

So weird that he'd hung around the house for a while. She'd been fidgety and seemed anxious for him to leave. He'd wondered if it had anything to do with the news that they were looking for a third car in Kyle Robard's accident.

He'd screwed up his courage and asked her flat out if she had anything to do with Kyle Robard's death. Swear to God, at the mention of Kyle's name she'd turned as white as death...and then she'd denied it.

He hoped to hell she got better at it before it counted.

He'd been physically ill by the time he'd left the house. He'd also been way behind schedule.

Bryce grabbed a cue as Toby racked the balls.

Some guy at the next table was talking really loud. Something about Kyle Robard's accident.

Bryce glanced at him. It was the guy who'd come to their house asking about the funeral—and where they'd been on the night of the accident. Trowbridge.

What if it all came out here, now, in front of Toby and half the town?

Bryce mumbled to Toby, "Somebody needs to tell that guy to shut up."

Toby glanced over. "He's pretty ripped. Don't think it's going to be me."

Trowbridge *was* about a hundred-and-fifty percent muscle.

Panic grabbed Bryce's gut, but he couldn't see a way to stop the train wreck.

Then he thought, if they knew... if they knew for sure, his mom would be in jail right now.

She wasn't.

This was his opportunity to hear what the police were thinking. His stomach crawled up his throat as he listened.

"Trowbridge, you're full of shit," the guy with the deputy said. "They wouldn't let you have the senator's kid's case."

Both men looked to be well into a good drunk.

"No, man," Trowbridge said. "I got the call, so it's my case—and I'm going to get to the bottom of it. Senator'll owe me big time. There are footprints all over out there that don't add up. That chick that hit the kid says she doesn't remember—like nobody's used that line before. But I'll get her to tell me."

Bryce was breaking the balls and missed entirely.

Toby laughed. "Thought you said you'd played pool before."

The guys at the next table changed their topic to some girl's ass across the room. And before Bryce and Toby's game was finished, Trowbridge and his buddy left the table and went to the bar.

Bryce totally screwed his game because of the anger boiling under his skin. He couldn't stop thinking about Abby Whitman and the many ways she was fucking up his life.

Abby crawled into bed certain that no matter how tired she was she wouldn't be able to sleep—and not just because of her fear of sleepwalking. The look on Jason's face as he'd left her to go downstairs had haunted every breath since. She could swear she could still taste his kiss, even though it had been hours ago.

But she soon relaxed, soothed by the security of his nearness.

As sleep quickly claimed her, she realized for the first time in her memory she'd relinquished control, and it felt so very right.

Just as Jason was heading up to bed at eleven, he heard Abby's cell phone ring in her purse. He only debated for an instant before he reached in the side pouch and pulled it out. If it was her father needing assistance, it couldn't be ignored.

The ID screen said it was Courtney.

Jason's finger hovered over the green button. His curiosity made him press it. As he did, he rationalized that it could still be a family emergency.

"Hello, this is Abby's phone."

"Who is this?" Courtney's voice was rough, as if her

vocal cords had been slightly damaged. It made Jason's skin prickle; even from a distance Courtney could torture her sister without even meaning to.

"This is Dr. Coble. Abby's sleeping. Can I take a message?"

"Oh my God, is Dad all right? She was supposed to call me!"

He wondered if she knew Abby had been in an accident. He doubted it. Abby was so protective of her family, sparing them unnecessary upset. And it hadn't made the national news. "Mr. Whitman is fine. I'll have Abby call you in the morning."

"Why are you..." she paused. "*This* is why she's making Dad see you; you're sleeping with her!"

"No, I'm not." Her tone had hit his hot button and it took an effort to keep his voice neutral. "And I've referred your father to another doctor."

"What are you doing there if she's sleeping, then?" She sounded like a jealous lover.

What the hell difference did it make if he *was* sleeping with her sister? Abby was a grown woman.

Even in this short conversation Jason figured out a few things about Courtney. The first being that she was resentful of anything that gave her sister happiness.

He decided to let her stew in her own jealousy. "I'll let Abby explain it all to you tomorrow."

"You'd better sleep with one eye open—"

Jason disconnected the call before he said anything he'd regret. Good God, that woman needed psychological help. He had no doubt she lorded Abby's guilt over her at every opportunity.

He'd seen cases like this. Traumatized children whose

well-meaning families had only exacerbated the situation by doing what they thought was protecting them.

He gritted his teeth. Had anyone ever given consideration to what that was doing to Abby?

When Bryce and Toby left Jeter's at eleven-thirty, they took Bryce's car.

"Dude, something's got you pissed," Toby said.

Bryce was too angry to keep it in any longer. But he couldn't tell the complete truth. "My parents are divorced. I think they could get back together. Except my dad's getting all messed up with this woman."

"Bummer. Who is she?"

"Abby Whitman. She's using that accident she was in as a reason to hang all over him. Dad feels he's gotta save her."

Toby was quiet for a minute. When Bryce looked over at him, he had a weird kind of smile on his face.

Finally Toby said, "How about we stop by the liquor store and get something to help you chill?"

Bryce hesitated. He couldn't get caught. Not now.

But he didn't want to look lame in front of Toby. They'd just started hanging out. Toby understood stuff. Bryce's high school friends didn't have anything to worry about except passing U.S. History and who they were going to take to the prom.

Maybe a drink would stop this feeling like he was coming out of his skin. He could handle a little alcohol. He wasn't his mother.

"Sure," he said.

Bryce parked on the street, around the corner from the liquor store. He tried to give Toby some cash, but Toby refused to take it. Bryce sank low in the seat and watched for familiar cars while he waited for Toby to come back out. All he needed was to get caught. Then he'd lose his car and wouldn't be able to fix anything.

Toby reappeared with a brown paper bag and got in the passenger seat. "I'd say we could go to my grandmother's, but she gets all bitchy when everybody's not over twenty-one. But I've got another place in mind."

"Okay. I need to swing by my house first, check on my sister."

"Is she hot?"

Bryce shot him a disgusted look. "She's *seven*."

A few minutes later, Bryce turned onto his street. "Fuck."

"What?" Toby asked, quickly tucking the bag with the booze under the seat.

"My dad's car's still here. He was supposed to come and pick it up."

"So?"

Bryce pulled in the driveway. His mom's car was in the garage where it belonged. "I'll be right back."

Toby nodded.

His mom was in her bedroom with the television on. She'd fallen asleep with the remote in her hand. Bryce tiptoed over and gently pulled it from her grasp, smelling her exhaled breath as he did. He caught a whiff of alcohol.

She opened her eyes and smiled. "Glad you're home safe." Then she turned over and closed her eyes. At least she wasn't passed out cold.

He clicked off the TV. Then he checked on Bren.

Watching his sister sleep, he got all worked up again.

Both his mom and Jason seemed to be making a royal effort to screw him and Bren over. Didn't they know how sad Bren was? Didn't they care?

He locked the house and went back to his car.

"You good?" Toby asked.

"Yeah. I wanna check one other thing."

"It's your party."

Bryce drove to Jason's. The lights in his house were all off. Abby Whitman's car sat in the drive. Bryce slammed his palm against the steering wheel. "Goddammit."

"That her car?" Toby asked.

Bryce nodded.

Toby shook his head. "Not good, man."

Bryce gritted his teeth until his jaw ached. Not good at all.

CHAPTER 16

An hour after he'd gotten into bed, Jason still lay sleepless, thinking of Abby just a few feet away. It had blindsided him how quickly he'd become emotionally involved with her. Up until now, he'd not even considered the possibility of another woman in his life, even in a casual dating capacity. But what he had for Abby wasn't a casual date kind of feeling.

He'd been drawn to her the day in St. Andrew's. He'd been so impressed with her kind and pragmatic interaction with Maggie. Although he'd initially been looking for a way to avoid waiting with Lucy and her family, that intent had been quickly forgotten when Abby had turned around and looked at him with those bourbon-colored eyes.

He'd felt as if he'd taken a step into an elevator shaft, sans elevator. Even recalling that feeling made him feel foolish and adolescent—grown men living in reality didn't react like that. But he couldn't deny it, and truthfully he wasn't sure he wanted to. It had made him realize he was still alive, not the walking, talking shadow man he'd been for the past couple of years.

Those hours at Jeter's had given him a glimpse at some very appealing possibilities.

When he'd seen her in the hospital lobby, bruised and battered, it had been a kick in the gut. And he'd responded in a very un-Jason-like way; dumping his colleague and getting personally involved in solving her problem.

Then tonight when they'd found her place broken into and that threat on the mirror, he—a man of control and logic—had been as close as he'd ever come to putting his fist through a wall.

He was on a slippery slope for certain. And there were a thousand reasons why he shouldn't allow himself to slide any further.

The fact that he was lying here with a hard-on just thinking about her said he was failing miserably in gaining a handhold to stop his freefall.

There was a loud thump in the room next door that made him sit bolt-upright in bed. He listened intently for a sound of movement.

A soft rustle was followed by a footfall on the carpet.

He quickly got out of bed and went to the dark hall. There was no light shining beneath Abby's door.

Should he knock? What if she was just going to the bathroom? He felt a little like a stalker hovering near her bedroom door like this.

He heard a drawer slide open.

"Abby?" he whispered. If she was awake she should hear him.

No response.

If she was sleeping, he didn't want to wake her. The instant he opened the door to check on her, the alarm would go off.

He waited. And listened.

More rustling.

And then the door swung open and the alarm wailed.

Abby started to run, bumping into him on her second step.

He wrapped his arms around her and called her name. At first she struggled, then her eyes seemed to focus and she blinked. "Oh!"

Moving forward with her in a bear hug, Jason reached up and shut off the alarm.

He smiled down at her. "See, I told you I'd hear you the second you set foot on the floor." He didn't admit that he'd been lying there awake thinking of her.

She didn't look comforted in the least. She pushed herself away from him. Her gaze traveled down to where she'd certainly felt his arousal, but she quickly caught herself and snapped her gaze up to his face.

"I told you this was a bad idea," she said.

He tried to make light of her sleepwalking by pretending he misunderstood her comment. "Hey, a guy can't be held responsible for what his body does while he's asleep."

She did not look amused. "You know that's not what I meant." She was trembling.

He sighed and ran a hand through his hair. "Look at it this way. You can sleep easy knowing I'll hear you if you go sleepwalking. This was a great test run. Go back to bed and go to sleep." He took a step backward, into the hall.

Closing her eyes, she shook her head and gave a sound of exasperation. Then she closed the door in his face. He heard the alarm switch back on.

"Good night," he called through the door.

He didn't get a response.

For the next forty minutes, he lay on his back, studying the ceiling, listening to her soft footsteps as she paced in Bren's room.

He had to keep his priorities straight. What Abby needed from him right now was support and protection. She did not need to worry about him having sexual fantasies about her while she slept in the next room.

And after this mess was behind them? He was going to have to play a game of wait and see, which normally suited his nature just fine. But Abby had already made him go against his nature. He didn't think wait and see was going to be an easy task.

He turned on his side, crossing his arms over his chest, and tried to change his course of thinking. If he was going to lie here awake, he might as well be productive.

He organized what he knew concerning Abby's accident in a logical, unemotional fashion. When he looked at it, he only had two solid items: Abby's account of what had happened after she awakened, and Trowbridge's search for a third party responsible for the 911 call on Kyle's cell phone. No way could any conclusion be drawn from those scant details. He needed more; evidence from the accident scene itself.

With Abby's permission, he'd go with her to the sheriff when she met with him to tell him about the headlights, and—if by some miracle the hypnosis worked—what they discovered tomorrow in Savannah. Hopefully, the sheriff could fill in some of the blanks.

His main concern right now was the connection

between the accident and the person threatening Abby. The obvious, due to the words on the mirror, was the 911 caller.

But what if Jason missed the truth by making that assumption? He'd seen it happen in investigations plenty of times.

Perhaps the threat wasn't linked to the accident at all. Jason had a limited view of Abby's life. Maybe after she'd rested, they could take a wider look.

For now, he had only questions. Was the vandalism at the cemetery coincidence, or linked? Abby had said she couldn't pinpoint when it had happened. And it was incongruous with the break-in; in the cemetery things had been taken, iron that could be sold as scrap.

He tried to approach from a logical, suspect-oriented viewpoint. Who was angry enough at Abby to threaten her life? Who could feel that Abby had grievously wronged them?

Because he was working with only the details of the past few days, the list he compiled was short: Courtney. Senator Robard. Jessica Robard.

Courtney was in New Mexico.

Senator Robard had lost a son. But he had too much to lose (which, judging by his treatment of his wife, he prized beyond family love) to stoop to break-ins and threats. If the senator wanted something done, it would be by another's hand. Not impossible, but unlikely considering the risk.

Jessica Robard. Much more likely. She had been depressed in the first place, and was now out of her mind with grief. She'd slipped away without her husband's knowledge before. The only problem was the words on the mirror. That message made no sense coming from Jessica. But again, she was out of her mind with grief; who knew what her thoughts were. Maybe she feared Abby had seen something having to do with Kyle that would ruin his reputation—which was all Jessica had left of him.

It came back around to his original thought. The anonymous 911 caller was most likely the key. A witness to the accident? Or someone involved in the accident? Someone linked in some way with Kyle Robard? Abby's suggestion of an underage drinker made sense. Had someone been riding with Kyle and taken off on foot? Had someone been racing him? There were plenty of kids who used that road as their own personal racecourse.

Jason wondered if the sheriff had questioned all of Kyle's acquaintances. He'd have to ask. A kid would act out like this, threats on the mirror, vandalism.

But would a kid have a bump key or know how to pick a lock so cleanly? Preston didn't have a lot of break-ins, and certainly none that had been linked to teenagers since Jason had been in town.

Anyone smart and experienced enough to break in so cleanly would surely be smart enough not to risk driving a car down a quarter-mile-long narrow lane and chance getting trapped. The road in front of Abby's property was too narrow and bordered on both sides by deep drainage ditches. Where would they have hidden a vehicle?

Jason fell asleep with that thought on his mind.

A few hours later, he awakened with a possible answer.

Abby roused slightly. Enough to realize she wasn't in her own bed. Then she remembered. Jason—she was in his daughter's room. And she'd gone sleepwalking in the night.

It wasn't as if she hadn't expected it. All of the triggers were there, sleep deprivation, stress, a break in routine. Still it had made her heart race and her bowels weak when she'd startled awake. All of the precautions had worked this time. But what if the battery on the alarm failed next time? What if she didn't make enough noise for Jason to hear her?

With a groan, she rolled onto her back and fisted her hands in her hair. Although her night's sleep made her feel human for the first time in days, it was so not worth the risk to stay here again. Her sleepwalking was a malignancy that couldn't be excised, a disease with contagious side effects that threatened everyone around her.

As she drew in a breath of surrender to the power of the darkness inside, she smelled it. Coffee and bacon.

She realized she hadn't eaten at all yesterday. Jason had offered food upon their return to his house last night, but she'd been too exhausted to eat.

It had been years since she'd awakened to someone making her breakfast—and she would never wake to it again. Until this moment, she hadn't realized how much she missed that feeling of security and belonging that came with someone cooking for you while you slept.

Belonging. The word struck a chord. She thrived on her independence, had never allowed herself to long for anything different. Life was what it was, not a storybook ideal. But for this brief moment, she permitted herself to imagine Jason in the kitchen making her breakfast under different circumstances.

It was a lovely and stimulating thought. No doubt if

she was a normal woman she would pursue those circumstances. But for her, sexual relations were fleeting; long-lasting entanglements virtually nonexistent. She didn't think if she shared that intimacy with Jason, she would ever be able to let him go.

A small place in her chest felt cold and empty as she realized that, sooner or later, Jason would be making breakfast for a normal woman, a woman who deserved him. A woman who was not Abby.

Aggravated with her self-pity, she threw off the covers and got out of bed. She had never dallied in daydreams. Now wasn't the time to start. She made the bed and went to her overnight bag. She'd only brought enough for one night, as that was all she would allow herself. Today she would come up with a way to secure her cottage from intruders—maybe a thick crossbar like they used in the old days, or a heavy slide bolt on the inside. She'd figure out something.

As she rummaged in her bag she was stunned with the bizarre combination of things she'd thrown in it: orange nylon sweat pants and a purple cashmere sweater, green running shoes and nylon stockings. Only her underwear was coordinated, although wholly inappropriate—a black lace thong and bra.

"You're gonna be one good-lookin' babe this morning." With a sigh she gathered her clothing, switched off the alarm, and headed to the bathroom.

She took a quick shower. Hunger outstripped pride and she went downstairs barefoot, with wet hair and no makeup. Dressed as she was, her pride was useless.

Jason was standing over sizzling bacon and didn't hear her come to the kitchen doorway. She took a moment to watch him. He wore well-molded jeans and a light-gauge black sweater that showed those muscles that Abby had been crying all over for two days.

Damn, he looked every bit as good making breakfast as she'd imagined. What a shame this would be her only opportunity to witness it.

He must have heard her sigh, because he turned around. He gave a startled jerk, his eyes widened, and he nearly dropped his spatula. Immediately, he censored his expression. "Morning." He said it tight-lipped, suppressing his grin.

"Go ahead, laugh," she said. "I look like Bozo the Clown fresh out of the dunk tank."

He accepted her invitation and sputtered into laughter.

"Hey, I said laugh, but I meant tell me I'm perfectly lovely," she chided as she walked into the room.

By the time she'd reached his side, he'd grown more subdued. "As I was just about to say, you look lovely this morning." His voice dropped when he added, "Really."

He got that look in his eye, like he was going to kiss her again.

She took a step away.

He took the hint and retreated to safer ground. "Guess I should have supervised your packing."

"Yeah, yeah. Feed me." She walked closer and sniffed the French toast he had on the griddle. "Smells great."

"Sit," he said. "How do you take your coffee?"

She pushed her wet hair behind her shoulders and sat down at the table. "Like my men: hot, white, and weak."

"Aren't we sassy this morning?" He set a coffee-filled mug and a carton of half-and-half in front of her. "You must have slept."

She looked up at him, hovering just behind her right shoulder. "I did. Thanks to you."

"I should love hearing a woman say that." He paused. "But not after she's asked me to lock her alone in a bedroom."

Their playful conversation felt like sparks on her tongue and effervescent bubbles in her chest. She chuckled appropriately and concentrated on adding cream to her coffee. *If I'd had my druthers, I wouldn't have been alone.*

He shuttled the rest of the food to the table.

When he sat down next to her and offered her the bacon platter, she took two polite pieces instead of the six her stomach was demanding. He grinned and shoved another two onto her plate.

Well, he was only two shy of her desires.

As they poured maple syrup—the real thing, she noted—on their French toast, he said, "I was thinking last night about the person who broke into your house."

She looked at him, those effervescent bubbles in her chest evaporating. "And?"

"Whoever it was seemed knowledgeable—with the lock and all. Would someone like that risk driving back on your lane with no other way out?"

As she chewed she thought. "You think they walked in?"

"Maybe." He took a sip of coffee. "Doesn't your property front the river?"

"They came by boat?" She got that feeling that Great-Gran Girault used to call someone walking on your grave. The intruder coming by river hadn't even crossed Abby's mind. The riverbank was overgrown and the dock had decayed to a few weathered pilings years ago. That kind of knowledge of her property opened many disturbing possibilities.

"It's something to consider. It'd be less risky than the road. They could come in with motor and lights off. No one would ever know they were there."

She had no idea why that idea made the entire break-in seem more creepy, but it did.

"I'd like to go out and take a look," he said. "See if it appears someone landed a boat back there recently."

She retreated to their earlier mood in order to hide her increased uneasiness. "That'll work great, because I clearly need to rearrange my outfit."

"Aw, and my eyes were just getting used to the clashing colors and stopped hurting."

They finished eating without further conversation. Abby was too hungry to initiate any more conversation that might take her appetite away. But once she'd cleaned her plate and they were rinsing the dishes, she said, "Something about that message on the mirror has been haunting me."

He stopped in mid-motion and looked at her. "I would hope so."

"The wording, I mean. The reason why didn't hit me until this morning while I was in the shower. The night after the accident I received a phone call around two in the morning. There was a lot of background noise. The person—I couldn't even tell if it was male or female— was obviously drunk and crying. They said, 'please don't tell...please.' I thought it was someone drunk dialing. But now I'm not so sure."

He set down the plate he'd been rinsing. "Did you tell the police?"

"No. It didn't seem like anything—until last night."

"Do you have caller ID?"

She huffed. "No, and don't lecture me on it."

"Maybe we'd better call the sheriff and meet with him before we go to Savannah. They could be working on getting the phone records."

"I'd rather not. A few hours won't make that much difference. I want to see what we find out under hypnosis before we see him."

"I'll call tomorrow morning and set up an appointment with him—if that's all right with you."

"Be my guest." Normally she was a do-it-myself kind of gal. But she had to admit, it was nice letting Jason make this call. She wanted the sheriff to know someone as intelligent and well-educated as Jason Coble was on her side when she tried to convince him that she'd been sleep-driving when the accident happened.

He said, "We probably won't be back from Savannah until late. It's a two-hour drive each way and we're not meeting Sonja until six."

Sonja. Sounded exotic. She was probably European and brilliant. Abby already didn't like her.

When they went out to Jason's driveway, the Explorer appeared odd to Abby. She was almost to the driver's door when she realized it was sitting lower than it should be.

Jason had been more astute and was already down inspecting the tires on the passenger side. He said, "All four are flat."

"Well, crap." One spare wasn't going to do her any good. And getting tires on Sunday wasn't in the cards in Preston.

Jason stood and looked across the hood of the Explorer, concern on his face. "They've been cut."

Cut. As in done on purpose. It hadn't been the bad luck of driving over nails spilled on the road. Then it sank in, and she felt as if she'd taken a fast drop over a hill in a speeding car. Someone was following her. Following her! She started to shake.

"Who would know to look for my car here?" It was a ridiculous question, but she had to ask it. "I mean, it's not even really my car."

Jason looked around with fire in his eyes; as if there was a snowball's chance on the Fourth of July that the person who'd done this would still be nearby. "I'm liking this less and less. Call the police."

"We're inside city limits. Should I call the sheriff's department or city police?"

"Call the sheriff."

Abby dug in her purse for the card Officer Fisher had given her last night. It had the non-emergency number on it. When she explained what she needed and why, the man who'd answered the phone transferred her to Master Sergeant Kitterman, an investigator.

It being Sunday, Master Sergeant Kitterman wasn't in his office. She left a voice mail in which she explained everything all over again.

When she got off, Jason was just putting his own cell phone back in his pocket. "Bryce'll be here in a few minutes to run us to get my car. What did the police say?"

"Apparently I'm now in the hands of an investigation officer."

"That's good news."

"Then why did I feel like a criminal when the guy on

the phone said 'all reports and investigations pertaining to Abby Whitman are now to go directly to Master Sergeant Kitterman'?"

"Abby, it means they think the incidents surrounding you are connected in some way. They're not leaving it in the hands of various patrol officers. Now it'll be looked at as a cohesive case."

She wondered if her case would be getting this much attention if she hadn't killed a senator's son, but kept the thought to herself.

"We should leave your car untouched until we hear from someone at the sheriff's department," Jason said. "If you don't mind, I still want to check the river before we go to Savannah. There's rain in the forecast."

"No problem." There was absolutely no way she was going to meet a woman named *Sonja* dressed like this.

Jason picked up her overnight bag and she followed him to the street to wait for Bryce. He set her bag on the grass next to the curb and remained quiet—in a preoccupied way. He had a look similar to the one he'd worn last night after he'd seen the words on the mirror. A look that said he'd like to inflict bodily harm on whoever was doing this.

Bryce arrived a couple of minutes later. His hair looked as if he'd just tumbled out of bed, and his expression was surly as a bear dragged out of hibernation.

Jason opened the rear passenger door for Abby. She got in and he handed her bag to her, and then got in the front passenger seat.

Bryce eyed her overnight bag. She settled it on the floor by her feet, as if out of sight truly was out of mind.

He asked Jason, "Why didn't you come get your car last night?"

"It got late," Jason said vaguely.

Abby shot him a look that he didn't seem to notice. Why hadn't he explained that she'd only spent the night because of a break-in, and had slept in Brenna's room?

Bryce didn't say another word the entire way to Jason's car. But he did keep a nasty eye on Abby in his rearview mirror most of the time. It felt every bit as accusatory as Gran Girault's had been, but for a much different reason.

From the back stoop of Abby's cottage, she could see the flat, dark water of the broad Edisto River as it made a meandering curve and headed away from the property. The old boat dock was hidden from view, built where the river's course dipped more deeply into Whitman land.

"The dock is off to the left," she told Jason as they descended the steps. "Through that grove of trees."

They walked in silence until they came to the path that led through the grove.

Abby stopped and looked at Jason. "I suppose we won't mess up any footprints by walking on the lane."

"It's too loose and sandy to hold one." He took her hand.

She immediately withdrew her hand from his and felt as if she'd peeled a layer of her own skin away. God, she'd never wanted anyone like she did him.

Was it simply because she knew she couldn't have him?

As they walked, she sensed him looking at her. She kept her gaze ahead and put a little more space between them.

He said, "I'm hoping the riverbank is a different story."

"Oh, it is. It's a muddy mess," she assured him. "Mom used to get so mad at Dad when we were little and he took us down here. We made castles out of the mud like other kids made sandcastles on the beach—except tidal mud stinks."

"I hadn't thought of the tide, didn't know it reached this far inland. Let's hope it didn't wipe out any footprints we might find."

"It's pretty muddy even beyond high tide line," she assured him.

They reached the end of the lane. The rotting pilings rose first out of dry sand and shell where the dock used to meet the lane. Then the thick posts marched through the grasses and out into the dark water of the river where the barges would carry the rice away from the plantation—the skeleton of a time long gone. The dock had been maintained for pleasure craft as long as the house had been occupied. This dock was just one more casualty of Abby's disorder.

Jason said, "Wait here." He picked his way carefully toward the river.

It didn't take but a few seconds before he called to her, "Better get the police out here."

Abby's heart beat faster as she followed Jason's footsteps until she was right behind him. At the edge of the river was a three-foot-wide area where the tall grasses and reeds had been broken over. In the middle of that was a depression in the mud that looked to have been made by the bow of a small boat. There were plenty of footprints around it.

The sight made Abby's skin crawl. Someone out there was very calculated in what they were doing. What did they have planned next?

CHAPTER 17

Apparently having a second new development in a matter of hours warranted disturbing Master Sergeant Kitterman on a Sunday morning. Thirty minutes after her call, he arrived at Abby's instead of a patrol officer.

He was a whiplike man with a receding chin and thinning hair. But Abby quickly saw his appearance was a disguise; there was nothing weak about him. He held himself as if it was difficult to keep his energy in check. Even as he introduced himself to her, his sharp eyes seemed to be taking in everything around him.

His questioning glance landed on Jason.

"This is Jason Coble," she said. "A friend."

Kitterman said, "The sheriff told me of your involvement. I hadn't realized it was personal." Although this was a statement, it had the feel of a question.

"Sergeant Kitterman." Jason shook his hand, not taking the bait on the questioning tone.

"Let's have a look at what you found."

As Abby led him to the river, Jason followed just behind.

Kitterman asked, "What made you think of checking for a boat?"

"I didn't. Jason did."

"Is that so?" He cast a glance over his shoulder. "What prompted you to look here?"

Jason said, "The narrow lane and no other way out. It seemed unlikely that someone who had enough finesse to break in without damaging locks would put themselves in a position to be trapped."

Kitterman nodded his approval.

When they reached the ruins of the dock, Abby indicated where he would find the evidence.

Jason stood next to her with a hand on the small of her back as she watched Kitterman survey the muddy bank.

In a moment he returned. "Looks like it was probably a small fishing boat. Wouldn't need deep water. There are some good-quality tracks. Can't tell if there's anything unique enough about them to do us any good. I'm going to need my casting kit and camera." He looked at Jason. "Would you mind staying here while Abby and I go get the equipment?"

Jason shot a curious look at Kitterman, but Abby couldn't decipher what was behind it. "No problem."

"So, Abby," Kitterman said as they walked back toward the house. "How long have you known Dr. Coble?"

"I've known who he is, you know, just around town, since he moved here. We've just recently become friends."

"Are you and he dating?"

Dating? She and Jason had become much closer over the past four days than dating could have provided. Her

circumstance had acted as a crucible, burning away all of
the frivolous and extraneous bullshit that dating entailed.

She answered, "No. He sort of got sucked into helping
me after my accident. He's a nice guy that way."

"So you aren't romantically involved."

She thought of their kiss. Although she'd felt a connection entirely new and exciting to her, one that shot
right to her core, it didn't qualify as a romantic entangle-
ment. "No." It made her a little sad to admit it aloud.

"Was he with you when any of these events
occurred?"

"I stayed at his house last night, after the break-in
and the message on the mirror—I assume you know of
that?"

"Yes."

"So he was with me when my tires were slashed during the night."

He looked pointedly at her. "He was *with* you, the
entire night?"

"Well, no. I slept in his daughter's room." She stopped
walking and threw up her hands. "Oh, you've got to be
kidding! There is no way in hell that Jason had anything
to do with any of these things."

"I'm just asking questions, Ms. Whitman, that's how I
get the information to do my job."

Her ears burned with indignation. "Listen, all of this
crap started after my accident."

"As did your friendship with Dr. Coble."

"Again, not possible." She rubbed her temple. "There
are a couple of things I need to tell you about the accident . . . so you have all of the information to do your job."
She told him of the headlights and their abrupt about-face

the night of the accident, as well as the pleading call she'd received in the middle of the next night.

He didn't respond with as much as an eye blink. "Have you had any contact with the Robard family since the accident?"

The question brought hot shame to her cheeks. "No. I...I'm just not sure what the right thing to do is in a case like this." She looked up at him. "Should I, do you think?"

"I was thinking more in the context of them contacting you."

"Oh." It sunk in. "Oh!"

"Until we get your phone records and find the source of that middle of the night call, we have to keep open minds."

She nodded. "But that doesn't explain the headlights."

"They may or may not be linked. It might just have been kids up to no good scared off by the approaching police cruiser."

She said, "We think that whoever made the 911 call is getting worried that I'll identify him, and he's trying to scare me off."

"I'll listen to the 911 recording, see if I can get anything off of it; but the report says that the caller didn't say anything. They found the accident by locating the cell phone signal. I'll also get your phone records, maybe we'll get lucky. Don't hang your hat on it. It really could have just been a drunk." He paused. "When you say 'we think,' I assume you're referring to yourself and Dr. Coble."

"Stop making statements like that—like he's up to something. He's just trying to help me." She strode on ahead a few steps, unwilling to listen to this innuendo anymore.

Abby grew more distant with every passing mile on the two-hour drive to Savannah. By the time Jason parked his car in front of Sonja's house near Forsyth Park, Abby was like a stranger sitting next to him.

He was glad he'd given Sonja all of the information she would need on the phone to hypnotize Abby. It would make things go more smoothly once they were inside.

He reached across and took her hand. "Don't expect too much."

She looked at him, her eyes clear from her night of sleep. "If I'm anything, Jason, I'm a realist."

The truth of that statement stabbed at his heart. How long had it been since she'd allowed herself to dance with dreams?

She got out of the car and closed the door. She was still standing there looking up at the house when Jason reached the curb.

"This is an amazing house," she said.

"And inside is an amazing woman."

A shadow flickered in her eyes just before she lowered her lashes, hiding from him.

"What's wrong?" he asked.

Her gaze snapped back to his face, the shadow replaced with steely determination. "Nothing. Let's go."

Abby walked up the steps to the porch, resisting the urge to take Jason's hand. Resisting mostly because that urge sprang from proprietary feelings she had no right to have, not a need for support.

Sonja's house reinforced all of Abby's suppositions of the woman. An imposing Greek revival, it truly was magnificent. Its age provided just enough imperfection to make it interesting. The setting sun filtering through the giant trees highlighted the azaleas blooming around the porch foundation: vibrant pink and snowy white, new life against old brick and stucco. This place looked like a watercolor painting, the kind tourists bought in local art galleries while vacationing in Savannah.

Jason rang the antique doorbell and Abby braced herself to face a woman whom he considered amazing.

Sonja—the name said tall, blond, exquisite, brilliant, worldly. Amazing.

The door opened to a tiny woman with short salt-and-pepper hair, dressed in a pink skirt-suit, pearls, and ivory heels. She looked like an aging pixie in Southern gentlewoman attire, complete with a button nose and sparkling eyes.

Abby feared this was the magnificent Sonja's mother.

Jason stepped close and gave the woman a brief hug. "It's so good to see you, Sonja."

Abby exhaled her relief loudly enough that Jason cast a curious look her way.

Luckily Sonja reached out her hand, giving Abby a reason not to explain.

"This must be Abby," Sonja said, her voice smooth and gracious and oh-so-Southern.

"Hello," Abby said. "I really appreciate you seeing me." *And not being some Euro-hottie past love of Jason's.*

"Come in, you two. Can I offer you an iced tea or something?"

Abby politely declined, anxious to get on with the hypnosis. Thankfully, Jason declined, too.

Sonja took them into an elegant front parlor filled with a mix of beautiful antiques and comfortable upholstered furniture. The late-day sun streaking through the tall windows gave the rich jewel tones of the decor more brilliance. It was a room that beckoned a person to curl up with a good book.

This evening Abby was the book. And she hoped that book would be filled with answers.

Sonja directed Abby to the sofa and asked Jason to close the interior shutters.

Sonja took a seat in one of the chairs near the sofa. "I can see you're anxious to get started, so let's begin. It's most important that you feel comfortable. First, I need to know if you want Jason in or out of the room."

Abby looked at Jason. He hadn't taken a seat and was lingering near the wide doorway to the entry hall. Respectful.

He'd come all of this way with her; Abby couldn't imagine taking this step alone. "I'd like him to stay."

"All right," Sonja said. "Jason, you know the rules."

Jason offered Abby an encouraging smile. He wondered if she was as wound up inside as he was. He felt as if he was about to open the door to a closet. Would it be empty? Would it hold forgotten treasures or hellish nightmares? Or would the hinges be rusted closed and refuse to open at all?

Abby was so hopeful that this would provide her answers. He'd done his best to prepare her for disappointment. But, he now realized, he hadn't prepared himself as well. His insides were twisted with dread. No matter what lay ahead in this hypnosis session, he couldn't see anything but upset and pain for Abby.

He wanted to hold her hand, give her a loving anchor as Sonja delved deep into Abby's defenseless subconscious. But Sonja was right, he knew the rules. He took a seat at a small table set with a chess board that was located behind the sofa, where he would be out of Abby's sight. This would be like watching as Sonja performed surgery on Abby, but this procedure would lay bare things much more vulnerable than internal organs. And unlike surgery, Abby would feel the pain—and she would remember.

Jason pressed his back against the chair and braced himself for what was to come.

Sonja, ever the prepared professional, had left an unlined notepad and a pen next to the chess set, in case he needed to communicate with her during the hypnosis.

She instructed Abby to lie back on the sofa and close her eyes.

Jason settled in for what could well be a long wait, almost hoping Sonja's attempt to hypnotize Abby would fail. Even though Abby was a woman who guarded herself well and therefore not an ideal candidate for hypnosis, Sonja was extraordinarily good at what she did.

It took a full forty minutes of Sonja's soothing Southern voice before Abby was in the proper mental state. Even though Jason couldn't see her, he could hear the alteration in her breathing, could feel her release control one slender thread at a time. And as each fiber slid free of her fingers, it immediately sought out his heart and wrapped tightly around it. With each beat, his own tension escalated.

"Now Abby," Sonja said softly, "we're going to go back to that night, the night of—"

Abby broke in. "There's smoke."

"Smoke?"

"It's dark. I don't know how I got to the living room."

Sonja shot a questioning look at Jason. He motioned for her to continue.

"What living room?"

"In our house."

Jason tensed

"Abby, I want you to know you are perfectly safe now," Sonja said. "There is no danger to you whatsoever in answering my questions. Where is the smoking coming from?"

"The dining room. I can see bright flames in there—hear them. It's so hot. The smoke stings my eyes." Abby sucked in a sharp breath. "Courtney's screaming." There was a break in Abby's voice. "She sounds hurt and terrified. She's in the back of the house. But it's too hot to go that way...."

Abby fell silent.

"Abby? What happened?" Sonja asked.

"I don't know. Everything is gone now."

With his heart breaking with sympathy and his entire body thrumming with tension, Jason quickly scribbled a note. *Ask what she remembers before the living room.*

Sonja did.

Abby was silent for a moment. "I was reading in bed until very late. I was only allowed to read until ten-thirty. But it was *Little Women,* I couldn't stop." There was a smile in Abby's voice that tugged at Jason's heart. "I pretended to be asleep when Momma checked on me at eleven. Just after I turned my light out I heard Court get up to go to the bathroom. I must have gone right to sleep. That's all I remember."

Jason wrote, *Time?*

"What time did you turn out your light?" Sonja asked.

"It was almost two."

Sonja looked up at Jason, brow raised in question.

He shook his head. There was no reason to push Abby any more about the fire. She'd come to find out about the accident. They needed to get it done while Abby's mind was still open.

"All right, Abby. We're going to leave that time. I want you to tell me about the night four days ago, the night of your accident. Begin when you left Jason in the Jeter's parking lot."

"I wish he'd kissed me."

Jason saw Sonja's smile in the dim room. As much as he was pleased by Abby's admission, he felt like a real creep. This was akin to reading a private journal without permission. Even though he supposed Abby *had* given her permission when she'd elected to have him stay in the room.

He motioned for Sonja to move forward in time.

"Did you drive straight home when you left Jeter's?"

"Yes. I stopped in the shop to check messages. I thought about working, but it was bedtime, so I went on home."

Sonja raised a brow. "Do you go to bed at the same time every night?"

"Yes. It's part of the ritual."

"Ritual?"

"The one Dr. Samuels created for me when I was a kid. It helps with sleepwalking."

"So you went through your ritual. Then what?"

Jason was a little disappointed that Sonja hadn't asked what the ritual entailed. Again, he was ashamed of his voyeuristic desires. But the more time he spent with Abby, the more he wanted to know everything about her.

"I wonder if Jason will really call me. I think about him for a while. Then I go to sleep."

"What is the next thing you remember after falling asleep?"

"Red lights."

"Where?"

"I don't know."

Jason scribbled a note on his pad and held it up.

"How many red lights?" Sonja asked.

"Two."

He scribbled another question.

Sonja nodded. "Are they in front of you?"

"Yes."

"Can you see anything else?"

"No. Now it's black."

"What do you remember next?"

"I hear gravel dropping around me."

"Did the sound wake you?"

"Yes…no, I was waking up anyway. But it isn't gravel. It's glass. It fell off me when I moved. My head hurts. My feet are wet."

As Abby talked about the glass, something that had been nagging Jason since he'd first heard her story came into focus. He wanted to know if there was any other broken glass on the van and if the crash investigation team had a theory about how the driver's window had been broken. Glass on the inside of the van would indicate it had been broken by a blow from the outside.

"What do you see?" Sonja asked.

"It's so dark. The fog is hanging over the water. My

van's sitting at an angle. One of my headlights is shining under the water."

The picture she'd just painted sent chills down Jason's arms. She was alone, disoriented; she had to have been terrified.

The questions continued. Jason listened as Abby recounted the same scenario that she'd told him about the time after exiting her van until the police arrived. Except that she hadn't told him of her panic prompted by the idea of gators and snakes in the water. His chest had squeezed tight and his fingernails bit into his palms when she described her fear.

When Abby had finished telling about her ride in the ambulance, Sonja looked up at Jason with a raised brow again.

He nodded and she began to bring Abby out from under.

Sonja began the process, making certain that Abby would remember everything after she awakened.

Jason was mulling over Abby's responses when he heard Sonja call his name.

He shook off his distraction and looked at her.

"I said I think Abby could use some iced tea. Would you be a dear and help me in the kitchen?"

He knew Sonja wanted to question him privately to see if they'd achieved Abby's goal. But he wasn't ready to leave Abby just yet, so he lingered when Sonja left the room.

He moved to stand in front of Abby. She was now sitting on the sofa, looking as if she'd just awakened from a nap. His heart was raw from listening to her, but she appeared calm. Her strength astounded him.

He reached down and touched her cheek. "There are two amazing women in this house."

She smiled and put her hand over his. "I suppose since I remembered the time between leaving Jeter's to going to bed, my memory loss of the rest of the accident can't be from the bump on my head. I was sleepwalking. And it's just like you said, I don't have any memory of it."

He wondered if she remembered her recounting of the fire. Abby was a woman who focused on a goal. And her goal here was the accident. He almost questioned her about it, but couldn't bring himself to do it. Not now.

He looked into those brown eyes, so much darker in the dim light, and said only, "I'm sorry."

He didn't remind her that her hypnosis had been of some value. Although she'd been fairly certain of it, they now knew for a fact she'd gone home after Jeter's and gone to sleep. But that wasn't what Abby had come here for. She wanted answers about the accident.

He left the room without bringing up the red lights. She needed a break, a bit of time to digest what she'd just gone through. They could dissect all of this later. Right now he wanted to thank Sonja as quickly as good manners allowed, and get out of here. He needed some time alone with Abby, as much for his sake as for hers.

CHAPTER 18

Jason was quiet after they left Sonja's, probably because he knew it was useless to rehash the same old details of her accident over again. And honestly, Abby was grateful. She'd thought she'd been realistic in her approach to this session, taking a nothing-ventured, nothing-gained attitude. So the hollow well of her disappointment caught her off guard. She reminded herself, she was no further behind now than she had been. And yet it felt as if she'd lost significant ground, surrendered the field of battle. She had no other defense to launch.

Maybe she was just looking for a way to rid herself of blame for Kyle Robard's death. Maybe it was time to step up and accept full responsibility publicly.

That idea led directly to another, more practical, thought. Would the people who'd already ordered flowers for Kyle still want to keep those orders? Abby would have to call each one and make certain before she processed them; those outside Preston might have no idea she'd been involved in the accident. She'd grown accustomed to providing funeral arrangements for people she knew, even for her own family. But this was an entirely different thing: flowers for someone she'd...killed.

How could Jason even be interested in someone like her, a person who killed people and didn't remember?

A little voice said, *He's a psychiatrist; he can't help himself from trying to figure out why you're so damaged.* As long as he was helping her, she should be grateful. Beyond that, there wasn't going to be anything anyhow. She turned her thoughts away from analyzing Jason's motives and back to her work.

She felt ghoulish just thinking about doing the arrangements for Kyle Robard's funeral. It felt entirely wrong.

Nausea gripped her stomach and her hands began to tremble. Could she even do it? And how would people feel about it if she did?

She couldn't make a profit, that was for certain. Perhaps she could donate any money beyond the material costs to whatever philanthropic organization the Robards chose.

Still, would having her trademark arrangements at the funeral cause more anguish than comfort to Kyle's family?

She shook her head, as if she had a prayer of dislodging troublesome thoughts.

All of this circuitous thinking was obliterating the languid calm she'd experienced as a side effect of her hypnosis—and she certainly wasn't making any headway toward resolution.

Then she glanced over at Jason. His eyes reflected the streetlights as he drove. His profile was the picture of serenity. As she looked at him, that calm reasserted itself, little by little.

How could his silent presence still the whirlwind that continually kicked around inside her?

What would it be like to orbit around him, she a moon to his planet? Would his gravitational pull keep her steady, prevent the swirling winds from organizing into storms? Or would it overpower her and send her crashing into him, resulting in the destruction of them both?

As she stared at him, wondering, she noticed they were going around Reynolds Square—which was in the opposite direction from Highway 17, the route that led north toward Preston.

Just as she opened her mouth to ask where they were going, he glanced over at her and said, "I thought we should get some dinner before the drive."

"Oh, okay." She wasn't hungry, but it wasn't right to make Jason starve.

He stopped the car in front of a restaurant on Abercorn Street. The beautifully lettered sign over the front porch said, "Olde Pink House." With a name like that a person expected a clapboard cottage near the river, not a large Georgian-style house with a thick-columned porch. It was pink, she'd give it that.

The restaurant looked like a place for special occasions, fine jewelry, and high heels.

As if to confirm her thought, a young couple emerged, nicely dressed, heads close together, arms around one another. They laughed as they descended the steps, as if sharing a secret understanding that no one else in the world would appreciate.

A yearning arose from deep inside that knotted in the base of Abby's throat. She would never have anniversaries, or any other event marking a couple's milestones.

She swallowed, and then cleared her throat. "Um, I don't think I'm dressed for a place like this."

When she'd changed out of her clown costume, Jason had told her it was important to dress comfortably for the hypnosis. Consequently, she was wearing a pair of near threadbare jeans and her favorite—and thus well-worn—bulky sweater.

"We don't look that bad," he said. "I doubt they'll refuse to feed us."

He didn't look bad. No sir, not bad at all. She realized it didn't matter what Jason wore, his confidence carried him through. She'd bet he would somehow manage to get served barefooted and shirtless.

"Besides," he said, "it being Sunday night narrows our choices."

"Okay." She sighed dramatically. "Don't be embarrassed when they turn me around and show me the door."

He laughed and reached for her hand. "You're too beautiful for that to happen. Beautiful people get seated no matter how they're dressed. It's good for business."

She nearly gave a glib and sarcastic response, but he looked like he meant every word. With a squeeze of his hand, she said, "Thank you. That was very sweet."

"I'm not sweet. I'm truthful and straightforward." He raised their entwined hands to his lips and kissed the back of hers.

A little taken aback, and afraid of embarrassing herself by letting him know just how deeply that simple gesture had affected her, Abby said, "Your momma sure raised you right."

He gave her that half-crooked smile that made Abby's insides do a bouncy little dance.

He said, "I'll be sure and tell her when I speak to her next."

With that, Abby realized she knew nothing about his life before Preston. "Does your family live here in Savannah?"

"My parents live in Atlanta. My sister, Katie, lives in Colorado; she married a ski patrol guy. They met when she was on vacation during college."

"So has she made you an uncle?" she asked.

"Four times over." He looked pleased by the fact. "Katie's oldest is eight and can already out-ski her."

The very idea of an eight-year-old on skis in the Rocky Mountains made Abby's stomach flip over. "I've never been in the mountains. Seems...dangerous."

"The Rockies are amazing. And if you're trained and do like you're supposed to, it's probably less dangerous than swimming in the ocean."

She frowned. "Don't do that, either."

"We're going to have to get you out there a little more, embrace a few risks."

She didn't like risks, or even the *idea* of risks. She'd carefully arranged her life to avoid them. But the idea of looking down a breathtaking mountain, blinded by glistening snow, face chapped by a cold wind while holding Jason's hand got her heart pumping from something other than trepidation.

She thought of the couple who had just exited the restaurant, sharing their unified existence, their mutual life experiences, and her heart ached for what she would never have. The reemergence of her sleepwalking had stamped out any glimmer of hope she might have secretly held deep inside.

Before she destroyed the light mood, she shut down that avenue of thinking. She redirected the spotlight of conversation back onto him.

"Do you visit Katie and her family often?" she asked. "Does all of your family ski now?"

"Lucy doesn't like cold weather or snow, even for vacation, so up until last winter we did summer trips. I took Bryce and Brenna out last winter. It was great. Bryce took to skiing right off, the faster the better as far as he's concerned. Bren's a little more cautious—thank heaven."

"And you?" she asked.

"Let's just say it's too bad we weren't shooting it on video. Could have made some cash on *Funniest Videos*— or at least been made famous on YouTube. When it comes to snow, I'm much better on a sled—nice and low to the ground."

Abby laughed, but she couldn't imagine Jason ever being awkward. He was just too…manly. She bet he looked hotter than hell wearing ski goggles and a parka— even if he was falling down a mountain slope.

Jason leaned closer and looked into her eyes. "I like to hear you laugh."

She felt his nearness as if her skin had been brushed by a warm breeze. Then he touched her with his hand, a gentle sweep across her forehead as he moved her hair away from her face.

Her heart sped up as she held his gaze. She moistened her lips. Her entire body buzzed with anticipation, and yet he didn't move to kiss her.

"I've never met anyone like you, Abby Whitman. I wish we weren't sitting in a car in a public place…."

Heat shot to intimate places that had long gone untouched. Abby closed the space between them; her hands framed his face and she kissed him. She started gently, intending no more than a single kiss. But when he buried his hands in her hair and leaned across the console, gentleness gave way to a driving desire she'd too long suppressed. She opened her mouth and the bolt of pure hunger shot through her body when his tongue probed deeply.

She pressed her feet against the floor in an effort to get closer to him, her breasts tingling with the desire to be touched. To hell with anniversaries and milestones. She wanted now.

Once again he read her well. His hands slid gently down the length of her throat, setting off fireworks everywhere his fingertips touched. She moaned into his mouth as his hand cupped her breast through her sweater. She wanted more; she wanted his hands on her skin. She wanted a moment she could hold on the long, lonely nights ahead. The word echoed through her head, *want . . . want . . . want . . . .*

She was just guiding his hand under her sweater when his cell phone rang.

He broke off the kiss and cursed under his breath. "This had better be important."

He gave her one more quick kiss before he snatched his phone off the console.

Abby bit her kiss-swollen lower lip, trying to keep the taste of him as long as she could.

Jason frowned at the caller ID, then answered his phone. "Hey, Bryce. Everything okay?"

Abby wondered if Bryce could hear the trembling in

Jason's voice, or notice his lack of breath. She herself was as breathless as a teen on the verge of third base. She worked on regaining some composure—which was hard as hell because she couldn't tear her eyes away from Jason.

As he listened to Bryce, Jason's face, moments ago so relaxed and handsome, tensed. "Oh, crap." He rubbed his forehead. "I didn't realize it was so late. Let me talk to her."

Abby heard the drone of Bryce's voice again.

Jason answered, "I'm in Savannah. I took Abby to see Sonja—" He stopped as if interrupted. "Yes, that Sonja, and yes it was about the accident—"

After a moment of listening he said, "Not much. She remembered seeing taillights, but that's about it." He listened. "I don't know. These things are impossible to predict. Put Bren on, will you? And Bryce... thanks for calling."

The next voice that came on the phone was too soft to even hear its cadence from Abby's side of the car.

"I'm so sorry, Peanut. I had to come down to Savannah and lost track of time." He listened for a moment. "Yes, I do think Father Kevin would appreciate being included in your bedtime prayers." A pause. "Sleep tight and I'll talk to you tomorrow. Love you, Peanut."

Jason had a frown on his face when he disconnected the call. He sat for a moment, looking out the windshield. Then he muttered, "I feel like a real shit."

"Why?"

"Over a year and I've never missed making Bren's bedtime call."

She cringed. He'd forgotten because he was preoccupied

with her problems. "You're a good father, Jason. Anyone can see that."

He blew out a long breath. "I don't know. Bren's retreated into herself so much since the divorce. Maybe she would have done better if I'd stayed...at the time it seemed like it was a clear choice. Our marriage was dead and no amount of CPR could revive it. My leaving forced Lucy into sobriety at least."

Abby swallowed her questions about the particulars concerning the death of that marriage.

"Jason, this isn't a perfect world with perfect families and perfect choices. We all do the best we can with what life gives us. Was Bren upset about you not calling?"

He looked a little puzzled. "Not really. She actually seemed more concerned about Father Kevin."

"See, you're raising a selfless and giving child. That's what good parents do. And you *did* speak to her before bed. So stop beating yourself up."

Then he turned to Abby, reaching across the car to stroke her cheek. "You're a kind and selfless person, too. See how you're making me feel better?"

She could make him feel even better yet—but it certainly wouldn't be selfless. So Abby just smiled and kept her hands to herself.

After a moment he said, "It's so hard for her. I want to do what's best...."

"From where I'm sitting, you're doing a great job with your children."

He smiled softly. "Thanks."

"Now," Abby put her hand on the door latch instead of on Jason, "let's get you some dinner."

As they got out of the car, Abby put a firm foot down

on her disappointment. Still, she couldn't help but wonder what might have happened if Bryce's call hadn't come exactly when it had.

As if under unspoken truce, Jason and Abby enjoyed dinner as if Abby's life wasn't playing out like a melodrama. They also avoided discussing the inappropriateness of their behavior in the car.

Abby was grateful, once again, for his ability to tune himself to her mood. Just as she'd needed sleep last night, she needed to pass a couple of hours like a normal person tonight.

They conversed like friends, looked at one another like lovers, and connected in ways Abby found wholly new in a relationship with a man. This dinner with Jason had nourished more than her body. It had jump-started a part of her that had lain dormant, and Abby was glad to discover it wasn't dead.

Unfortunately, it made her want things she could never have. But then, it didn't have to be all or nothing, she assured herself. Maybe they could meet on this slip of common ground, at least for a brief time. She would have to be happy with that.

The only sour note in the meal was his refusal to allow her to pay the bill. He had already done so much for her; it seemed little enough reward. But he held steadfast.

At her final protest, he said, "You already complimented my momma. Don't make her ashamed of me now."

She took her hand off the folder that contained their check. "Fine. I'll just have to figure out another way to show my appreciation."

His roguish expression made her realize the innuendo of what she'd just said.

"I was thinking of a nice houseplant," she said in a reprimanding tone that lowered his suggestive brow. "Or a garden gnome."

"No gnome, please." He raised his hands in mock horror. "The one in your shop already bit me in the leg."

She laughed. "Oh, yeah, Siegfried, my attack gnome. Better than a watchdog."

When he laughed, she decided she loved hearing his laugh as much as he'd indicated he liked listening to hers. It was a very, very nice feeling.

It was nearly ten-thirty when they left the restaurant. And Abby decided it was time to address reality again.

As he drove north on Highway 17, she said, "I suppose I should talk to Sergeant Kitterman tomorrow morning, now that he's on the case. I'll admit to him that I was sleep-driving. It'll sound like some petty excuse I'm making up if I wait until they've concluded their investigation of the accident and find me at fault." She paused. "Not that I'm saying it excuses me from responsibility—it'll just look like a pathetic cry for sympathy. You know what I mean?"

Jason was quiet for a bit. "I've been thinking. Do you remember saying something about red lights to Sonja?"

"I did? I don't remember that part."

"You said, 'Red lights,' then when Sonja asked you what about them, you said there were two, but that was all you remembered. Then everything went black."

"Hum. I did have that dream...."

"I wonder if the two got scrambled in your mind, or if it really did have something to do with the accident. If it's memory, maybe that third party they're looking for was there *before* you. Maybe you woke up and saw red lights in the road and that made you veer off into the swamp. Or maybe it was Kyle's taillight you saw."

She frowned, trying to recall anything about the red lights in her dream. "In my dream they were like car taillights, two about five feet apart, a couple of feet off the ground."

"Let's suppose there was a car in the road and you swerved to miss it. Maybe Kyle was already dead. Maybe the 911 call had already been made. If so, that person would have a very good reason not to want to be identified."

She could hardly let herself hope. "Someone else was in the accident with Kyle?"

"And you came upon it afterward."

She looked at Jason. "God, do you think it's possible?"

"Someone is risking a lot to warn you off." He reached across and took her hand. "Which leads me to the other thing that's been bothering me. You said there was glass on you when you awakened in the marsh... from where?"

"The driver's side window."

"Were any of the other windows broken or cracked?"

"Not that I know of. The windshield was fine. But it's not like I took a good look around the van before I got out and went to the road."

"We'll call Kitterman first thing tomorrow. We need to find out exactly what kind of damage your van sustained. And we'll see how our ideas about the red lights fit with the accident investigation findings."

"Okay." She watched the road for a while, thinking that this trip hadn't been a waste after all. Unfortunately the questions it raised could only lead to more unsettling findings. Who would be so callous as to flee a scene with a fatality? And who would be so desperate to keep their identity a secret that they'd be willing to threaten her? Were they willing to carry out that threat?

She leaned her head against the side window and watched the shadows move past as they traveled down the road. What would she do without Jason?

As the miles rolled underneath the car, Abby grew drowsy, holding onto Jason's hand and the spark of hope in her heart that she hadn't killed Kyle Robard after all.

CHAPTER 19

Maggie sat in the living room with her photo album in her lap. It was quiet. Uncle Father was working late in his office next door. He'd been so sad today. He used to be happy on Sundays.

She worried that she wasn't doing her job—God had sent her to take care of him, after all.

She opened the album, feeling sad, too.

Uncle Father had made this book for her when she'd first come to live with him. Already the pink fabric edges were getting fuzzy even though she was extra careful with it. It had to last her whole life now. There would never be any new pictures of Momma and Daddy.

She traced the curve of her mother's cheek in one of the pictures. It was a really old one. Maggie was seven. Both Maggie and her mother had on hospital clothes. A tube went into Maggie's arm. It was after she had had her big operation; the one that fixed her heart. She sat on Momma's lap and held Momma's long braid like a rope. That's what Maggie missed most about her mother. The smell of her hair and the way it felt when Maggie helped her brush it. Momma's hair was orange-gold, like Maggie's. But Maggie's didn't feel the same. And it didn't smell the same.

Maggie turned the page. Momma and Daddy were dressed up, going to a fundraiser. (When Maggie was little and didn't know better, she had thought it was a fun-raiser. She'd always been so mad that she had never got to go see the fun.) It was for Momma's and Daddy's special group, COC. Maggie had kept this picture because this was the night when Momma came home so happy because some rich man had promised a lot, lot, lot of money.

Because of COC, sometimes Maggie got to fly to places where most of the people had beautiful brown skin and black hair and there weren't hardly any trees. But sometimes she had to stay with Grandma, because Daddy said it was too dangerous. When it was dangerous, Maggie didn't want Momma and Daddy to go, either. But Momma said they had to go help the children who didn't have parents anymore.

Two years ago it was dangerous, and they went away. They didn't come home.

Now Maggie didn't have parents.

Grandma moved to a place like Tidewater Manor right after that. It was in New Jersey, where Maggie used to live. That's when Maggie had come here to live with Uncle Father.

It was God's plan. Uncle Father needed her.

But sometimes she felt so sad. Sometimes she just wanted to brush Momma's orange-gold hair.

Maggie ran her finger over Momma's hair in the picture, trying to remember how it felt. It was getting harder and harder to remember—

The alarm on the back door went off, startling Maggie and making her heart beat fast.

She waited for Uncle Father to shut it off. But it kept screaming.

"Uncle Father?" she called, starting to sweat with fear.

A loud clatter came from the kitchen.

Maggie jumped up and dropped her album on the floor. "Uncle Father?"

She started toward the kitchen, but stopped.

The back door had been locked. All of the doors were locked and their alarms on. Uncle Father had made sure.

She leaned toward the kitchen. "Uncle Father?"

The air was moving through the house, like the door was open.

She grabbed the phone and dialed Uncle Father's cell phone. He said to call right away if she got scared. He promised he would come right over from the church.

She heard it ringing through the phone.

And then she heard it playing the ring tone... in the house.

"Abby?"

Abby roused and blinked, orienting herself. They were passing the tractor supply store on the edge of Preston.

"We're almost home," Jason said.

"Oh, sorry. I didn't mean to fall asleep."

"You needed it. You're still running on a deficit." He reached over and ran a hand over her hair. "How are you feeling?"

Like I want to finish what we started before dinner. The taste of intimacy he'd shown her had only ignited her need for more. But more probably wasn't in the cards.

Jason didn't seem the kind of man to take a relationship halfway, to live only for the moment.

She said, "Good."

"While you were asleep, I was thinking about some of the things you said while you were with Sonja. Do you remember talking about the fire?"

She did, vaguely. And she immediately wanted to turn her mind away from the memory. "A little."

"Sonja thinks that since you jumped right into that memory, perhaps you still have unresolved issues."

"Well, duh." Irritation shot through her veins. "How am I supposed to *resolve* the fact that I burned down a house that had been in my father's family for over a hundred and fifty years? How am I supposed to *resolve* ruining my sister's life? How do I *resolve* the pain I caused? Just how does one do that?"

"It will never go away, I understand that. But you can forgive yourself. Accept it for the accident that it was. I think that's what Sonja meant." Jason's tone was steady, unresponsive to her anger.

Abby sat there looking out the passenger window. "I don't want to talk about this now."

He reached over and took her hand. "Abby, please. Just work with me for a bit here."

She didn't respond.

He asked, "Where did the fire start?"

She sighed. He was not going to leave this alone.

"In the dining room," she said through tight lips. She closed her eyes and saw the charred pile of rubble that had been left in dawn's light the next day. Blackened bones of a home, still exhaling the last of its life in tiny smoke trails. "The house was fully involved when we got out. By the time the fire department arrived, they couldn't save it."

And Courtney—oh God, Courtney, her baby sister. Abby could still hear her screams. Sometimes they woke her from a dead sleep. Other times they came from the blue light of day.

Right now their echoes haunted her in a way that both broke her heart and turned her stomach. She kept her face to the window to hide the freshness of the pain. Forgiveness. Jason had no idea what he was asking of her.

The car was slowing, pulling to the curb in front of the brightly lit Shell station.

She didn't look at him when she asked, "Why are we stopping here?"

"Because I want to look at you."

She turned, her lower lip between her teeth.

He was looking at her with such intensity that she immediately looked away.

Reaching around, he gently touched her chin. "Look at me, Abby. I want to help you."

"Fix me," she corrected, as she turned his way. "You want to fix me and it can't be done."

"What?" He looked as startled as if she'd just accused him of being a thief.

"It's what you do. Fix people. But there is no fixing me, Jason."

"I am not trying to fix you. There's nothing to *fix*." He sighed and ran a hand over his face. "I'm not trying to upset you, either. I don't know much about what happened, and what you told Sonja raised some questions."

"Like what?" She'd tried to ignore him; she'd tried to start an argument. Nothing worked. He wasn't going to give up. It was probably best if he knew it all, then he would understand why she'd made the life choices she had. And maybe, he'd find a way to have a relationship with her and live with them.

"Did they have a theory on how it started?" Jason asked.

"I lit an antique oil lamp that was on the sideboard, and then knocked it over. Sleepwalkers aren't very graceful."

"Why did they assume it was you?"

"Because I'd done lots of everyday things before, turned on the TV, took a bath, went out and planted flowers, turned on the stove.

"And that lamp was a big deal. We always burned it during Sunday dinner, some family tradition that was started way, way back. I'd just been given the privilege of lighting it the Sunday before."

For a moment, he looked thoughtful. "How long had you been having trouble with sleepwalking before the fire?"

She gave her head a slight shake. "Maybe a year, maybe a little less."

"You woke up in the living room—"

"I was sleepwalking."

"But you said the fire was going strong."

"The oil accelerated it. It was an old house."

"How did you get out?"

"My dad found me unconscious in the living room—"

Abby's cell phone rang. It was so unexpected, so shrill in the quiet of the car, she jumped as if she'd been pinched. She pulled it out of her purse. "It's Maggie."

She answered.

"Abbbeeeeee! Help!" Maggie cried. "I n-n-need help...."

CHAPTER 20

A bby's hand tightened on the phone. She fought the panic that threatened to sweep away reason. Maggie needed her; she had to keep her head.

She gestured toward the street ahead and whispered, "Drive!" to Jason. Then into the phone, she asked, "Maggie, are you at home?"

"Yes. Oh, Abbbeeeeee...."

Abby nodded as Jason glanced at her for confirmation. His face showed none of the panic that was ricocheting like a stray bullet inside her.

"I'm on my way, sweetie."

Maggie cried, "There's blood...I don't know what to do...."

"Whose blood?" She could barely croak out the words.

"Uh-uh-uncle Father's."

Abby felt a little rush of relief that Maggie wasn't hurt. "What happened?"

"I don't knooow." Maggie's voice was on the verge of hysteria. "He's in the kitchen."

"Can he talk?"

"He's trying to." Maggie's speech was getting thicker and more difficult to understand. "I don't know what he's saying...his mouth is bleeding."

It sounded like trying to speak to him on the phone would be useless.

"I'll be there in three minutes. But Maggie, I want you to hang up the phone and then call 911."

"I don't want to hang up—" She broke off in a sob.

"It's okay. I'm almost there. But your uncle needs a doctor. Call 911 now, Maggie."

She heard a pitiful, thin whine, but the phone disconnected.

"Father Kevin is hurt," Abby said to Jason. "I have no idea how badly."

Jason was already pushing the speed limit. The streets of Preston were deserted at midnight on Sunday. The stoplights had switched to flashers. Jason only slowed before he went through two that were flashing red.

When he swerved to the curb in front of the rectory, Abby was out before the car stopped moving. She ran up to the lighted front porch. The door was locked. She sprinted back down the steps and around the side of the house. The back door was standing open, light spilling from the kitchen into the yard.

Abby recognized the high-pitched squeal of an add-on door alarm like hers and her heart did a stutter-step.

By the time she made it to the back door, she heard Jason right behind her.

Father Kevin was in the middle of the kitchen floor, a chair from the table overturned next to him. There was a smear of blood next to his head on the floor, as if he'd

landed face-first then rolled over. His left eye was purple
and swollen shut and his nose looked broken.

Maggie wailed, "He wouldn't let me do it!" She was
kneeling next to her uncle, trying to wipe away the blood
on his face with a wet kitchen towel. Her face was red
and wet with tears.

Abby went to Maggie's side and knelt. Jason shut off
that damn alarm and went to Father Kevin's other side.
Jason gently removed Maggie's hand from where she was
trying to clean her uncle's face.

She immediately threw her arms around Abby, bloody
rag and all. "I tried. He wh-wh-wouldn't let me."

"What wouldn't he let you do?" She rubbed Maggie's
back to soothe her.

"Call 911." Her mouth was muffled against Abby's
neck. "He knocked the phone out of my hand."

Abby saw the bloodstained cordless phone lying halfway across the room near the refrigerator. Father Kevin
was obviously delirious with pain.

"It's okay…it's okay," she crooned softly. "See, I
brought Dr. Coble. He'll help your uncle."

Abby watched Jason assess Father Kevin. When
Jason gently examined Father Kevin's mouth, one of his
front teeth appeared to be either missing or broken off
at the gum line. Jason's hands moved over the priest's
body, asking if various areas were in pain. Father Kevin
groaned when Jason touched the man's ribs.

"Maggie, can you get some ice from the freezer?"
Jason asked.

Abby shot him a look. "I'll get it." Didn't he see how
upset Maggie was?

"No. I'll get it," Maggie said, releasing her death grip around Abby's neck and sniffling loudly. "It's my job."

Abby closed her eyes and let out a long breath. Jason knew exactly what Maggie needed.

Abby mouthed, "Sorry." But Jason's focus was back on the priest.

"Do you think you can sit up?" Jason asked.

Father Kevin gave a slow, shaky nod.

Jason assisted him into a sitting position, which clearly caused Father Kevin some pain.

Maggie returned with a bowl of ice.

"Maggie, put some of that ice in a clean dishtowel. Then we can hold it on your uncle's face while we drive to the hospital."

Father Kevin expressed his displeasure loudly, if not understandably.

Jason said quietly, "We have to go to the hospital." While Father Kevin continued to sound his muted protest, Jason handed the keys to Abby. "Bring the car around to the alley. It'll be shorter."

"Shouldn't we call for an ambulance?" Abby asked.

Father Kevin shook his head sluggishly, mumbling.

"We can get him there faster," Jason said. He looked at Abby, "Go. Hurry."

By the time Abby stopped the car in the alley behind the rectory, Jason and Maggie were halfway across the backyard with Father Kevin between them.

"Open the front passenger door," Jason said, huffing with exertion. "It'll be easier to get him in there."

Once they had him inside and the seat belt around him, Jason got behind the wheel. Abby and Maggie got in the back.

Father Kevin started shaking. Maggie leaned forward and tried to give him the ice-filled towel. He didn't seem to notice.

"Buckle up, girls." Jason put the car in gear and shot out of the alley.

"But he needs ice," Maggie said.

Abby made certain Maggie had her belt on and then took the ice pack from her. "I'll see what I can do."

Instead of putting on her own seat belt, Abby pressed herself against the back of the passenger seat and gently applied the ice to Father Kevin's mouth—which looked only slightly worse than his left eye.

The hospital was only ten minutes away. Jason made it in eight.

Jason returned from the coffee machine and stood in front of Abby and Maggie. They were seated side by side in a couple of wood-armed upholstered chairs in the emergency waiting room. Abby handled Maggie as well as an experienced mother. She was caring, yet not over-protective and coddling; which would only validate and fuel Maggie's fear.

At least she'd stopped asking if her uncle was going to die. Abby had nipped that right away.

But the stress was taking its toll. Maggie's teeth were starting to chatter with her trembling.

Jason handed her a cup of hot tea with plenty of sugar. "Drink some of this, Maggie. It'll make you feel better."

Maggie looked up at him as if he were Superman. "You saved Uncle Father."

"No, honey," he said. "*You* did."

Maggie didn't smile her trademark smile, but she did

sit up a little straighter when she accepted the tea. She wrapped her hands around the warm cup and he could see there was still a little blood crusted under her fingernails. His heart ached for her. Father Kevin was all she had, and to have found him like that....

He asked, "Do you know what happened to your uncle?"

Maggie took a small sip of tea, then shook her head. "He had been in his church office. I was looking at pictures and the alarm went off. I heard a loud noise. I guess he fell in the kitchen and hurt himself."

Abby looked at Jason. He didn't believe Father Kevin had hurt himself that badly by falling in the kitchen any more than she did.

Jason lifted his chin, asking Abby to walk away with him.

"I'm going to get a drink of water," she said softly to Maggie. "It's just across the room there. I won't be out of sight."

Once they were beyond Maggie's earshot Jason said, "He did say he fell; I understood that much when they were checking him in."

"It must have been someplace other than the kitchen. Maggie said he'd been next door. Maybe he fell at the church. The steps outside his office are old and pretty steep."

"Makes more sense than tripping in the kitchen. Would also explain the open kitchen door." He glanced over at Maggie. "They said someone can go back and sit with him. I don't think it should be Maggie. And she'll be more comfortable out here with you. I'll go."

"Okay." She looked at him with the same kind of veneration and confidence that Maggie had.

He liked it, but he didn't deserve it.

"Keep us posted." She turned to go back to Maggie.

Pausing with his hand on the door that led to Emergency, he looked over his shoulder at her. She was sitting with her arm around Maggie. Her head tilted to the side, her dark hair resting on the top of Maggie's head.

Abby was the one who deserved to be adored. She did everything in her power to protect the people she cared for. Yes, she deserved to be adored...and she deserved peace. And right now he could only offer one of the above.

He forced himself to stop looking at her and opened the door into the Emergency area.

It was nearly four-thirty in the morning when Abby and Jason delivered Father Kevin and Maggie back home. They were met there by Father Kevin's housekeeper, Mrs. White, whom he'd had Abby call from the hospital. She was a widow and was willing to stay as long as she was needed. It was clear by her fussing that Father Kevin would get much closer attention here than he would have had he been admitted into the hospital. And she had a good relationship with Maggie, which made Abby feel a little less like a heel leaving her.

Maggie had made it perfectly clear as soon as they'd arrived that taking care of her uncle was *her* job. Mrs. White could cook and clean and do laundry all she wanted; Father Kevin was Maggie's.

As they drove away, Abby felt the letdown from her adrenaline rush. She stifled a yawn.

"You were right about the church steps," Jason said. They'd avoided talking about the accident while

Maggie was with them. "Before they gave him that dose of Demerol, he managed to convey that he'd tripped at the top and fallen all the way down. He landed on his face on the sidewalk."

Abby cringed. "He sure looked like he'd kissed the concrete. I hope he has a quick recovery; the fundraiser is right around the corner."

"Well, with cracked ribs, he sure won't be golfing. But he should be recovered enough to attend."

"What about preparations?" Abby asked. "He always does all of that stuff himself."

"Not this year." Jason looked over at her. "This year he has a committee...me."

"Really?" She shouldn't be surprised, not with the way Jason had jumped right in and helped her during her crisis. "I had no idea you were involved with COC."

"Just the golf outing, as a participant—at least until this year. It looked like Father Kevin could use an extra set of hands."

"You've noticed, too, then...that he seems ill?"

Jason glanced at her. "Yeah, even though he insists he's fine. Has Maggie said anything to you?"

"No. Well, other than she thinks he's planning on sending her to Tidewater Manor when he can no longer take care of her."

"Seriously?"

"I think Maggie misunderstood a telephone conversation she'd been eavesdropping on. There's no way—even if he is dealing with a serious illness—that he'd send Maggie to Tidewater." She paused. "Didn't they ask him medical questions in the Emergency room?"

"Not while I was present."

"You're a doctor," Abby said. "What do you think?"

"I'm a doctor, Abby, not a psychic. I can't diagnose people by reading their auras."

She laughed. "Isn't that sort of what psychiatry is all about?"

The look he gave her could have withered a lesser woman. "Very funny."

He turned the corner at the Sunrise Bakery. The lights were on and workers were milling around behind the counter.

"I think we should try to get a few hours' sleep before we talk to Sergeant Kitterman," he said.

"Really, you've done enough. I don't expect you to hold my hand every step of the way." She didn't relish the idea of going to talk to Kitterman alone, but how long did she think Jason could ignore his own responsibilities? "Don't you have a practice to run?"

"Monday is my day off. I just have a couple of patients to check up on. So I'd like to go with you, if you don't mind. I'd like to hear what evidence they have; maybe we can piece together how all of these things are linked."

Abby tried not to think of someone out there stalking her, making threats. Were they willing to do more? Or was it at an end? If only she'd been able to remember more under hypnosis.

"I'd appreciate you coming along. I'll call you after I've talked to Kitterman and set up a time. You'll have to come and pick me up though, since the Explorer is on four flats at the moment."

"Abby, you're not sleeping at your house. It's too dangerous."

"It's almost daylight."

"Big deal. We don't know what time the guy broke in; daylight doesn't mean much when the house is as isolated as yours."

"Jason, I agreed to one night. And I proved I couldn't make it through without sleepwalking. Let's not tempt fate. I have the alarms at home. I'll even pile furniture in front of the doors if it'll make you feel better."

"Well, you *don't* have the alarms. One of them is on Brenna's door. By the time we mess around with re-installing it at your house, we'll burn valuable time when we could have been sleeping. *Besides*," he said, as if matching her argument for argument, "until we have our chat with Kitterman and have a better idea what's going on, I'm not leaving you alone."

"I have work to do. *You* have work to do."

"One step at a time, and in this order: Sleep. Talk to Kitterman. Come up with a plan to keep you safe." As if she'd consented, he made the turn toward his house.

It would just be for a few hours. And she had the alarm on the bedroom door. "All right. But this is the last time."

He gave her that half-crooked grin and winked.

She socked him in the arm. "Listen buster, don't push your luck." She didn't admit that she did feel much safer staying with him. But she couldn't trade his safety for hers.

It wasn't yet dawn, but it was no longer nighttime dark when they climbed the stairs at Jason's house. They both stopped in the hallway where they would part ways, lingering as if they were daters on a front porch.

"I'm afraid Bren's room doesn't have room-darkening shades," he said.

"No problem. I actually prefer sleeping in the light."

The way he looked at her was so laced with pity that she wished she hadn't admitted it. It made her feel weak. She'd worked too hard to temper herself against weakness to succumb to it now.

"Stop looking at me like that," she snapped.

"Like what?" His tone was just as prickly as hers had been. "Like I care about you?"

"Like you feel sorry for me. I'm living my life the way I choose. Save your pity for someone who needs it."

"Pity? Man, I need to work on my relationship skills if that's what you think I feel for you." He stepped closer, so close to her that she felt his body heat, and yet he didn't touch her. "You stir up all kinds of feelings in me, woman—and not a one of them resembles pity."

She had to tip her head back to look him in the eye. The emotion she saw there was intense, profound...and blazing hot. The heat in his gaze shot straight to her soul, igniting all of the longing he'd stirred last night. Only now they weren't sitting in a car in a public place.

Her breathing was so shallow that she began to get lightheaded. Or maybe it was just that all of her blood was rushing to places far from her head. And she wanted Jason to touch those places.

Still he kept his hands to his sides.

She reached for his hand and noticed a fluttering ripple pass through him. When she placed that hand under her sweater on the bare skin of her waist, he drew in a sharp breath.

It felt as if she'd waited a lifetime to have him touch her like this.

His fingers inched around her waist until they reached

the small of her back. Then he pulled her to him, laying claim to her mouth with his own.

Abby's hands slid beneath his black sweater, touching his firm midsection and gliding upward until they rested on his chest.

He responded with a demanding kiss, his tongue probing deeply, his teeth then nipping at her lower lip. He unfastened her bra and pressed her hips into his with his other hand.

She teased his nipples and he groaned softly. She felt empowered as she led him along a sensual path that could lead to only one destination. She broke off the kiss and pulled his sweater over his head. Then she began kissing a trail from his neck to his navel. As she swirled her tongue around his belly button, her name left his lips on a hushed breath.

She looked up at his face. "Who needs pity now?"

"Good God, Abby. I surrender and beg for mercy." He wrapped her in his arms and kissed her again.

Her sweater joined his on the floor. And he began exploring her body as she'd done his. His mouth discovered every inch of sensitive skin and she closed her eyes and enjoyed the sensuous journey. By the time he reached her navel, she was shaking with need and he was on his knees in front of her.

Suddenly she felt a cold place where his mouth had just been. She opened her eyes and looked down at him. His eyes were shining, his mouth curled in a seductive smile. "Say it," he urged.

She could barely hold together a thought. Her confusion must have been evident.

He said, "Surrender to me."

She hesitated.

He traced her navel with his fingertip that then dipped just below the button on her jeans.

Could she? Could she surrender completely to him and then let him go?

His lips teased her skin from her ribs to her waistband, while his hand slid between her legs and cupped her through her jeans.

Then he began to move his hand.

"I surrender," she said breathlessly. "I surrender and beg for mercy."

His smile was wicked as he slowly unzipped her jeans.

CHAPTER 21

At some point during the exquisite tour of sensual torture, Jason had carried Abby into his bedroom. They'd come together in an explosive climax that had nearly sent Abby's world off its axis. Now they lay sated, limbs intertwined.

Her head on his shoulder, she listened to the rhythm of his slow and steady breathing, loving the fact that the air she inhaled had just been inside his body. There was something about it that was every bit as intimate as their erotic lovemaking.

He'd been asleep for a few minutes now, and Abby was struggling to stay awake. She just couldn't leave him, not yet.

When she caught herself dozing off, she forced herself to get up.

Jason surprised her by grabbing her hand and pulling her back into the bed.

She rolled to his side and kissed him. "We need to get some sleep."

"I wasn't suggesting anything else," he said with an innocence that mocked the past hour.

She resisted the urge to kiss him again. "I can't sleep here."

He wrapped his arms around her and held her tightly. "Yes you can. I'll wake if you get up...I just proved it."

"Jason."

"Don't talk. Sleep."

She sighed and relaxed against him. He was warm and molded perfectly against her. She would allow herself a few minutes more. Once he drifted off again, she would lock herself safely in the other room.

It was already ten o'clock; time to face the day. Jason was anxious to talk to Kitterman, and yet reluctant to wake Abby, who was sleeping softly in his arms.

For a long moment, he watched her sleep, the dark sweep of her lashes relaxed against the curve of her cheek. He'd never seen her unwound like this, never seen her so peaceful. He wished he could help her find this kind of calm in her waking hours, too.

He'd have to step carefully, lest she misinterpret his actions as pity.... He smiled; that misinterpretation had led to some mighty fine clarification a few hours ago.

For a woman so strong and so guarded, Abby had given herself passionately and unreservedly. And he valued it for the rare treasure it was.

When she'd agreed to stay in his bed, he'd known what she was up to. So he'd out-waited her, allowing himself to fall asleep only after he was certain she was deep in slumber.

Now he hated to wake her—and not just because she

was exhausted. He loved the places where her utterly relaxed body touched his. He loved the feel of her sleep-warm hair as he stroked her head. He loved the innocent vulnerability of her relaxed mouth. And although it was far too soon to make such a statement, he felt he could fall in love with her. Deeply. Eternally.

That he would keep to himself, however. He'd already taken her one step beyond her self-imposed boundaries. He wanted her to want him as much as he wanted her before he pushed her further.

First they had to catch whoever was making these threats against her; he had to make her safe. He worried that once that happened, she would lock her heart away from him. She would once again become that belle that rang solo.

One step at a time.

He kissed her cheek lightly.

She stirred slightly and snuggled closer to him.

"Abby," he whispered, his lips against the top of her head. "Abby, wake up."

Her movement was so swift and unexpected that she was out of the bed and on her feet before he could react. Her panicked eyes went from the bright window to the clock. With her hands in her hair, she said, "Oh God! I fell asleep."

She looked incredible, naked in the streaming morning sunshine, her dark hair spilling over her bare shoulders and brushing her breasts. He had to fist his hands to keep from grabbing her and dragging her back to bed.

"Yes, you did. And everything is fine," he assured her.

She drew in a sharp breath and glared at him. "But it might not have been."

"I told you I'm a light sleeper. I can tell you what time it was every time you shifted positions if it'd make you feel better."

She was already snatching up stray articles of her clothing, following the trail from the bed out his bedroom door. "This was a mistake."

"Abby," he called. "Wait."

The bathroom door slammed.

Jason flopped back onto his pillow, the heels of his hands over his eyes. "Dammit."

After a moment, he got up himself. This was not the time to try and change her mind.

Jason had taken a big step back after Abby had fled the bedroom. She appreciated the space he gave her, but it wouldn't change her mind. She was too big a threat to him; and she obviously couldn't count on her own will-power to prevent disaster.

By tacit agreement, they both let the subject of their relationship lie and went about getting the day in order.

While she called Kitterman to set up a meeting time, Jason went into his home office to make some calls concerning his patients. When he returned to the kitchen, she said, "We're to meet Kitterman at the Sheriff's office at twelve-thirty. I need to stop by home to shower and change."

Jason checked his watch. "Let's go, then."

Once they were in the car, Abby focused on watching the town pass by. It was easier than trying to make small talk.

Jason swung the car into the parking lot of the Sun-shine Bakery, his gaze fixed on his rearview mirror.

"What?" Abby asked, turning in her seat to look out the back window.

He looked, too. "Nothing. I'm just edgy. I thought I saw that gray Impala a couple of cars back."

"He didn't pass by."

"I know. Like I said, just erring on the side of caution."

"Maybe there's reason to be cautious. That car kept circling the block when I was at the hardware store buying my door alarms. And then when I passed out in front of your house, I'm pretty sure I saw it go by."

"Under the circumstances, I'd say we need to be vigilant, not just cautious. Next time, we'll try to get a license plate number to give to Kitterman. It needs to be checked out."

She nodded, wondering how many times that car had been around and she *hadn't* noticed it. Her body gave an involuntary shudder.

He reached for her hand and gave a reassuring squeeze. He lightened his tone. "As long as we're here, I'll run in and get some bagels and coffee to go. Preferences?"

"Cranberry with butter."

He frowned and looked at her as if she was crazy, but didn't say anything disparaging about her choice.

While he was in the bakery Abby watched the traffic flow on the street behind her. What if the Impala had turned the corner a half-block back when the driver saw Jason pull into this lot?

Her scalp tightened with apprehension.

The Impala didn't reappear in the traffic going either direction.

Jason returned with a cup carrier and a bag. He handed

both to her when he got in. She took out the cups and put them in the cup holders.

"You want your bagel now?" she asked.

He shook his head. "I'll eat it on the way to the Sheriff's office."

She nodded and folded the top of the bag more tightly before she set it in the back seat.

They fell back into silence as they sipped their coffee and drove out of town. Abby tried to organize her thoughts for their meeting with Kitterman. How accepting would he be about her sleep-driving? At least she had Jason with her to make it sound more credible.

They were on the road out of town when Jason suddenly put on the brakes.

"What's wrong?" she said.

Jason let off the brakes and drove on, glancing in his side-view mirror. "Bryce just drove past, going the other way."

Abby looked behind them and saw the back of Bryce's dark blue Honda Civic. "Isn't he supposed to be in school?"

Jason was pulling his cell phone out of his pocket. "Yes, he is."

He dialed and waited, long enough that Abby knew Bryce wasn't answering.

"Maybe it was just a car like his," she suggested.

He shook his head. "It was him." Jason dialed another number. "Lucy, is there a reason why Bryce isn't in school right now?"

Abby couldn't help the little spark of jealousy that flared when she realized Jason was speaking to his ex—it didn't matter that it had to do with their son. Logic and emotion just didn't mix. She wondered how Lucy would feel if she knew that Abby and Jason had just slept together.

It doesn't matter how I feel or how she feels, because it's not going to happen again.

Jason's face hardened, the muscle in his jaw tightened as he listened. "Because I just passed him on the road...Yes, I'm sure...All right, let me know what you find out." He disconnected the call.

"I can call and move our meeting with Kitterman back," she suggested. "If you need to stay here until you figure out what's going on with Bryce."

"Bryce is seventeen, not ten. He doesn't need to be chased down. He just needs to know he's been caught."

"Okay then." She looked out the window.

"Sorry. I don't mean to take it out on you. It's just...there's something going on with him and I can't figure it out."

She gave him a reassuring smile. "Like you said—he's seventeen."

Jason didn't look like he thought it was normal teenage stuff, but he didn't move to discuss it further with her.

She supposed she shouldn't feel badly, but it stung just a little that he didn't want her to help talk through his problems the way he helped talk through hers.

The tension in the car made the ride to her house seem longer than it was. Finally, Jason turned onto her lane. "Let's hope you haven't had a visitor again while you were gone."

She sat there looking at the front door of her beloved cottage and felt violated all over again. "Let's hope." She opened the car door and got out.

The cottage door was locked and appeared undisturbed. Abby unlocked it and stepped inside. "I'll only be ten minutes."

She left Jason in her living room and ran up to the loft.

As she was stripping off her clothes, Jason called up, "Do you smell something?"

She paused and sniffed the air. "Nothing but old house. Everything in here except the couch and my mattress is ancient. Sometimes the drains get a little stinky when they haven't been used."

He made a noncommittal noise. She could hear him moving around downstairs, as if searching for the source of the odor.

She turned on the shower and got in before it was fully warm. If she didn't hurry they were going to be late.

As she washed, she tried to ignore the places on her skin that were irritated from the scrape of Jason's unshaven face and the intimate soreness from their lovemaking.

She quickly shampooed her hair, then got out and wrapped in a towel. After running a comb through her hair, she picked up her blow dryer and bent over at the waist, flipping her hair so she could dry it upside down. She was just about to turn on the switch when Jason yelled, "Stop!" and wrenched the dryer from her grasp.

She jerked upright, her hair falling over her face. She shoved it out of the way and Jason was standing there with terror in his eyes. "Gas. That's what I smelled. Gas."

She took a long sniff. "I don't smell it."

"It's stronger downstairs. Your pilot light was out on your stove."

She sniffed again and decided it was there, lying beneath all of the other smells she'd grown so accustomed to.

"I've opened all windows downstairs and shut off the gas at the tank." He set the dryer on the sink ledge, but he didn't unplug it. Then he took her hand and said, "Grab some clothes; you can get dressed outside."

"The smell isn't that strong." She lagged back, trying to sort out propane gas from the other odors.

"It's less strong up here, but I think it's strong enough that if you'd started that dryer, you'd have gotten more than you bargained for. It's a damn lucky thing that we took the alarm off the front door. It might have been enough to ignite it."

She felt as if she'd been kicked in the face. How much closer could they have come?

He tugged her hand. "Stop standing there sniffing and get some clothes."

She didn't explain that she was stunned, not sniffing. On the way to the stairs she grabbed clothes from the laundry basket on the floor.

Once they were outside and what Jason considered a safe distance from the house, Abby went behind an overgrown boxwood hedge to dress. Silly, she realized; Jason was familiar with every inch of her body already.

When she came out, Jason was closing the front door—gently. "We'll have to leave the windows open for now. I want to check the shop; give me your keys."

"Oh." She realized she'd been rushed out without picking up her purse. "They're in my purse on the coffee table."

He started back to the house.

"Hey! You can't go back in there; you just made me come out here naked."

Jason ignored her and re-entered the house, leaving the front door open behind him.

Ten seconds later, there was a concussive *whoosh* and orange-yellow flames shot out of the windows and door, rolling in huge balls toward the sky.

CHAPTER 22

Jason!" Abby screamed as heat blasted her face.

She ran toward the house on trembling legs. The initial ball of flame had dissipated. She made it up the steps, shielding her face from the heat with her hand. The skin on her forearm felt like it was starting to blister.

Fire licked over every surface inside the house. Smoke was building rapidly.

"Jason!" She squinted but couldn't see him. He should be somewhere between the front door and the center of the room.

Please, God, let him be alive. It was a prayer she didn't expect to have answered as she braced herself to run into the burning house.

Just as she started to dash through the door, she was slammed off her feet so violently that she was thrown off the steps. She hit the ground on her back, her breath knocked from her lungs, her head feeling as if she'd been whacked with a board. Jason was on top of her.

As she wheezed, she looked into his scraped and bloodied face. She blinked, unable to believe her eyes.

She managed to raise her hand and touch him, just to make certain he was real and not caused by her bump on the head.

He was.

He had a sprig of azalea stuck in his hair. He was panting, nearly as breathless as she was, but he managed a half-smile before he rolled onto his back beside her.

When she could finally get some air into her lungs, she croaked out a single word. "H-how?"

Jason rolled to his knees. "Can you get up? We need to get away from the house."

She nodded.

He helped her to her feet. They stumbled, arms around one another, away from the house. When they were nearly to the car, they collapsed onto the ground again.

"I can't believe...." Abby struggled to even out her breathing. "How?"

He didn't seem to hear her. He pulled his BlackBerry out of his pocket. "Thank God I didn't kill it." Then he dialed 911 to report the fire.

Abby looked at her cottage. The structure was brick, but she didn't hold much hope that anything inside could be saved, no matter how quickly the fire department arrived.

Through the windows she saw the dancing flames. Suddenly she was transported back to the night fire had destroyed the big house.

She closed her eyes and saw bright flames against the night sky. The plantation house had been constructed of wood and had burned fast and furiously, the fire a ravenous monster consuming everything it touched.

And then the screams began, shrill and pain-filled.

Although the shrieks were inside Abby's head, she instinctively covered her ears. That only made the sounds more intense.

She felt Jason's hands on her wrists, gently pulling her hands away from her ears. "It's all right, Abby."

It was then that she realized she was yelling for it to stop.

He leaned close. "Look at me, Abby. Look in my eyes."

When she did, it felt as if a cool breeze blew through her burning soul.

"That's it, baby. No one is screaming. It's just you and me."

Then the shaking started. It began in the center of her chest and radiated to her extremities. The harder she tried to stop it, the more fiercely she shook.

He pulled her to him and cupped her head, pressing it against his shoulder. She clung to him, reassuring herself that he was alive and unharmed. That this fire had not claimed one she loved.

And she did, she realized in that moment. She loved him.

After a few moments, she had herself back under control and she leaned away from him. She touched the scrapes on his face. "I thought you were gone." She felt a tear slide down her cheek. "I was so afraid...I couldn't stand it if—"

He cut her words off with a soft kiss on the mouth. "You were going into that fire to try and save me?"

"I couldn't leave you in there." She swallowed convulsively. "How did you get out?"

"I saw the little lamp you normally have on the table beside your front door. It was on the floor in the far corner of the room. When I got closer, I saw the glass on the bulb was broken and its timer had been moved with it. And it was about to switch on. I dove out the back window just in time."

"My God," she whispered.

"Yeah, I know, it was too close."

Her next thought overshadowed her elation over his survival. "The pilot light didn't go out by itself," she said hollowly.

"No, I don't think it did." He said the words cautiously, as if fearing his confirmation would set off a new round of tremors in her.

Instead of shaking, every muscle in her body tensed, and she ground her teeth until they hurt. Anger dominated her emotions. Someone was after her and had almost killed Jason. She was a danger to him in ways she hadn't even imagined.

Great-Gran Girault's accusations rang in her memory: *"It ain't natural. That girl is cursed, I tell you. She's a danger to everyone."*

It was true.

Abby got to her feet and walked a few feet away, turning her back to the fire consuming her home, and on Jason.

Things could be replaced. But Jason...dear God.

He came and stood close behind her. "I know what you're thinking."

"I don't think you do." She hugged her middle and closed her eyes.

"Abby, the fact that I'm here with you might have saved you—and it didn't kill me."

Just because we got lucky. She didn't respond.

He took her by the shoulders and turned her to face

him. "This happened because someone *out there* is dangerous, not because of you."

She rolled her lips inward and bit them. Finally she said, "It still all goes back to my sleepwalking."

"Which isn't your fault," he said emphatically.

She heard an approaching siren.

Drawing herself up and squaring her shoulders, she asked, "How did he know when to set the timer to come on?" It turned her blood to cold sludge thinking someone was trying to kill her.

"Maybe he didn't want you here. Maybe he wanted it to serve as another warning. If it did…more than that, well, there was nothing to make it look like more than an unfortunate accident."

"Or maybe he's watching us," she said, looking at him, gauging his reaction. His words might twist things to soothe her, but his eyes wouldn't lie.

Jason gave a slow shake of his head but didn't spare her when he said, "Maybe he is. Which should make him easier to catch. But it doesn't really matter. What matters is we have to figure this out before he gets more serious—or luckier in his timing."

Abby stood as if frozen when the fire truck roared into the lane. She watched with odd detachment as the firefighters scrambled around her, shouting to one another, dragging hoses and putting water on the fire.

It didn't matter if they saved the house. Jason was right; the only thing that mattered was stopping this before someone was hurt.

It had been difficult to dodge the newspeople gathered to report on the fire, but somehow Abby and Jason had managed. The last thing she wanted was to make a stupid statement to the press that would make things worse.

Now everyone except a single fire truck had packed up and left. According to the firefighters, this last truck would be here for quite a while, making certain there were no hot spots. But there was no reason for Abby and Jason to remain. They'd moved their meeting with Kitterman to four-thirty. They were going to have to get going.

Abby walked to Jason's car without looking back.

Once seated in the passenger seat, she used his Black-Berry to make a call to her father to let him know there had been an *accidental* fire caused by a gas leak and that she was fine. Once she convinced him the emergency was over and he didn't need to get a neighbor to bring him out to the property, he immediately insisted she move in with him until her place was repaired.

Reluctantly, she looked at the brick shell, its roof collapsed and still smoking. "Repaired" was a gross understatement. Reconstructed would be more like it. She kept that to herself.

There was no way she could move in with her father. She couldn't be trusted, and he wasn't in any shape to protect himself from whatever dangers she'd come up with while sleepwalking. Stress played a major role in her sleep disorder; she didn't see it going away anytime soon. Besides, after what just happened to Jason, it was clear the farther she was from her dad right now, the safer he'd be.

"I think I'm going to set up a little apartment in the back of the shop temporarily," she said with forced cheer. "That way I can still be close to work. You know how late I have to work sometimes. It's better that I don't have to drive back to town in the middle of the night." That should convince him.

"Good idea, Jitterbug. But you'll need a place to stay until you get that set up."

This was why she had put off calling him. She knew it was going to be lie after lie. She didn't lie as a general principle, and never to her father.

She sucked it up and spun another one. "I have a friend who's already offered to bring over a bed and some basic things for me to use. So I'm all set." She had to get off the phone before he came up with another thing that forced her to lie. "Listen, I need to go now. I just wanted you to know I'm fine. But my cell phone was in the house, so you'll have to call me on the shop phone if you need me."

"I think I should come out there," he said.

"No need, Dad. Besides, I'm going to be helping move the bed and all over, so I won't be here."

He was quiet for a moment. Then he said, "You're just as damned independent as your mother."

"I'll take that as a compliment. Gotta go. Love you, Dad."

"Love you, Jitterbug. Call if you need anything."

"Will do." She disconnected the call and handed the phone back to Jason. "I feel like such a slimeball, lying to him like that."

"Think of them as white lies."

She huffed. "Call them whatever color you want, they're still lies." But she knew they were necessary.

At four-twenty-five, Abby followed Sergeant Kitterman into the sheriff's office conference room. Her head throbbed with each footstep. She had dirt skid marks on the back of her shirt, a scraped elbow, and no clothes except those on her back. But she looked a lot better than Jason. The EMTs had cleaned his cuts and scrapes, which were numerous. She'd noticed him flexing the fingers of his left hand and repeatedly bending and straightening his left elbow, as if trying to work out a tingling nerve in his funnybone.

God. There was nothing funny about it. Any of it.

Abby could only imagine how much worse his injuries would have been if that window had not been open. His close call was the nail in the coffin of their near-relationship. She brought nothing but bad to those she loved. Once she and Jason were finished here today, they were going their separate ways. He would fight it, she knew. But she had to be strong.

As he followed her down the hall, their echoing footfalls on the tile floor tapped out a farewell. She'd developed a connection with Jason unlike any she'd experienced with anyone. It seemed cruel, to have so much that she could not have laid before her.

Even after this short time, Jason Coble was going to be a hard habit to break.

Kitterman stopped in front of an open door, his arm extended, inviting them to enter the room ahead of him. "I appreciate you still coming today. I know you've already been through the wringer."

"I want to do everything I can to help catch this guy before he really hurts someone," Abby said. Her insides were still quivering from that moment when she'd thought Jason had been killed.

They sat down at the conference table on which several manila folders were stacked beside a small tape recorder.

Kitterman said, "Sheriff Hughes gave the go-ahead to share what we have with you. But first I want to get this newest development on tape." He turned on the recorder and said to Jason, "Tell me again exactly what happened before the fire erupted."

Jason recounted the entire ordeal once again, from first smelling gas to the moment he dove out the open window. As Abby listened she could have sworn she was becoming feverish. She felt clammy and chills ran just beneath her skin.

"So this lamp and timer were normally in the house?" Kitterman asked.

"Yes," Abby said. "Obviously I don't keep the lamp on the floor. When we came in I was in a hurry because of our appointment here. And Jason was preoccupied with finding the gas leak. It's a small lamp; we didn't notice it wasn't in its usual place."

"Propane gas is heavier than air," Kitterman said. "It would pool and travel across the floor; the highest concentration would be there."

Abby shuddered at the calculating nature of whoever had done this. How well did this person know her? How closely was she being watched? Had he checked out her stove on the previous break-in, or had he improvised?

Kitterman said, "I'm sure the fire marshal will get his report to me ASAP. He knows the urgency." He tapped the top folder on the stack. "Since there's a good chance this is linked to your accident on Thursday morning, let's take a step backward, Ms. Whitman. I've read all of Deputy Trowbridge's notes and looked over the other evidence. I'd like to hear your account of what happened."

Abby shot a glance at Jason. He nodded encouragingly.

"That's one of the reasons we wanted to talk to you," Abby said. "I'm fairly certain that I was sleepwalking, or sleep-driving, at the time of the accident. That's why I can't remember anything before I woke up in the swamp."

He raised a brow, but didn't say anything.

She explained her history and her experience with Sonja. Occasionally Kitterman would look over at Jason, as if seeking corroboration, but he didn't interrupt her.

When she was finished, Kitterman asked, "So you've done plenty of everyday things while sleepwalking?"

"Yes," she said. "I only know that I've been up and moving if I've done something to leave a clue—or if I awaken while I'm still out of bed."

"Had you driven in your sleep before?" Kitterman asked.

"Not to my knowledge."

Her answer seemed to take him a little by surprise, as if it was just now sinking in that she truly did not have any memory of what she did while sleepwalking.

He sat quietly for a moment. "Perhaps if we make this public knowledge—the sleep-driving and amnesia, that is—whoever is threatening you will stop."

Jason put his palms on the table. "In my experience, people who have never had somnambulism aren't going to readily believe that: one, Abby could have driven; and two, she won't remember eventually. Certainly not someone hiding something he's willing to go to these lengths to protect. He may even see her claim as a ruse to hide the fact that she *does* know. It could force him to act more aggressively."

Kitterman screwed his mouth to the side, considering. "You may be right. Along those lines, it's feeling to me like this person has more at stake than just being identified as the 911 caller. It's just an old cop's gut, but I think there's more."

Abby said, "I've been assuming it was kids who weren't supposed to be out, maybe drinking. Maybe it was even someone who was with Kyle...another motorcyclist, even. You think it's more nefarious than that?"

"I'm just trying to equate the risks this person is willing to take with what he wants to remain secret," Kitterman said.

"To a kid," Jason said, "depending on the circumstance, getting caught out after curfew or underage drinking might be enough. When you're dealing with teenagers, logic and proportional reactions aren't involved in the equation."

"True enough," Kitterman agreed. Then he looked at Abby. "Tell me what you remember from the accident."

Abby was a little surprised that he seemed to accept that she'd been asleep while driving, but she wasn't about to question him about it. Instead, she went through what she did after waking in the van.

As she spoke, Kitterman leaned back in his chair, one hand fiddling with a pen. Once in a while he would nod slightly. Abby wondered if these nods were at things that she said that aligned with the evidence, or if he did it as a matter of course when he was listening.

When she finished, he said, "I've been down to the impound and checked out your van. There's very little damage to the body, other than scrapes and a broken driver's side headlight. I've also been to the scene and studied the photos taken that night. I can't figure out how the driver's side window got broken."

Abby sensed Jason sitting up a little straighter next to her. He'd been interested in the broken glass, too.

Jason asked, "Was there any other broken glass on the van?"

"No," Kitterman said. "And it takes a pretty strong sharp blow to shatter safety glass like that. It had to come from outside the vehicle because the glass was all over the inside of the van and we didn't find a single trace on the road or along the tracks into the water.

"Ms. Whitman, you said you remembered red lights, like taillights."

"I remembered it under hypnosis, but I can't say that it happened with certainty. I had a dream that was very similar. And I can't recall anything before or after that glimpse of red lights, so I'm doubting I truly saw them."

"Has the investigation team come up with a theory about how the accident happened?" Jason asked.

Kitterman said, "It's clear that the motorcycle and Ms. Whitman's van were traveling in opposite directions. But the skid marks the van left on the pavement are too far from where the motorcycle left the road to indicate they were the result of trying to avoid a collision."

She leaned forward, suddenly every nerve humming. "As in *I* didn't hit him? Is that what you're saying?"

"Or you didn't hit the brakes until after impact," Kitterman offered matter-of-factly.

Her heart sank like a rock in a pond.

Impact. Even the word sounded horrible.

"Are you sure the motorcycle actually did make contact with another vehicle?" she asked with guarded hope.

"Yes, of that we're certain. We'll need lab confirmation for the paint found on the motorcycle to know if it matches your van—it was white. There are thousands of white vehicles around. But from what I saw of your van, I don't think it'll be a match."

Abby grasped that shred of hope, but didn't allow herself to believe, not until she was certain she hadn't killed Kyle Robard.

Jason asked, "What about the fingerprints on Kyle's phone, any luck there?"

"There were two fingerprints on the phone that were not the victim's and good enough quality to do us some good. They likely belong to the same person. Until we have something to compare them to—they didn't match any in the database—they're useless." He leaned forward slightly and looked at Abby. "We do know they are not yours."

Abby felt a little vindicated and hoped Officer Trowbridge had received the news and choked on it.

Kitterman tapped his pen against his chin. "The castings from the shoe imprints around the body have told us that there were at least two other people on the scene besides Ms. Whitman. The imprints near the motorcycle and body are all over each other, which isn't unusual at an accident scene where people are disoriented or upset."

He opened a folder and showed Abby and Jason photos taken of the castings. One shoe was smooth-soled. The other was grooved and patterned, like an athletic shoe. They were both large, so Abby assumed they belonged to men—or boys.

Jason said, "So there could have been multiple vehicles."

Kitterman said, "That's a lot of traffic out on that road in the middle of a weeknight. I'm betting on multiple people in one vehicle. Also, alongside Ms. Whitman's bare footprints on the pavement where she came out of the marsh, there were muddy shoeprints from both of these shoes—also leaving the marsh."

"Maybe they checked on me too before they called 911," Abby suggested.

"Possibly. The castings I took by the river yesterday went to the lab today. They called a short while ago. They class-match one of the pairs of shoes at your accident scene."

"Class-match?" Abby asked.

"They have identifiable tread markings to say they're the same brand and size. We don't have anything that will single them out to a *particular* pair of that brand and size, at least yet. The experts have yet to analyze them."

"It can't be a coincidence," Jason said. "It has to be the same guy."

"We don't speak in absolutes until we have absolute proof, but I'd be hard pressed to disagree too strongly," Kitterman said. "And if they do match absolutely, then the person at the accident scene is certainly the person who broke into Ms. Whitman's house."

"What about the other things: the phone call, the vandalism at the cemetery, and the slashed tires?"

"*Likely* connected, not absolutely," Kitterman said. "The phone call came from a pay phone at the Silver Star Tavern. Of course nobody remembers seeing who made it. The fingerprints on the iPod from the cemetery are all too smudged to be of use. It does have an engraving on the back, '226.'"

Jason shook his head; those numbers were about as useless as smudged fingerprints. "How are we going to get absolutes?"

"We're following all of the leads we can. Other than the prints—which as I said do no good without a match—we only have the prayer card from St. Andrew's."

"That could have come from me," Abby said. "I was at that funeral, and I did most of the flowers."

Kitterman looked at her. "But the fingerprints on it don't belong to you. They match those found on Mr. Robard's cell phone."

Abby and Jason looked at one another. There was a very short list of people who had attended that funeral. And Abby knew most of them personally. Could someone she knew actually have tried to blow up her house, possibly with her in it?

She must have turned pale, because Jason put an arm around her, and Kitterman got up and returned with a bottle of water and set it in front of her.

He stood there, looking down at her. "I don't have to caution you to be alert and careful until we catch this guy."

As she unscrewed the cap on the water bottle, she shook her head. She wasn't the only one in danger. She had to separate herself from Jason.

CHAPTER 23

Abby walked beside Jason as they left the sheriff's office, feeling as if she had ants crawling all over her. She even caught herself absently trying to sweep them off her skin a couple of times.

"I don't know what I was expecting," she said. "But I don't feel we've made any headway—other than the fact that I now know *two* people are out to get me."

Jason tried to take her hand, but she moved slightly to the side, out of reach.

"If there's one thing I've figured out over the years it's that when two people share a secret, one of them is very likely to give it up. Because there was only one shoe imprint at your place, it could mean the second person doesn't agree with what the first is doing, or may be completely ignorant that it's going on at all."

She thought for a moment. "Then maybe the police need to let the public know I'm being threatened. If the second person is against it, or doesn't know...wouldn't they be more likely to come forward?"

"It's *more* likely that person number one will view person number two as a bigger liability than you are."

She frowned. "Oh. Well, we can't put someone else in the crosshairs."

"He, or she, may already be. Who knows what's happening that we don't know about?"

"At least no one else's house has been torched," Abby said.

Jason didn't say anything. Abby could read his thought on his face well enough: *Not yet.*

They got into Jason's car and left the station. On the way out of town, they stopped at a Wal-Mart so she could pick up some necessities. Jason had to pay because Abby's purse, along with her cash and backup credit card, had gone up in flames. At least Jason had escaped unscathed. For that she'd sacrifice everything she had ten times over.

It seemed now, just when she needed to put more distance between them, she'd become more dependent on him than ever. At least he hadn't argued with her this morning when she'd said sleeping together had been a mistake. He must feel it, too.

Although it would make things easier, his acquiescence settled on her like a damp fog. She would never again experience the magic of his touch, the perfect symphony of their joining. She'd never bared her true self to anyone as she had him. He was the one person who truly knew her and accepted her completely, without excuses for the ugly truths.

She pushed those thoughts from her mind. They were only going to make her mood more morose.

It was nearly dark when they headed back to Preston. They grabbed sandwiches at the McDonald's drive-thru before hitting the highway. Hers tasted like cardboard, but Abby forced herself to eat it. She was enough of a damsel in distress; the last thing she needed was to become a fainting flower.

As she choked down her cheeseburger, she started sorting through the practicalities of her situation.

When she'd swallowed the last bite, she wadded up the wrapper and put it back in the bag.

"I've waited too long to cancel the flower orders for the Robards," she said. "Maybe some folks have already figured out the situation and called to cancel. But I need to get to the shop and start working."

Jason stopped with a fry halfway to his mouth. "Seriously?"

"I can hardly just ignore the orders at this point. The viewing starts tomorrow."

"No, I guess not."

"I probably don't have enough flowers on hand. I'll work with what I have tonight and have more delivered first thing tomorrow. And since I'll be working through the night, you won't have to babysit me."

"You can't think I'm going to let you be out there by yourself."

"Whoever set that fire knows I don't have a place to stay. He won't know I'm working. He won't be back tonight."

"And what crystal ball told you that?"

"Jason, sooner or later you're going to have to leave me. You have your own responsibilities."

"Then it'll be later. I have an air mattress. I'll sleep at the shop while you work."

"Don't be ridiculous."

"I'm not the one who's being ridiculous."

Abby huffed, but stopped arguing. It was pointless. She guessed he might well be safer at the shop if whoever was after her thought she was staying at his house. And it was just for one night.

At least that was the justification she gave herself.

While Jason went upstairs to get his air mattress, Abby used his phone to call the tire store. After having an investigator check the Explorer for evidence, Kitterman had given the go-ahead to have the tires changed. He was less definite about when her van would be released. So getting the Explorer up and running was the first step in regaining her independence.

The thought of truly separating herself from Jason brought a mixed bag of emotions, none of which she wanted to examine at the moment. So instead she focused on the giant magnolia tree outside his front window. It only reminded her of him, straight, strong, unbendable—and yet majestic in beauty. Everything about both of them spoke of strong Southern principles. Exactly the kind of man she would be looking for—*if* she were looking for a man.

When the voice message system answered, she was so lost in thought she was a little startled. After stuttering for a moment, she left a message asking them to replace the tires on the Explorer as early as possible tomorrow morning.

After she finished her call, she heard Jason talking upstairs. Soon he came trotting down the staircase with the air mattress box under one arm, his cell pressed to his ear.

"What do you mean you let him go out?" he said crossly. "Lucy, he skipped school today."

He listened.

"Yes, I do think it's a big deal. Did you even find out how

he spent his day?" He paused and listened again. "I don't care how often you skipped school when you were his age. We can't act like it doesn't matter to us—" His mouth tightened and his eyes grew stormy. "Don't pull that on me. You always do that when you don't agree with me. He's my son, too. His being upset lately means he needs less freedom, not more. I'm going to call him." He disconnected the call.

He looked like he'd just hit his finger with a hammer. He handed the mattress box to Abby. "Can you take this to the car?"

"Sure." She went outside feeling just a little tweaked. She knew it was stupid. His conversations with his children were no business of hers. But he'd been there every step of the way with her; she'd like to reciprocate with a little support in his difficulties.

It was nearly ten minutes before he came out of the house and got in the car. He was still frowning.

"Everything okay?" she asked.

"Bryce didn't answer his cell. Which means he's in bigger trouble when I do finally talk to him."

Jason sounded as angry as she'd ever heard him, so she didn't question why if Bryce hadn't answered it had taken him so long to come out.

It wasn't quite twilight when they pulled into Abby's lane. Spanish moss moved ghostlike in the ancient trees lining the way. The smell of scorched wood and wet ash burned her nose, a bitter reminder that she wouldn't be going home for a very long time.

Although she was braced for it, the sight of the blackened shell of her cottage sucked the breath from her lungs. She quickly turned her eyes away.

She was glad Jason didn't offer a litany of platitudes

and promises about rebuilding and a better future. He allowed her to feel the rawness of her loss.

Once they were inside the shop, Jason knelt to inflate the air mattress. That's when she saw the likely reason he'd been so long in coming out of his house—and probably why he'd sent her on ahead of him.

"What in the hell is that?" she said, pointing at the handgun tucked in the back of his waistband. She knew it hadn't been there before they stopped at his house; he could not have gotten inside the sheriff's office with it.

He stood and faced her. "I've had a few crazy incidents while working with law enforcement. I have a permit."

"Who gives a shit? Why do you have it now?"

"Because it's more effective than your attack gnome or throwing pottery at someone if they try to break in here."

She crossed her arms over her chest. "Is it loaded?"

"Wouldn't be much good if it wasn't."

"I don't like it."

He stepped close to her. "Neither do I. But it's here and it's staying."

"What if you shoot a kid?" She glared up at him.

"You mean the kid that tried to incinerate us both? The kid that destroyed your home?"

Closing her eyes, she sighed. "It just seems so... extreme."

Jason framed her face with his hands. "I'll do whatever it takes to protect you." He kissed her quickly, before her emotion-burdened reflexes could avoid the contact.

Although she knew she should pull away, her mouth opened to his, her hands grasped his waist, and she buried herself in the sensations he set off in her body. It was very effective at blocking out reality.

By the time she broke from him, they were both breathing heavily. If this was the kind of restraint she had, she simply could not allow herself to be alone with him in the future.

"I'd better get to work," she said, stepping away from the temptation to touch him again.

"Can I help?"

"No. Go to sleep." Her work was the only corner of her life that was still firmly in her grasp. And it was a safer place to bury herself from her troubles than in Jason's arms.

Jason lay on the air mattress watching Abby work, his gun within reach on the floor beside him. The wind was kicking up, stirring the occasional soft creak and rattle and the random tap-tap of tree and shrub branches. He tuned his hearing to the song of the old building, so he would be able to pick out those notes that didn't belong.

The room was dark except for the light right over Abby's worktable, where she stood in a pool of radiance, like an angel.

She'd put her hair up and her hands moved with sureness as she assembled her creations. He liked watching her when she was like this, in command. It was the way she was meant to be. After a short while, he would have bet money that she'd not only forgotten about the gun she'd been glaring at, but had completely forgotten he was in the room.

He must have closed his eyes and begun to drift off when some shift in the sounds around him snapped him back awake. He jerked to a sitting position, listening. Abby was no longer in the cone of light at her work table.

He jumped up off the mattress and reached for the gun he'd left on the floor next to him.

It wasn't there.

CHAPTER 24

*C*hrist! How could he have fucked up this badly? Jason's heart was rioting in his chest and his mouth had gone dry as he turned in a full circle, scanning the shop. He didn't hear anyone moving.

Cool air moved against his cheek. A door or window had been opened.

"Abby?" he called softly as he moved quickly deeper into the building.

He passed the flower cooler. The area grew darker as he moved farther from the single source of light over the work-table, but his eyes were well adjusted to the dimness.

The back door was standing wide open.

"Abby?" he whispered loudly.

Only the wind whispered back.

He glanced around for a makeshift weapon and picked up a garden shovel propped near the door. Gripping it tightly, holding it over his shoulder ready to strike, he moved through the doorway. He restrained his movement, inching quietly when he wanted to run wildly, yelling her name.

He scanned the area near the building. It amazed him how much deeper the night was out here than in town.

Trees swayed and shrubbery shivered. Spanish moss fluttered in the old oaks. But he saw no humanlike movement.

Check for a vehicle first. He turned to the right and walked close to the building toward the front.

His car was there. No other.

The river.

His gut tied itself into a tight knot as he thought of Abby being dragged to a boat, taken from him forever.

He started to run toward the path to the old dock. As he passed the corner of the building, something snagged his ankles, sending him sprawling face-first on the ground. He heard the shovel hit the ground somewhere off to the right.

Rolling toward the shovel, he grasped blindly for the handle; the crack of a gun right next to him stunned him into stillness.

He looked up. Abby stood not three feet away, holding his gun with both hands, aiming it in his direction.

"What the fuck?" he said at the same time she said, "Oh my God!"

She lowered the weapon.

He scrambled to his feet. "You almost shot me!"

"I told you a gun was a bad idea." She shoved it into his hands. Then she added, "You were safe; my first shot was up in the air."

"What are you doing out here?" he demanded, his heart still rocketing around inside his chest.

"I thought I heard something."

He grabbed her by the arm and hauled her toward the

back door. "If you hear something, you're supposed to wake the person who knows how to use the gun."

"Don't yell at me."

"I'm not yelling."

"You are—"

"Shhhhh!" he said. He strained to listen. There, beneath the wind, was the distinct sound of a boat motor.

Abby's eyes grew wide. "I told you I heard something."

His grip tightened on her arm until she said, "Ouch."

"Sorry." He loosened his hold. "Let's get back inside."

When they were once again behind a locked door, Abby said, "I left the door open so you could hear if I saw someone and called for you." She held herself in smug confidence. "Should we call the Sheriff?"

He wanted to shake her, an urge spurred by fear, not anger. Instead of shaking her, he crushed her to his chest and buried his face in her hair.

"Don't you *ever* take a chance like that again," he said.

Her felt her trembling and realized just how false her bravado was.

She whispered, "Not a chance."

By the time Sergeant Kitterman finished his search for evidence—only finding a repeat of the footprints on the riverbank—it was eight o'clock and fully light.

Abby needed to get the flowers to Randall and Roberts Funeral Home. She had to be back out here by ten to receive the flower order she'd placed while Sergeant Kitterman was combing the property looking for traces of their prowler.

As Kitterman drove away, Abby asked Jason, "If the Explorer is still flat-footed can I use your car?"

Jason was scheduled for office hours today. Already he'd had to call and cancel a nine o'clock appointment.

"I'm sure if you call people and explain the situation—"

"This is my job, Jason. It'll only take me a couple of hours and then I'll come straight back to your house."

He pulled his BlackBerry out of his pocket. "Maybe I can rearrange—"

"No." She cut him off. "You see your patients. I can get Dad to come out with me if it'll make you feel any better."

"I thought you weren't telling him." He eyed her with suspicion.

"I won't have to. I've got plenty of excuses to get him out here. He always wants to help."

"Two hours?" he asked.

"Tops. The delivery is at ten. I should be finished by noon. Drop the flowers at Randall and Roberts; I'm at your place before one o'clock."

"If it's only two hours, maybe we can get a deputy to stay with you," he suggested.

"That'd be great." She started toward the front door of the shop. "You call and see if it's doable while I load the flowers." Fat chance. The sheriff had made it clear they were understaffed due to budget cuts and spread entirely too thin to work effectively.

When she came back out with an arrangement in her hands, Jason was smiling. "A deputy will be here from ten to twelve." He ducked and put the gun into the glove box of his car.

"Easy as that?"

He hesitated and shoved his phone in his pocket. "Yep."

She eyed him, wondering what he'd said to convince the sheriff to assign a deputy to her for those two hours.

She said, "Thank you."

Randall and Roberts Funeral Home was located in an old yellow and white Victorian diagonally across the street from St. Andrew's. Jason pulled his car into the alley and parked by the rear entrance. Abby walked on ahead with the first arrangement as Jason got the next one out of the backseat of his car. She was already through the door when he noticed the Robards' Cadillac sitting on the street at the side of the funeral home.

He hurried toward the door, hoping Abby wouldn't run into them. He also hoped Jessica had stayed home until the viewing began late this afternoon. Even with the medication he'd prescribed, this day would push her to the limit.

Belatedly, another thought sprang into his mind. Was the casket already in the room where Abby would have to place the flowers? He didn't want her to go in there alone. He took the back steps two at a time.

Just as he put his hand on the door handle, he heard a woman shouting. The shrieking got louder when he pulled the door open.

"Get out . . . get out . . . get out . . . get out!"

He set the flowers on a table by the door and ran toward the voice, which led him to the big room with wide double doors at the front of the building.

He walked into a scene from a soap opera. Abby was standing frozen in the middle of the room, a stricken look on her color-drained face. In her hands she held the empty flower container. Flowers and greenery were strewn around the floor as if tossed by a tornado. That tornado had been Jessica Robard.

Ken held his wife from behind, wrapping his arms around her to prevent further attack. Jessica strained against him, her face a furious red, her teeth bared.

"You took the only thing I live for! I don't want anything you've touched near him!" She thrust her body forward, trying to break her husband's hold.

Ken saw Jason. "For God's sake, do something with her!"

For a split second, Jason hesitated. His instinct was to go to Abby. His responsibility dictated he help Ken calm Jessica.

He put a hand on Abby's shoulder as he passed her. He said quietly, "Go out in the hall. I'll be there as soon as I can."

Abby didn't move.

He squeezed her shoulder slightly. "Abby, please."

She broke out of her stunned state and nodded, backing away as if afraid to expose her back to Jessica.

Jason moved directly in front of Jessica, blocking Abby from her view, crushing delicate flowers underfoot with each step.

He said her name quietly, repeating it until she looked him in the eye. "Will you come and sit with me for a minute?"

She was breathing as hard as if she'd run a sprint, but she'd stopped straining against her husband.

Jason prompted, "Will you?"

She gave a nod and seemed to relax a little more.

He shifted his gaze to the senator. "Let her go."

Ken Robard released her the way one would a wild animal, cautiously with slow, steady movements.

Jason took her lightly by the elbow. "Let's go sit down."

"She won't take her medication. You have to do something," Ken said. "I can't have her acting like this this afternoon."

Jessica slapped her husband so hard her handprint was immediately visible. "You bastard! You don't care about anything except your career. You don't care about me...or Kyle." She looked at Jason. "He was off screwing who knows who and I was all alone when I found out our son was dead. I'm always all alone—"

"Jessica!"

"It's true!"

"I was working—"

"Give Jessica and me a few minutes, will you, Senator?" Jason put an arm around her and led her to a sofa at the end of the room.

It took fifteen minutes to get her calmed and semi-rational. All the while Jason had to force himself to stay put, to not leave her and go to Abby.

Finally, Ken came quietly back into the room. He stood in front of his wife with his hand extended. "Let's go home," he said softly, with so much love in his eyes that Jason was amazed at his quick transformation. "You can rest for a while."

All of Jessica's fight had been used up. She slowly reached out and took his hand, then stood. They walked out of the room without another word, Jessica moving beside her husband robotically. She'd promised to take her medication. For her sake, Jason hoped she kept that promise.

He followed them out, concerned she'd fly into another rage if she saw Abby. But Abby wasn't in the hallway.

He found her in the office, sitting with Jim Roberts. The color had come back to her cheeks.

She stood up. "Jim and I were just talking. He's going to hold all of the flowers in the back until I bring the rest of them. I'm going to replace all of the cards that have my logo with plain white ones. That way people's condolences will be delivered, and maybe Mrs. Robard won't be so upset."

She was acting as if that whole scene hadn't transpired. Jason looked at her for a moment, trying to read the emotions beneath the surface.

She started toward the office door. When he didn't fall in behind her, she said over her shoulder, "Well, come on. Help me unload the last of these flowers."

He looked at Jim Roberts, who shrugged and said, "She's sure handling this well."

Denial is not handling it.

Jason hurried to catch up with her. She was nearly to the back door when he did. "Abby," he said, catching her arm.

She turned to face him and he could see how hard she was fighting to maintain control. "Please, Jason. Don't. Just let me do this my way."

He removed his hand and gave her a nod. "Let's get those flowers in here."

Ten minutes later, they were at the Verizon store, getting Abby yet another cell phone and activating it. There was no way he was letting her out of his sight without one.

When they reached his house, he got out of the

passenger side. He noticed the Explorer was still in the driveway, but it was without wheels, sitting on four jack stands.

"Okay." He set his hands on the top of the car and leaned down to look at Abby through the open door. "Straight to the shop. No detours. And don't even get out of the car if the deputy isn't there when you get there."

"That's the third time you've said that. I think I've got it." She reached for the glove box latch. "I don't want this." She picked up the gun and held it out to him with the tips of her finger and thumb, like it was the reeking carcass of a dead squirrel.

He didn't take it. "Keep it in the glove box—just in case."

"Jesus, Jason, I nearly shot you last night."

"I'll be here, safe."

She did not look amused.

"The deputy will have his own gun," she said. "I don't need one."

She was probably right; she had no business with it. It was as likely to be used against her if she hesitated— and she no doubt would. When she'd thought he was an intruder, she shot up in the air.

He finally leaned inside the car and took it from her. While he was still hidden from view, he tucked it in the front of his waistband, under his shirt; no need to freak out the neighbors.

"Call me when you get there," he said. "And before you leave to come back."

"It's the middle of the day. I'll have a deputy. I'm going to be cautious. Stop worrying. I'll be fine."

She hit the button for the power window and put the car in gear.

He stood there watching her drive away, his instincts shouting not to let her go.

Once she turned the corner, he finally left the street. He was halfway to his front door when his cell rang. He reached in his pocket, thinking Abby was making a sarcastic point to call when she reached the next block. But it was Lucy's number on the screen.

"Since you were in such a snit yesterday," Lucy said, "I thought I'd let you know the high school called. Bryce didn't show up again today. Now you deal with it so it's done properly."

He took a long breath to rein in his temper. "Did you find out where he was yesterday?"

Jason let himself in the front door and made his way into his office.

"He got home late and had homework to do," Lucy said defensively. "I was waiting to discuss it with him when he got home from school today."

"Homework? He'd skipped school." Jason unlocked the outer door to the waiting area, then went to his desk.

"It was a project that was due."

He sighed. "Due, like today...when he didn't go to school again?"

"Don't talk to me like I'm an idiot. How did I know he wasn't going to school today? He's been in such a foul mood lately, he hardly talks to me at all."

"Have you checked with his friends? Is anyone else missing from school today?"

"How am I supposed to find that out?" she asked. "The school won't give out information on other students.

And if they're not in school, I doubt their parents know about it."

She was right. Still, it pissed him off that she hadn't dealt with this last night. "Call me when he gets home."

He heard his patient come into the waiting area.

"All right," she said.

He disconnected the call, put his phone on silent, and went to greet Mr. Brubecker, his first appointment of the day. He wasn't sure how in the hell he was going to keep his mind on his work with Bryce off who knew where and Abby running around alone.

During the session with Mr. Brubecker—who always spent at least the first twenty minutes complaining about his wife of forty years—Jason's eyes kept straying to his BlackBerry. It was on his desk, shielded from his patient's view by a stack of books.

Finally, a text message came in. He discreetly checked it.

Deputy Bigelow and I are having a party. Wish you were here.

Jason suppressed his smile and refocused on Mr. Brubecker, who was finally getting around to discussing his medical condition.

Two hours and three patients later, Jason broke for lunch. He hadn't heard from Abby telling him she was on her way back into town yet. He almost called her, but didn't want to delay her getting her work finished. He wanted her back here so he could keep a protective eye on her.

Silly, he thought, she was with a deputy sheriff, who should be perfectly capable of guarding her. But when it came to Abby, he trusted no one as much as he did himself. He was invested in ways no officer of the law performing his duty ever could be.

He tried to call Bryce again. When his son didn't answer, Jason texted him, betting he was more likely to read it than to check his voice mail.

You're busted. Call me ASAP.

Jason began to assemble a mental list of places he was going to search for his son if he didn't hear back from him by the end of the work day.

Just as he was headed from the kitchen to his office, he got the call from Abby. His heart lifted at the sound of her voice.

"All packed up and headed to Randall and Roberts. Deputy Bigelow and I just parted ways at the end of the lane. I should be at your house in forty-five minutes or so. I have to change the cards on the arrangements already at the funeral home, and set everything up in the viewing room."

"Let the staff take them into the viewing room," he said, his hand tightening on the phone.

"Probably a good idea."

He'd been braced for contention, probably something about professional presentation or some such thing he'd have a difficult time arguing against. He was still waiting for a "but" when she said, "Listen, can you leave your kitchen door unlocked? That way I won't interrupt you when I get there."

"All right," he said. "And Abby?"

"Yes?"

"Be careful."

Abby drove slowly toward town; she didn't relish the thought of going back into the funeral home. But, she assured herself, the viewing was still three hours away. The Robards had had their private time with their son this morning—which Abby had unwittingly interrupted. So the chances of another scene with Mrs. Robard were slim.

Abby had managed to do her work by blocking out the fact that these arrangements were for a boy whose death she was responsible for. As soon as she had the delivery behind her, she was looking forward to locking herself in Brenna's room and taking a nap. Maybe she could just stay there until morning. It would be the best way to make certain she didn't give in to her desires and go to Jason's bed again. She'd proven she was too weak to leave when she should.

Just as Abby was making the curve in the road, she saw a blue Honda Civic off on the shoulder ahead with its flashers on. She reduced her speed.

There, standing at the front bumper, was Jason's son, Bryce. He had a hand in the air, waving to stop her.

"Oh, buddy, you are so busted," she muttered.

She pulled onto the shoulder, right behind the Civic.

CHAPTER 25

J ason had just seen his first patient of the afternoon out
the door when a text message came in from Abby.
phone almost dead stopping to c dad c u later

"Dammit, Abby." He was dialing her number when
Brenna came in the door his patient had just exited.

"Hi, Daddy."

"Hi, Peanut." He disconnected before he finished dialing. "This is a surprise." Sticking his head out the office
door, he looked out into the drive for Lucy's or Bryce's
car. Neither was there. He was, however, pleased to see
the new tires on the Explorer because he might just have
to go drag Abby back here and lock her up. "How did
you get here?"

"Mom dropped me off. We got out of school early
today. Bryce wasn't home. She said to tell you she had
some errands and she'd pick me up later."

"She just dropped you off?" His voice tightened with
anger.

"She saw Mrs. McCutcheon come out and walk down
the driveway, so she knew you were here working."

He realized he was grinding his teeth. He put on a neutral face and asked, "Have you had lunch?"

"Yep."

"Do you have homework?"

"Nope. And Father Kevin cancelled PSR this week, so I don't have that stuff, either. Daddy, do you think Father Kevin is sick?"

"I don't know, baby. Maybe. But he had a fall this week and broke some ribs. I'm sure that's why he cancelled class."

"Oh, no. I bet that hurt." She looked pensive for a moment. "I pray for him every night."

"That's the best gift you could give him," Jason said, marveling at his daughter's extraordinary compassion at such a young age.

"Okay, then." He clapped his hands. "I have my last patient in a few minutes. Do you want to watch a DVD or something?"

She lifted a shoulder. "Sure."

She was so used to having her life blown by the winds of her mother's whims that she wasn't nearly as affected by this impromptu visit as Jason was. What was Lucy thinking? All she had to do was call. He always took Brenna when he got the chance. But, Jesus, to dump the child on the curb! After he got Bren set up in the den, he'd be calling Lucy. How freakin' irresponsible.

When he was popping in *Charlotte's Web*, he said, "So was your brother home for dinner last night?"

"Yeah," Brenna said. "Mom's real mad at him."

Jason stood and put his hands on his hips. "So am I."

"I don't know why. He's lost it before and nobody got this mad."

Jason narrowed his eyes. "Lost what?"

"His iPod. He lost it again. It's his new one, the one Mom bought after he lost the white one." Then she tilted her head. "Why are you mad at him?"

"Mom replaced the white one?"

"Yeah." She slapped her hand over her mouth and her eyes grew large. "Oops! I wasn't supposed to tell that. Please don't tell Mommy that I told you."

"Don't worry." He started to walk away, miffed that on top of everything else, Lucy was teaching their daughter to keep secrets from him. Then he stopped and turned back around. "Bren, what color is his new iPod?"

Her eyes were focused on the TV screen. "Silver. It's cool. Mom had his real dad's birthday put on it."

Jason flashed hot, his mouth instantly dry. *226. 2-26. February 26.*

Could his son have vandalized the Whitman cemetery?

All of the things that had happened to Abby over the past days raced through Jason's mind. The police stressed the events were *probably* connected to the accident. Probably. Not absolutely. Jason had been so focused on the incidents all being done by the same person that he hadn't seen what should have been obvious early on. The attacks were inconsistent. There were two entirely different levels of things happening to Abby: Vandalism and mischief versus death threats and attempts on her life. Careless loss of an iPod in the cemetery versus a break-in so sophisticated that there was no trace of evidence.

Bryce didn't have access to a boat, so Jason felt sure he wasn't behind the more serious issues. But, damn, why hadn't Jason seen the inconsistencies sooner?

Jason paced outside the den. He went back over the

events around Abby's slit tires. Bryce had made no attempt to hide his displeasure when they'd taken Abby into the house after she'd collapsed on the street.

That morning when he'd come to pick them up he'd been moody. Jason had written it off to a teenage boy being abruptly awakened. Abby's Explorer had been sitting in the driveway and Bryce hadn't even asked why they hadn't driven her car over to pick up Jason's.

Why would Bryce take such a sudden turn? He was always responsible beyond his years, so protective of his mother and sister—

Protective! That was the key.

Brenna's words from a telephone conversation a few days ago came back to him: *"Bryce said if we're all real good, you'll come home. I've been good, Daddy. When are you coming home?"*

Abby was a threat to reuniting their family. Even though Jason had been clear, he'd thought the children understood...but what if Lucy was feeding them something different?

He dialed Bryce's cell. It rang six times and rolled to voice mail—as it had every time Jason called him for the past two days.

Then he called Lucy's cell—and the same thing happened.

Goddammit, where was she?

He looked at the clock. His next appointment was due any minute.

Jason tried Abby's cell. It went directly to voice mail. Battery must be completely dead.

Then he heard Mr. Jefferies come into the waiting area. Jason was tempted beyond words to tell the man that he had a family emergency and couldn't see him now. But Steve Jefferies had some serious problems; it would be irresponsible to cancel the appointment.

Stop panicking. Abby was fine. She'd gone to see her dad. Maybe she'd be here by the time Jason was finished with Mr. Jefferies. And maybe Lucy would be back, too. Then Jason could hunt down Bryce and demand some answers.

He took several deep breaths and went to take care of business like the level-headed professional he was supposed to be.

Maggie walked through the front hall and saw Uncle Father with his head stuck in the coat closet. He was making grunting noises, like he was having trouble with something.

"Uncle Father, what *are* you doing?" She used the same tone that Mrs. White used on Maggie when she thought she was doing something silly.

He jerked his head out of the coats. He looked like she felt when she got caught sneaking cookies before dinner.

"Oh. I thought you were in your room," he said. "Is Mrs. White here?"

He was breathing hard. His face looked like it really hurt and it made her sad to look at him.

"She went to the grocery store. Do you need help?" she asked.

"I was trying to get the video camera case. The strap is caught on something way back in there. I'm having trouble getting back there with these sore ribs."

"Uncle Father," she sighed and shook her head, "I'm

supposed to do things like this for you." She got on her knees and crawled under the coats.

She found where the camera strap was caught on an umbrella and untangled it. When she pulled it out and stood up, Uncle Father had tears on his face.

"It's okay," she said, patting his shoulder. "You'll get better. I don't mind helping you."

"I know you don't." He smiled, even though he was still crying. "You're a very good girl."

"Why do you want the video camera?" she asked.

"I need to take some video of the church for the insurance company."

"You're supposed to be in bed. Do you want me to take the pictures?"

"No, no." He wiped his face dry. "I need something to do. Lying around is too boring."

"I know!" Maggie hated not having things to do. Now that Uncle Father was feeling a little better, she wished Abby would call her to work on flowers again.

He said, "Could you carry the bag over to the church for me and get the camera out and ready to record?"

"Sure." She smiled and picked up the bag. Maybe it was too soon to work with Abby again. Uncle Father did still need her.

As soon as Mr. Jefferies left Jason's office, he went into the den.

"Did Abby come in?"

Bren looked up from her show. "Nope." Then she added in a disappointed voice, "Is she coming here?"

"She's supposed to." Jason's nerves were buzzing with worry; this wasn't the time to address her attitude toward

Abby and the future of their family with his daughter. That conversation would take lots of TLC.

He went into the kitchen and called Abby's father.

"Mr. Whitman, Jason Coble. Is Abby there?"

"Hello, Jason. No, I haven't seen Abby for a couple of days."

"If she comes by, would you have her call me?" Jason wondered if the man would remember.

"Sure. I'll leave a note on the refrigerator, so I won't forget."

"Thanks."

Jason hung up. He looked up the number for Randall and Roberts, then called there.

Jim Roberts answered.

"Hello, Jim, this is Jason Coble. Has Abby dropped off the rest of the flowers for the Robard funeral yet?"

"No. And she's cutting it pretty close. It's not like her."

Jason's stomach dropped to his knees. "She hasn't called, either?"

"No."

"Have her call me when she shows up." *If she shows up.*

As he disconnected the call, Jason closed his eyes. Where in the hell was she?

He thought about the text message. Something about it had bothered him when he'd read it, but Bren had arrived and the thought had skittered away.

He brought it up on the screen again.

phone almost dead stopping to c dad c u later

Then he brought up her previous text.

Deputy Bigelow and I are having a party. Wish you were here.

Shit! That second text didn't sound like Abby sent it.

"Brenna!" Jason called as he hurried into the den. "Shut off the TV, sweetie. We need to go do something."

"Daaad, it's almost over."

"You can finish it when we get back." Jason shut off the TV himself. "This is an emergency."

With the word "emergency," Brenna looked at him with fearful eyes and grabbed her shoes. "What kind of emergency?"

"We need to find your brother." *And Abby.* Jason prayed the two were in different places.

"Is he okay?" Brenna asked in a small voice.

Jason stopped and put his hand on the top of her head. "I'm sure he's fine. He just isn't where he's supposed to be."

"So he's in trouble." At least she looked more sad than afraid now.

"Maybe. Now go get in Abby's Explorer," he said. "I'll be right out."

He watched her from the window as she got in the SUV. Then, just in case, he went to the gun safe and got out his handgun. Then he untucked his shirt and slipped the gun in the back waistband of his pants.

As he grabbed the Explorer's keys from the kitchen counter where Abby had left them, he called Sergeant Kitterman. The police could comb the roads for Abby much more effectively than Jason could. Jason's first responsibility was to find Bryce; he just couldn't turn his son over to the police for vandalism until he talked to him first.

When the Sergeant came on the line, Jason said, "I can't get a hold of Abby and she didn't show up at the funeral home after she parted company with your deputy."

"What's she driving?" Kitterman asked.

"My car. A silver Nissan Altima." He gave Kitterman the license plate number. "I spoke to her when she was pulling out onto the road from her lane. That was about twelve-fifty."

"I'll be in touch," Kitterman said and hung up.

When Jason got into the Explorer, he asked Brenna, "Do you know where Bryce likes to hang out? Is he friends with anyone in particular now?"

"He's all into this comic book stuff. He took me to the comic shop one day after school."

"The one on Market Street?"

She nodded. "Are you going to yell at him about the iPod?" She looked like she wanted to melt into the seat.

He reached back and patted her on the knee. "Don't worry, your secret is safe. There's something else I need to talk to him about."

"You said it was an emergency," Brenna said.

"It is. Bryce didn't go to school today like he was supposed to."

"I know that. Mom was mad because he was supposed to babysit me after school."

"And he's always home when he's supposed to babysit you. So I want to find him and make sure he's okay."

She frowned. "You think he had a wreck or something."

Jason backed the Explorer out of the drive and muttered, "Or something."

Jason took his daughter by the hand and led her in to the comic and card shop. It was filled with pimply-faced teenage boys and a few Goth-looking girls. There were two aisles. Bryce wasn't in either one of them.

Jason went to the register. It was manned by a guy wearing a black T-shirt with skulls on it. He had spiky hair and a goatee. He was too old for the spiky hair and T-shirt by about a decade.

After Jason introduced himself, he asked, "Do you know my stepson, Bryce Patrick?"

The man smiled. "Sure, he's in here all of the time."

"Has he been in here today?"

The man's eyes went narrow and he got busy straightening the comics in the case. "Hey, I don't get in the middle of family crap."

"I'm worried. He didn't come home, and it's not at all like him."

The man looked at Jason. "Well, if it's like that." He shrugged. "You know how it is, man, parents come in here all of the time trying to make it seem like I'm supposed to keep track of their kids—usin' me for a babysitter."

Jason just waited.

"Yeah, Bryce was here earlier. Left with Toby about eleven o'clock."

"Toby?" Jason didn't recall any friends named Toby.

"Toby Smith. His grandma lives in town. He and Bryce seem to be tight."

"His grandma? Toby doesn't live in Preston?"

The man shook his head. "Visits a lot lately, though."

"Do you know where his grandma lives?"

The man looked perturbed again. "Dude, you're pushing your luck. It's not my job to keep track of every freakin' one."

"Hey." Jason cast a glance at his daughter. "Easy." Then he asked, "Do you happen to know if they took Bryce's car? I didn't see it out there."

"Well, then I'd say they took Bryce's car, wouldn't you?"

Jason decided since he'd already crossed the line, might as well ask one more question. "Do you know what Toby drives?"

The man huffed. "Gray Impala."

Jason's breath locked in his lungs. "Dark tinted windows?" Under the circumstances, that Impala had been around Abby too many times to ignore.

"Yeah. Now get outta here, you're freakin' out the customers."

"Does Toby have access to a boat?" Why would he go after Abby? Had he been the one to place the 911 call? Or did it have more to do with Bryce? Dear God, he hoped not.

"How the hell should I know!" The man lowered his voice. "Get out."

Brenna was already tugging on Jason's hand, trying to drag him to the door.

Once out on the sidewalk, Jason knelt in front of his daughter. I don't want you to worry. Bryce is probably just off with this friend having fun."

She nodded solemnly.

"Let's take a walk around the block." Jason wanted to see if that gray Impala was parked nearby.

Bren took his hand and walked silently by his side.

They made the circuit. No gray Impala. That gave Jason hope that Bryce and Toby had gone separate ways.

Jason's cell phone rang.

It was Kitterman. "We found your car about a quarter mile from Abby's lane."

"And Abby?" Jason asked, his heart swelling with fear.

"No. It looks like she just pulled to the side of the road. One of the tires is flat. The flowers are still in the backseat. No purse. No sign of struggle."

"She lost her purse in the fire. She did have a cell. Was it in the car?"

"No."

"She's not answering it. Can you use it to locate her?"

"As long as the battery is still in it."

"I think it's dead."

"Doesn't matter; as long as it's inside the phone we can locate it. Give me her number."

Jason recited it, then he heard paper tear and Kitterman tell someone to start locating it.

Jason asked, "Did someone check to make sure she didn't walk back to the shop? That'd be her nearest phone if her cell's dead."

"She's not there."

Jason explained his theory that someone other than Abby had sent that last text message. Then he said, "There's a car that may be involved. I've noticed it enough times to make me suspicious. A late model gray Impala with dark-tinted windows. I just found out it belongs to a guy named Toby Smith."

Jason was so dry that his tongue rasped against the lining of his mouth as he explained how the driver of that gray Impala had befriended his son. He stopped short of saying Bryce had vandalized the cemetery and slit Abby's tires. He'd give Bryce the chance to turn himself in. Things would go much better for him that way.

"Do you think it's more than coincidence that he's hanging out with your kid?" Kitterman asked.

"I don't believe in coincidence."

"Neither do I," Kitterman said. "I'll get this info out to our patrols. And I'll see if I can find anything on Toby Smith. Have any idea what he looks like?"

"No. But you can ask the owner at Hi Flying Comics in Preston. Toby hangs out there." Jason was certain that the police would have better luck getting information out of the owner than he could.

He almost asked Kitterman to have the patrols keep an eye out for Bryce's car. But he wanted to check all of his friends' houses and their hangouts before he got the police involved in locating his son. Besides, he didn't want the police to divide their attention from finding Abby.

"All right," Kitterman said. "I'll keep you posted— hang on."

There were muffled voices, as if Kitterman had covered the mouthpiece with his hand. When he spoke to Jason again, he said, "The battery must be out of her phone. We can't locate it."

Jason closed his eyes and sent a rare prayer to heaven for Abby's safety.

What had seemed like a really good idea a few hours ago didn't look so great now that Bryce had Abby unconscious in his back seat, her hands bound behind her with duct tape. What had sounded like a logical plan to fix more than one problem, now felt more like he'd started an avalanche.

Why hadn't he thought this through more completely? What if he scared the crap out of her and she told anyway? Then both he and his mom were in deep shit.

He beat his palms against the steering wheel. Fuck. Fuck. Fuck.

Tears burned his eyes. He sniffed and refused to cry. That only backed them up in his chest until he felt he'd choke on them.

Get a grip!

It was done. He couldn't undo it. God! He should have gone with his instincts and made certain she hadn't seen him. It would have been harder to do, but then he could just dump her somewhere and no one would ever know.

He kept driving around country roads, afraid to take the next, now necessary, step.

His cell rang. Shit, it was probably his dad again.

It wasn't.

"Where the hell are you?" Toby sounded pissed. "Something go wrong?"

"No."

"Then why aren't you here yet?"

"I don't know, man." He ducked his head and swiped the sweat from his forehead on his T-shirt sleeve. "I just don't think we should do this. It was a bad idea."

"Too-fucking-late. There's no going back now. Get your ass here, before the cops find you."

Bryce shot a look at his back seat. How long would the chloroform Toby had given him to use keep her out?

Toby was right. How would he explain if the cops stopped him?

All he could do now was hope the plan worked.

"I'll be right there."

CHAPTER 26

Jason called Bryce again, not expecting him to answer. He regretted sending that text message. It might only serve to delay Bryce's response since he now knew he was in trouble.

Jason drove past all of Bryce's friends' houses, the park and Jeter's arcade. His son's car wasn't at any of those places. He decided to head out to Abby's. Maybe he could find a clue the police had missed—or maybe Bryce was out there breaking windows. Either was a long shot, but it beat the hell out of sitting still doing nothing.

As he drove past Randall and Roberts, he saw Lucy standing on the side street, talking to a man in a suit. Jason circled around the block. He had to double-park and put on his flashers because the streets were so packed with cars calling on the Robard family. He felt more comfortable leaving Brenna in the car on this little traveled side street for a couple of minutes than letting her hear what he was about to say to her mother.

When he got out, he realized the man Lucy was with was Senator Robard.

From the immediate guilty looks on both Lucy and the senator, it didn't take a nuclear physicist to figure out there was something going on between them. Apparently that was one accusation Jessica Robard had right.

Jason now understood at least one of the secrets that had been making Lucy act strangely of late. He hoped this was the only one. And he hoped there would be no fallout from this poor judgment that would affect the children.

The senator made a quick comment to Lucy, then disappeared back into the funeral home.

"What are you doing here?" Lucy snapped. It was clear she'd been crying.

"Jesus, Lucy, really? You dropped off our daughter at the curb, without even making certain I was available, so you could hook up with the senator at his dead son's viewing?"

She sniffed and turned her back on him. "You don't understand."

"Oh, I'm pretty sure I do. And so will anyone who got a look at you two out here."

She looked at him with venom in her eyes. "It doesn't matter. He doesn't want to see me anymore—just because he's feeling guilty because he was with me when Kyle had his accident. I have to make him see—"

"I thought I made myself perfectly clear." Jason didn't have time for Lucy's drama; he'd stopped to deal with an issue. "When you drop Bren off, either you walk her in, or call me to come out and get her."

"If you're so worried about perverts, maybe you should move your office out of the house."

Jason referred all pedophiles and sexual deviants—not that there were many seeking help in little buttoned-up

Preston—to another doctor who specialized. Lucy knew that. But he didn't take the bait.

"If you ever pull a stunt like this again—"

"What? What are you going to threaten me with now? Jesus, you treat me like I'm a twelve-year-old!" she snapped.

Twelve-year-old was about right, but that wasn't his current argument. "This isn't about you and me. It's about keeping Brenna safe. Now I'm going to get her out of the car and you're going to behave like a responsible mother and take her home."

"Bryce was supposed to be home to watch her—"

"Yeah, about that," Jason said. "Do you have any idea where he is?"

Her gaze shifted away. "He's an adult."

"He's a *boy* who needs to know his parents give a shit where he is and what he's doing."

Her head snapped up. "Well, *you* are not his parent."

He literally bit his tongue to keep words that would only inflame the situation inside his mouth. "Listen, I have to go. Will you take Brenna?"

"Of course. Stop making it sound like I abandoned her."

Jason knew he was partly to blame for the derailing of this conversation. "Okay...all right." He went to the Explorer and opened the rear passenger door. "Come on, Peanut. You're going home with Mommy now."

Although he'd shielded her from hearing the argument, her serious eyes said she was well aware it had transpired. He felt like a heel.

Before he left her at Lucy's side, he hugged her. "Everything is okay, sweetie."

"Love you, Daddy."

"You, too." Then he said to Lucy. "If you hear from Bryce, have him call me."

She turned and walked away without another word. Bren followed solemnly behind. He watched until they got into Lucy's car before he turned for the Explorer.

He'd almost shared his fears about Bryce with Lucy. He wanted her to know Bryce's sudden shift to deviousness and irresponsibility was serious. At the same time he feared that if she knew, she would do whatever she could to help Bryce cover his tracks. God knew, Bryce had done it often enough for her.

Just as Jason was heading back to the Explorer, he heard a girl call, "Dr. Coble! Dr. Coble!"

He looked up and saw Maggie on the porch of the rectory. "Wait, Dr. Coble!" She sounded panicked.

Maybe she knew something about Abby.

Jason trotted across the street. They met on the sidewalk at the bottom of the rectory steps. She was holding a video camera.

"What is it, Maggie? What's wrong?"

"I wasn't supposed to look at the video. Uncle Father told me it wasn't finished and put it on his desk at home. I just wanted to see the pictures of the church, I promise, that's all I wanted to do." Maggie was talking so fast her words slurred together.

"Whoa, slow down. Why are you so upset?"

Her blue eyes widened. "I saw this—and I didn't know what to do. I prayed to St. Jude—and he sent you! He answered my prayers."

"Why did you need to pray to St. Jude?"

"This!" She held up the small video camera. "Uncle Father...he...he's dying!"

Bryce got out of his car in front of the old tin-roofed fishing shack where Jason had taught him how to gut and clean a fish. It was in the woods by the river—far enough from the road that they could leave Abby here and no one would happen across her.

"Put up a fight, did she?" Toby asked, eyeing the scratches on Bryce's face and arms.

"You said it would knock her out right away."

"Did I? Maybe I was wrong."

"Damn right you were wrong." None of this was going according to plan. "I wish we hadn't started this."

"Man, I'm hanging my ass out for you," Toby said as he walked to the passenger side of the car. "It's *your* mom we're protecting. You want her to go to jail?"

"No, but, if the hypnosis didn't make Abby remember, maybe she won't ever—"

"*You* told *me* that your dad said she remembered tail-lights. Sounds to me like it's already started. Do you want to wake up every day for the rest of your life thinking that this will be the day they come and haul your mom off to jail? Besides, this fixes two of your problems at once. She won't tell on your mom for killing the senator's kid *and* she'll stop screwing your dad."

Bryce regretted ever confiding in Toby. If Bryce had kept his worries to himself, he wouldn't be in this mess right now.

"I've been thinking," Toby said, opening the rear passenger door. "We need a more permanent solution."

"Permanent?" Bryce opened the driver's side rear door.

Abby was on her side, her wrists duct-taped together. Her hair covered her face.

"Yeah, like as in for eternity," Toby said.

The plan was to let her know they meant business, maybe threaten to hurt her dad, make sure she was too frightened to ever tell and "persuade" her to stop seeing Bryce's dad. Stupid as it sounded now, it had seemed logical when Toby had laid it out.

Bryce looked at Toby, trying to figure out if he was serious. Toby was an excellent bullshitter, loved to yank your chain.

"Nah," Bryce said. "Stick to the plan."

"No, dude. Can't you see? This is way better."

"I was on board for scaring her," Bryce said, wondering at what point he actually thought he had control of this situation. "Not...that."

Toby took a look at Abby's bound hands. "Aww, Jesus, is that the best you could do? Cross the wrists, man, don't tape them side by side."

"She's out. What does it matter?" Bryce said, almost wishing she'd awakened and gotten free before they got here. "We're sticking to what we'd planned."

"Shut up and grab her feet," Toby said.

Bryce's heart was beating too fast and he was getting lightheaded. "You're shittin' me." Toby had to be messing with him, seeing how far he could bluff Bryce into going.

Toby looked him in the eye. "No man. This is the *only* way."

He looked dead serious.

Bryce had had enough. He put his hands on his hips. "Why do you care what we do with her? She didn't see you, you can walk."

"Because you're my friend, man. And this bitch is fucking up your life."

"We stick to the original plan," Bryce said firmly, his heart's erratic beats pounding in his ears. Once he showed Toby he couldn't be pushed, maybe he'd stop this ridiculous game. "She's my problem. I decide what happens to her."

Toby shook his head, as if Bryce was missing the entire point. "Why put a plug in the dam when you can drain the whole lake? This will take care of everything for good."

Bryce pressed his lips together and shook his head, too afraid that if he opened his mouth, his voice would show him for the frightened kid he was.

"Did you get the gun from the glove box of your dad's car?" Toby asked.

"It wasn't there." Thank God. Now maybe Toby would shut up about killing her.

Toby gave Bryce a soulless grin that made him want to puke, and pulled a pair of latex gloves out of his pocket. "Then we'll have to improvise."

CHAPTER 27

Maggie's face was streaked with tears. She tugged on Jason's arm, bobbing up and down a little as she held the video camera in front of his face. "I don't want Uncle Father to die! You have to do something!"

"Hold on, Maggie," Jason said. "Where is he?"

"I don't know! I can't find him."

"What makes you think he's dying?"

"This!" She shook the video camera. "He *said* it."

Jason needed to get moving. Find Bryce. Find Abby.

"Where's Mrs. White?"

"Shopping. I was supposed to be babysitting Uncle Father and I lost him. He was supposed to be taking pictures of the church. But he wasn't—" She flipped open the little screen and pushed a button. "Look!"

Jason and Maggie stood in the afternoon shadow of the rectory so Jason could see the screen, at least a little. The picture was dark. He squinted and leaned close, shielding the screen from as much light as he could. It was Father Kevin. It looked like he was in...a confessional.

"Let's go inside where I can see this better," he said.

Maggie immediately started up the steps, pulling him along with her. "We have to hurry."

Once inside, Jason took the camera from her and hit play.

The sound was low. He turned it up.

"With my death, I am committing myself to eternal damnation. I do it of my own free will, a sacrifice that must be made. I see no other way than to embark on the path I now take. Once I am dead, both my beloved Maggie and my sister's life's work will be saved."

Maggie said, "See. He's dying!"

Jason shushed her, feeling his entire world was spinning out of control. What in the hell else could happen today? "Hold on, we need to listen." He rewound the video and listened to what he'd missed.

"A few months ago I discovered gross misuse of funds and illegal transportation of goods in the organization, Children of Conflict, of which I am director. Using the face of Christian charity, this money has gone against everything Jesus Christ our Lord and Savior stands for.

"Through murder and intimidation, threats and blackmail, they have taken control of our organization. I am certain the helicopter crash which claimed my sister and her husband's lives in Afghanistan was no accident. Unfortunately, I have no proof. God will sit in judgment on those who are responsible.

"But I do have proof that COC has been diverted from its Christly work. All proof, including a letter from my sister written before her death, is being held by a person of my choosing, who will upon my death deliver it to the authorities. That threat of exposure is the only thing that has kept me alive this long. They have demanded I turn the papers over, or they will take my dear Maggie from me. They feel assured that as an ordained priest, I will not take my own life. They underestimate my commitment against the vileness of their purpose. I have decided I would rather commit my soul to eternal damnation than be a party to their evil deeds.

"Someone has been sent to intimidate and manipulate me." He absently touched his swollen face and Jason knew the priest's injuries were not caused by a fall down concrete steps. "I would gladly give my life, but cannot sacrifice my beloved niece. And now the poison is spreading—and I am responsible."

At this point Father Kevin closed his eyes—actually one eye, as the other was still swollen closed—and took a deep breath. That breath set off a coughing spell that was so clearly painful that Jason winced."

"In a moment of confusion and desperation I was too weak to do what I know must be done; that night I put my death in the hands of God. I am ashamed to say that the life that was taken was not my own, but that of Kyle Robard, an innocent. I called for help, but I'd been followed and was forced to leave the scene. These people have gone to a lot of time and trouble to establish their system. They are not about to let my conscience get in the way.

"Now Abby Whitman's life is in danger because she was at the wrong place at the wrong time. At first I thought she was keeping my secret voluntarily, but now know differently. I have to end this."

At this point, Father Kevin made the sign of the cross and began: "O my God, I am heartily sorry for having offended you—"

Jason stopped the video with his heart beating violently

in his chest. Father Kevin was sick all right, sick at heart.

COC served children in war-torn countries—Afghanistan, Northern Africa—hotbeds of terrorism and illegal arms trade. Who knew what kind of things Father Kevin's organization was being used for.

And if the priest was responsible for Kyle Robard's death, well, that had pushed him completely over the edge.

Father Kevin's car *was* white. Taillights…Abby saw taillights. She must have come upon it while Father Kevin was still there. That's why he'd made that pleading call for her not to tell.

But there was no way that Father Kevin broke into Abby's house and left that message on the mirror.

…*now I know differently.* Father Kevin knew who had been threatening Abby. If he could find Father Kevin…

"You're sure he's not in the house?" Jason asked.

"Uh-huh."

"Did you check to see if his car is in the garage?"

"It's not. It's been gone for days. Uncle Father has been driving the church van."

No doubt while his car was being repaired.

"And the van?" Jason asked. "Is it here?"

"No."

"I need to look at your uncle's desk in the church. Maybe there's a clue about where he went," he said.

"Okay." Maggie led him through the house and out the back door. Passing the key rack, she picked up a set of keys attached to a crucifix keychain.

"Are those keys usually there?" Jason asked.

She stopped and tilted her head. "Only if Uncle Father is home."

Jason urged her on, hoping there would be a clue in his office that could lead him both to the priest and whoever had Abby.

Once they reached the side door, Maggie fumbled with the keys, selecting the one for the outer door. Jason had to fist his hands to keep from snatching the keys and trying them himself. Finally she found the one that opened the door.

He followed her down the hall to Father Kevin's office. Once inside the door, Jason looked around the cluttered office for something obvious. Of course it wasn't going to be that easy.

He went to the desk. There was a smudged double old-fashioned glass sitting next to the blotter. On the blotter were doodles of the COC logo.

Jason tried to open the desk drawers. All but the large center one were locked. He rifled through that one. It yielded nothing but the norm: pens, pencils, paperclips, tape, a pair of reader glasses, and a pad of Post-its.

"May I see those keys?" He put his hand out and Maggie handed them over.

Luckily, there was only one key small enough to be the desk key. The top drawer held a nearly empty bottle of Scotch. The store receipt was still taped to it. Father Kevin had bought it yesterday.

Abby's middle-of-the-night caller had sounded drunk.

Jason quickly went through the rest of the drawers, including the file drawer. After glancing in each of the hanging folders, he decided Father Kevin had been very careful not to leave clues here.

The police had checked all garages in Preston, looking for a white vehicle with appropriate body damage and hadn't come up with one. If Father Kevin had been forced from the accident scene, whoever was watching him wouldn't have allowed his vehicle to be repaired locally.

Jason called Kitterman and, with a stomach full of frustration and dread, explained what was happening with Father Kevin. "We need to have your patrols looking for the church van. Maybe we can find him before he does something rash." Jason chose his words carefully; he hadn't been able to convince Maggie to leave his side.

"Got it," Kitterman said. "Is there a chance he's out there on the same road executing his original plan?"

"Doubtful. People normally resort to a different...tactic second time around." Jason paused. "Whoever is here watching him is after Abby. Could be Toby Smith—the gray Impala guy." Jason still could not understand how Bryce fit into this. Vandalism was one thing, but could he actually have gotten caught up into something bigger?

Jason kept thinking of how Father Kevin's face looked after his "accident." Those injuries were inflicted by a person with no conscience. God help Abby—and Bryce, too—if that's whose hands they were in.

"If you've been seeing his car, you're probably right. We're already looking for him and his vehicle. No luck yet. I doubt his name is Toby Smith, but we're searching DMV and credit cards to see if we get a hit."

Desperation clawed at Jason's insides. Then he realized it could be even worse. "What if Bryce is still with him?"

"I think it's time to track your kid's cell phone."

The instant Bryce saw the knife, *his* knife, in Toby's gloved hand, his breath became trapped in his lungs. Toby was fucking serious.

"How'd you get my knife?" Bryce asked, feeling his cargo pants pockets. Abby still lay in the back seat of his car. Both rear doors were open with Toby on the passenger side and Bryce on the driver's.

"You make a horrible criminal. I've had this knife since this morning," Toby said in a light tone—as if they were talking about catching fly balls or the latest DC comic issue. But there had been a silent shift in him; same friendly guy on the outside, but beneath the skin there was a dark and sharp-edged undercurrent that scared the crap out of Bryce.

"We're not going to cut her," Bryce said with as much authority as he could force into his voice. He tightened his throat to keep from puking. "Just tie her up and leave her here for a while. Let her know we're serious. Stick to the plan."

"Don't be a pussy. She'll promise anything now, but once you let her go, you're toast. It'll be easy. We'll dump her in the river. Maybe nobody'll ever find her and you won't even have to come up with an alibi."

The ice in Toby's eyes made Bryce swallow his protests. Toby looked like a shark about to go into a frenzy over bloody chum. He was set on killing Abby Whitman. The dude was a psychopath. And Bryce had no doubt, Toby wouldn't hesitate to kill him if he got in the way.

He blinked rapidly against the tears burning his eyes. He couldn't let Toby know how scared he was.

God, how was he going to get out of this and keep Abby alive, too?

Toby was three inches taller, thirty pounds heavier, ripped, *and* he had the knife. Bryce had to outthink him, play smart, and hope someone had found his dad's car and was looking for Abby right now.

He was gauging if he'd be able to jump in the driver's seat and take off before Toby could get in the car.

Not likely.

He'd taken the battery out of Abby's cell phone right after he'd sent the text, just like Toby had instructed. If Bryce could get the battery back into her phone without Toby noticing—they might use her phone to locate her.

Then he had another idea. But he needed a little time. He forced a shaky laugh. "Guess you need to teach me some shit, huh?"

"You have no idea," Toby said. "First, I'm going to teach you how to keep bitches like this from ruining your life."

Toby ducked and leaned into the car.

"Wait!" Bryce yelled, bending to look at him across the car's interior. *Stall. Stall. Think of a way out of this.* "Don't kill her in my car! She'll bleed all over."

"See, learning already." Toby saluted him with the knife. Even when talking murder, he still showed the innocence of a hometown hero—as long as you didn't look deep in his eyes. "Besides, I'm not going to kill her. You are."

For a stunned second, Bryce said nothing. Toby held his gaze, never blinking.

He just handed you the ball. Grab it and run.

"I guess she *is* my problem," Bryce finally said. "You've risked enough for me, man. It'd be safer for you not to be here when I do it. That way the police won't come after you as an accessory."

"You'll need help carrying her down to the river." He spoke as if this was a matter of simple logistics.

Cold shot through Bryce so severely his teeth chattered.

"Um." Bryce swallowed and clenched his teeth. "Guess we should get her out of the car first."

"That'd be a good start."

"Go on and pull her out your side," Bryce said. "Maybe she'll wake up when she hits the ground. I want her to know she's going to die." He tried to sound callous, but to his ears he just sounded scared.

When Toby reached for Abby, Bryce turned his back and reached into his pocket. He kept his phone close to his body and typed in a message to his dad. It had to look innocent, just in case Toby got a look at it.

gone fishing

He heard rustling behind him as Toby pulled Abby from the car. Bryce hit send, then put it back in his pocket and groped for Abby's phone and battery. Once he had the battery back in it, he could stash it someplace Toby wouldn't see it.

Suddenly, something pricked the middle of Bryce's back and he nearly shit his pants.

"Dude," Toby said. "You disappoint me." The knife-point pushed a little deeper.

He heard Toby moving again and realized he'd crawled across Abby to get to Bryce's side of the car.

Toby moved out of the car and stood behind him, somehow maintaining steady pressure on the knife. Bryce kept his back to him, trying to get the battery in place with one hand while it was still in his pocket.

Toby's left hand reached around, palm up. "Give it."

Bryce hesitated.

The knife stabbed deeply enough that Bryce felt a trickle of blood run down the small of his back.

Sickened with defeat, he dropped the cell and the battery into Toby's hand.

"And yours, too."

Bryce pulled out his cell and put it in Toby's hand.

"I actually thought you might have the stomach for it," Toby said. "I'm rarely wrong. Let's see what you were up to.

"'Gone fishing.' How clever. Now the clock is ticking." Toby almost sounded excited.

"It's late. If I didn't tell Dad something, he'd be looking for me." It was a desperate grab; he doubted Toby would believe it.

Toby flipped out Bryce's battery. Then he dropped both phones on the ground and stomped them with his heel. "I suppose you know this is a game changer. But Plan B isn't so very different from Plan A. Either way you murder Abby Whitman. It's just a matter of murder—or murder-suicide."

Toby had been setting him up for days. He was so fucking stupid!

Bryce started to see lights dance before his eyes. He forced himself to keep breathing. Plan A or B. Either way Abby was dead. Either way, for all intents and purposes, Bryce was, too.

He prayed for the strength to keep his head; it was his only ticket to safety. His dad always said people never did anything without a reason. That if you could unearth that reason, you could figure out a way around it. Bryce had to figure out Toby's reason if he was going to stay alive.

"Why do you care if she's dead or not?" Bryce asked, willing his voice not to break.

"I don't," Toby said. The knife continued to press

against Bryce's back. "She's just a job. I never leave my work unfinished, and I never leave a trail. That's why they pay me the big bucks."

"Who wants her dead?" What could she have done to make someone hire a crazy bastard like Toby?

"I'm afraid that's classified information," Toby said.

"What does it matter? You're going to kill me." Bryce felt the tears rolling down his cheeks and was humiliated by his fear. He should be strong. He should fight. But he was going to die like a coward.

"And I'm sorry about that. I kinda like you. But I do have professional standards to maintain, no divulging the client, ever." He jabbed again with the knife. "Now, let's get your girl out of the car, shall we? She's starting to wake up."

CHAPTER 28

Someone was lightly slapping Abby's cheeks, calling her name. Nausea rolled in her stomach.

Birds chirped and frogs croaked. A breeze moved over her.

I'm outdoors.

Sleepwalking?

"Abby. Wake up." It sounded like Jason's son.

She forced her eyes open.

Daylight.

Green leaves blurred overhead. An indistinct face between her and the leaves.

She was lying on the ground.

The nausea swelled.

Rolling to her side, she gagged with dry heaves.

After a moment, she gasped to regain her breath with her eyes watering.

"Abby?" Bryce. He was leaning over her.

She tried to get up, but her arms were bound behind her.

That realization shot adrenaline coursing through her body, clearing her head. Her heels scrabbled against the ground in an effort to get away.

She had stopped behind his Civic. He'd asked her to
get jumper cables from his back seat. When she'd leaned
in, he'd come from behind and covered her nose and
mouth with a cloth.

Get away! She scooted on her rear end, legs frantically
pumping to put more space between them.

Bryce's face and arms showed the scratches from the
struggle she'd put up earlier. But he didn't look angry.
And he made no move to stop her as she pushed away
from him.

"I'm so sorry," he whispered with hitched breath. She
now saw his face was wet with tears.

She tried to ask, "Why?" but all that came out was
a croak. On the second attempt, it came out as a raspy
whisper.

Bryce said nothing, but he cast a glance over his shoulder.

Now she saw there was someone standing just behind
him. Someone with a handgun pointed at his head. Her
view of his face showed his profile…there was something familiar about him.

"What's going on?" she demanded.

The guy with the gun ignored her question. "This
really would have been less painful for you if Bryce had
brought the gun from the car. Where did it go, Abby?"

"I gave it back to Jason." Her answer was automatic—
and stupid. She had to start thinking.

The guy made a *tsk*ing sound. "You've been screwing
up my plans for days now. I really should have killed you
that night in the marsh. You can thank Father Kevin for
the gift of these last days." Then he tapped the barrel of
his gun against the side of Bryce's head. "Get her on her
feet, man. Time's a wastin'."

Marsh? Was this the 911 caller? What did Father Kevin have to do with it?

Father Kevin. Something...it finally clicked. This guy had been in the church sanctuary after she and Maggie had returned from Tidewater Manor. The profile of his nose was very distinct.

Bryce got up and grabbed Abby under the arms, hauling her to her feet. The world spun around her; dizziness caused her stomach to roll once again. She swayed and would have fallen, except Bryce grabbed her by the shoulders and steadied her.

"Walk," the guy with the gun said.

"Who are you and want do you want?" Abby planted her feet and refused to move. She wasn't going without a fight.

"Aw, for Christ's sake," the guy said. He slapped her across the face.

Abby staggered, but stayed on her feet.

"Hey!" Bryce lunged toward the guy and was met with a stiff backhand that sent him spinning to the ground.

"You two need to stop making things harder on yourselves. Now get moving."

Bryce's lip was bleeding. He swiped it with the back of his hand and got up off the ground. He put a hand on Abby's upper arm and urged her to start walking.

"No!" she said.

The guy extended his arm, putting the gun barrel against Bryce's temple. "Have it your way." He was about the pull the trigger.

"Stop!" Abby shouted.

She had to keep them alive as long as she could. Maybe they could somehow get out of this. She turned and started moving in the direction the guy had pointed.

She had no idea where they were. She scanned the area, trying to get her bearings, but came no closer to figuring it out. When she stumbled, Bryce put an arm around her waist to help her along.

Leaning close she whispered, "What the hell is going on?"

Bryce kept his eyes straight ahead and said, "We're going to die."

By the time Jason finished talking with Kitterman, Mrs. White had returned from shopping. He quickly explained the situation—telling her she'd have to wait for answers to her endless string of questions—and left Maggie in her care.

Just as he was going out the front door of the rectory, a text message came in.

It was from Bryce. Finally.

gone fishing

"What the . . . ?" Why had he sent this now, after avoiding Jason all day?

And Bryce hated to fish. Jason had tried to get him interested, but had given up when Bryce turned twelve.

Bryce *hated to fish*.

Oh, my God.

Jason sprinted to the Explorer. As soon as he put it in gear and started moving, he called Kitterman. "I know where they are."

Bryce was about to piss himself by the time they reached the river. But he wasn't going to cry like a little kid while Abby's eyes were dry and focused.

Toby had thumped him in the head with his gun

when Bryce had spoken to Abby. They'd been moving in silence ever since. Moving slowly. Abby seemed to be faltering more; a couple of times her knees buckled completely. When he'd caught her to keep her from falling down, she looked in his eyes in a way that told him she was buying time.

It was a good idea. Maybe Jason would figure out the text message and call the police.

Or maybe they were only delaying their deaths by minutes. Either way, it was a good move.

They played up her incapacity until Toby threatened to shoot her on the spot and make Bryce carry her body the rest of the way.

As they trudged along, Bryce realized the place Toby had dug the knife in his back was bleeding worse than he'd thought. There was a sticky trickle of blood creeping down the back of his right leg.

Reaching the river, Bryce saw Toby had an aluminum fishing boat tied at the old dock. Bryce had been so freaked since he'd gotten here, he hadn't even noticed Toby's car wasn't anywhere to be seen.

The normally sluggish river was running high and fast because of the spring storms. Toby was right; there was a damn good chance no one would find either of their bodies.

Toby had them walk out to near the end of the weathered dock. Because it was high tide, they were well out over the water. Bryce saw the cold brown water moving through the gaps where there were missing boards and knew that even if they dove for the river, their chances were slim.

"On your knees, Abby," Toby said.

When she didn't comply, he kicked the backs of her knees. She went down hard.

"You move and I shoot Bryce first."

"So you're the one who called 911 at the accident scene," Abby said.

"Nope," Toby said.

"Then why are you doing this? And why bring Bryce into it?"

"Shut the fuck up. You're wearing on my nerves," Toby said.

"Like I give a shit," Abby said.

Toby delivered a quick blow that sent her sprawling onto her back. Her head hit the dock with a thud.

The gun didn't move from Bryce's chest.

Toby reached down, grabbed her hair, and pulled her to a sitting position.

Her nose was bleeding. Bryce watched the deep red drops hit the weathered wood. Soon there would be so much more.

Toby reached into his pocket with his left hand. He pulled out Bryce's knife and handed it to him. "This whole fucking mess is her fault. Here's your chance to make her pay."

Bryce squared his shoulders and glared at Toby. He did not take the knife. "You're the one getting paid. I'm not going to do your work for you."

"Oh, I think you will," Toby said. "If you take care of business, I'm going to let you live."

"I don't believe you."

Toby tilted his head slightly. "Dude, it's this—or you're as dead as she is."

Bryce was breathing so hard and fast he was starting to get dizzy. "You'll kill me anyway."

"Nah, I told you, I like you. I'm giving you a chance. Water's high. Tide's going out. Her body might not be found. There's a good possibility you'll get away with it. It's a no-brainer, dude. You kill her. Or I kill you both."

Toby extended the knife to him.

"No."

Toby stepped closer and put the gun to Bryce's temple.

Bryce squeezed his eyes closed and felt tears run down his cheeks.

"Bryce, no," Abby said. "Don't do it. Make *him* kill me."

I don't want to die. Oh God, I don't want to die.

He opened his eyes—and put out his shaky hand for the knife.

Father Kevin drank the last of the scotch, letting it linger blissfully on his tongue before swallowing. For a moment, he stared at the small revolver on the passenger seat of the church van. Then he picked it up. Somehow it felt lighter in his hand than when he'd handled it an hour ago.

He got out and left the van there, at a seldom-used boat launch less than a mile away from the accident that began to unravel it all.

He walked through the woods along the river until he found a quiet spot where the sun cast brilliant rays through the old trees.

He sat for a long moment with his hands over his face, his knees bent in front of him, his elbows on his knees. The brown flow of water before him had a hypnotic effect. He'd been fighting the memory of that night for days. Now he let it wash over him, one last time:

The dark narrow road unfolded in the beams of his headlights. The windows were down. Sweat trickled down his temples, teasing the flesh in front of his ears, feeling like the advance of a column of ants. It was after two a.m. His mouth held the taste of the scotch he'd been drinking since midnight. The moist wind whipped around him, swirling through the car like the breath of a demon.

Papers rustled on the floor of the back seat: church bulletins and prayer cards.

Knowing the curves that lay ahead, he shut off his headlights and put his death in the hands of God.

His eyes closed and he forced himself to keep his foot on the accelerator.

All sounds became more acute. The slap-snap *of bugs against the windshield. The soft flutter of papers reminded him of butterfly wings…angel wings…the wings of death.*

He began a whispered prayer—and heard a motorcycle engine, wound tight, racing…

His eyes snapped open as he reached to flip on his lights. Too late—

Father Kevin gasped at the memory of the impact. His eyes opened to the reality of daylight.

Dear God, forgive me for taking that boy's life.

Oh, what a cowardly fool he'd been. He had thought the despair of that night was the worst he could possibly feel. He'd been wrong.

He tucked the revolver into the inside pocket of his windbreaker—he was dressed in secular clothing. He would not commit this sin in holy garments. Then he walked into the water until it swirled high around his calves, the pressure promising to draw him away with the current.

Then he knelt, his knees sinking deeply into the muddy river bottom, the insistent water tugging at his hips.

He closed his eyes and the weight of all he had done settled on his shoulders.

His sins were many. He knew this baptism would serve no purpose. But he wanted the Lord to know that no matter how flawed he'd been as a man, even in the disgrace of this final sin of his death, he was recommitting himself to Jesus Christ.

He gripped his rosary, bowed his head, and made the sign of the cross.

Abby was still blinking from the blow to her face. Her scalp throbbed from the man hoisting her by the hair. But she was not going to give him the satisfaction of showing fear.

She looked up to glare defiantly at him—and saw that Bryce had the knife in his hand.

"Don't," she whispered.

Bryce grimaced and raised the knife high.

His yell filled her ears. And the knife came plunging down in a flash of silver and pain.

CHAPTER 29

The Explorer fishtailed as Jason made the sharp turn onto the dirt road that led to the shack where he and Bryce had cleaned the fish they'd caught while boating years ago. Its discovery had solved one of the negatives of fishing; Lucy refused to have fish cleaned at the house. Unfortunately, the second negative never disappeared. Bryce had always been bored out of his mind.

The shack had been abandoned long before they'd happened across it. And Jason had just discovered how much farther it was from town by road than by water.

Bryce's car was parked in the tall weeds in front of the shack. Three of the Civic's four doors were open.

Jason slammed on the brakes and the Explorer skidded to a stop.

The shack wasn't more than a rusty metal roof, a single room with half-walls and a plank floor. The top half of the walls had once been screened, but those screens had been reduced to a few scraggly, fluttering remnants. The old screen door hung askew, no longer a rectangle that fit its opening.

Bryce was nowhere to be seen. Neither was Abby. Nor the gray Impala Jason had expected to find.

That didn't mean Toby wasn't here. He'd used the river before. And Bryce had clearly felt threatened or he never would have sent the text message that led Jason here.

He picked up the gun he'd laid on the passenger seat, jumped out, and crouched low near the vehicle, scanning the area.

No movement in the woods or the shack.

He listened.

There was a siren, but it was still far away. A police helicopter thudded somewhere in the distance; Kitterman had said he was dispatching one, as well as water patrol, in case of a chase.

The absence of the Impala said that if there was going to be a chase, it would be on the water. Jason thanked God for Kitterman's forward thinking.

He carefully moved away from the Explorer. When no one shot at him, he started running toward the river.

The sirens got closer.

The sound of a gunshot tore through the quiet. Birds startled en masse from their roosts in the trees.

The river was still about forty yards away; Jason could only see a small sliver of brown water at the end of the path through the trees. He pushed harder, arms and legs pumping. His heart felt like it was going to explode in his chest. He pressed on, his lungs burning, fear rising like bitter bile in his throat.

Dear God, please let me be in time.

But that gunshot...Jesus, that gunshot. Neither Abby nor Bryce was armed.

The dock was off to the left of the path. Jason erupted recklessly from the cover of the woods.

There was only one person on the dock. A guy Jason presumed to be Toby aimed his gun at the water and fired...and again. The sound of repeated shots covered Jason's careless approach.

Jason's feet hit the long dock. The vibration made Toby stop firing and look over his shoulder.

He spun and pointed the gun at Jason. But Jason had already stopped and aimed.

He fired first.

The bullet hit Toby's right hand; his gun clattered to the dock. He immediately reached down for the gun with his left hand.

Jason fired again, this time hitting him in the left knee. Jason was a doctor; he'd spent a lot of time perfecting his shot to maim, not kill.

Toby went down, his foot knocking his gun off the edge of the dock.

Jason ran somewhat closer, his aim now on Toby's head. He cast swift glances toward the water, but didn't see a sign of Abby or Bryce in the river.

"Where are they?" Jason shouted, praying for an answer that contradicted what logic told him.

"You're too fucking late." Toby started to push with his good leg toward the boat.

"Stop!" Jason held himself in place, resisting the instinct to move closer. He had to stay far enough away so Toby couldn't take Jason's legs out from under him. This guy was a killer. He wasn't done fighting yet.

The sirens grew louder, then stopped.

Toby scooted closer to the boat.

Jason fired again, hitting Toby's right calf.

The helicopter thumped closer, hovering over the water. The wash from its blades pressed Jason's clothes against his body. The turbulent gusts tossed tree branches and sent ripples across the surface of the river. Jason squinted against the wind and saw two officers with flak jackets and rifles in the chopper's open doorway.

The loudspeaker bellowed, "Drop your weapon."

Jason carefully placed his gun on the dock beside him and held his hands where they could easily be seen.

Then he yelled, "Check the river! They're in the river!"

He pointed downstream, keeping his hand movements slow and away from his body.

Feet pounded the dock. Jason spun around, hands in the air, and faced two officers who luckily knew him. He shouted as he kicked off his shoes, "Tell them not to shoot me. They're in the water. Have the helicopter search!"

Officer Bigelow reached for his radio and started talking.

Jason dove off the side of the dock.

Even with her eyes wide open, Abby couldn't see anything except the blurred image of Bryce's face inches from hers and a swirl of something darker in the water. Blood?

Hers or his?

He had come at her with the knife. There had been the pain of impact; she didn't think the knife had hit her, but she couldn't be sure. Then they'd tumbled over the edge of the dock. As she'd fallen, she'd heard a shot, followed by Bryce's grunt of pain.

Now he was holding her under the water. It was so cold she felt as if knife blades were flaying her flesh from her bones. Her lungs burned and felt ready to burst.

She struggled against his hold, but with her hands behind her, she was helpless.

She twisted her wrists against the tape.

He dragged her deeper.

The zing of bullets entering the water was getting quieter. Abby wasn't sure if they were moving away, or if she was losing consciousness. Everything had been so acute when she'd hit the water; now her senses were muffled. The sounds were less distinct, the pain rolling into numbness.

The current held her with a grip of its own. Without the use of her arms, she wasn't sure that she'd be able to surface even if he did let her go.

Even so, she kicked at him. He was drowning her. She writhed in panic, but he held tight.

Drowning. Drowning. Air. She had to get air.

Jason dove deep, ignoring the needles of pain caused by the cold temperature. The water was so murky, he would have to be right on top of them to see them. He flung his arms, feeling for skin or clothing.

Had they both been shot? Were they dead already?

The current was moving him away from the dock. Away from the *whump* of the helicopter.

He surfaced for air and discovered he'd been carried about twenty yards downstream. The helicopter was moving slowly along the course of the river, the two police officers leaning out, searching the surface of the water.

Jason's chances of finding Abby and Bryce were ridiculously slim, but he had to try.

He dove again.

He couldn't stay under as long this time. When he was forced to surface, a patrol boat was fast approaching from upstream. It slowed as it reached him.

One of the men on board called to him. "Here!" He tossed a life ring on a line. "Grab this!"

Jason ignored it and took a deep breath.

"Don't!" the man yelled. "We have divers on the way. Get out before we have to rescue you, too."

His limbs burning with exhaustion, Jason dove again.

The bullets had stopped—or they were far enough away that Bryce could no longer hear them. His lungs ached. He struggled not to suck in water.

His grip on Abby was growing weaker; luckily her strength against him was fading, too. His left arm was going numb and his shoulder felt as if it had been skewered.

He couldn't let her go.

Had to hold on...hold on...hold...

Jason heard the muffled drone of the boat's motor. He continued to grope blindly with no results. He was having a more difficult time keeping himself oriented in the water; the cold temperature was robbing him of his senses. And the current seemed to pull more insistently on his tired limbs.

He couldn't give up. Not until he found them.

Finally, he was forced to come up for air. Almost as soon as his head popped above the surface of the river, something snagged him around the chest.

He looked behind him. One of the men in the boat held a long pole on which there was a hook that encircled Jason.

The man was pulling him closer to the boat.

No! He had to keep going.

He struggled only briefly. He realized his limbs were so fatigued that if he located Abby or Bryce, he wouldn't have the strength to pull them from the water.

As soon as the officers had hauled him into the boat and laid him on the deck, he gasped, "Keep looking. Find them."

As he lay there heaving in great gulps of air, he tried to tell himself that they were alive. Even if they'd been shot, the water was cold. There was a chance. He had to cling to hope.

The boat's motor revved up.

One of the men said, "We're using fishing sonar. We'll find them, sir."

If only he sounded like he believed it would be in time.

Abby's right hand finally pulled free of whatever had bound her. At that same moment, she felt Bryce's hold on her relax. His eyes closed and his body started to separate from hers.

She grabbed the front of his shirt with her right hand. Stroking with her left, she began desperately kicking toward the surface.

The current tugged, but the light was growing stronger. Almost there!

Finally, she burst through the surface, gasping, her need for air overwhelming all else.

Coughing and sputtering, she struggled to pull Bryce's face above water. Her strength was failing.

With a frantic gaze, she looked to see which bank was closer. They were maybe thirty feet from the right bank, the bank they'd started on, still moving downstream. Luckily, the dock and the guy with the gun weren't in sight.

She heard a helicopter, but couldn't tell how near it was. She prayed it was looking for her.

She wrapped her right arm over Bryce's right shoulder and across his chest, hooking her hand in his left armpit. Then she rolled onto her back beneath him, supporting his head with her chest. She sucked in a breath and yelled, "Help!" Her second cry was cut off as the water came up over her mouth.

She started swimming toward the bank, pulling with her left arm and scissor kicking. The shore didn't seem to be getting much closer.

She might be able to make it alone. But she would not let Bryce go. She couldn't. Not ever.

Rolling onto her back again, she took deep breaths. She tried calling one more time.

"Here!" a man yelled. "Here!"

Abby rolled onto her side again, kicking toward the bank. A man was slightly downstream, chest deep in the river, hanging on to the limb of a huge tree that had fallen into the water. "Here!" he encouraged. "You can make it."

Abby kicked with all she had, pulling with her left arm. She had to get over there before they passed the fallen limb.

It was coming fast.

Almost.

She gave a big kick and stretched her arm out as far as she could.

She wasn't going to make it.

Just as she passed, the man lunged out and grabbed her wrist. He clung to the branch with his other hand, strung between the tree and Abby like a man on whipping posts.

She looked at his battered face and realized it was Father Kevin. His teeth gritted with strain as the current tried to pull her away from him.

Abby kicked furiously, holding tightly to Bryce.

Finally she reached the spot where the flow eddied around the fallen tree enough that it gave her a boost to swing closer to Father Kevin.

He kept pulling until she could grab a branch herself.

She realized he was standing and put her own feet on the river bottom.

Father Kevin tried to take Bryce from her, but she wouldn't let him go. She steadied herself by holding various limbs until she reached the point where she could no longer float Bryce along with her.

Father Kevin immediately moved to Bryce's feet. They hauled him out of the water, more dragging than carrying him.

Once Bryce's torso was over solid ground, they set him down. Abby and Father Kevin were breathing like sprinters. Bryce wasn't breathing at all.

Father Kevin checked for a pulse. Then he put the heels of both hands on Bryce's abdomen and pressed fast and hard. Once. Twice. On the third try, water bubbled out of Bryce's mouth.

Father Kevin moved quickly, turning Bryce's head to the side until the water stopped coming. Then he repeated it.

Then he checked for breaths.

"Come on," Abby wheezed.

Father Kevin began CPR, alternating between breaths and compressions.

Abby didn't have the strength to blow air into Bryce's lungs. She was about to take over compressions when she heard the helicopter. It was getting closer.

She got up and hurried back into the water, out from under the canopy of trees, until she was knee deep, waving her arms overhead. "Help!" Her cry was weak and useless against the sound of the rotors.

The helicopter swiveled in the air, hovering over the water in front of her. A voice came over a bullhorn. "Help is coming."

Abby frantically gestured toward Bryce and Father Kevin. But the helicopter continued to hover. It was only when the voice on the speaker told her again that help was coming that she realized there was no place for the helicopter to land.

She looked upriver and saw a boat fast approaching.

She slogged out of the water and fell onto her knees next to Bryce.

"I can take over compressions," she said, noticing the growing dark stain of blood on Bryce's left shoulder.

She placed her hands in position, purposefully not looking at the duct tape clinging to her left wrist. As she watched Father Kevin, waiting for him to give breaths, she noticed the cut over his eye had pulled open.

Just before he administered the second breath, Bryce sputtered and drew a breath on his own.

Abby choked on a sob of relief.

Father Kevin looked to heaven, closed his eyes, and began to move his lips in quiet prayer.

Bryce wheezed and coughed; more water bubbled out of his mouth. Abby made certain his head was turned to the side so he didn't aspirate it back into his lungs.

She heard the boat's hull scrape the bank and feet splash through the water. She didn't take her eyes off of Bryce. She laid her hand on his forehead and muttered encouragement, "Hang in there...You're doing great...We're safe...Help is here."

She heard the helicopter move away.

A man fell to his knees on the other side of Bryce. Abby took her hand away from Bryce's face and switched to holding his hand.

"He's been shot," she said. "In the back."

Guided by the blood seeping into the sleeve of Bryce's T-shirt, the man's hands immediately went to Bryce's left shoulder.

"Dad?" Bryce's whisper was shaky.

Abby's gaze snapped up and her exhausted heart did a triple-flip in her chest. "Jason."

His eyes met hers for a brief second, long enough to give her the strength to fight collapse, then he returned his focus to his son's injury.

"It looks like it went through," he said. "That's a good thing, son."

Jason and two other men from the boat helped Bryce on board and stretched him out on the deck. One of the men kept pressure on Bryce's wound and the other put a blanket over him.

Then Jason turned back to Abby. His hands ran over

her face, her shoulders, searching for wounds. "You're not hurt?"

She took a look down at herself for the first time. "I'm fine." Bryce had thrown himself at her hard enough to sell the act of stabbing to Toby, but he hadn't struck her with the knife. "Fine."

Jason's hands framed her face. "You saved him."

She closed her eyes and fell against him. His arms instantly came around her. Finally, the terror left her and all she felt was the beating of his heart next to hers.

She whispered against Jason's neck, "He saved me."

Then she pulled away and looked toward Father Kevin, who had held himself apart from the scene once others had arrived. "And he saved us both."

Jason nodded to the priest, then he lifted Abby onto the boat.

As soon as the man in the boat had Abby sitting down and a blanket around her, Jason returned to Father Kevin.

Jason faced the priest, which meant his back was to Abby. He put a hand on Father Kevin's shoulder and leaned close. He was talking so softly Abby couldn't hear.

Father Kevin's head bowed. He covered his eyes with one hand and his shoulders shook. After a moment, he reached inside his jacket and handed something to Jason. Then the two men walked to the boat.

"I can drive myself back to town," Father Kevin said as they approached. Abby noticed he kept his gaze on his feet when he spoke.

"You go with me," Jason said. His voice wasn't harsh, but it said he wasn't going to back down. "We'll get the van later."

Once on board, Father Kevin moved to the bow of the boat, away from everyone. Jason sat next to Abby, pulling her close with one hand and holding Bryce's hand with the other.

"It's going to be okay, son."

Bryce started crying. "I did things, Dad—"

"Shhhhh," Abby said softly, putting her hand on top of Bryce's and Jason's. "Don't talk now."

Bryce looked at her, his eyes clouded with pain and regret.

Abby smiled and said, "You saved me."

Bryce blinked and looked away.

She had no idea how Bryce had gotten involved with the man who wanted to kill her. But she didn't want him to say too much now with two officers on the boat.

When she looked at Jason, she saw tears in his eyes.

Abby decided she'd do whatever she could to protect both Jason and his son from more heartache.

CHAPTER 30

Jason had convinced the police to wait until the next day to take Bryce's statement. Although his gunshot wound hadn't required surgery, he didn't need to be put through the stress of questioning until he'd had some rest. After his lungs had been filled with river water, there was a high likelihood of lung infections. Besides, Toby was safely in custody and Jason wanted to hear it all from Bryce's lips first. His son might need a lawyer when he spoke to the police.

Lucy had arrived shortly after they'd gotten to the hospital—hysterical and demanding answers that no one had as yet. She'd left Brenna in the care of her grandparents. Throughout the afternoon, Constance and John had been in close phone contact, monitoring not only Bryce's medical status but Lucy's mental state. Jason was thankful for the latter. Anything he said only made her worse.

Jason had spent thirty minutes on the phone with Bren, giving her the edited, non-nightmare-inducing version of why her brother was in the hospital. A couple of times during the conversation, the reality of what had happened crashed in on him so enormously that he had to stop and take deep breaths before he could go on.

When Bren had said she couldn't understand why anybody would want to hurt her brother, Jason had had to bite back the words that threatened to spill forth; that the world was an ugly place filled with greedy and misguided people. Instead he'd told her that he couldn't understand it, either. By the time he'd hung up, she was as calm as she was going to be until she saw Bryce with her own eyes. And Jason was almost wishing he'd killed Toby Smith.

At eleven p.m. Jason and Lucy accompanied their son from the ER to a private room. Lucy hadn't said more than a handful of words to Jason since she'd made it clear that he was not Bryce's parent or guardian and had no business in the ER at all. Bryce had put a quick stop to that. Lucy had been miffed. Jason was proud.

Now she walked ahead of him behind the gurney, as if he weren't there at all.

Fine with him. He was there for Bryce, not to fight for parental rights with Lucy.

Once the nursing staff had left, Bryce said, "Mom, I need to talk to Dad for a minute."

She couldn't have looked more stricken if Bryce had slapped her. Her mouth came open and then closed. Her hurt gaze moved from Bryce to Jason and back. Finally, she surprised Jason—and Bryce, too, judging by the look on his face—when she nodded and said, "I'll go get some coffee."

"Did they catch Toby?" Bryce asked as soon as Lucy had gone.

"Yes." Jason didn't tell him that he'd shot the bastard three times.

"I was so stupid." His chin weakened slightly as he

fought tears and his eyes were clouded with pain medication. "I didn't know; really I didn't."

"Know what?" Jason asked, stepping closer to the bed. He'd planned on waiting until morning before making Bryce relive the horrors of the day. But Jason sat down; he would listen as long as Bryce needed to talk.

"That he wanted to hurt Abby. I never...I never would have taken her there if I'd known that."

Jason forced himself to ask a question he didn't want to. "Why did you take her there?"

Bryce clenched his teeth and looked away. In a small voice, he said, "I wanted her to leave us alone. Toby said we should try and scare her."

"Did you slash her tires and vandalize the cemetery on her property?"

With an audible swallow, Bryce nodded. He kept his face averted. A tear slid down his cheek.

"Were those Toby's ideas, too?" Jason shouldn't offer his son an out, but logic and responsibility were warring with his aching heart.

Bryce shook his head. Then he looked at Jason again. "Well, not the tires. He suggested the cemetery thing. But I didn't even know it had anything to do with Abby. It was just a place to get out some frustration."

Jason reminded himself of what it was to be seventeen; how emotions dug deep with claws that made pain override all thought, both rational and otherwise.

"You'll be accountable for those things," he said. "You can tell the police tomorrow when you tell them everything else."

Bryce nodded. After a long moment, he said, "I think Mom is in trouble."

Jason listened with a breaking heart as his son recounted the past week. Jason was achingly proud of Bryce's willingness to accept responsibility for his part in what had transpired—and furious with Lucy for putting him in the position to misconstrue things in the first place.

"I wish you'd come to me when you thought she was drinking again," Jason said.

"I was afraid you'd take Brenna," he said softly, his attention focused on his right hand picking at the blanket. "That's what Mom said you'd do."

It took an act of sheer will to keep from marching out of the room and wringing Lucy's neck. "We're a family, you and Bren and me. We'll always be together." Jason took a breath and blew out his anger. "And you don't have to worry about your mom being charged with the accident that killed Kyle Robard. She wasn't there."

Bryce's gaze snapped up. "But she wasn't home... and she acted all weird. The car was scraped. She *lied* to the police."

"She had other reasons. I'll let her explain them to you. As for the drinking, she and I will be discussing that. All I want is for you and Bren to be safe."

Bryce lowered his gaze and nodded. "I know."

"And Bryce," Jason said.

Bryce looked up.

"Your mom and I are not getting back together. It would be bad for all of us." Jason leaned forward and slipped his hand behind Bryce's neck. "But I will always be your dad." He kissed his son on the forehead.

Bryce nodded. He kept his eyes averted, but Jason saw fresh tears pooled in them. After a second, Bryce sniffed and then said, "Toby said he was paid to kill Abby. Why?"

Jason thought about the far-reaching ramifications of the investigation that would surely be coming. He didn't want his son to have any part in it. "Toby works for some really bad people. It had nothing to do with Abby, or you. You two were just collateral damage."

A light knock sounded on the door, and Lucy peeked in. "May I come in now?" Her entire demeanor had changed. She seemed almost meek.

Jason stood, glad for the interruption. He wasn't sure how much of Father Kevin's story would become public knowledge, and he didn't want to tell Bryce more right now. "Sure. I think this guy needs to get some sleep. I'll be down the hall."

Lucy nodded as he passed her going out the door. She said softly, "She's still here."

Jason glanced at Lucy, waiting for the barb, the sarcastic jab. It didn't come. "Thanks." He knew Abby was waiting; she'd refused to leave, but his heart still lightened. Right now he needed her; needed to touch her, assure himself she was safe and whole.

It was late enough that the corridor lights had been dimmed. The only sounds were the soft chatter from the nurses' station and the drone of a television somewhere up the hall.

Jason went to the little lounge near the elevators. Abby was alone in the room, dozing in an uncomfortable looking chair.

He stood there looking at her for a long moment. She wore scrubs and hospital socks. Her elbow was propped on the arm of the chair, her temple rested on her fisted hand. Her hair had been pulled into one long braid that draped over her shoulder. She had a whole new set of bruises on her face. For the second time today, he wished he'd killed the man who'd given them to her.

He walked over and sat next to her, hoping to hell this was the last time he saw her in a hospital, battered after a traumatic event.

She roused, blinking, as if disoriented. Then her eyes landed on him and she smiled tiredly.

"How is he?" she asked, sitting up straighter and stretching her neck.

Suddenly all of Jason's words became tangled in his throat. He reached out and rested a hand on either side of her head. He pulled her close, until her lips met his.

She grasped his wrists, her hands cold and trembling.

He kissed her long and hard, the taste of her reassuring him that he hadn't lost what could have so easily been taken today.

Finally, he ended the kiss and rested his forehead against hers. She laced her fingers behind his neck and they just sat there, blending into one, breathing in and out in unison.

Whatever lay ahead with Bryce, Jason knew he could deal, because Abby would be there to help him through.

A moment later, she pulled away and wouldn't meet his eyes. "I'm glad he's going to be okay." She stood up and ran her palms over the thighs of her scrubs. "I'd better be going."

He stared up at her in confusion. Then he realized how exhausted she must be.

"I'll drive you home."

At the word "home," her eyes clouded. "If you don't mind, I'll hang onto that air mattress for a few days ... until I can get something better set up in the shop."

He stood and reached for her, but she shook her head and backed away.

"Stay with me, Abby. I need you," he said.

"And I'll be here for you—as a friend. I owe you so much."

Anger snapped like lightning in his veins. "Owe me! You don't *owe me* anything. I love you." The admission surprised him, but he realized how true it was. "I love you."

The words seemed to hit Abby like a blow. She staggered back a couple of steps. "Jason...I thought I made myself clear. I can never live like a normal woman...a normal couple. I'm offering my friendship. That's all I can give."

"Why?"

"Nothing's changed. I still sleepwalk—"

He took a step closer. "I'm not afraid of you and your sleepwalking."

"But I am." She stepped around him. "Please don't make this harder for me." It was a whispered plea that raked across his heart like eagle talons.

He watched her walk away, his heart sitting bloody and bruised in his chest.

Abby waited until she stepped into the elevator to wipe the tears from her cheeks. Then she blinked hard, trying to vanquish them completely. She'd been preparing the entire evening to separate herself from Jason. Still it felt as if she'd just skinned herself alive. The pain was all encompassing, raw and stinging.

This was a before-and-after from which Abby would never recover. The pain might dull, she may grow more accepting, but her heart would never heal.

When the doors opened on the lobby level, Sergeant Kitterman was standing there.

"I was just coming up to get you," he said.

Her heart settled somewhere around her knees. She'd hoped she might avoid giving her statement until tomorrow. Right now all she wanted was to crawl off and be alone, lick her wounds, and deal with the fact that her time with Jason was over.

With a nod of resignation, she exited the elevator.

Kitterman gestured toward the door to the chapel, which was off to the left of the elevator. "Let's go in here."

Abby supposed they'd have as much privacy there as anywhere. Visiting hours were long over.

Kitterman opened the door and allowed her to go in first. It was dim inside the chapel. A low wattage spotlight shone on a cross on the front wall. There were five rows of empty pews.

She glanced over her shoulder to Kitterman to ask where he wanted to sit when a shadow in the corner beside the door moved. She tensed, then the silhouette stepped into the light.

"Father Kevin," she said. She hadn't seen him since the police escorted him off the boat.

Kitterman said, "You have ten minutes. I'll be right outside." He turned to Abby. "I'd like to speak to you afterward."

She nodded.

Father Kevin took her elbow and guided her to the rear pew. They sat side by side.

"It's so peaceful in here," he said, his voice wistful.

"Yes." She reached over and put her hand over his.

"Thank you for saving my life. It sounds like you did it more than once."

He turned his eyes toward the illuminated cross. "If it weren't for me, you wouldn't have been in danger in the first place."

"Maybe. Maybe not. I was sleep-driving. If you hadn't been out there on that road, I might have killed myself." As soon as the last words left her lips, she cringed. Jason had said Father Kevin was trying to validate Suicide Road's name that night, driven by desperation to untangle COC from some illegal activity.

"That man, the one who...," she couldn't bring herself to finish. "He was threatening you, too?"

Father Kevin nodded. "He was going to shoot you that night in the marsh. I convinced him that since the goal of his employers had been to keep their activities a secret, putting a bullet in an innocent woman on a country road would be counterproductive."

"He was close, though," she said. "He broke out the glass."

Father Kevin nodded and swallowed.

"None of this was your fault," she said.

He leaned forward, his elbow on his knee, and cradled his forehead in his hand. "I handled things badly."

"Jason said these people were using COC before you were the director."

He sat for a moment, his eyes closed. Then he licked his lips and said, "I'm not supposed to tell anything, but you deserve to know. It started when my sister and brother-in-law needed money for Maggie's heart surgery. It was supposed to be a one-time thing. They were to transport some unnamed cargo along with their COC relief supplies. In addition to paying for Maggie's surgery, there were some very large donations made to COC that went toward their work." He looked at Abby. "They were desperate—Maggie was their only child. Of course," his gaze shifted to the cross again, "it didn't stop after one shipment—that's when they started threatening Maggie's life. My sister finally discovered they were moving weapons, used to make orphans of the very children they were trying to help."

With a shake of his head, he said softly, "I learned firsthand how the desperation to protect a child robs you of everything, including your principles." He buried his face in his hands and a sob broke free.

Abby put a hand on his back. "Like I said, none of this was your fault. And your sister did what she had to do to save Maggie. So did you."

After a moment, he straightened and sniffled loudly. "Maggie and I are leaving tonight—going into protective custody. The U.S. marshals are already here."

"Now? You have to leave now?"

"Before the people who hired Toby find out what's happened." There was still fear in his eyes, but his shoulders were more square than Abby had seen them in weeks. He was a man on the path to redemption.

"Can I at least say goodbye to her?"

Father Kevin shook his head. "I had to fight to get a minute with you myself. Maggie can't ever know any of this. She's too innocent; too vulnerable."

Abby bit her lower lip. She sat staring at the subtle pattern in the commercial carpet. She might never see or talk to Maggie, or Father Kevin, again.

Just one more before and after.

There was a light knock on the door. Their time was up.

Abby and Father Kevin stood. She wrapped him in a hug. "Tell Maggie I love her and I'll miss her."

Father Kevin broke away and left without looking at her.

Abby sank back down on the pew, unable to watch him walk out of her life. She sat motionless for several minutes, absorbing the peace, the silence.

It wasn't until she heard him clear his throat that she realized Kitterman had come in the chapel as Father Kevin had exited.

Kitterman stepped forward and handed her a paper cup. "Herbal tea."

He didn't seem like the herbal tea type. Her thought must have been written on her face. When he handed it to her, he said, "It's soothing, but won't keep you awake once you get home."

The tea wouldn't be responsible for her wakefulness, but she would not sleep. Every time she closed her eyes she saw the cloud of blood in the water, Bryce's still face as they'd pulled him from the river. Jason's son had nearly died saving her.

"Thank you." As she took the cup, every muscle in her body protested. Her pulse pounded a rhythm in her head. Hot tea couldn't hurt.

Kitterman sat on the pew in front of her, turning to look at her with his arm on the back of the seat. "I figured this was as good a place as any for our interview."

Interview. He made it sound so innocuous. What she said could have Bryce under arrest for kidnapping, at the very least.

She nodded and lowered her gaze to the cup she was turning in her hands. She'd been dreading this. Up until now, she'd managed to remain vague about how she'd ended up at the fishing shack.

To delay a bit longer, she asked a question for which she knew there was no answer. "How long do you think Father Kevin and Maggie will have to remain in witness protection?"

Kitterman shrugged. "Depends on the investigation and prosecution. Could be months...or forever, depending upon what the Feds uncover."

So much loss—and all of it was out of her hands.

Kitterman informed Abby that she would still need to make a formal statement at the station, but he wanted to have a basic understanding of what had transpired.

Abby nearly told him he'd have to wait, but she didn't want her attitude to make her less credible when she tried to convince them to go easy on Bryce. She began by talking about awakening at the fishing shack and ended when she climbed into the boat with Jason and the officers. She hoped Kitterman would somehow not ask how she'd gotten to the fishing shack in the first place.

Once she got to the end, Kitterman squashed her hopes. "Tell me about leaving your car on the side of the road."

"I was driving toward town. And I saw a stranded motorist and pulled over—"

"Motorist?"

"Yes." She took a sip of tea, trying to figure out a way to explain what happened without sending Bryce directly to jail. Kidnapping was serious; although he was only seventeen she feared they would make an attempt to try him as an adult. How could she minimize this and keep the focus on the real villain in this situation?

"Just to make this easier for you," Kitterman said, "we found chloroform and duct tape in Bryce's car. So I already have a pretty good idea of what happened."

"Well, then you know—and I don't need to relive it." She tried to sound like she was at her breaking point. But it didn't look like Kitterman was buying it. He just sat there waiting.

She sighed. "He was on the side of the road. I thought he was having car trouble, so I stopped. He asked me to get the jumper cables from the backseat of his car. I don't really remember much more than that."

"They took scrapings from your fingernails in the ER. There was skin under them. From the looks of Bryce's face and arms, it's probably his."

"He was being manipulated," she said. "That guy was trying to frame him for my murder. Bryce didn't know what he had planned. If not for Bryce, I'd be dead. He saved me by knocking me into the river—and got shot in the process."

"Duly noted."

"What's going to happen to him?"

"That'll be up to the prosecutor. I'll do what I can to keep things in perspective."

"I'll do whatever you think will help him...talk to the prosecutor, judge, whatever."

"I'll pass that along." Kitterman got up and closed his notebook.

Abby couldn't help but feel she hadn't done enough.

CHAPTER 31

It had been five days since Abby and Bryce nearly lost their lives. And five nights in which sleepwalking had been usurped by nightmares that jolted her awake several times a night, sweating and gasping for breath.

At least she couldn't set her shop on fire with a nightmare.

Jason and her father were helping her arrange a functional space in the rear of the carriage house. Throughout the process Jason had vacillated between trying to convince her to stay in Bren's room, voicing arguments for them to continue their relationship, and tense silences.

It had taken all of her will not to reach across those silences and make promises she could not keep. It would be better this way for them both; no sense in ripping off a Band-Aid slowly and prolonging the pain.

It was nearly midnight; her father had left two hours ago. She and Jason were just finishing the last details of the plumbing. Abby's limbs were heavy with exhaustion.

But the exhaustion felt great. Her brush with death had made everything feel so much...more. Including her feelings for Jason.

She was torn between relief and despair that the project was finished and they would no longer be spending all of their spare time together.

He packed up the last of his tools and then stood in front of her.

Abby stuffed her hands beneath her arms to ensure they behaved.

Putting his hands on his hips, Jason took a deep breath. And then he said, "I know you think you're protecting me. But I don't need protection. I think it's time to stop denying what's between us."

"I'm not denying it. I'm choosing not to act on my every desire. I'm an adult. I know my actions have consequences." The words were true—and so very bitter on her tongue.

"Abby—"

"Jason, no. There's no future and I can't ask you—"

He reached out and grabbed her so quickly she didn't have a chance to move away. He crushed her to him, kissing her the way she'd been fantasizing about for days.

Within seconds, her pent-up desires obliterated the fortress of her restraint. The demands of her body outshouted the whispers of rationality.

Her hands moved beneath his shirt and she felt his muscles tighten with her touch. That tiny response sent her senses reeling. And when his hands slid under her clothes, it was like an electrical current shot through her. Since that moment when she'd thought her life was over, her entire body had become supercharged. Jason didn't know it, but he could practically make her come just looking at her with longing in his eyes.

Within seconds they were both frantic with desire. They ended up making love right there in the tiny bathroom; her bare back against the wall, her sweat-slickened breasts against his chest, and her legs wrapped around Jason's naked hips.

When it was over, they clung to one another, breathless, their bodies still intimately joined.

Abby rested her face in the curve of his neck. "Maybe you should put me down," she whispered.

"This wall is the only thing holding us up," he said weakly. "If I move a muscle, we're both going to end up on the floor."

"In that case," she kissed his neck, tasting salt and passion. "Stay right where you are."

"I think I'll keep you right here like this forever."

Forever. Tears stung her eyes. The agonizing truth was she had to let him go.

No matter how painful, loving Jason was one before and after she would never regret.

They'd made love again on Abby's new bed. They were lying face to face on the full-size mattress—Abby's statement that she would always be sleeping alone. Jason didn't like the look that was shadowing Abby's eyes. It was as if this was goodbye.

He wasn't ready to give up, probably never would be. If he had to make adjustments to his expectations in order to keep her in his life, so be it.

He said, "Let me stay tonight." If he could spend

enough nights sleeping next to her without disaster striking, maybe he'd be able to ease her into acceptance.

"Jason..."

"One night," he said. "That's all I'm asking." He glanced at the clock. Two thirty-eight. "It's more than half over already." He slid his arms around her and tried to snuggle close, as if she'd already agreed.

She stiffened, it was like trying to snuggle with a tree trunk.

"It only takes one night to ruin the rest of your life." She rolled off the bed and reached for her robe. Shrugging it on, she cinched the belt tight. "Just ask Courtney."

Jason snagged her hand and pulled her to sit back down on the bed. He said, "I don't think you're nearly as dangerous as you think."

She opened her mouth, but he raised a hand and said, "Hear me out."

"Okay." Her mouth agreed, but her eyes had already shut him down.

"I haven't brought this up before now. You've had so much to deal with, but I've been thinking this ever since your hypnosis. There's a good chance you didn't start the fire that burned your family's house."

"Of course I did," she said, pulling her hand from his. "And I'm surprised you'd stoop to something like this to try and stay in my bed all night." In fact she was stunned; it was totally unlike him.

He gave her a scathing look. "I realize this is bad timing, but it has nothing to do with that. I think it's worth asking some questions. I'd bet once the flames were out, none of your family discussed the details of that night again. Especially with you and your sister."

Her brows drew together and she frowned. He'd hit the nail on the head. Parents always wanted to shield their children from trauma; unfortunately sometimes they missed the truth because of it.

"When you awakened in the living room, you said the dining room was already engulfed in flames."

She nodded. "The oil from the lamp—it must have made the fire escalate faster."

"Maybe. And maybe it had been burning for a while before you even came downstairs."

She sat quietly, thinking—the fact that she wasn't actively arguing gave him hope.

"And right after you awakened, you heard Courtney screaming in pain—on the other side of the burning dining room. Why, if she was up because she smelled smoke, why hadn't she awakened your parents? Why was she downstairs?"

Her eyes widened as she shifted her gaze toward him. "You're trying to blame my sister for the fire?" Defensiveness laced her words.

"I'm just saying that maybe it's time for your family to have an honest talk about that night. Because you were a sleepwalker, everyone *assumed* you started the fire. What does she remember of the fire?"

"Nothing, thank God." She crossed her arms over her chest.

"So you can't say with absolute certainty that you started the fire."

"I *can* say with absolute certainty that I do sleepwalk, so it really doesn't change anything, now does it? It doesn't matter."

"Of course it matters. Just like it matters that you

didn't cause the accident that took Kyle Robard's life. It's the difference between a relatively harmless sleep disorder and feeling that you're responsible for another person's bodily injury."

"I could have hurt someone while I was sleep-driving."

"And you *could* hurt someone while driving awake. That doesn't keep you from getting in a car."

Abby rubbed her forehead. "Listen, you need to go. I'm really too tired to argue about this."

"I don't want to argue. I just want you to think about it." He got up and went into the bathroom to get his clothes. He slipped on his jeans and came back to the bed, where she sat staring into space.

"I'll leave." He ran a hand over her beautiful hair. "But don't think you've seen the last of me. I'm making the informed decision to take the risk of being with you...minimal though it is."

"We'll see next week, after you see my sister's scars. Then you'll have the proper perspective of the risk."

He slipped his T-shirt over his head.

Courtney was coming for her father's appointment with the Alzheimer's specialist. Jason might just have a few questions for Abby's sister himself before she left here.

He leaned down and kissed the top of Abby's head.

Then he left, hoping with all of his heart that she would have that difficult conversation with her family. How could they all go through their lives just assuming— and letting Abby carry the burden?

CHAPTER 32

Since her arrival yesterday, Courtney had been the most civil Abby could ever recall. She'd come out of the airport wearing huge sunglasses, a long-sleeved turtleneck, and with her hair styled close to her face; her usual in-public attire. The instant she'd seen Abby, she dropped her carry-on and grabbed her into a fierce hug.

She'd kept saying over and over, "Thank God you're alive. Thank God that maniac didn't kill you."

At first Abby had wondered if Court had been drinking during the flight, but she'd seemed cold sober.

Not so now. The two of them sat in the darkness of their father's backyard, deep into their second bottle of wine. It was chilly and they were both wrapped in bulky sweaters they'd dug out of a closet inside. Abby had a serious buzz going and Courtney had admitted she rarely drank and was well beyond tipsy. Abby had always dreamed of moments like this with her sister, but never truly felt they'd experience one.

Perhaps their father's illness would bind them in a way nothing had before. It was sad to think so.

The doctor's appointment had gone well. He felt that their dad was still in the very early stages. The doctor had high hopes that the medication would significantly slow progression of the disease. There was no cure. At least for the immediate future, they wouldn't be completely losing the father they knew.

Courtney refilled both her and Abby's glasses. "I almost wish I wasn't leaving tomorrow."

"Really?" Courtney normally detested every moment she was forced to spend in Preston.

"I said *almost*."

They were quiet for a while. Then Courtney asked, "When you thought you were dying, what went through your mind?"

Abby took another sip of wine. That moment was something she'd continually turned her thoughts away from ever since she'd made it out of the river.

She sighed and spoke the truth. "I wondered if anyone would miss me."

Her sister rolled her head against the back of her chair and looked over at Abby. Even in the dimness, Abby could see the ropy scars on the left side of Courtney's face that pulled the corner of her left eye slightly downward.

"That's stupid." Court sounded like her old self. "You have a life. You have ... people."

"Hey, you asked. That's what I thought," Abby said. "I'll never wake up with another person's head on the pillow next to me. I'll never have children. When I'm gone the hole will be so small, it won't take long for it to close up like it was never there at all."

Jason's comments the other night had been repeating themselves in her head for days. At first she'd been so defensive about his assumption that her family would let her believe she'd set that fire without absolute proof had kept her from thinking rationally. She'd spent a lot of hours recalling everything she could about the fire and what followed. Jason had been right. Once the initial assumption had been made that she'd been the one to light and overturn the lamp while sleepwalking, it had become a non-topic.

Abby knew her parents had closed that door in order to protect her and her sister as much as possible. Even Courtney had resorted to backdoor comments and innuendo. Any direct mention of the fire ceased to be.

Before Courtney had arrived from New Mexico, Abby had broached the subject with her father. He'd squirmed in his chair as she'd poked and prodded his memory. In the end, she'd learned nothing new—and her father had been in tears.

Could she put her sister through the same discomfort, just for her own selfish peace of mind?

Courtney had gone through years of therapy; maybe somewhere along the way, she'd recovered memories just like Abby had under hypnosis.

Abby took a long drink of wine and then asked, "What do you remember about the night of the fire?"

She heard Courtney's sharp intake of breath.

Abby kept her eyes on the stars, as if looking at her sister would be that much more invasive, that much more hurtful.

Courtney was silent for several minutes. Then, in a cold voice, she said, "You know I don't like to talk about the fire."

"Yeah, well, neither do I, but I think it's time we

stopped acting like our tongues will fall out if we mention it. It's time to stop ignoring and deal." She turned to face her sister. Courtney's arm rested on the arm of the Adirondack chair, her hand holding her wineglass by the stem.

"Why are you asking this now?" Courtney asked, her voice a quiver in the darkness.

Abby reached across the few inches between them and put her hand on her sister's arm. She imagined she could feel the scars beneath the yarn of Courtney's sweater. "I remembered some things under hypnosis recently. I was wondering if in any of your therapy sessions you remembered what happened. It's time to let this memory bind us, not tear us apart."

Courtney kept her eyes averted and remained stone silent.

Abby gave a sigh of disappointment and took her hand off her sister's arm. She'd taken another sip of wine before she heard a sob catch in Court's throat.

"I didn't mean to upset you," Abby said. "I just… wondered."

It took a couple of false starts before Courtney managed to choke out, "I'm so sorry."

"Sorry about what?"

Courtney sniffled. Her voice wasn't much more than a squeak when she said, "That you live all alone."

"It's not your fault," Abby said.

After a moment, Courtney said, "Yes, it is."

"My sleepwalking has nothing to do with you. You're two thousand miles away and I'm still doing it."

"You d-don't un-un-understand. I should have told you a long time ago…." Courtney's gaze moved to the night sky; Abby saw tear tracks on her cheeks in the moonlight.

Abby's skin prickled all over, waiting to hear what her sister had to say.

"You didn't start that fire." Courtney turned to look at Abby. "I did."

Abby felt the world spin around her. It took a minute for her to find her voice. "*You* started it?" She shot to her feet. "You started it— and all of these years you let me and everyone else believe I did it!"

Courtney got slowly to her feet. Her wineglass slid off the arm of the chair and shattered as it hit the paving stones of the patio. "I didn't know at first, honest I didn't. I didn't remember anything about the fire until a few years later."

"A few years…like how many?" Abby struggled to keep from lashing out. She didn't want Court clamming up. She wanted to hear it all.

Courtney turned her back to Abby and crossed her arms over her chest. The night was still; it was easy to hear her hushed voice when she said, "I was nearly eleven before things began to come back to me. At first I thought they were just dreams. It was a long while before I remembered enough to put it all together. So it wasn't like one day I just remembered and didn't tell."

"But—"

Courtney spun around and cut her off. "You always got to do everything. You were always perfect. I was always the baby. I hated it."

"Oh, Court…." Abby reached out, but her sister stepped backward and waved her off.

"I snuck downstairs after everyone was asleep and lit

the Sunday lamp. When I was reaching to turn down the wick, I knocked it over. The oil spilled and the fire spread so fast. I tried to put it out, but it kept getting worse. I was so scared, I ran and hid in the butler's pantry. The fire seemed to follow me, like it was looking for my hiding place. My pajamas caught fire and I ran out through the kitchen."

"Why didn't you tell us! My God, you let me go on believing I did this to you." Abby gestured to the left side of Courtney's face.

"I didn't know at first. I was only six!"

Abby shook her head. If only Courtney had awakened their parents instead of hiding, both of their lives would have been so much different.

Courtney added, "By the time I remembered it was long over. I was afraid everyone would think I'd lied in the beginning. They'd think I knew all along and just wanted someone else to take the blame."

"So you've spent every day since then making sure my guilty feelings kept everyone from talking about it…making sure I *stayed* feeling guilty."

"It wasn't like that. It was just too late—"

"God! Too late for what?"

"Too late for me!" Courtney shouted. "Nothing was going to fix me. Maybe I wanted you to hurt, too. But when Dad called and told me about you nearly drowning…I thought…I thought I might never be able to make things right."

Anger tightened like suffocating bands around Abby's chest. "And you think this makes things *right*?"

"I know I've been selfish—"

"Oh, you are way beyond selfish." Abby turned and

walked away, fury blurring everything except the ground immediately in front of her steps.

An hour later, Abby stood on Jason's front porch, ringing the doorbell. It was late, but his lights were still on.

He turned on the porch light and then opened the door. Surprise registered on his face, "Abby? What's wrong?"

She stepped into his arms and buried her face on his shoulder. She hadn't planned on crying. Then again, she hadn't planned on coming here. She'd just started walking and her feet brought her to his door of their own accord.

It wasn't fair to him. Her appearance here was selfish. And yet, it was only right to tell him he'd been right about the fire. Problem was, now that she'd laid eyes on him, she couldn't manage a coherent word.

Her mind raced with unanswerable and disturbing questions. If Dad hadn't been sick, would Court ever have come back? If she hadn't been drunk would she have confessed the secret she'd guarded so carefully all of these years? God, Abby might never have known the truth. The entire serendipity of it all made her insides quiver and her palms sweat. Was life nothing more than a long string of coincidences set to topple like a line of dominoes?

As Jason held her, gently rubbing her back and murmuring to her, the anxious quivering in her began to subside.

At some point Abby heard the door close. He must have shoved it with his foot, because his hands stayed on her.

Finally she gathered herself together and lifted her face. "Sorry. I didn't know I was such a basket case."

His hazel eyes were clouded with concern. "What's happened?"

"Can I beg a cup of coffee?" Her buzz had worn off in the hour she'd been walking. But she was chilled to the bone, and it wasn't entirely due to the cool temperature.

He held her hand as he led her back to the kitchen and had her sit at the table. After setting a tissue box in front of her, he started a pot of coffee.

"I'm giving you decaf," he said. When she glanced up at him he added, "Your nighttime rules."

Once the coffee was brewing, he sat across from her and extended his hand across the table. She hesitated before she put hers into it. The instant their skin touched a sense of rightness and order settled over her. Holding Jason's hand made her world feel just a little less random.

His warm fingers closed around hers. He didn't prod, he just waited until she was ready to talk.

Swiping a tissue across her nose, she finally said, "You were right."

He half-smiled. "No doubt. But which thing are you talking about?"

Abby couldn't suppress her smile. "You're so damn arrogant sometimes."

"I'm simply truthful and realistic," he said, feigning affront.

Suddenly, she couldn't even imagine dealing with this and not having him to confide in.

"I questioned Courtney . . . and I didn't set the fire that destroyed our house. She did."

There was no surprise on his face. He nodded.

"I just can't believe she let me think I did it for all these years." The thought still had her reeling.

"Did she always know?"

"She *says* not. She said she started remembering things when she was eleven."

"The same age you were when the fire occurred."

"Yeah. Do you think that had something to do with her memory kicking in?"

"Hard to say. Trauma has a way of working to the surface like a festering splinter, no matter how deeply buried. But there's no timetable."

Abby shook her head and blew out a long breath. "But she still kept it to herself. Why? Does she hate me that much?"

"I'm sure Courtney's emotions are more complex than simple hate. And her reasons will take some serious digging to figure out. Remember, you're talking about a child, not an adult, and one that's suffered serious trauma. From what you've told me, she had everyone jumping through hoops to make it up to her. That's a lot to back-pedal on."

"Okay, when she was a kid. But Jesus, she's twenty-six years old."

"And now she told you."

Abby pulled her hand away and pressed her lips together. "You sound like you think she's justified."

He got up and moved to stand behind her chair. He massaged her shoulders with magic fingers. "No. I'm just trying to make you see that once the misconception was out there, how hard it was for her to undo it. She needed to make sure everyone still believed, so she never let anyone forget it. The question is, now that you know, what are you going to do with the knowledge?"

She frowned. "What do you mean?"

"Are you going to let it put the final nail in the coffin of your relationship with your sister? Are you going to hold onto the past, or are you going to look to the future? Think about the freedom she just handed you."

"Freedom? What are you talking about?"

"You've ordered your entire life around the idea that your sleepwalking harmed others. Now you know it hasn't. You're finally free to live your life as you choose."

"I still sleepwalk."

"So do thousands and thousands of other normal people, living perfectly normal lives. We'll adapt."

She looked up at him. "We?"

"Now that you know your sleepwalking is as harmless as the next person's...yes, *we*. You and me."

The enormity of that reality took her breath away. Could she dare hope for a normal life, a normal love?

As she sat there, it settled upon her like a gentle mist. She supposed it was a sort of freedom. Freedom to do all of the things that she'd thought would forever be denied her. Freedom to weave her life into the fabric of others. So many *good* befores and afters.

Jason went on, as if he felt she still needed convincing. "I'll strip my room bare and install alarms on the doors and windows. I'll set squeakers all over the floor. I'll do whatever it takes to make you feel safe sleeping with me. All I'm asking is for a chance for us. Courtney's truth has just freed you to take that chance."

She closed her eyes. The past had done so much damage already.

"I get it." She sighed. "But can't I just wallow in self-pity and indignation for one night?"

He kissed the top of her head. "I think you've earned that right."

After pouring her coffee and adding cream, he set it in front of her. She looked at it for a minute without comment.

"Did I get it wrong?"

With a sigh, she said, "I really only wanted it to warm up." She stood and put her arms around his neck. "But there's a much better way to get rid of this chill."

"I'd be obliged to help in any way I can," he said with that grin that set off the bubble machine inside her heart. "And now that you know you're not nearly as dangerous as you'd thought, I plan to keep you until morning."

"I'm not sure I'm ready—"

"Sometimes you just have to close your eyes and take a leap of faith, baby. I promise to catch you when you fall."

"I have no doubt that you will." She kissed him, and the bone-deep chill that had enveloped her began to fade.

THE DISH

Where authors give you the inside scoop!

♥ ♥ ♥ ♥ ♥ ♥ ♥ ♥ ♥ ♥ ♥ ♥ ♥ ♥ ♥ ♥ ♥

From the desk of Susan Crandall

Dear Reader,

After a good friend of mine finished reading one of my suspense novels, she asked my husband how he could sleep next to me at night, knowing how my mind works. After I'd given her a good dose of stink-eye, I really started thinking. Not about how dangerous it is for my dear husband—although that could probably be debated. Many of us do it every night without pause, but think about how much trust it takes between two people to fall into innocent, blissful, and completely *defenseless* sleep next to that other person.

But more important to this book is the question: When in our lives are we more vulnerable than when we're sleeping? I mean, it starts when we're children with the monster in the closet or the bogeyman under the bed. And for sleepwalkers, that vulnerability multiplies exponentially; their fears are real and well-founded, not imaginary.

Think about it. You go to bed. Fall asleep…and never know what you might do during those sleeping hours. Eat everything in your refrigerator? Leave the house? Set a fire? It would be horrifying. Even worse, you will have absolutely no recollection of your actions.

As they say, "From tiny acorns mighty oaks do grow." The disturbing vulnerability induced by sleep-walking was the seed that grew into SLEEP NO MORE.

As for my husband...the poor man continues to slumber innocently next to me while my mind buzzes with things to keep the rest of you awake at night.

Please visit my Web site, www.susancrandall.net, for updates and extras you won't find between the covers.

Yours,

Susan Crandall

♥ ♥ ♥ ♥ ♥ ♥ ♥ ♥ ♥ ♥ ♥ ♥ ♥ ♥ ♥

From the desk of Sherrill Bodine

Darling Reader,

You know I can't resist sharing delicious secrets about some of Chicago's best stories!

When I discovered that my friend, the curator of costumes at the history museum, was poisoned by a black Dior evening gown (don't worry—he's perfectly well!) and that it happened at a top secret fall-out shelter that houses some of the most treasured gowns in Chicago's history, I knew I had to tell the tale in A BLACK TIE AFFAIR.

After all, what could be more irresistible than a

time-warp fantasy place that houses row after row of priceless gowns that were once worn by Bertha Palmer, the real-life legendary leader of Chicago's social scene?

For those of you who may not be familiar with her, Bertha leveraged her social standing and family fortune to improve lives and to champion women's rights. So I thought, how perfect it would be if her gowns helped the women of Chicago once again, and one woman in particular!

It wasn't long before my heroine, Athena Smith, was born. I gave her two fabulous sisters who are just as devoted to fashion as Athena is—and, of course, as I am—and I determined that a couture gown would change her life forever. One of Bertha's gowns would poison Athena, just as that Dior had poisoned my friend, and that would throw her back into the arms of her first love, notorious bachelor Drew Clayworth. Of course, that's just the tip of the iceberg of this story because, as we all know, the course of true love never does run smooth.

Find out what other surprises and tributes to my beloved Chicago I have in store for you in A BLACK TIE AFFAIR. And never forget that I love giving you a peek beneath society's glitter into its heart.

Please tell me *your secrets* when you visit me at www.sherrill bodine.com.

XO

Sherrill Bodine

♥ ♥ ♥ ♥ ♥ ♥ ♥ ♥ ♥ ♥ ♥ ♥ ♥ ♥ ♥ ♥

From the desk of Amanda Scott

Dear Reader,

What sort of conflict between the heads of two powerful Scottish clans might have persuaded Robert Maxwell of Trailinghail to abduct Lady Mairi Dunwythie of Annandale, the heiress daughter of a baron who defied certain demands made by Maxwell that he believed were unwarranted? Next, having abducted the lady, what does Robert do when Lord Dunwythie still refuses to submit? And why on earth does Mairi, abducted and imprisoned by Robert, not only fall in love with him but later—long after she is safe and a powerful baroness in her own right—decide that she wants to marry him?

These are just a few of the challenging questions that faced me when I accepted an invitation to consider writing the "true" fourteenth-century story of Mairi Dunwythie and Robert Maxwell—now titled SEDUCED BY A ROGUE.

The invitation also came in the form of a question—a much simpler one: Would I be interested in the story of a woman who had nearly begun a clan war?

Since authors are always looking for new material, I promptly answered yes.

A friend had found an unpublished manuscript, dated April 16, 1544, and written in broad Scotch by

"Lady Maxwell." Broad Scotch is a language I do not know.

Fortunately, my friend does.

Lady Maxwell related details of how two fourteenth-century Dunwythie sisters met and married their husbands. ("Dunwythie" is the fourteenth-century spelling for Dinwiddie, Dunwoodie, and similar Scottish surnames.) SEDUCED BY A ROGUE is the story of the elder sister, Mairi.

Relying on details passed down in Maxwell anecdotes over a period of two hundred years, Lady Maxwell portrayed that clan favorably and Mairi's father as a scoundrel. The trouble, her ladyship wrote, was all Lord Dunwythie's fault.

So the challenge for me was to figure out the Dunwythies' side of things and what lay at the center of the conflict. That proved to be a fascinating puzzle.

Her ladyship provided few specifics, but the dispute clearly concerned land. The Maxwells thought they owned or controlled that land. Dunwythie disagreed.

The Maxwell who had claimed ownership (or threatened to *take* ownership) was just a Maxwell, not a lord or a knight. However, Dunwythie was *Lord Dunwythie of Dunwythie*, and that Annandale estate stayed in Dunwythie hands for nearly two hundred years longer. In the fourteenth century, landowners were knights, barons, or earls—or they were royal. So, clearly, Dunwythie owned the land.

Next, I discovered that the Maxwells were then the hereditary sheriffs of Dumfries. Sheriffs ("shire-reeves") were enormously powerful in both Scotland

and England, because they administered whole counties (shires), collected taxes, and held their own courts of law. The fact that Annandale lies within Dumfriesshire was a key to what most likely happened between the Dunwythies and the Maxwells.

The result is the trilogy that began with TAMED BY A LAIRD (January 2009) and continues now with SEDUCED BY A ROGUE. It will end with TEMPTED BY A WARRIOR (January 2010).

I hope you enjoy all of them. In the meantime, *Suas Alba!*

Amanda Scott

http://home.att.net/~amandascott
amandascott@worldnet.att.net